Praise for
Nancy Thayer and *He*

"[*Heat Wave*] should draw raves from [Ms. Thayer's] female fans everywhere . . . a beautiful story . . . a finely drawn and lovely fiction whose mood sticks with you when you're finished, and adds more than a few heart-wrenching moments as well."   —*The Barnstable Patriot*

"[Thayer] captures the essence of summer."   —*The Charleston Gazette*

"*Heat Wave* tells the moving story of a woman who, after her seemingly perfect life unravels, must find the strength to live and love again."
        —*Cape Cod Today*

"A riveting read for the summer."   —*Romance Reviews Today*

"*Heat Wave* is filled with both tenderness and tough situations. It is an engrossing look at love and friendship and how both are constantly evolving."   —*The Roanoke Times*

"Thayer has the knack of creating likeable characters who grapple with problems that will strike a chord with many readers."
        —*The Boston Globe*

"This latest from the popular Thayer should make good beach reading."
        —*Library Journal*

"Thayer delivers a gentle but fast-paced story of second chances in *Heat Wave*. Populated with endearing characters, this story deals with the very real subject of grieving, and how family and friends are so important to have around to carry on with life. An important message wrapped within a heartwarming story."
        —Wichita Falls *Times Record News*

"Nancy Thayer's gift for reaching the emotional core of her characters [is] captivating."   —*Houston Chronicle*

Heat Wave

NANCY THAYER

Heat Wave

A NOVEL

Ballantine Books Trade Paperbacks
New York

2012 Ballantine Books Trade Paperback Edition

Copyright © 2011 by Nancy Thayer
Random House reading group guide copyright © 2012 by Random House, Inc.
Excerpt from *Summer Breeze* copyright © 2012 by Nancy Thayer

Published in the United States by Ballantine Books,
an imprint of The Random House Publishing Group,
a division of Random House, Inc., New York.

BALLANTINE and colophon are registered trademarks of Random House, Inc.
RANDOM HOUSE READER'S CIRCLE & Design is a registered trademark of
Random House, Inc.

Originally published in hardcover in the United States by Ballantine Books,
an imprint of The Random House Publishing Group,
a division of Random House, Inc., in 2011.

Epigraph by Edith H. West. Used by permission.

This book contains an excerpt from the forthcoming book *Summer Breeze*
by Nancy Thayer. This excerpt has been set for this edition only and
may not reflect the final content of the forthcoming edition.

LIBRARY OF CONGRESS CATALOGING-IN-PUBLICATION DATA
Thayer, Nancy.
Heat wave : a novel / Nancy Thayer.
p.   cm.
ISBN 978-0-345-51832-3—ISBN 978-0-345-51833-0 (ebk.)
1. Nantucket Island (Mass.)—Fiction.   2. Domestic fiction.   I. Title.
PS3570.H3475H43 2011
813'.54—dc22   010053759

Printed in the United States of America

www.randomhousereaderscircle.com

2 4 6 8 9 7 5 3 1

Book design by Mary A. Wirth

For Charley
My Man

Acknowledgments

. . . . .

While writing this book, I consulted the superlative Diane Pearl, M.D., and her excellent office staff: Diane Cabral, Julie Reinemo, and Janet Chaffee. Also, Greg Hinson, M.D., was kind enough to talk with me. I based most of my medical information on what my sister Martha Foshee, R.N., told me, and I want to thank them all. Any medical mistakes are entirely my sister's.

Thanks to Ann Balas of The Anchor Inn. Any mistakes about innkeeping are completely mine.

I also want to thank my talented, irrepressible friends Susan McGinnis, Laura Gallagher Byrne, Charlotte Kastner, Pam Diem, and Melissa Philbrick for being there when I needed them. Also thanks to Pam Pindell, who let us use her studio, and Jill Burrill, Laura Simon, Jean Mallinson, Tricia Patterson, and Deborah Beale, my literate, literary buddies. Mimi Beman, you're with me every day.

Thanks to Josh Thayer and David Gillum for consistent patient support with the mysteries of computers.

Thanks to Emmett St. John Tutfield Forbes, for making me fall in love again, and to Sam Wilde Forbes and her husband Neil Forbes, wonderful parents to my darling Ellias, Adeline, and Emmett. And

Sam, thanks for your brilliant response to my emergency phone call from New York!

Thanks to Jan Dougherty for keeping me literally in line. Great thanks to Anne Kronenberg, who has helped me believe, and trust, that fiction and reality are different.

Thanks to Jean Gordon for her help and especially for keeping me supplied with that wonderful health food, Jamaican rum cake.

Thanks to Karen White of Tantor Media for her excellent reading and careful questions for the *Beachcombers* CD.

I'm grateful to the entire team at Ballantine, especially Libby McGuire and Gina Centrello, as well as Junessa Viloria, Kim Hovey, Katie Rudkin, Quinne Rogers, Jean Lisa, and Penelope Haynes. Special thanks to Kate Collins. Lasting thanks to Dana Isaacson.

My editor, Linda Marrow, has a riding-crop mind and an angelic heart, an amazing combination, which fills me with admiration and gratitude.

Thanks, too, to Christina Hogrebe and Peggy Gordijn of the Jane Rotrosen Agency, and to my agent, the unique and fabulous Meg Ruley.

The house is good
The beams are strong
The sun streams in
The whole day long
A hundred years
Or more it's stood
Swept by sea winds
The house is good

—Edith H. West

Heat Wave

1

. . . . .

Some days recently, Carley Winsted had experienced moments of actual happiness, when her heart gave her a break. She'd forget Gus's death and focus on the sight of her daughters or the sparkle of sunlight on the ocean—and lightning-fast, guilt zapped her. How could she be happy even for a moment?

She *had* to be happy, because she needed to be a role model for her daughters. She wanted to show them how to get through the dark times, to relish the good in each and every day.

Today she just needed not to be a coward.

It was the end of December, the end of the year. The end of the worst year in Carley's life. High on a cliff overlooking the deep blue waters of Nantucket Sound, Carley stood in her bedroom, her heart racing with anxiety.

Thank heavens her girls were with friends this morning. She couldn't let them see her like this. They had enough to deal with. Their beloved father, Carley's dear Gus, had died a month ago. His death had been unexpected, unpredictable, *wrong*, caused by an un-diagnosed heart defect that had been lying stealthily in wait for years. Gus had been only thirty-seven. Carley was only thirty-two.

Cisco was twelve.

Margaret was five.

It was unbearable. Yet it had to be borne.

She'd been doing pretty well, she thought, but this morning her grief was overridden by a gripping panic, which was ridiculous, really.

After all, it wasn't as if she were a peasant being thrown into the lion's den. She was only going to her father-in-law's office to discuss finances with him. Okay, fine, finances had never been her strong suit. She'd gotten married at twenty, she'd never had a real job, Gus had handled the money, she had taken care of the house, the children, food and clothing, their lives. But she was not a financial *idiot*, and Gus knew that. Gus had left this house entirely to her. It had no mortgage. It was completely, legally, hers.

So why had Russell asked her to come to the law office to meet with him? Such a cold, businesslike place—why hadn't he come to her house to talk with her in the living room as he always had? True, Carley had not always been on the same page as Annabel and Russell. They were different in so many ways, and the truth was, her in-laws were difficult to please. But they shared a mutual love for their son, her husband, Gus, and for his and Carley's daughters, Cisco and Margaret.

Carley gave herself a careful, critical once-over in the mirror. Her tailored gray suit was loose on her, but that was to be expected. She'd lost weight since Gus's death. So had Russell and Annabel, even Gus's best friend, Wyatt. Carley was tall and lanky, and now whip thin. In this suit, she looked elegant, even haughty, although anyone who knew Carley knew elegant and haughty were so not her. Russell had to know that after being around her for thirteen years.

But since Gus's death, both Russell and Annabel had been . . . different. More openly judgmental. Carley's only defense was to be prepared. She slipped her feet into her highest heeled boots.

Her appointment with Russell was set for eleven o'clock. Her *appointment*! Gus wouldn't have put up with this formal crap. "Come on, Dad, just tell us what you have to say, and we'll work it out." That's what Gus would have said.

2
. . . . .

Carley met Gus on Nantucket one summer night when she was nineteen. The air was hot and muggy and she was whipped from waiting tables.

She'd just finished her second year at Syracuse with less than sterling grades. She wasn't upset about the grades. No one was upset about the grades—her parents were engrossed with their work and all her life Carley had been advised not to compare herself to her older sister, Sarah, who was brilliant at science and a jock as well, so no one was pressuring Carley to perform.

It was just that now, approaching her junior year, Carley felt a little lost. Sarah had always yearned to be a nurse when she grew up, an emergency room nurse. Her father was a much-respected and eternally busy dentist. Her mother and her best friend ran a day care center.

Carley had no idea what she wanted to be.

She thought she should want to be *something*. Rosie, her best childhood friend, wanted to go into the Peace Corps and become an immigration lawyer. Another friend wanted to teach in elementary school. Carley had believed she'd be inspired by some teacher or subject once she got to college, but that hadn't yet happened. She was listlessly declaring education her major.

One thing was crystal clear to her: she loved being on Nantucket. It was her third summer working here, and it seemed she was always happy here, no matter what her job was. Of course, it was always *summer*, when the days were drenched with sunshine and the air smelled of salt and roses and she was surrounded by friends. She kind of even liked her wait job. Some of the customers were jerks, but most of them were on vacation, tanned, relaxed, happy, and ready to give a big fat tip.

Still, she couldn't make a career out of waiting tables. First of all, her restaurant closed for the winter, but more important, island life was staggeringly expensive. She shared an attic room and tiny shower-stall bath with four other women and rent still took up a large chunk of her paycheck.

She wasn't worried about it, though. Not worried about a thing. Tonight some girlfriends had heard rumors of a party out on Cisco Beach and Carley decided to ride out with them. She smelled like the curried fish stew she'd been serving all evening, so she stripped down to almost nothing—shorts and a halter top, bare feet, her hair skinned back into a ponytail to keep it off her neck. The minute she arrived at the party, she nabbed a bottle of beer and chugged it down.

She was in a restless, devil-may-care kind of mood that summer. She was an accident waiting to happen, and subconsciously, that was probably what she wanted to be.

That night at the beach, she was light and supple, riding the tide of life wherever it would take her, and loving the motion. Bonfires were illegal on the beach, but someone had set up some grills and hibachis that gave off flickering golden lights and filled the air with the rich aroma of roasting hamburgers and hot dogs. Tables sunk into the sand held plastic cups and gallons of wine. Trash barrels stuffed with ice and beer leaned crookedly in the sand. Friends screamed with glee when they saw each other, as if they were reunited after years apart, and as darkness fell, people seemed mysterious, exotic. Music from a CD player had people dancing at the water's edge, with partners or alone.

Carley talked with friends, drank a couple of beers, and then she and Rhonda, one of her roomies, started dancing with their shadows. Oh, that night—the heat of the air, the cold shock of waves lapping over her feet, the sounds of laughter, and the beat of music—she was a primitive thing for a while that night, dancing in and out of the waves that surged up the shore. It wasn't just the alcohol, it was the essence of the night, the sheer joy of being young, and she felt sassy, free, *eternal*, somehow part of the world and still very particularly herself.

Late at night, a man came over, took her hand, and led her up to a log someone had left on the beach as a seat.

"You need a hamburger," he said.

Carley threw her head back and laughed. "I need a hamburger?"

"I've been watching you. You've been dancing for a long time. You're about to fall down. I think you need a hamburger and some water and if you sit here, I'll bring them to you."

As she dropped down on the log, her head spun and her legs suddenly gave way. She landed hard on her bum. "Oops." She grinned up at the man. "I think you may be right."

Carley never had been able to drink much. She went straight from sober to pass out on three glasses of wine, seldom enjoying any kind of high. That night she'd only had two beers, or maybe three. She wasn't exactly drunk. Perhaps she was just a bit tired. And she couldn't remember when she'd last eaten.

The man returned, bearing a paper plate in one hand and a bottle of Perrier in the other.

"Thanks." She chugged the sparkling water. "That tastes sublime! I had no idea I was so thirsty." She held the hamburger with both hands. "Yum."

"I'm Gus," he said.

"I'm Carley," she told him.

They didn't go to bed with each other that night, although around three a.m., when most of the others were dragging themselves away for a few hours of necessary sleep before their workday began, they did begin to kiss. The log was not a comfortable site for romance. Twice they clumsily tumbled into the sand, laughing through their kisses. Rhonda straggled up to Carley, saying she was driving back to town now, if Carley wanted a ride. Gus asked Carley if he could see her the next night, and Carley had chuckled, feeling warm and dreamy and tired and sexy.

"Yeah, and somewhere with lights might be good," she told him. "So we can see what we look like."

The next night, sober, she had liked the way Gus looked. Anyone would. He was striking, with unusual black eyes and thick black hair. He was older than Carley, already a lawyer, working at the family firm on the island. He loved the island, he had grown up here. He knew who he was and what he was, and that impressed the hell out of Carley.

That night, they had slept together. He took her out to dinner at a posh restaurant, then brought her to his apartment. The sex hadn't been amazing, at least not for Carley, but it had been friendly, and that was very nice. Afterward, Carley joked, "Ah. Seduced by a hamburger."

Then Gus took her home to meet his parents, and she did fall in love.

Gus was a Winsted, whose family had helped settle Nantucket in the 1600s. His mother Annabel was a Greenwood, and her family had deep island roots as well. Gus's father, Russell, had grown up on the island in the Winsted family's enormous brick house on Main Street, gone off to Harvard, and returned as a lawyer. Annabel was the only child in her family, and when her parents died, she inherited the Greenwood house, another historic Nantucket mansion, this one set at the end of a road on a cliff overlooking the Sound. Gus was an only child, too. "It had just worked out that way," was as much as elegant Annabel ever offered in explanation.

Russell and Annabel were both striking to look at. Tall and slender, Russell clad his storklike body in elegant pin-striped suits and handmade monogrammed cotton shirts that had belonged to his father and his grandfather. At home, he poured his daily scotch from an antique crystal decanter embossed with silver leaves. And he had that glossy ebony hair, those piercing dark eyes that gave Gus such intensity.

Annabel, Gus's mother, was a lean beauty with honey-colored hair worn in a careless twist and soft brown eyes. She was Carley's mother's age—forty-nine—but she went around in jeans and turtlenecks and Docksiders.

Carley knew her own mother would consider Annabel a lightweight, a frivolous and even selfish woman. But it was hard to measure up to Carley's mother's standards.

Marilyn Smith and her friend Bernice ran a day care center in East Laurence, New York. Marilyn was a passionate reformer, trying to bring comfort and affection to as many small children as she could—as long as they were other people's children. She had been a dutiful mother to Sarah and Carley until they turned ten, then Marilyn considered them old enough to take care of themselves. More than that, she considered them lucky, *too* lucky, and had no interest in any of their problems, which were, after all, only the problems of spoiled middle-class children. Carley's father, a dentist, worked hard as well, and came home late and tired. The family seldom ate dinner together but made sandwiches or heated up frozen dinners in the microwave.

But Russ and Annabel relished daily life—that was the mesmerizing, seductive quality the Winsteds had. Everything was centered around the home. Life was about family and friends.

Annabel and Russ both loved cooking. They grew some vegetables and herbs and experimented with sauces. They both had brown rubber waders that they wore when they pushed their way over the sand and through the water to pick mussels off the jetties; one of their favorite meals was mussels steamed with garlic, a warm loaf of homemade bread, a fresh salad, and wine. In the summer, Annabel roamed the moors to pick wild blueberries for pies and jellies; in the fall, she picked beach plums and made jam. Because Annabel and Russ were great sailors, Russ was always taking off from his law firm—it was his family's firm, he could take off whenever he wanted—to go sailing for the day with Annabel on their catboat, often returning with fish for dinner. They were both gregarious and loved entertaining, filling the house with people who gathered in the kitchen drinking wine and talking while Annabel and Russ put together some of their spontaneous catch-as-catch-can pizzas.

Not that they were obsessive about cooking. Sometimes Carley would drop by to find Annabel curled up on a sofa, reading. "I can't put this book down!" she'd say. "We'll have to order takeout tonight." Annabel and Russ were voracious readers. They attended all the lectures the library and museums gave. They loved art, too, and covered the walls of their house with works by island artists. They were involved in politics, and attended town meetings faithfully. The high school plays brought them out for at least one performance and often more. They were right *there* in their lives. They were not trying to get anywhere else; they weren't competitive or envious; they were that rarest of human creatures: genuinely happy people.

Of course, they had started off with more than many people ever had. They had each inherited an old Nantucket mansion. Their lives grew out of the island history like a flower from a new dawn rose, climbing, blossoming, part of a thick twisting stem deeply planted in the island's sandy soil, and proud to be in that sandy soil.

The Greenwood house that Annabel had grown up in—the house where Carley had made her home for the past thirteen years—was a rambling old wooden structure with a definite summer feeling about it. The redbrick mansion Annabel and Russ lived in was the more formal Winsted home. Behind the house, the large yard was walled with redbrick fifteen feet high, making the garden a private enclosure, a little Eden few people ever saw. Here Annabel grew her vegetables and flowers, and played with shaping privet bushes into whimsical shapes, one of her favorite pastimes. Inside, the rooms were large and high-ceilinged, with fireplaces, most of which worked, silk drapes pooling on the floor, and comfortable sofas and chairs mixed in with antique pieces. Like the ones at Carley's home, the kitchen and bathrooms were ancient, floored with ceramic tiles, fitted with claw-foot bathtubs that would have been delightful if the porcelain weren't almost worn through. Both houses required endless vigilance and maintenance, and endless amounts of money.

The first time Carley entered the Winsted house, she didn't notice the paint peeling from the walls or the faded ancient Oriental rugs. She thought the metal kitchen cabinets with the inset sink, considered "modern" in the 1940s, were charmingly old-fashioned. She didn't see the cracks in the plaster around the fireplaces or the way the bookshelves, overburdened with books, leaned dangerously sideways. The house had such a quality of excellence and experience and age. It felt like a wise house, a comforting house, a house that had witnessed holiday festivities and political gatherings and the solemnity of birth and death, and had stood at attention, with pride, through it all.

Carley loved the *idea* of the way the Winsteds lived. She wanted to be casually elegant, too. She yearned for Annabel and Russell to like her. She could imagine spending time with Annabel, learning so very much from her.

The older Winsteds seemed pleased by Carley that first night Gus brought her home. Certainly they charmed her, asked her questions, laughed at her slightest attempt at whimsy, treated her with gentle warmth.

As they drove away from his parents' house, Carley glanced shyly at Gus. "I think they liked me."

"Of course they liked you," Gus replied. "Who wouldn't?"

She smiled contentedly.

Then Gus said, "Although they wouldn't like it if I got too involved with you."

"Really? Why not?"

"Because you're not an islander. Not 'one of us.' "

"Does that really matter?"

"You'd be surprised how much it matters."

Carley chewed on her lip. She was already worried about something that could be a real problem between them. This made her feel even worse. She decided to wait a few days to tell Gus. She wanted to be sure.

3
. . . . .

She hadn't been on the birth control pill. The truth was, she'd been fairly naïve sexually. She'd had one serious boyfriend during high school, and no one since then. She hadn't planned to hook up with anyone on the island. She hadn't planned to get serious.

She hadn't planned.

Apparently, the first condom Gus used when they were together was old. By the time Carley went to be fitted with a diaphragm, she was pregnant. It was almost impossible to believe. She wasn't frightened or sad or happy or anything at all. Just confused.

"I don't want you to worry," she told Gus. "I—I can deal with this." Actually, she hadn't thought how she would deal with it. It still didn't seem real; it seemed as if, once she left the island, this fantasy land, and set foot on the mainland, the real world, her pregnancy would vanish.

"Maybe you shouldn't deal with it," Gus said. "Maybe we should get married."

"*Married?* My gosh, Gus, we hardly know each other."

"Yeah, but I like what I know," he told her. "We seem to get along awfully well. And the idea of having a family appeals to me. I'm ready for it. It will give me *gravitas*."

Well, she thought, I never thought I'd marry a man who said *gravitas*. The entire situation seemed dreamlike, as if she were trying on a life like a dress she might decide to buy, or not. She was not passionately swept off her feet by Gus. She liked him a lot. She thought she could come to love him. She thought his immediate response to her announcement of pregnancy indicated that he loved her, even though he hadn't said as much.

"What will your parents say?" she asked.

Gus winced. "It's not going to be easy. But we'll do it together, Carley. We won't back down."

Later in their marriage, Carley would wonder if Gus married her as proof that he was not controlled by his powerful, charismatic parents. Was she his rebellion? His glorious revolution? Certainly, until Cisco's birth, there was dissension in the family.

Gus invited his parents out to dinner. This was unusual. Annabel loved to cook, and Nantucket restaurants were crowded and expensive in the summer. Also, Gus was a partner specializing in real estate in his father's legal firm, along with Gus's best friend Wyatt Anderson, so his father knew exactly how much money Gus made. His parents would be just as likely to chastise him for wasting money as to praise him for taking them out.

Carley thought Gus's intention was to break the news to his parents in public, where they wouldn't cause a scene, although Annabel and Russell were never the sort to make a scene.

They went to The Languedoc. They were dressed conservatively, the men in blazers and ties, the women in summer dresses. Annabel wore pearls. Carley wore fake pearls. Carley pulled her long brown hair to the back of her neck in a puritanical bun.

Gus waited until the waiter had taken their dinner orders and brought them more wine before dropping the bomb. "Mom. Dad. Carley and I are going to get married. We're going to have a baby."

Annabel responded by turning her head to one side, as if she'd been slapped. She cast a meaningful look at her husband.

Russell remained jovial, as if this were a trivial matter. "Well, well. Gus, this is a surprise. You and Carley haven't known each other very long—"

Annabel interrupted. "And Carley doesn't know the island *at all*. Do you, dear? I mean, you've never been here in the winter. Perhaps you think it's all pleasure and parties on the beach, but believe me, we have long, lonely, isolated winter months. Even people who've grown up here, who *love* the island, find it difficult."

Smoothly, Russell took up the argument. "Even though it seems we're wealthy, we're not, really. I suppose you could say we're house poor. I mean, what I'm trying to say, what I'm sure Gus has told you, is that we're not like a lot of people who fly off to some Caribbean island for a month or so in the winter to get some sunlight. We're stuck here on this windy stretch of sand all during the coldest months—"

Gus interrupted. "Carley knows that. I've told her all that. She's not a dunce and she's not a fortune hunter or whatever you want to call it. We love each other, and we love the idea of raising a family on the island. She's met my friends. They love her. I've taken her through the house. We've talked about fixing it up—Carley has wonderful ideas. She can do much of the work herself. She can paint. She can hang wallpaper."

At those words, Annabel went white. "The *house*." She put her elegant hand to her chest, as if her heart hurt. "Gus, that is my family's house. It's historic. It should be restored by someone with knowledge and the proper skills."

"Come on, Mom, it's a wonderful old house, but it's not Monticello. You and Dad promised it to me when I got married. I'm getting married. Carley and I will raise our children there."

Annabel turned to her husband, her expression a silent cry for help.

Russell cleared his throat. "Perhaps there is some other way to resolve this. Perhaps a sum of money—"

Gus's voice growled out low and threatening. "Don't you dare."

Both Russell and Annabel drew up, clearly startled at their son's tone.

"This is your grandchild we're talking about," Gus reminded

them. "This dinner is meant to be an announcement and a celebration."

Annabel tried to smooth the troubled waters. "If you are happy, Gus, then so are we. It's just that it's all happened so fast."

"I am happy, Mom," Gus assured her. "Happier than I've ever been in my life."

Carley and Gus married quietly and settled into the Greenwood house like a pair of nesting birds settling into an enormous drafty box. Carley and Gus hung wallpaper and Gus painted while Carley sewed up curtains for the baby's room. They went to movies and parties with friends. They bought furniture, they bought pots and pans, and Gus's belt tightened from eating Carley's delicious food.

Then Carley went into a long, difficult, agonizing labor and gave birth to their first daughter, Cisco. Carley was no longer the unmotivated drifting airhead of her family. She had her *own* family. She was the wife of a lawyer, the mother of a baby girl, the chatelaine of a historic house, a member of the Winsted clan, and a resident of an island thirty miles out at sea.

When Cisco was born, Annabel and Russell took one look at her tiny face and melted with love. In the hospital, holding the infant, they both wept tears of joy. Later, Annabel brought over a variety of gourmet casseroles for Carley and Gus and joyfully did endless loads of baby laundry while Russell went to the pharmacy and the grocery store.

One morning while Carley was tucked up on the sofa with the infant sleeping in her arms, Annabel curled up in the chair opposite and gazed upon mother and child, her face radiant with adoration.

"You *are* a clever girl," Annabel praised Carley. "I've never seen a more beautiful child in my life. Carley, please forgive me for being so damnably mean when we first heard you were pregnant. I had no idea how much I would adore this little child, and you brought her to us."

"Thanks, Annabel." Carley shifted on the sofa, trying to get comfortable. "I had no idea how much I'd love her, either."

"She's just so completely bewitching." Annabel leaned forward, love-struck.

Carley chuckled. "I don't suppose your opinion has anything to do with the fact that Cisco has the black hair and eyes and pale skin of the Winsted clan, does it?"

Annabel pressed her hand to her chest in mock surprise. "How could you suggest such a thing?" she teased lightly, then admitted, "Of course it does. I'm wild about Russell's coloring, and thrilled that Gus has it, and over the moon that my granddaughter has it." She cocked her head and offered brightly, "I do think Cisco has your nose."

After that, Carley and Annabel became comrades, devoted to the baby, satellites revolving around the sun that was Cisco. When Carley was pregnant again, she and Gus learned from the ultrasound the baby was female. When they told Russell and Annabel, Carley sensed the very slightest moment of disappointment that the baby was not a boy. At once, Annabel lightened the atmosphere, crying out, "Oh, thank heavens! I have so much fun buying little-girl clothing!" And when Margaret arrived, she and Russell both adored the new girl as much as they adored Cisco.

Annabel was a forceful personality. Yet over the years, Annabel managed to be available for emergencies, parties, little treats and surprises, without ever intruding on Gus and Carley, without ever attempting to manipulate or steer their lives. Carley sensed this took some amount of self-restraint on Annabel's part, and she was grateful.

4
. . . . .

Gus had died, quickly, one evening in his office. The small law firm was housed in a handsome old brick Greek Revival house on Centre Street. Russell usually walked there from his brick home a few blocks away on Main Street, stopping to chat with shopkeepers along the way. It was a fifteen-minute walk for Gus from his house, but it was cold the day he died, so he'd driven. When he hadn't come home for dinner that terrible night, Carley had called Russell, who had returned to the building and found his body.

Carley had already fed the girls and sent them off to their rooms. She'd been mildly anxious about Gus but more pissed off that he'd be so late for dinner. She paced the house, waiting for Russell to call. Instead, there was a knock on the door.

Carley found her father-in-law standing there, pale, confused.

"*Gus.*" Russell could scarcely speak.

Behind him, a police car pulled up to the curb and the police chief, a friend of the Winsteds, stepped out.

"Heart attack," Russell gasped.

Her first reaction was a rush of adrenaline, a frantic sense of dread and urgency, a need to *move*, as if she could still prevent it if only she *did something*. She wanted to push Russell aside, to rush down to the office, to get to her husband.

"I'll go to the office." She tried to pass Russell, who blocked the doorway.

"Honey, we've already phoned an ambulance and the coroner."
Russell stood very straight in his suit and dark wool coat, but he was
trembling.

Carley bit her lip to hold back her anger. Gus belonged to her
and her daughters! How dare Russell—her thoughts derailed. Oh,
her *daughters*, whose father was *gone*! She slammed to her knees
with terror.

Kellogg, the police chief, approached through the darkness into
the light of the front hall. His uniform and grizzled face provided a
welcome sense of authority. Bending, he took Carley's shoulders and
gently helped her stand. "I'm sorry, Carley. This is a terrible thing.
Let's get Russell inside. Let's all have some brandy."

Numbed, grateful to be told what to do, Carley led Russell into
the living room. They sat on the sofa while Russell spoke about
finding Gus dead at his desk. Chief Kellogg brought them each a
glass of brandy. Carley could only stare at hers.

"Mommy?" Cisco and Margaret had come downstairs and stood
in the doorway to the living room, looking curious and so vulnerable in their pajamas that Carley's heart broke for them.

Cisco asked, "What's going on?"

"Oh, girls . . ." Carley set her glass on the coffee table and walked
over to her daughters. She knelt before them, taking their hands in
hers. She looked into their deep, beautiful eyes, their ebony Winsted
eyes. Their father's eyes. "Daddy died. He had a heart attack. He was
in his office. Your grandfather found him. Chief—"

"No!" Cisco wrenched her hand away from her mother's. "I
don't believe you! I want to see him! Where is he?"

Chief Kellogg answered, his voice low. "He's at the hospital
now."

"Let's go there!" Cisco's eyes were wide. "Maybe they've done
CPR."

Russell rose from the couch and approached his granddaughters.
He bent toward them. "Cisco. Honey, I found your daddy. I saw him.
I called an ambulance and the police. They did try to resuscitate
him. They tried all possible means."

"Mommy." Margaret's high voice trembled. "I don't want Daddy to be dead."

"I know, sweetheart." Carley pulled Margaret against her. Her younger daughter was crying, obviously frightened and confused, but also seeking and receiving the consolation of her mother's embrace. Cisco, Carley feared, was going into shock. Her fists were clenched, and her jaw shuddered.

Carley looked at Chief Kellogg. "Could we phone Dr. Kunadra and ask him to come over?"

Kellogg nodded once, abruptly, and pulled out his cell.

Russell offered, "Cisco, come sit with me."

Cisco didn't move. She couldn't *seem* to move.

Kellogg said to Carley's father-in-law, "Russell. We have to tell Annabel."

"Dear God." Russell's face sagged. He staggered backward, just slightly, and Carley reached out for him.

"Cisco, take Granddad's hand," Carley quietly demanded.

Cisco's paralysis broke. She took Russell's hand and led him into the living room. Carley followed, settling on the sofa, holding Margaret on her lap, and wrapping her free arm around Cisco.

"Shall I go get Annabel?" Kellogg asked.

"I'll go," Russell said. "I have to be the one to tell her. Then we'll come back here."

"I don't think you should drive," Kellogg warned. "I'll take you."

Russell looked at Carley and the girls.

"We'll be all right," she said, just as a knock sounded on the door and Sunjay Kunadra, their physician, entered.

Russell and Chief Kellogg left. With infinitely soft hands, Sunjay took Carley's pulse and ordered her to drink some of the brandy. Margaret asked him to take her pulse, too, and he did, pronouncing her perfect. Sunjay took a seat, pinching the crease in his expensive trousers as he did, and in a gentle voice, asked who he could call. Carley had trouble thinking, but Cisco said at once, "Maud. Vanessa."

Margaret added, "And Wyatt. He's Daddy's best friend."

Sunjay made the calls. He sat across from Carley and her daughters and explained in his mild, scientific manner that Gus had had a heart attack. They would do an autopsy to find out the cause. Sometimes these things just happened.

Time lurched forward. Chief Kellogg, Russell, and Annabel came into the house. Annabel, elegant in a blue sweater and slacks, was rigid with self-control, but when she saw her granddaughters, a small cry burst from her throat and she stumbled. Her husband helped her to the sofa.

"Go to her," Carley whispered to her daughters. Cisco and Margaret obeyed, wrapping their grandmother tightly in their arms.

Wyatt arrived from his house in Madaket. He made more phone calls. Vanessa and Maud came, hugging Carley and the girls. Everyone was weeping. The immediate protection of shock faded; the air of the room was thick with grief, with misery. Annabel's self-restraint dissolved, and a terrible wail broke from her. Margaret fled back to Carley's arms and even Cisco looked frightened.

"Let's make hot chocolate for everyone," Carley told her girls, leading them from the room as Russell cradled his wife against him. The three went into the kitchen together and with an almost ceremonial rhythm measured the milk, stirred in the cocoa and sugar, heated the pan, and poured the liquid into the cups. Cisco, older and stronger, carried in the tray with the cups. Margaret carried her favorite bunny teapot full of hot chocolate.

By midnight, everyone left. Carley brought the girls into her bed, and watched them until they fell asleep, which wasn't long, because they were completely exhausted with grief. She took the sleep medication Sunjay had given her.

Over the next few days, the world went on.

Her family had come up to help, all of them, her father, mother, sister, and Sarah's partner, Sue. They'd been efficient and loving. They'd taken Cisco and Margaret off to the beach or to the library or simply for a walk, to get them away from the suddenly saddened house. They made coffee and food for the many good friends who showed up to express their surprise and their sorrow, to offer help.

They arranged the funeral, talked with the minister, cooked for the reception, thanked those who brought hams and quiches and desserts, lugged in cases of sparkling water and juice and wine, and cleaned up the explosion of glasses and plates left scattered around the house afterward.

When her parents returned to their home in East Laurence, they took Carley and her daughters with them for the Christmas season. It was the custom for Carley and her family to go to her parents' every other year, and this year they did as always, driving into Manhattan to see the tree at Rockefeller Center, strolling the streets to gaze in the amazing shop windows. This year, of course, the holiday was muted for them, surreal, uncomfortable. They felt awkward together, awkward alone. They gave presents, but didn't know whether to be happy about them. They didn't know how to have Christmas dinner without Gus at the table. They didn't know how to *be*.

It was good to return home at the end of December. Just unpacking in their own rooms brought a sense of normality to Carley and her daughters. They still mourned and talked daily of missing Daddy, but their lives were going on. Cisco continued with ballet. Margaret played dolls with Molly. Carley said prayers of thanks every day to Gus, for her daughters, and for their home, their true shelter against the storm.

Their house, which had once been Annabel's family's house, was large and built to last where it stood on a cliff overlooking Nantucket Sound. The front and back gardens were spacious, fenced, and planted with climbing roses, honeysuckle, hydrangea, and lots of bushes for hiding behind. Her friends liked gathering at Carley's, to sit on her wide porch while the children played games in the garden. In rainy or cold weather, the children could run shrieking up and down the stairs and especially into the attic, while the mommies sat in the kitchen drinking tea or wine, telling secrets.

This house was hers, free and clear. The mortgage was paid off. With her father at her side, she had attended the reading of Gus's will, the contents of which she already knew, since Gus had talked it over with her when he made it. He left everything to her, the house, his money, his life insurance.

So why had her father-in-law asked her to come into his office for a "little talk"? When Russell phoned her yesterday, he'd been silky smooth as always, but firm and more businesslike than she'd ever heard him. Her appointment was for eleven o'clock. Her father-in-law had seen her in jeans and tee shirt, in a bikini, even in a hospital gown after giving birth. For this appointment, Carley wore makeup, neat and light. She felt an instinctive need to appear mature, capable, responsible. Inside, her heart quivered with fear, though she didn't know why.

But she *did* know. She was certain that Russell was going to talk with her about financial matters. That was why he wanted to meet in the office rather than in her home.

Leaving her bedroom, she clattered down the stairs to the first floor, into the large room that had once been Gus's office.

For a moment she stood in the doorway, looking into the room the way tourists view a museum setting: Gus Winsted's office. The room had a fireplace. The mantel held sailing trophies and pictures of the girls. Gus's desk was directly across from the fireplace, the handsome old mahogany desk of his grandfather's. One wall was lined with shelves for his books and photos. He had a leather sofa facing a television set.

A comfortable executive leather chair towered behind the desk. Carley had sat in it before, but not often. Gingerly, she lowered herself into its depths. She'd opened some of Gus's desk drawers before, too. The middle drawer held pens, rubber bands, scissors, Post-it notes.

The left drawer held the checkbooks. And his computer was angled toward him from the left.

Carley looked around the room. It was daylight. No shadows.

"Gus," she said aloud, "I have to do this. I don't want to intrude, but I've got to take charge of our lives."

She opened the desk. Gus had been secretive about money.

When she asked him for details, he only told her, not quite conde-scendingly, "Honey, don't worry. We have enough."

Now she found files about house insurance, health insurance, car insurance. No life insurance file. That was odd. Files about in-vestments, savings, loans, stocks and bonds. She booted up the com-puter and lost herself in the maze of Gus's financial dealings. Two years ago, the amount in the various accounts had been substantial. Now it looked as though most accounts were closed. She couldn't find any sign of a savings account, or a money market account. Gus and Carley shared a checking account, and over the past few months she'd withdrawn just enough to pay the household bills. She'd intended to transfer money from the savings account into the checking account when she had time—but where was the savings account?

Desperately, she scrolled and clicked through his computer. She turned to the deep drawer on the right side of the desk and clawed through the files. It didn't make sense.

Her heart raced. So this was what Russell was going to talk about with her.

She had no money.

Forewarned is forearmed, Carley told herself, although she wasn't certain what she was armed with. She did feel less frightened. Money matters were scary, but they weren't *death*. They could be dealt with.

She pulled on her favorite coat—a light wool, very chic—then took it off. It had a swing cut, which seemed frivolous. She pulled on her good old black wool coat, grabbed her purse, and left the house. She would walk to the law firm. Fifteen minutes of fresh air and deep breathing would do her good. She set off toward town.

Nantucket seldom got as much snow as the mainland, and as she walked along, she found the sidewalks dry and clear even though a dusting of white scattered over the yards. Close to town, a white gravel drive circled in front of the law offices, providing parking space for their clients or the Winsteds. She climbed the steps to the handsome black door and turned the knob. She stepped inside.

The reception room was empty. Claudia, their secretary, was absent, her computer off, her desk tidied.

Carley peeked into the other downstairs room. Dick, their paralegal, was gone, too, and the kitchen/storage area where they made their coffee and kept their supplies was vacant. But she heard footsteps upstairs.

The offices and long conference room were on the second floor.

From force of habit, she turned right, toward Gus's office, before correcting herself and turning left.

Russell's door was open. As Carley entered, he rose, smiling. "Carley, my dear."

"Hello, Russell." She went around the desk and kissed his cheek.

"Hello, Carley."

Her nerves already on edge, Carley flinched at the unexpected sound of Annabel's voice. Spinning around, she saw her mother-in-law perched on the leather sofa, elegant in a suit and Hermès scarf.

"Hello, Annabel. I didn't realize you were going to be here." Crossing the room, she bent to kiss Annabel's cheek. *Thank heavens I wore a suit,* she thought, settling herself on the other end of the sofa.

Russell lowered himself into his desk chair and sat for a moment, staring down at a pile of folders in front of him.

"Carley, it's often hard to discuss money, especially during times of such sorrow. I'm not sure how much you understood during the reading of Gus's will."

Carley nodded. She'd been lost in a blur of distress that day. Numbers had melted and slid away in her mind.

But she was firm when she answered, "I know Gus left me the house. Free and clear."

Annabel made a sudden little sound, a whimper of pain.

Russell continued pleasantly, "Of course. We are well aware of that. We have a copy of the will. He left you all his money, too, except as you will find out, and I apologize for bringing this up at this difficult time . . ." Russell took out his handkerchief and wiped his eyes before continuing. "Gus made some bad investments last year."

"I'm aware of that," Carley told him.

Russell raised his eyebrows. "You are? Well. Well, then, perhaps all this won't come as such a shock to you." He cleared his throat. "I have no idea about how much of the financial aspect of running this house Gus shared with you, but it's a huge house, and it requires a lot of maintenance. Also, of course, for your family, there is the basic cost of living, groceries, clothing, car insurance—" He stopped suddenly. His face caved in. He looked old and very sad. "Carley, my dear. Gus left you no money. Well, enough, I suppose, for a month or two, if you're careful."

"The insurance policy?" Carley began.

"It appears he was unwise. He cashed it in."

Carley's fingertips went cold. She knew the symptoms of panic attacks, and fought to stave one off. Deep breaths, she told herself.

Russell cleared his throat. "Carley. Annabel and I have been talking."

Carley forgot the breathing as her mind sharpened in self-defense. "Okay."

"We think you and the girls should come live with us."

Carley stared.

Annabel leaned forward, her voice rich with concern. "The house is too big for you to live in alone with the two little girls. It will be too *lonely*. In our house, we've got room for everyone. Think how much better it will be, especially for Cisco and Margaret, to have three adults living with them, not just one."

Carley chose her words with care. "Annabel, Russell, what a kind offer. But the house is our *home*, mine and Cisco's and Margaret's. The girls have grown up there. Their bedrooms are there. The yard they play in, the attics they play in. It would be terribly disruptive, disorienting, to ask them to move."

"They have bedrooms in our house," Annabel pointed out.

"True. And of course they'll still spend overnights with you; they love doing that. That won't change. But we need, the three of us, to learn to get on with our lives there, in our home."

"If the three of you lived with us," Russell said carefully, "perhaps the girls wouldn't miss their father quite so much."

"Oh, Russell," Carley argued. "The girls adore you, but Gus was their *father*, and nothing can protect them from missing him. I may not be stating this well, I'm overwhelmed, I'm *sad*, and I'm heartbroken for my daughters, but I don't think anyone can be a substitute for their father."

"If you live with us," Russell continued, "we'll take care of all your expenses. If you don't live with us, you'll have to find work."

"And that would mean," Annabel added quickly, "that the girls would become latchkey children."

A flush of anger shot through Carley. "No, that won't happen."

"But how can it not?" Annabel asked, tilting her head delicately.

"I have some ideas," Carley said, lying through her teeth. "I'm not ready to discuss them with you yet, but I will, soon. I'm grateful for your concern, but—" Tears pressured the backs of her eyes. Her mind was spinning. She stood up, unsteady in her high-heeled boots.

Her father-in-law hurried toward her. "Carley, please. We're all overwrought. We're not going to come to any sensible conclusion right now. Won't you just think about our offer?"

Emotion made Annabel's voice tremble. "Carley, we just want to take care of you."

"I understand," Carley said. "And I'm grateful." But her teeth were clenched as she left the room.

6

.....

She strode home, fueled by anger and determination, her thoughts in a whirlwind. It was lunchtime, but she wasn't hungry. She had to keep moving. Tossing her good suit on the bed, she pulled on jeans and a long-sleeved tee. She tied her sneakers, yanked on her parka, wool hat and gloves, and slammed out the door. She jogged down the dog-legged route past houses, cottages, and concession stands to the long stretch of Jetties Beach where the winter waves surged and spat like her thoughts.

Her worries churned repetitively through her mind like the wheels of a train. What could she do? What could she do? How could she make money?

She would call her father, first of all. He had offered, when he came up for the funeral, to help Carley financially. She would gladly take him up on that offer now. She had no intention of being dependent on him, but he could spare enough to get her through a few months while she found a solution.

A solution. A job.

What she wanted to be, fortunately—and now, perhaps unfortunately—was just what she was. A stay-at-home mom with a big house and lots of friends. Growing up, she'd never had a dream career—lawyer, nurse, pilot, belly dancer—so it had been a continuing delightful surprise, each day, that completely by accident she'd achieved a life that seemed exactly right for her.

So, first, her father. Next—next, she would sit down with
Vanessa and Maud and brainstorm ideas. They were bound to come
up with something.

Vanessa Hutchinson and Maud Parsons were Carley's two best
friends on the island. On the planet, actually. Maud and Vanessa
were best friends, too, and for some inexplicable reason, their trio
worked. They'd met thirteen years ago, when Carley had just married Gus and moved to the island. Their husbands were fishing, sailing, and football-watching buddies, so they were thrown together a
lot, part of a larger young married gang who spent New Year's Eve
together, and sailed to Coatue for an all-day Fourth of July picnic,
and turned out to cheer the local high school football team, where
once Gus had been linebacker and Toby quarterback.

Gus Winsted, Toby Hutchinson, and John Parsons had been
born on the island and had grown up here. Gus's best friend, Wyatt,
was another island man who attended the picnics or football game
parties, but he was single. Each time he brought a different knock-
out girlfriend who caused the three husbands to stare, suck in their
guts, and straighten their shoulders.

"Hey!" Vanessa would snap. "Down, boys!"

"Yeah, you *pillars of the community*," Maud would chip in.

Then the three women would exchange glances sparked with
mirth and mischief, because all three women secretly agreed that
Wyatt Anderson was center-of-the-sun *hot*. When he came around,
they stared at him as much as their husbands did at his dates. Wyatt
had wavy brown hair and truly green eyes and no insidious flab
creeping over his belt buckle. He was relaxed and good-natured, unlike their husbands, who were always stressed-out and cranky, or at
least so it seemed. John Parsons taught English in the high school
and worried constantly about not making enough money, and Toby
was the local pediatrician. He didn't worry about money, but he was
always overwhelmed and hopeless at home.

Carley, Maud, and Vanessa loved their husbands, but as the
years passed, they were just naturally drawn into their own little trio
by the need to discuss female matters. At least that was why, they

explained to their husbands, they spent so much time on the phone with one another. *Yeast infections,* they'd murmur, or *PMS,* and their husbands would scurry away as if they had the flu. The three women served on many of the same committees, too, but really what bonded them was a similar sense of humor, a love of the sting of sarcasm, and a general sense that everyone should just *relax.* When cornered at a cocktail party by Beth Boxer, one of their extended group by virtue of her husband, and a savagely gossip-mongering little rat terrier of a woman, they would look at each other with deadpan faces and slowly twitch the left eyelid, their signal for "Get Me Out of Here." Later, they would collapse with laughter and clever Maud would do an eerily perfect impersonation.

Maud was petite and Audrey Hepburn pretty. Carley was lanky, brown-haired, and athletic. Vanessa was tall, voluptuous, and raven-haired. So they weren't like peas in a pod. They weren't like anything, really. They weren't rebels, they were just young wives and mothers who shared a sense of humor, and that got them through some pretty hard times. And through some funny times, too.

Six years ago in January, the town was hit with a flu epidemic at the same time a gale force wind blasted a blizzard across the island, dropping mountains of snow, toppling trees across driveways, tossing the huge ferries in the harbor around like toys in a bathtub. This was the side of Nantucket life the tourists never knew about and it wasn't pretty. The DPW wasn't prepared for snow removal of this magnitude because it so seldom snowed with such fury on the island. Roads were blocked. Shops were closed. Schools were closed. Worse, the ferries carrying the necessities of life—fresh milk, bread, orange juice, cough medicine—couldn't make it over from the Cape because of the wind. People shared their baby aspirin and ginger ale as if it were gold.

When the front finally passed and the sun came out, life returned to normal. The children, over their flu, went skipping energetically back to school and the husbands shaved off their caveman bristles, took much-needed showers, and went back to work.

Carley could never remember who it was who made the first phone call. Probably Maud; she was the most imaginative. She suggested they fly to the Cape for the day, to shop, see a movie, have a girls'-night-out dinner, and fly home on the last plane. Carley asked her mother-in-law to have her daughters and Gus over for dinner, and Annabel was delighted. Margaret was only a little over one then, but she'd spent a lot of time with her grandparents and loved being in their home. Everyone would be fine for one day without Carley.

It was a brilliant escape from reality. They shopped like women just set free from a sensory-deprivation tank, shrieking with joy over the January sales and discovering the pretty young women they still were under all their practical L.L. Bean fleece. When they finally settled around the table at the Mexican restaurant, their arms, necks, and ears jangling with new, totally unnecessary jewelry, they ordered the most extravagantly unusual margaritas on the menu.

"Oh my gosh!" Maud stretched her arms above her head. "I feel like I've just been let out of prison. Carley, you have two kids, too, but you have *girls*. Believe me, little boys are different. Manic. Little animals. Sometimes I watch them run through the house bellowing and the entire history of the world comes clear before me."

Carley snorted. "Cisco and Margaret were easy, I guess, even though they were both so sick. It was Gus who was driving me crazy. We *all* had the flu, but with Gus it was like the last act of *Romeo and Juliet*."

For years, Vanessa had been trying to get pregnant, and it hadn't happened—or as Vanessa always insisted optimistically, it hadn't happened *yet*. Still, she waved her hand. "No, no, you haven't seen sick until you've seen *the doctor* sick. True, Toby worked at his office all day, and true, he did have the flu, but he so seldom gets sick, he acted as if he had cholera. The coughing, the sneezing, the whining—I'd bet good money he didn't do that at the office. And could he ever ask for two things at the same time? No. First, could I bring him tissues. Then a blanket, because he had to languish on the sofa, watching TV. Then a whiskey, mixed with the scientifically precise amount of soda water. Then some crackers. No, not the wheat thins. Just plain saltines. Then—"

Carley and Maud were laughing with Vanessa, sipping their drinks, eyeing their jewelry, when they suddenly became aware of a man standing in front of their table. He was wildly handsome in a Ricky Martin way, wearing a satin shirt unbuttoned for full exposure of his own fine gold chains, and he was young. They were around twenty-six. He was probably twenty-one. His skin was like honey, his lips full, his dark eyes deep with sexual promise.

He swept his thick-ebony-lashed eyes across the three of them. He said, "¡Hola!"

The three women stopped laughing. For a long moment they just stared, lips clinging to their margarita glasses.

Vanessa, who spoke some Spanish, replied, "¡Hola!"

At this, the Ricky Martin clone leaned toward them, and putting his hands on the table, unrolled a series of silken Spanish words toward them with such speed not even Vanessa could understand him.

"¿Perdón?" Vanessa asked.

And then the spell was broken by the arrival of their waiter, not nearly as handsome as Ricky Martin. In rapid-fire Spanish, with many gestures, the waiter made it clear that the young man was bothering the ladies and should leave them alone *pronto*.

Ricky Martin shrugged sadly, and walked away, turning only to say, "*Las tres enchiladas.*"

"What?" Maud demanded of Vanessa. "What did he say?"

"It sounded like he called us enchiladas," Vanessa told her.

"Yeah," Carley agreed. "I heard that, too. *Las tres enchiladas.* Why would he call us enchiladas?"

"Well, obviously, he *didn't* call us enchiladas," Maud said. "He must have said something that *sounded* like enchiladas."

Carley suggested hopefully, "Maybe in Spanish *enchilada* is a compliment. Like in French they call someone *ma petite choufleur.*"

"I don't think so," Vanessa dryly disagreed.

"Well, I'm going to buy a Spanish dictionary!" Maud decided.

"I'm going to go through every word that sounds like enchilada until I find one that he might have meant."

"Girl," Carley teased, "you are desperate for a compliment."

After that night, they called themselves Las Tres Enchiladas. When people asked them why, they said it was too complicated to explain, which made people like Beth Boxer, the gossip of their married group, suspect all sorts of erotic misbehavior. That made it all the sweeter. Really, the word sparked a touchstone in their spirits, reminding them vividly, for just a moment, of that evening of freedom and lighthearted camaraderie. It brought back the jangling jewelry, the silken non-mommy clothes, the salty margaritas, and the hooded-eyed young man.

It was good for them to have a tight little clique in those days because shortly after that night, Maud's husband John left her for a much younger woman. He moved to California, never called his sons, and was systematically late with child support checks.

Maud struggled along financially, writing children's books. She illustrated her books, too; she was very talented. Her *Flip and Bob* books, about two harbor seals (brothers, like Maud's sons) and their adventures in the waters around Nantucket, became popular, bringing in the income Maud truly needed.

Maud had wanted daughters. She'd dreamed of having three little girls she could dress in identical white dresses with blue sashes. Instead, she had her two boisterous, energetic, noisy boys, named Spenser and Percy by her English-teacher ex-husband. After John left her, Maud often called Carley and Vanessa in a panic; her two sons were accident-prone, or perhaps, Carley thought, they were just normal. Carley drove Maud and the boys to the emergency room when Spenser fell out of a tree and broke his arm. When Percy stuck his soggy chewing gum in his older brother's hair Vanessa drove over to help Maud cut it out because Maud couldn't get Spenser to calm down and sit still.

And when Carley's husband died, Maud and Vanessa had been her rock, her parachute, her safety net, her emotional 911. Carley didn't know how she'd have survived without them.

Tomorrow morning Vanessa was coming over to help Carley make several dozen cookies for the bake sale Margaret's kindergarten class was running to raise money for a trip to Boston. Carley would talk things over with Vanessa then, and make plans to see Maud, too.

Perhaps Carley could start a bake shop? She loved to bake. But there were already too many good bakeries on the island. Was there something she could sell on eBay? Should she take a course online? What kind of course? The wind whipped the waves up so that they crashed down on the sand in a relentless roar. The low winter sun sparkled on the water, sending shards of light into her eyes. She couldn't think. She needed help. She'd be tired enough when she got home to be calm around her girls, and tomorrow she would begin again.

Saturday morning, Carley whipped her hair back into a high ponytail and slid her feet into flip-flops. She went down the back stairs.
Sounds led her to the den, where Cisco and Margaret sat side by side
on the sofa, munching cereal out of the box and staring at the television set. They were not supposed to watch television in the morning, but since their father's death, Carley had relaxed the rules.
Cisco and Margaret seemed normal now, after the first crushing
weeks of sorrow and shock. And that was what mattered, that her
girls were healthy and happy.

"TV," Carley said, disapproval in her voice.

"It's not TV," Cisco argued sweetly, tossing her mother a glowing smile. "It's *Swan Lake*."

Carley couldn't help but laugh. "You're going to grow up to be a
lawyer."

"Just like Daddy and Granddad!" Margaret squealed. "I am,
too!" She'd seen the DVD of the ballet before and didn't really care
about it, but she couldn't pass up the opportunity to be with her
sister.

And *there!* Carley thought, her heart lifting. Margaret mentioned her father without sadness, without crying. She was *healing*.
They all were. She gave herself a moment to soak in the glory of her
daughters. Their black hair, ebony eyes, and snowflake skin, direct
genetic echoes of their father, gave them a fairy-tale-princess aura.

Like their mother, they were tall and lanky, which sometimes made them clumsy. As adults, they would be stunners.

She tore her eyes away. "I'm making coffee. Vanessa will be here soon."

While she drank her coffee and ate her granola, she flipped on the computer and scanned the newest recipes for cookies. She loved cooking and baking, loved experimenting with unusual ingredients. The kitchen was at the front of the house, facing the street, giving the long living room and den the fabulous blue views of the waters of Nantucket Sound. She'd see Vanessa's SUV when she arrived.

Carley was sipping her second cup of coffee as Vanessa parked her car, lifted out a bag of groceries, and came up the walk.

No doubt about it: Vanessa was gorgeous. A sex bomb. Carley and Vanessa were the same age and the same height, but Vanessa's figure was voluptuous while Carley was wide-shouldered, small-breasted, and angular. Carley's hair was a glossy brown, manageable, no bother, but Vanessa had wavy black hair that bounced and tossed around her face in sensual curls as rounded as her body. Men always did a double take when Vanessa walked into a room.

Vanessa was just naturally *nice*. Humorous, easygoing, and generous, in spite of a life that had more than its share of woe. The only child of two only children, Vanessa lost her father when she was in college, and during the past year her beloved mother had died of Parkinson's disease. Fourteen years ago, she'd married Toby when he was in med school and in spite of her fertility goddess looks, hadn't been able to get pregnant. Some women might be bitter, but not Vanessa, who loved life and people, who had a great, exuberant excess of energy and compassion. She was a natural giver. She sat on almost all the major nonprofit boards on the island: The Boys and Girls Club, A Safe Place, the library, the AIDS network, and the hospital. She was definitely the kind of woman to make lemonade. Or, today, cookies.

Of course she was wearing a dress. She was the only female on this windy island who regularly wore dresses. She insisted she couldn't find jeans to fit, but really Vanessa had developed a kind of camouflage of loose dresses covered with looser sweaters to make less of a display of her shape. Her arms were full of bags of flour, chocolate bits, butter, and sprinkles, and when she came in the front door, she was laughing.

"I couldn't help it, I sampled some of the chocolate, the bag was just leaning there, tempting me."

Carley lifted one of the bags into her own arms. "You've got chocolate on your chin."

Vanessa followed Carley into the kitchen. Together they unpacked the groceries.

"There's fresh coffee if you want it," Carley told her.

"Yum." Vanessa knew this kitchen as well as her own. She took a mug off a shelf and poured herself a cup of the fragrant brew.

Cisco strolled into the room. Lanky and trim in the tee shirt and boxers she wore for pajamas, she edged herself onto the corner of the table. "Whatcha doin'?"

Vanessa gave Cisco a big hug. "Good morning, darling. We're going to make cookies for the bake sale. Want to help?"

Cisco hugged Vanessa back. "No, thanks. I'm going over to Delphine's to practice."

"When's your next recital?" Vanessa asked.

"I'm not sure," Cisco told her. Her face grew wistful. She was longing to wear pointe shoes, but at twelve, she was not yet allowed. Lost in her reverie, she slid off the table and wandered out of the room.

"She's such a beauty," Vanessa observed.

"I'm not thrilled about this ballet obsession," Carley confided. "Cis worries about her weight, and she's already a little twig. I don't want her becoming anorectic."

"Honey, she's not. Enjoy this phase. In a flash, she's going to be getting her teenage hormones, complete with periods, breasts, zits, and mood swings."

Carley rolled her eyes. "Oh, help."

As they talked, they moved around Carley's kitchen, sharing the work with familiar ease. Carley was proud of her kitchen. It was the

one part of the venerable old house she'd insisted on having reno-
vated. It had two ovens, and a rack hung with pots, skillets, and
utensils over a central island. She'd had the two rooms that once
had served as pantry and butler's pantry opened up to make one
large room, and a long pine kitchen table with comfortable captain's
chairs stood at one end of the kitchen, next to a small desk where
the household calendar and computer were kept. Her kitchen was
the command control center of her own domestic world. Sometimes
she thought she'd rather be here than anywhere else.

She set out the measuring cups, mixer, and bowls. "How's
Toby?"

Vanessa shrugged. "Busy. Too busy. We really could use another
pediatrician on this island. Well, I knew what I was getting into
when I married a doctor. Or I thought I did. Most days we scarcely
have time to talk before he falls into bed, exhausted."

Vanessa measured out two cups of flour, then stopped and
looked directly at Carley. "Carley, sometimes . . . sometimes Toby
kind of bores me."

Carley gave Vanessa a gentle smile. "Every marriage goes
through phases like that."

Before Vanessa could reply, the front door opened. Footsteps
sounded down the hall and Maud appeared, her two exuberant sons
at her side.

"Hi, Carley! Hi, Vanessa!" Maud's enormous blue eyes were
wide in her heart-shaped face, and she looked rather like a child
herself, with her turned-up nose and brown hair cut in an easy
Dutch-boy bob. Under her quilted jacket she wore black tights and
a leotard, which made her look even more petite. She kicked off her
clogs and settled into a chair. Recently she'd been dropping her boys
off at Carley's while she went for an hour of yoga. "I've got a few
minutes before class. Tell me everything."

"Chocolate chips!" Spenser yelled.

"Chocolate chips!" echoed his brother Percy.

"Cookies *later*," Vanessa told them sternly.

Margaret ran into the kitchen. "Percy! Spenser!"

"Hide and seek!" Spenser yelled.

The three children exploded out of the room.

Maud rolled her eyes. "Wild things."

"Want some coffee?" Carley asked. "It's fresh."

"Sure. No, it will make me pee. Any gossip? What are you doing?"

Vanessa told her, "Making cookies for the bake sale."

"Oh! You should have asked me. I would have helped."

Vanessa gave Maud a steady committee woman stare. "And that would be before or after yoga?"

Maud dodged the issue. "Vanessa, it should be against the law to look that gorgeous in such baggy clothes!"

Vanessa smirked. "Flattery will get you nowhere."

"What can I say?" Maud leaned her flower-face in her hand. "I'm selfish, unaltruistic, and useless. I've never baked for a good cause in my entire life. You two are admirable, and I admire you, I really do."

"Oh, stop," Carley ordered. "You write fabulous books that make children happy."

Margaret raced into the kitchen, hair flying. A pink barrette had slipped down and dangled from one clump of black hair.

Maud caught Margaret in her arms and kissed her. "Slow down."

"Can't!" Margaret giggled, and raced off, down the long front hall. Seconds later, Spenser stampeded into the room, followed by Percy, who tripped over his shoelaces and did a perfect comedic pratfall onto the floor. The five-year-old didn't allow himself to cry.

"Ooopsie," Maud said.

"Shoelaces." Capable Vanessa captured the child. She held him on her lap and managed to tie the flopping laces even as Percy wriggled to get down.

"Which way did she go?" Spenser demanded.

"We'll never tell," Carley said.

The boys burst from the room, yelling with glee.

"All that energy," Maud sighed. "If I could only plug into it for half an hour."

"Tell me about it," Carley agreed. Pulling herself up straight, she announced, "Listen, you two. I need some advice. I need to make some money."

Vanessa's brow wrinkled with sympathetic distress. "Oh, honey. Of course, with Gus gone . . ."

Maud tilted her chair back and stared at the ceiling for inspiration. "Sell baked goods?"

"I've thought of that," Carley told her. "Too many great bakeries already on the island."

"Sell your body?" Maud teased.

"Right," Carley snorted. "That's an attractive thought."

"Sell your SUV and get an older, cheaper one," Vanessa suggested.

"That's not a bad idea!" Carley clapped her hands. "At the least, I can sell Gus's BMW. I know it's paid off, and we don't need two cars anymore. Why didn't I think of that?"

"I've got it!" Maud held her arms out wide, enclosing the entire cluttered kitchen. "Hold a tag sale."

Carley brightened. "Maud! What a good idea!" She sagged. "But it's almost January. Will anyone come?"

"Are you kidding? What else is there to do on the island in winter? Anyway, people always love tag sales. Hold it on a Saturday, in your garage."

Vanessa chimed in. "You'll make a fortune. I'll bet you haven't seen half the stuff lurking in the corners of this big old pile."

"True." Carley grabbed up a pad and pen and scribbled notes as she talked. "Things Gus and I brought home from vacation then wondered what in the world we were thinking. I'll have to be careful not to sell anything that has sentimental value to the Winsteds. Oh, I can sell the baby things, the crib, the high chair."

"Oh, no!" Vanessa cried. "Carley, don't get rid of the baby things!"

"Vanny, I'm a widow. I'm hardly going to have another baby anytime soon, if ever."

"Well, that's just sad."

Carley put her arm around Vanessa. "When you get pregnant, you'll want to buy all new baby things, wait and see." She took a deep breath. "I'm going to sell some of Gus's things, too. His clothes."

Maud groaned. "His parents will flip."

"They'll have to flip. I was going to give them to the thrift shop anyway. But why shouldn't I sell them? I need the money, and they're all such good quality. Shoes, overcoats, suits, shirts, and his CD collection, or most of it. I never did like most of his jazz."

"You should do that on eBay," Vanessa suggested.

"Maybe. A tag sale would be quicker."

"What will the girls think?" Maud asked.

"They both have piles of toys in the attic they've outgrown. I know—I'll tell them they can have their own table and keep any money they make."

"Selling their toys? It seems sad somehow," Vanessa said.

"No," Carley stated firmly. "It will help them learn a bit about the financial realities of the world."

"When are you going to hold it?" Maud asked. "I'll come over and help."

"Me, too," Vanessa said. "And Carley, I think you should have a table of baked goods. Everyone goes crazy for your scones and tarts. I bet they'd fly."

Carley stood in front of her kitchen calendar. "I'll have to put an ad in the paper. That comes out next Thursday, but I can make the deadline. I'll have to organize the girls to get ready. Oh." Doing an about-face, she scrunched up her face at her friends. "I'll have to tell Annabel and Russell."

Her friends groaned sympathetically.

Cisco appeared in the kitchen, dressed in leotard and track pants. "Mom, I'm going to Delphine's."

Maud stood up. "I've got to run. I'll come back for the boys later, Carley, before lunch, okay?"

"Sure, or they can have lunch here."

"Oh, bless you. I can do a few errands." She hugged Carley and pecked a kiss on the top of Vanessa's head. "Cisco, want a ride?"

"Cool."

"Come on, then, sweetie."

Cisco tossed her mother a kiss. Cisco looked thin, Carley thought, too thin, but for the moment she was simply grateful that her increasingly temperamental daughter was happy.

When Maud and Cisco left, the three children thumped around in the attic and Carley and Vanessa started back on the cookie project. They worked in peace for a few moments.

"I worry about Maud," Vanessa confided. "She's not seeing any man or even interested. She's been alone a long time."

Carley paused, a carton of eggs in her hand. "I worry, too. How can she meet anyone? She doesn't get out of the house at all. She's always with her boys or writing. She *has* started taking that intensive yoga class twice a week, and she needs it, really, because her writing and drawing are messing up her back and shoulders."

"But she's not going to meet a man at a yoga class."

"Probably not." Carley carefully cracked eggs into the mixing bowl. "Maybe she doesn't need a man."

Vanessa snorted. "If anyone needs a man, Maud does. She's so fragile I doubt she can open a peanut butter jar by herself." She slid a cookie sheet into the oven and set the timer. "What about Wyatt Anderson?"

"What about Wyatt?"

"He could date Maud. They'd be cute together."

"Wyatt would be cute with Cruella de Vil," Carley quipped. "He must know she's divorced. He's been at some of the parties and I haven't seen him chat her up."

"Maybe he just likes younger women."

"Oh, moan. Vanny, I'm sure Maud will meet Mr. Right sometime."

"I hope so." The room filled with the warm buttery aroma of cookie batter, eggs, sugar, and chocolate.

Vanessa dropped dough by the spoonfuls onto the cookie sheet. "At least Maud has two children."

"Oh, honey." Carley turned and embraced Vanessa, taking care not to get egg white on her clothes. "It's so unfair." Releasing her, she tried to be optimistic as she returned to her bowl. "Have you and Toby talked about adopting?"

"Not yet." Vanessa's voice was low, her face averted. "I want the experience, Carley. I want to feel a baby grow in my belly. I want to give birth."

Carley laughed. "Believe me, it's no walk in the park."

"I know that. Well, actually, I don't *know* that, but I want to." Vanessa turned away. "Sometimes I think I'm too intense about everything. You're just so easy with all of it, Carley. All the kids."

"I like kids, Vanessa. I like people. I like—" She held out her arms, indicating it all, the mess of the kitchen with the mixing bowls and bags of flour and coffee cups and glasses scattered everywhere. "My mother's run a day care all her life, and it has her entire heart and soul. Dad's a dentist, and he does a lot of free work, too. You've met my sister and her partner. Sarah's an emergency room nurse and Sue is a social worker. It takes a trauma or at least a head wound to get attention from my own family."

Vanessa laughed, then turned serious. "Do you miss Gus terribly?"

Carley said, "I do miss him. Every day." Briskly, she turned toward the sink and rinsed her hands. "I'm going to gain weight if I don't stop eating the batter. Come on, let's get these done."

It was early afternoon when the dozens of cookies were decorated and carefully covered with cling wrap, ready for the bake sale at four. Vanessa offered to drop Maud's boys back at their house, and she rounded them up and drove away. Margaret, exhausted by boy play, went down the street to her friend Molly's house to play with dolls, and Cisco phoned, just checking in, telling Carley that Delphine's mother had given them lunch and then they were going to walk around town.

Carley was alone in the house. It felt like being on an abandoned ocean liner in a calm sea just after a gale-force storm. She loved the chaos and clutter of people, but she loved the quiet, too. She walked through the house, returning the umbrellas the boys had used as swords to the umbrella stand in the hall, gathering up the toys and clothing—a headless doll, a striped sock, one of Gus's father's ancient hats—that had somehow been used in the children's games.

Margaret's bedroom had been ransacked by the children. The boys had crammed Margaret's shoes upside down on her stuffed animals' heads—they *did* look funny. Her pink duvet was balled up against the wall and the construction paper from her child's desk had been scattered around the room. Carley would have Margaret help her tidy it.

Cisco's room was perfection. The boys knew better than to enter Cisco's room—she was *twelve*. Sometimes, on special days, Cisco allowed Margaret in her room, but Margaret thought the sun shone out of Cisco's belly button, she treated Cisco's possessions like religious icons. She could spend hours trying on Cisco's shoes and sweaters and walking solemnly around the house in them, and she always put them away carefully, because the items were precious.

The master bedroom was tidy, too. Without Gus there to drop his clothes on the floor, his change on the dresser, his books and magazines on the tables, everything was easier to keep neat. At Christmas at her parents', in a burst of "I'm getting on with my life!" optimism, Carley had treated herself to a new bedspread and matching curtains in a floral pattern that Gus would have hated. Now the room looked luscious, but so feminine. So solitary.

There were three other rooms on the second floor of this spacious old ark. Two of the rooms were kept as guest rooms. One was a playroom, a lifesaver on snowy or rainy days. The children had left it in what Carley liked to consider a creative disorder. Doll carriages and cradles and toy stoves and refrigerators had been upended and piled together to make some kind of ersatz vehicle, no doubt a space ship.

There was also the attic. From its half-moon windows, views of Nantucket Sound glistened and sparkled into the far horizon, compelling the imagination out to foreign fantasies. Antique settees, fabulous old opera cloaks, boxes of china, oil paintings of some rather ugly ancestors, and other souvenirs the Winsteds hadn't yet decided to have valued, filled the large room, giving it a sense of otherworldliness. The kids loved playing up here. It was a Shangri-La for the imagination.

And it was chock full of all sorts of good stuff for a tag sale.

Sunday morning, Carley brushed Margaret's hair till it shone like black silk. She allowed her to choose one of her favorite, frilliest dresses. Cisco's outfit, for once, did not involve either tights or leotard, but rather a plain skirt and top. The older Winsteds always dressed for church and Sunday dinner, and Carley followed their lead. She wore a loose brown cashmere dress, high heels, and family heirloom gold jewelry Annabel had entrusted to her over the years. Out of her regular jeans and tee, she felt like an imposter or a changeling.

After church, Carley and her daughters stood with Annabel and Russell on the sidewalk, chatting with the rector and other members of the congregation. Carley knew her in-laws liked this, liked showing off their pretty, polite little granddaughters. Then, in the weak winter sunshine, they all walked over to the older Winsteds' house for Sunday dinner. Russell immediately went to the den to watch a news program. The females gathered in the kitchen. Annabel had put a small turkey in to roast early that morning, and the room was warm with delicious odors.

"How can I help?" Carley asked Annabel.

"Just heat up the veggies," Annabel told her. "I'll make the gravy."

"I'll set the dining room table," Cisco said cheerfully, tilting her head to be sure Carley noticed how helpful she was. Carley smiled, and she *was* proud of her daughter, but she would never understand why it was Cisco loved doing chores at her grandparents' and complained miserably about doing them at home.

Margaret was babbling, as usual. "Robin's dad built her a *tree-house*! Really, it's for Robin's older brother, and we have to wait till Robin's mother comes out to stand by the ladder when we climb up, but that's silly, because we are *very* careful climbing—"

"Margaret," Cisco said bossily, "you need to fold the napkins while I put the silverware around."

"Okay." Cheerfully, Margaret skipped into the dining room. She loved folding napkins.

"Russell," Annabel called melodically. "Could you open the wine?" She marshaled her troops. "Everything's ready. I'll have Russell help me carry in the turkey. The platter is heavy. You can each take a bowl of vegetables."

"This is like Thanksgiving, Nana!" Margaret cried as they gathered around the table laden with Brussels sprouts, sweet potatoes, and mashed potatoes and gravy, the girls' favorite food.

"Well, every day is Thanksgiving, I think, when our family is all here together," Annabel said quietly, and a shadow fell over the table as they all looked at the empty chair where Gus once had sat.

Russell broke the spell. "Tell me, everyone! Who wants white meat?"

Conversations at Annabel and Russell's house were always lively. They invited the children to talk about the news of their school—what was the school play this year? *Peter Pan?* Fabulous! Had they heard about the foghorn? Cormorants had pooped all over the fog sensor, so the foghorn thought it was perpetually foggy and the horn sounded constantly, even on sunny days. Cisco and Margaret almost fell off their chairs laughing.

Carley ate and chatted and felt calmed. It was as if she could actually feel the spin of her molecules slow. She loved the way Annabel's face glowed whenever she looked at Cisco or Margaret.

Annabel adored her granddaughters. She doted on them. The house, old and weathered, showed signs of Annabel's love and attention: she had painted the dining room trim and woodwork herself, just last year. On the old mahogany sideboard, among the heirloom silver, Annabel had set a vase of green holly. The cranberry sauce they ate with their turkey had been made by Annabel last fall. And on the far wall, among valuable if dreary oil portraits of Winsted ancestors, Annabel had hung a large photograph of her granddaughters swimming at Jetties Beach, laughing, gleaming in the sunshine like the treasures they were to Annabel.

The girls. They were what mattered. She needed to keep them safe.

She cleared her throat. "The girls and I are going to hold a tag sale."

Annabel's fork halted halfway to her mouth. "Really."

"In your yard?" Russell asked.

"And inside the garage. On the drive."

"Carley, I'm not so sure—" Annabel began.

In her excitement, Margaret interrupted her. "I'm going to sell my old Legos, I never play with them anymore, and the little toy barn with the animals, the silly little pig and cow and the horse and the—"

Carley put her hand gently on Margaret's leg. "No wiggling at the table, please."

"Are you selling . . ." Russell began, frowning. "How can I put this? Are you selling family items?" His voice was raspy, a sign of his emotional state.

"None of the real heirlooms, Russell," Carley hastened to assure him. "I wouldn't do that. Most of it will be the sort of thing Gus and I acquired during our marriage. All the baby stuff, for example, car seats and clothing, which is always needed. And," she continued bravely, her heart thumping in her chest, "I'm going to sell some of Gus's stuff."

Both her in-laws were silent.

Perkily, Carley continued, "Honestly, Gus collected so many gadgets. I think there's some kind of electronic weather monitoring device in every room of the house. He's even got—he even had—a mirror in the shower that electronically reported the weather. And the electronic putting machine and his electronic language translator—for thirty different languages!" For a moment, a terrible sadness overwhelmed her to think that Gus might once have dreamed of traveling to thirty different countries. But this was not the time for sorrow.

"And *my* things, too!" Carley chirped on. "My maternity clothing. Sweaters and other unfortunate gifts from years ago that I've put away and never used. And perhaps one of the tea sets, when Gus and I were married, we got at least four different tea sets, which is ridiculous, no one gives teas anymore—" She was chattering like a monkey. She forced herself to stop and take a breath.

Annabel touched her napkin to her lips. She laid her napkin in her lap and folded her hands over it. "Carley. I understand how grief can derail your logical thought processes, but really, my dear, this idea of a tag sale is just all wrong. It is not *appropriate* for a Winsted to hold a tag sale."

Carley struggled to keep her voice level and mild. "Annabel, I'm afraid it is terribly appropriate for *this* Winsted to hold a tag sale. I won't sell anything of importance to the family. But we do have so much *stuff*. And we can use the money. I apologize for discussing financial matters at the dinner table. I know you like to talk about more pleasant things." She looked steadily at Annabel, smiling.

Annabel looked steadily back, not smiling.

Carley turned to Margaret. "Sweetie, would you like more mashed potatoes?"

Margaret nodded enthusiastically. As her mother spooned them onto the plate—making a "pond" in the middle for the gravy—Margaret chirped, "And Mommy's going to make cakes and cookies for the tag sale, and I'm going to help her!"

Russell could not resist his granddaughter's excitement. "Well, then, I'll have to stop by and purchase something."

"Oh, Granddad," Margaret laughed. "You know we would always give you and Nana our cakes for free!"

Everyone at the table laughed, too. In the face of such sweetness, Annabel backed away from the subject of the tag sale, asking both girls about school. But when she glanced at Carley, her eyes were dark as thunder.

Monday, as soon as the girls were off to school, Carley climbed the narrow stairs and opened the door to the attic. She could tell, instantly, that something had changed. Things had been moved around. There was a very slight smell . . . of tobacco? She shook her head. Couldn't be.

Still, she closed her eyes and let her nose lead her. Past the drop-leaf table with the broken leg. Past the cardboard wardrobes of clothing old enough to be called vintage. Past one of the boudoir chairs . . . There. In the corner was a kind of nest. Cushions and pillows were piled around Cisco's CD player and a pile of CDs.

Carley smiled. Cisco and her friend had been up here in their own private aerie, listening to music, discussing life, love, and boys. Cisco had a new friend these days, a sloe-eyed girl called Polo who had just moved to the island. Polo was shy, but polite. She didn't seem to talk much, but Carley had heard her and Cisco giggling, and that gave Carley great hope that when Cisco finally realized she was not going to be a ballerina, she wouldn't be devastated. Polo had no interest in ballet.

So, good. Carley liked that about the house, how it provided hiding spots and private nooks for conversation.

She turned to search out the other boudoir chair, and her foot hit something. She looked down.

There on the wide old floorboards was an object of heavy glass, so wrong here in this place that for a moment her mind wouldn't make sense of it. Then she did make sense of it.

A glass ashtray. Full of cigarette butts.

Suddenly she was so angry she could have slammed her fist into the wall.

She and Gus had warned and *warned* the girls about the connection between smoking and cancer. They watched *Thank You for Smoking* together on a DVD. Cisco knew better than to smoke!

And to smoke up here in the attic! She might as well light matches in the middle of a haystack. All this old dry stuff, newspapers, books, photo albums, hats with feathers . . .

"Cisco, you *idiot!*" Her hands shook as she bent down to pick up the ashtray. She wanted to throw it hard against the wall. Instead, she carried it down to the kitchen and plunked it in the middle of the table: Exhibit A. When Cisco got home from school, Carley would have the evidence ready. She needed to decide on a suitable punishment. It really was a serious offense, smoking in the attic! How could Cisco, usually so intelligent, do something so stupid?

The smoking wasn't so very awful, Carley decided as she paced the room. All kids tried it sooner or later. It was almost a rite of passage. But to smoke in the attic! She didn't want Annabel or Russ to find out about this. As much as they adored their granddaughter, they were emotionally, symbolically, personally attached to their houses. They would freak out.

She couldn't focus on the tag sale now. She was too upset. She concentrated her energy on routine tasks: laundry, vacuuming, mopping the kitchen floor. She could do all this without thinking, which allowed her mind to rampage around the problem. She needed to find the right way to react to this. It had been a long time since she'd had a real confrontation with Cisco. She could tell that her older daughter was changing—her period had started just last month, and she was beginning to develop breasts, which had Cisco nearly ill with embarrassment. Carley wanted to handle this just right.

"Hi, Mom!" Cisco banged in through the back door as she always did, dropping her backpack on a kitchen chair and heading directly for the refrigerator. Another issue—diet soda—was an ongoing problem for Carley, who didn't want to buy the empty calories for her children, but who felt sympathy for Cisco, who begged and pleaded for them. They'd compromised. Cisco could have one a day.

Cisco's new friend Polo came in, curvy and smug, exuding a lazy sensuality. Polo had breasts, for sure. Carley told herself she ought to be thankful for Cisco's new friend—Polo was anything but anorectic.

Carley stared at them, feeling like a witch with a hairy wart growing on the end of her nose, gnashing her teeth and rubbing her hands together as she prepared to roast a child. Yet her children's safety was her responsibility and being a parent meant setting limits.

"Hello, Mrs. Winsted," Polo purred.

"Hello, Polo." Carley was sitting at the head of the table. "Cisco, Polo, sit down. We need to talk."

The girls exchanged glances. Cisco handed Polo a can of soda. The girls sat down as far away from Carley as they could get.

"What's up?" Cisco asked.

Carley nodded toward the ashtray in the middle of the table. "That."

To her surprise, Polo giggled. That made Cisco's mouth twitch. The girls shared a brief conspiratorial glance.

"Oh, Mom," Cisco said, as if she were bored.

Cisco's attitude took Carley's breath away. How had this happened? How had her daughter changed so enormously without Carley even noticing? And why did this make Carley feel so *violently* angry?

She kept her voice cold and in control. "This isn't some silly little prank, Cisco. You were smoking in the attic. You could have burned the house down."

"But we didn't." Cisco lowered her lids and slid a look over at Polo, who seemed to be stifling a laugh.

"No, you didn't, not that time. But you could have, easily. That attic is a tinderbox, dry and full of old materials. Oh, Cisco, you don't need me to spell it out, you *know* it's dangerous to smoke in the attic. And for heaven's sake, you shouldn't even be *smoking* at all! It's *terrible* for your health. Your father and I have warned you about it, and they've warned you about it in school, too."

Cisco stared steadily at the surface of the kitchen table. Her attention had switched away from Carley. Polo's hand was on the tabletop. Her index finger was moving in a definite beat. Da da da da da da. Cisco wasn't looking at Polo, her gaze was fastened to the table, but her index finger began to move in the same beat. Cisco's mouth curved in a slight smile. Polo didn't smile, but she looked *smug*. She looked sly.

In a flash, Carley understood. The girls were beating out the rhythm of a song by The Ting-Tings, which actually was a song Carley loved to dance to. *Shut up and let me go.*

Like prisoners, Cisco and Polo were tapping a message to each other.

Cisco and Polo against Carley.

Carley knew her mouth was thin-lipped as she spoke and she hated herself for it. But she knew, rationally, this was the right thing to do. "Since you two girls were the ones smoking together, the most sensible punishment I can see for this is to prevent you from spending any more time together. Cisco, you are not to bring Polo home for a week, and you can't go to her house for a week. No phone calls between the two of you, either."

"*Mom!*" Cisco erupted from her chair, her face red, her hands clenched at her side. "That's not fair!"

"It's my decision, Cisco, and I'm not changing my mind. It's obvious that you two think you're clever and cute with your smoking and your tapping, but smoking is a serious problem and it has to—"

"I won't smoke anymore, Mom! I promise! I won't smoke!" Cisco had tears in her eyes.

Polo looked bored. She sat very still, rolling her eyes to the ceiling, as if anything there were more interesting than what was in the rest of the room.

"Polo, perhaps I should phone your mother and explain why I'm imposing this restriction," Carley said.

"Go ahead," Polo countered smugly.

"Mom, NO!" Cisco was almost screaming.

"I'm out of here," Polo said. In one smooth move, she rose, shouldered her backpack, and loped out the kitchen door without another look at Cisco or Carley.

Cisco watched her friend go with amazement. When she turned to face Carley, her eyes blazed with disgust. "I hate you," she hissed. "You have no idea how much I hate you."

"Cisco, calm d—"

"You have just ruined my life."

"Oh, Cisco, I doubt that—"

"You know nothing about my life, *nothing*. You have no idea what you've just done. I hate you. I wish I didn't have to live with you. I wish I never had to see you again."

"Cisco, honey—"

"Don't touch me!" Cisco ran from the room. She stomped up the stairs and slammed the door, but the noise of Cisco's furious crying carried through.

Carley clasped her own hands together to try to stop them from shaking. If only Gus were here to help her make the rules. To help her take the force of Cisco's fury when Carley enforced the rules. At times like this, she felt alone and *hopeless*. The loneliness of her adult life would, like a river finding a crack in a dam, break through, flooding her with misery. She went into the living room, intending to curl up on her side on the sofa, just for a moment, just to catch her breath.

The front door slammed and two little giggling girls skipped in, Margaret and her best friend Molly.

"We're going to have tea with our babies," Margaret informed her mother.

As fast as Superwoman in a phone booth, Carley transformed herself into a calm and smiling mommy. "Great, girls. Do you want to take some juice and cookies up to your room?"

"Yay!" Margaret jumped up and down, then caught herself and stood quite still. "We'll be very careful not to spill," she promised solemnly.

Carley put together a doll-size picnic basket of cookies and juice in a thermos. She followed the little girls to the bottom of the stairs and waved to them as they went up. Really, she was listening for sounds of Cisco. The wailing had stopped. There was silence. Perhaps Cisco had fallen asleep, exhausted by her emotions. Or perhaps she was talking to Polo on her cell phone. Fine. Carley would phone her own friend.

"Maud, can you talk?"

"For a while. I've got to get the monsters from The Boys and Girls Club. What's up?"

Carley explained about the smoking, the insolence, Cisco's tantrum.

"Oh, sweetie, and you have to do this by yourself." Maud sighed. "My mother used to say to me, 'Just wait until your father gets home.' All I can say to my boys is, 'Just wait till your father gets home—oh, never mind, your father is three thousand miles away and doesn't give a shit.' "

Carley laughed, and relief flowed through her. "It's easy for me to fool myself into thinking Cisco and I are friends, equals, and sometimes we really seem to be. Other times, and this is definitely one of them, I've got to stand up and be a parent, even if she does hate me."

"Tough love is the best kind, especially with the smoking issue. Cisco's peers are going to be sampling drugs and alcohol pretty soon."

"Oh, Maud, don't even say that. It's terrifying."

"Yeah, but settle down. Cisco's got ballet. That will keep her steady, give her something to dream about, something to organize her life. I think I'll register my guys in karate this winter. If anyone can break boards with their bare hands, it's my two."

Carley laughed again, then added more soberly, "Isn't it hard, making and enforcing rules without another adult to help?"

"Actually, no. John was so hopeless. His head was always in a book, and when he wasn't reading, he was reciting poems to himself in his head. Sometimes I was certain he was looking at us and wondering who we were. I do miss being able to go out of the house at night, just to run down to the library or the convenience store. John at least would have protected the boys. I mean, doesn't your house seem awfully big to you sometimes, in the middle of the night?"

"Yes," Carley agreed solemnly. "Yes, it does."

"Back to the smoking thing. I think you did exactly what you should have done. Stand firm on this issue, and she'll get it that you're going to stand firm on the harder ones down the line— staying out late, drinking, all that."

"You're right, Maud. Thanks."

Cisco didn't speak to Carley at dinner that night. Afterward, she shut herself in her room and when bedtime came, Carley knocked on the door and looked in to find Cisco already tucked in bed and sound asleep. Or pretending to be.

The next morning Cisco went off to school still in high dudgeon, mouth set, eyes cold, posture stiff. She didn't hug Carley, but as she went out the door, she said, "I'm going to Nana's after school. Okay?"

"That's fine." Carley made her voice mild, and smiled at her older daughter, as if everything was good between them.

That afternoon, Carley's phone rang.

"Darling, it's Annabel. Do you have a moment to talk?"

Carley was on her knees at the back of the linen closet, digging
out all the delicate lace-embroidered tablecloths she hadn't used in
all the years of her marriage. She sat up straight and leaned against
the wall. "Of course."

"Cisco stopped by on her way home from school. She told me
about her and Polo smoking in the attic."

"Oh, gosh, Annabel, I should have told you. I—"

"I really think you're being too strict with her, Carley. Cutting
off communication with her best friend for a week? That seems
cruel, especially when her father died only two months ago."

"But—but—" Carley sputtered. "I thought you'd be just as upset
as I am. Smoking in the attic?"

"All kids her age try smoking."

Reluctantly, Carley agreed. "I suppose. Still, parents have to
make it clear that we disapprove. We don't want it to become a
habit."

"Don't be such an alarmist. It's not going to become a habit."

Carley was speechless.

Annabel continued, her voice full of warmth and love. "Darling, I'm sure they won't do it again. I've told Cisco that the attic
was a stupid, *dangerous*, place to smoke. She understands. She said
she won't do it again. I promised I'd speak to you. I told her I'd suggest that you consider lightening her punishment. The poor child
lost her father. She needs her friends."

Carley took a deep breath. Wasn't it only yesterday that she
bemoaned the loss of Gus's point of view, his opinion of how to
raise the girls? Why did she feel so resistant to Annabel's suggestion? Perhaps because Annabel had sided with Cisco against
Carley, because Cisco was Carley's child, not Annabel's. Because
Annabel was making herself the good guy and Carley the bad
guy.

Annabel obviously believed it was her place to interfere. Hadn't
Annabel and Russell asked Carley to bring the girls and live with
them? The hairs stood up on the back of Carley's neck at the

thought of her charming, powerful mother-in-law so silkily, smoothly, relentlessly taking over.

"Annabel, I appreciate your concern, but this is a matter between Cisco and me. I am quite concerned about her smoking, and very worried that Cisco, who is twelve, would be foolish enough to smoke in the *attic*. There are times when I need to set limits to stress my rules with Cisco, and this is one of them." She was glad she wasn't in the same room with her mother-in-law; her knees were shaking. Always before Gus had been the perfect buffer. Anything he said brought smiles of approval to Annabel's face.

"Well." Annabel cleared her throat. "It seems then I have nothing more to say than that I think you're making a mistake." With a faint click, the connection ended.

Did she just hang up on me? Carley wondered. But she didn't have time to worry about it. She had too much to do.

Just before dinner, Cisco came in, hugging her books to her chest, humming to herself.

"Hi, Mom." She was all sweetness and smiles as she slipped out of her parka.

"Hello, darling. Want to wash your hands and call Margaret? I've made tacos."

"Oh, yum." Cisco went out of the room, then turned back, as if she'd just remembered something. "Um, did Nana phone you?"

"She did, yes. We discussed your smoking in the attic. She is much less inclined to discipline you than I am. On the other hand, she's your grandmother and not responsible for your welfare and safety, not to mention morals. I thanked her for her advice but told her I'm not changing my mind."

"Mo-om!" Cisco's face darkened. "You are such a *stick*!"

"Probably," Carley mildly replied. She set the bowl of chopped tomatoes and shredded cheese on the table. This was one meal Cisco found impossible to resist.

Cisco's jaw clenched with anger. "I can't believe you don't—
honor—Nana!"

"I do respect and esteem Annabel, of course," Carley said. "But
Cisco, you are *my* daughter."

Cisco stomped from the room, muttering. Carley was sure Cisco
said *I wish I weren't.*

10
· · · · ·

Very early on the morning of the tag sale, Carley woke, jumped out of bed, and pushed open the curtains to check the weather.

The sun shone down on a bright, clear day. The Weather Channel had predicted temperatures in the forties today, and no precipitation.

Murmuring prayers of gratitude, she hurriedly pulled on her clothes and rushed down to the kitchen. At seven-thirty, Maud and Vanessa and Toby would arrive to help set up the sale. Until then, Carley could bake one more batch of cookies.

Cisco came thumping down the stairs, dressed in jeans and a red sweater. She headed robotically to the refrigerator, completely ignoring Carley's presence, took out the orange juice, and poured herself a glass.

"Sit down and have breakfast with me first, Cisco." She was worried about how thin Cisco was, but not ready for a fight first thing in the morning.

"I'm not hungry."

"We're going to be busy today. It's cold out. Our bodies need fuel and we won't have time to eat. Just some cereal."

Cisco hesitated, then slumped into a chair.

Carley put a bowl of granola and fruit in front of her daughter. She took a bowl for herself. "I've got the chart made out. I'm glad we're so organized. I hear people show up early for these sales, wanting to be the first to get to the good stuff."

Cisco couldn't resist. She was excited about the tag sale. Her friends were coming; strangers were coming, it was going to be like a party. She gobbled her breakfast down, then pushed back her chair. "Shall I go tie the balloons to the mailbox, Mom?"

As Carley and her friends were carrying out the tables and baby furniture and setting up, they heard the thud of car doors. Clusters of strangers bustled eagerly toward the yard. Toby, large and male and a figure of authority to those who knew him, took on the job of standing at the end of the driveway, warding people off. "Not open until eight o'clock, folks. Let them get set up."

For just a moment, before the sale began, Carley looked around the garage and the yard and was seized with a terrible panic. So many beloved or at least familiar objects, lying naked for strangers to touch and take. It was like having the inner life of their family revealed. It was like selling memories.

Suddenly Maud was at her side, whispering in her ear. "They're only *things*, Carley. Life is fluid. You have to let go and move on."

Carley threw Maud a grateful glance. "You're right. Thanks, Maud."

Cisco and Margaret artistically arranged their table of old dolls, rejected books, outgrown tutus, ballet slippers, and used clothing. Vanessa took charge of the baby furniture, receiving blankets, stuffed animals, and baby clothing.

Carley and Maud each took a table with the rest of the stuff: old clothing of Carley's, candlesticks, bookends, placemat and napkin sets, all wedding gifts that had never been used; stools, chairs, picture frames, and three different waffle pans. Also they sold the odd unused gifts accumulated over the years like the weed-whacking golf driver, the electric corkscrew, the digital measuring cup, and the speaking clock that spoke in such a depressed monotone that it creeped out the girls.

Framingham Burr, another friend of Gus's, volunteered to stay outside. A big man, he never noticed the cold, and he was pleased to run the table holding all of Gus's things: ice skates, tennis racquets, scalloping gear, electric foot massager, electric nose hair trimmer, electronic multiroom temperature monitor, and mounds of clothes from high school and college days, beloved sweaters, ties, and overcoats Gus hadn't been emotionally ready to give up but no longer wore, and had been banished to the basement.

The depressed clock said, "Eight." Toby stepped aside.

Dozens of customers poured up the driveway, charging toward the tables, almost desperately eyeing the merchandise, as if sure they would find a treasure. Some of them did. Cries of delight floated through the air as a little girl found one of Cisco's old ballet tutus. The elegant brass carriage clock, one of two Carley and Gus had received as wedding presents, was plucked from the table with triumph by a newlywed couple. An elderly woman happily paid good money for the dusty, outdated 1982 world encyclopedia Maud had convinced Carley to put out. People surged up to the tables, grasped items, shoved money toward her, or dropped the objects back on the table and rushed to another stand.

Carley looked over to see an extremely pregnant young woman with the Slavic cheekbones of the Russians who were working on the island. The man with her, Carley presumed her husband, was dismantling the crib Cisco and later Margaret had slept in as babies. Once again, a kind of regret, almost a panic, ran through Carley like a thrill. She watched Margaret approach the pregnant woman, holding out one of her favorite, softest, teddy bears.

"Would you like to have this for your baby?" Margaret asked.

The woman hesitated.

"It's a gift!" Margaret announced. "A gift for your baby. I love babies."

"Thank you very much." The woman took the bear and smoothed its fur, studying it. "It is a very special bear," she said to Margaret. "And you are a very nice girl."

Margaret grinned, wiggling all over with pleasure at the compliment. She ran to Carley. "Mommy, look, I gave that lady my bear for her baby!"

"That was nice of you, Margaret," Carley told her. "What a good, generous girl you are." Suddenly the day brightened for her—absolutely turned around. How proud Gus would be of his little girl, so instinctively kind and thoughtful. What a good thing it was that her daughters' crib was going to be used by that young couple from a country so far away. It made Carley feel more connected, somehow, to the wider world.

Maud leaned over. "You should have baked more."

Carley glanced down at the end of the table where she'd placed her gingerbread people, applesauce cake, pumpkin muffins, and her special chocolate, walnut, and a bit of everything else cookies. Every single crumb was gone. Carley didn't have a chance to answer Maud—she was dealing with a woman who wanted to buy the scarf Carley was wearing around her neck.

Around noon, things quieted down. The frenzy of eager shoppers ebbed as people headed home for lunch. Most of the items were gone.

Margaret was crying because she'd sold a baby doll that she realized had been her very favorite. Carley picked her up, took her into the house, and cuddled her while she drank juice and ate a peanut butter sandwich. Moments later, Margaret jumped off Carley's lap, yanked on her parka, and rushed back out to the action.

Carley returned to her table. No customers now.

Maud said, "I need a bathroom run. Can you give me a ten-minute break?"

"Absolutely."

Maud stood up, stretching. "My boys are out at Lauren's this morning. She said she'd bring them by around noon. If they get here while I'm in the house, don't let them buy anything!"

"I promise," Carley told her.

Maud went off and Carley settled in the chair at the table, grateful for a moment of peace. A few browsers were still roaming around the front yard. The table, so neatly organized this morning, was a shambles. She began to straighten it up.

"Carley, my dear." The minister from their church approached her. He was a dignified older man with a head of white bristly hair and runaway white eyebrows.

"Hello, Reverend Salter."

"May I sit down?" He gestured to the folding chair Maud had left.

"Of course."

He sat, neatly pinching the crease in his trousers. "I have a favor to ask you." He laughed. "People always look nervous when I say that. Let me jump right in—I want to find a place for my nephew, Kevin, to rent for a month or two this winter. He's working on his Ph.D. in history, writing a thesis on nineteenth-century New England farms, and he needs to do research at the historical association. He's an awfully nice fellow, and he's not impoverished, but he doesn't want to pay two hundred dollars a night to stay at an inn, and he would like to be in town so he won't need a car. If you could ask around, see if any of your friends had a room with a bath he could rent . . ." The minister paused.

"Of course," Carley answered. Reverend Salter tilted his head hopefully, like a dog hoping for a treat. "Oh! You're wondering if *I'd* like to rent a room."

"You do have a large house. And I can vouch for my nephew. He would be no trouble at all, I assure you."

Well, I could certainly use the money, Carley thought silently. Aloud, she mused, "There's a room off the laundry room. It has its own bathroom. It was a maid's room, once, I think. Kevin wouldn't have a private entrance, but if he came in the back door, he'd just go through the laundry room, he wouldn't have to go through the entire house . . ." She smiled. "Let me think about it, but this might work out for both of us."

"Thank you, my dear. Give me a call."

"I will. Soon."

Reverend Salter performed a courtly bow and took himself off. Carley sat smiling. The day was turning out very nicely!

Carley reached under her table and brought out the last few items, objects she doubted anyone would buy. A tin box that had once been filled with chocolates. A reproduction lightship basket filled with dusty potpourri she'd won in some raffle years ago. A very pretty Christmas ornament with a Nantucket lighthouse and the date 2004 painted on it.

She'd barely set them out when a group of women rushed over, inspected the items, and bought them.

"You're doing well," a man said.

Carley looked up to see Wyatt Anderson standing there.

Wyatt and Gus had been best friends since childhood. Wyatt's parents were Realtors, and friends of Gus's parents. Gus and Wyatt attended the same law school, and after law school, it had been completely natural and the realization of an adolescent strategy, for Wyatt to join Gus at Russell's firm. The two friends were as close as brothers even though they had such different energies. Gus was intense, somber, diligent. Wyatt tended to be more easygoing and slow-burning, with a smile that flashed like a lighthouse beacon, bright and engaging. Gus was shorter, more compact, more vivid, with his raven-black hair and eyes. Wyatt was taller, lanky, and handsome enough to make a woman drool. As boys, they sailed together, practical Gus as captain, energetic Wyatt as his willing crew. They won almost every race they entered.

While Gus eagerly jumped into the life of a married man with children, Wyatt had been a traveler, often sending Gus's girls postcards and dolls from exotic ports. Years ago, shortly after Cisco turned three, Wyatt had married a woman named Roxie, tiny, sexy, and city. She owned an apartment on Park Avenue, so Wyatt had spent most of his time there. After a couple of years, though, Wyatt had divorced Roxie and returned to the island, living by himself in a cottage in Madaket, his sailboat only a few yards outside, waiting in the water.

Gus and Carley raised their children, went sailing with their friends, formed an unofficial kind of club centering around their families. In the warm intimacy of their bed they agreed smugly that Wyatt wasn't cut out for family life, while Gus most certainly was. Carley tried to feel sympathy for lonely Wyatt, but for some reason, she just always felt awkward, bashful, even in the privacy of her thoughts. She was sure Wyatt thought of her as plain, weary, and boring in a settled mommy way. He was handsome, carefree, effortlessly flirtatious. It always embarrassed her that she found him attractive.

When Gus died, Wyatt had been everywhere, helping with funeral arrangements, driving people to and from the airport, taking the girls out for dinner and a movie. Through the blur of her grief, she was aware of his gentle kindness, and she was grateful. She hoped he knew that. She couldn't remember thanking him. But she couldn't remember much about those first terrible days.

"Hi, Wyatt. Haven't seen you for a while."

"I went off hiking." Wyatt looked around. "You've got a three-ring circus going on here."

"You should have seen it earlier."

"The girls look flush," Wyatt told her, nodding toward Margaret and Cisco, who sat at their table, smiling eagerly at some kids pawing over their last articles.

"They've struck it rich, getting rid of their baby toys."

"I know. Margaret charmed me into purchasing this." He held up an ugly plastic whale.

Carley laughed. "Just what you need!"

"How are you doing, Carley?" Wyatt's gaze was warm.

She couldn't think about Gus now, not in the middle of the tag sale. "Oh, I'm all right."

"Let me take you out to dinner sometime," he suggested.

Surprised, Carley went speechless. She was grateful when a customer approached and asked about a teapot. She was just taking the woman's money when Angie, Wyatt's current girlfriend, wandered up to the table.

The appellation "cute as a bug's ear" could have been designed

just for Angie Matthews. Petite and buxom, with a mop of blond
curls and freckles across her pug nose, Angie was as energetic, sassy,
and cheerful as any woman Carley had ever met. She was a sporty
girl, too, excelling in tennis, sailing, swimming, biking, and in spite
of her size, she could put away a phenomenal amount of beer.

"Hey, Big Momma, how are you?" Angie asked Carley, sweeping
up to smack a wet kiss on Carley's cheek.

How could Carley tell this butterfly *not* to call her "Big
Momma"? It made Carley feel like a moose. But she answered good-
naturedly, "The sale has been excellent!"

A neighbor approached Wyatt, holding up one of Gus's ancient
wooden tennis racquets, asking Wyatt's opinion. As Wyatt turned
away, Angie said, "Oh, I'm so glad! Because Wyatt's been so worried
about you. Financially, I mean. With Gus dead and all."

"We'll be fine," Carley responded stiffly. Her thoughts were in a
whirl. She couldn't tolerate the thought of Wyatt and this perky little elf pitying poor old widowed, downtrodden Carley. "Listen," she
said suddenly, "would you mind the table for just a minute? I've got
to go to the john."

"Sure, honey." Angie settled into the chair.

Carley hurried around to the back door, up the back stairs and
into the private bath off her bedroom. She was tired, but jazzed up
at the same time. She couldn't wait to see how much money she'd
made. She knew the tag sale was only a short-term solution to her financial problems, but it was a *start*. It would carry her for a while,
and it might be a first step in convincing her in-laws she could take
care of herself and her children. Her daughters loved their grandparents so much. Carley didn't want any sort of dissension between
them.

On her way out, she passed the door to the kitchen. Movement
caught her eye from the window at the side of the house. She
stopped dead, as if she'd run into a brick wall. In a way, she had.
What she saw did not make sense.

Maud and Toby—*Vanessa's husband*, Toby!—stood close together, quite obviously locked in a private world. They spoke

softly—Carley couldn't hear the words—then Toby leaned forward, and kissed Maud's neck, right beneath her ear. Carley gawked, astonished, flushing hot with embarrassment. This was no little peck on the cheek. It was a nuzzling, lingering, lover's kiss. Maud sagged against Toby, closing her eyes in rapture, her expression dreamy. The couple smiled at each other, spoke again, then slowly parted, returning to the front yard and the tag sale.

Carley just stood there with her mouth open, freaked out, even panicked. What should she do? What *could* she do? After a moment, she took a deep breath and returned to the tag sale.

Angie was still at the table, but standing up. She and Wyatt were talking to an older woman . . . Annabel.

In her beige suede coat, a silk scarf knotted at her neck, a fur toque warming her elegant head, Annabel radiated refinement.

"There's Carley!" Angie didn't try to hide her relief.

"We'll be off." Wyatt nodded respectfully to Annabel as Angie tugged his arm.

Angie waggled her cute little fingers at Carley. "Bye-bye." They strolled away.

Carley was alone with Annabel.

"Hi, Annabel." Carley kissed her mother-in-law on the cheek. Lightheartedly, she held up a rather ugly perfumed candle. "What do you think? Irresistible?"

"Not really," Annabel replied smoothly. "The girls tell me it's been quite a successful event." Pointedly, she nodded toward the table that once had held Gus's clothes and paraphernalia.

Frame had gone home, leaving Toby in charge, and there Toby was, talking to an eager customer. Vanessa was in the garage, at the baby table, demonstrating to a young couple how a baby-wipe warmer worked. Maud crouched down by the children's table, chatting with Cisco and Margaret. Annabel's voice buzzed at Carley; more people were arriving. In such a jumble, Carley decided, she must have misread what she saw, or thought she saw, going on with Maud and Toby.

"I suppose you were wise to hold this little tag sale," Annabel was saying. "Especially with the economy in such bad shape. This summer business was at an all-time low on the island and as we all know, the fall marks the start of the quiet season. The restaurants won't need waiters and the shops won't need clerks. The market is flooded with people looking for jobs."

And you have no qualifications was Annabel's subtext, Carley knew. *You and your girls will need to live with us.*

"Actually," Carley announced cheerfully, "Reverend Salter just told me his nephew needs to rent a room while he's here doing historical research. For perhaps two months. I could fix up the room off the laundry room. It has its own bathroom."

Annabel stiffened. "Really, Carley, I'd think twice about . . ." She could almost not say the words. " . . . *renting* a room. It seems . . . wrong, somehow. The house is a *home.*"

"I think it will be good for us," Carley retorted, keeping her tone as mild as her mother-in-law's. "We'll make a bit of money and have someone young around the house."

Before Annabel could respond, two young women burst up to the table, excitedly pawing through all the remaining place mats.

"Those will have to be ironed," Annabel warned.

"Oh, we're not going to use them for place mats," the young women giggled.

"I'll sell them half price," Carley told them. "Since it's afternoon." *I'll pay you to stay here*, she thought. The young women squealed with delight and rummaged deep in the pile, accidentally touching Annabel's elbow.

"I'll say hello to my granddaughters." Annabel started to walk away, then stopped. "We need to discuss this more, Carley."

Carley glanced at Maud's table. She wasn't there—she was over chatting away with Vanessa! Carley sighed with relief.

By three o'clock almost everything had sold. The crowd had diminished to an occasional car driving by with people surveying the yard and passing on. Margaret and Cisco, exhausted and bored, went into the house. Toby, Vanessa, and Maud helped fold up the card tables, gather up the trash, and move anything not sold into a cardboard box in the garage.

Vanessa and Toby drove away. Maud drove away. The lawn spread out before her, empty, unchanged, except for little chunks of sod dislodged by people's shoes.

Carley carried the various cigar boxes of money to Gus's desk in his office and locked them away in the bottom drawer. All at once, she was completely exhausted. She was even too tired to count the money. Her girls were in their rooms, adding up their gains and giggling with each other.

When the phone rang, she almost didn't answer.

"Carley? It's Lauren. Listen, I know how tag sales can wear you out. Want to bring the girls over for dinner tonight? I'll make spaghetti."

Framingham Burr's wife, Lauren, was part of Carley's extended girl group. A tall, broad, comfortable woman, Lauren lived in jeans and a cotton shirt in the summer, jeans and a turtleneck in the winter. Her husband was a successful real estate developer, and they had a farm with horses, dogs, cats, chickens, a vegetable garden, and an in-ground swimming pool. They had three children, healthy, active individuals who moved through the world with confidence. Cisco was always stunned into silence by the presence of fourteen-year-old Nicholas, while Margaret, dazzled by nine-year-old Rosalind, tried to ignore the childish ploys for attention by five-year-old Will.

"Oh, Lauren, how heavenly! Of course we'll come. Bless you!" Carley hung up the phone, reinvigorated. What thoughtful friends she had! What would she do without them?

And what did she owe her friends? Should she tell Vanessa she'd seen Toby kissing Maud?

No. No. Carley must have misunderstood a perfectly innocent gesture.

11
· · · · ·

Overnight a heavy snow had fallen, unusual for the island, and the girls were eager to get outside and make snowmen. Carley padded around the kitchen in yoga pants and a flannel shirt, yawning, checking the calendar for the week and supervising the girls' breakfast. It seemed to her that Cisco was only pretending to eat.

"Mom, Delphine's coming over after school to practice, okay?"

Carley turned on a winning smile. "It's okay as long as I see you eat three bites of toast."

"I'm not a baby!"

"I didn't say you were."

Cisco tore off a bite and swallowed almost without chewing. "There."

"That's one bite."

"Mom! Stop it!"

"Studies have shown that children are healthier when they've had a substantial breakfast, and one bite of toast is not a substantial breakfast. Two. More. Bites."

Cisco glared and sniffed disdainfully. But she ate two bites, and drank her entire glass of orange juice.

All during the school year, every Tuesday afternoon and Saturday morning, Maud dropped Percy and Spenser off at Carley's house while she went to her yoga class. Maud needed the classes desperately, she said—typing and drawing tied her muscles into knots. It was a friendly arrangement.

Today it was raining, so Margaret and the boys were in the attic when Maud arrived. Even though it was cold out, Maud wore, as usual, a tank top, yoga pants, and fleece-lined clogs. Maud was looking sexier than ever—she'd had her Dutch-boy bob expensively cut and shaped.

"Tea?" Carley offered.

"I'd love some."

Carley put the kettle on and then, on the spur of the moment, asked Maud, "What's up with you?"

"What do you mean?" Maud widened her eyes innocently.

Carley narrowed her eyes. "What *do* I mean?"

Maud turned red.

"Maud!"

"I'll just shut the door." Maud closed the door to the back stairs.

"Maud, the children are in the attic, they can't hear you."

"I need to be absolutely sure." Maud sat at the table and crossed her arms defensively over her chest. "If I tell you, Carley, you've got to promise not to tell anyone else."

Suspiciously, Carley narrowed her eyes. "I'm not going to like this, am I?"

"I don't know. It doesn't matter. It looks like you've already guessed." Maud trembled with nerves. "I need to talk to someone, Carley. But you have to swear to keep it secret. Swear on your children's lives."

"Maud! What's wrong with you? I'd never do that."

"All right, all right. Listen. Just swear you won't tell anyone else."

Carley hesitated. "Okay."

"Oh, Carley—" Maud lifted her huge blue eyes to Carley, and they were shining. "I'm in love."

"You're in love?" Carley echoed. She felt sick at her stomach.

"With Toby Hutchinson."

Carley sat down hard in her chair.

"Do you hate me?" Maud clutched Carley's hands.

Carley pulled her hands away. "Maud, of course I don't hate you," though for a moment she thought maybe she did. She had not misinterpreted what she saw, Toby's mouth on Maud's neck. "But dear God, what about Vanessa?"

"Carley! I wouldn't even have told you if I'd thought you were going to get all self-righteous on me. I haven't told *anyone*, I *need* to talk to someone about this. Can't you be on my side?"

"That's a complicated question, Maud." The teakettle whistled. Carley took a moment to catch her breath as she poured water into the pot and set out the teacups and saucers.

Maud jumped up and grasped Carley's shoulders. "Oh, Carley! Oh, Carley, we tried to stop ourselves. We tried to resist one another, but we couldn't. I've always liked Toby. He's the boys' pediatrician."

"Yes, he's our pediatrician, too." Carley edged out of Maud's grasp, picking up the teapot, setting things on the table.

Maud sat down again and took a deep breath. "Okay, so you're aware that he's wise and kind and gentle. I've always been fond of him for that. The boys adore him. He's always seemed to give us extra time, he hasn't minded if I've asked silly questions, and he takes us in right away whenever we have an emergency. I suspected he had a little crush on me. And at the autism benefit gala at the new yacht club last summer, Toby asked me to dance, and it was a slow dance . . . Stop it, Carley! Don't look at me that way. You've talked about lusting after other men sometimes!"

"That's true. But, well—have you slept with him?"

Maud turned bright red. Carley had her answer.

"Oh, *Maud!*" Carley's heart twisted with worry for Vanessa.

Maud leaned forward, eager, earnest. "Carley, it was paradise! It was ecstasy! It was the same for him."

Maud's passion astonished Carley. "But Maud, I mean, come on, that's more than a flirtation, that's taking it into infidelity, adultery—"

"Stop being so judgmental!" Maud sat back down and burst into tears.

"I'm not judging you, Maud. But, come on, Vanessa—"

"Mommy!" The back stairs door flew open and Margaret flew into the room, followed by Percy and Spenser. "We're hungry!" She stopped, and her dark eyes grew wide.

"It's all right, Margaret. Maud has something in her eye." As she talked, Carley hurriedly stuffed a box of cookies, a thermos of apple juice, and three paper cups into a small paper bag. "Here's a picnic, you can eat it in the attic, but not the second floor, okay?" It would mean crumbs in the attic, but Carley wanted the children as far away as possible.

Actually, she wanted *everyone* far away, just for a minute, so she could *think*.

Maud and Toby Hutchinson? Sexually passionate? Maud had discovered *paradise* with Toby Hutchinson?

Paradise. What was that like?

The children hurtled back up the stairs. Carley shut the door.

"Don't you want me to be happy?" Maud asked, almost begging.

"Of course I do. But . . . what about Vanessa? My gosh, Las Tres Enchiladas!"

"I can't even think about her, Carley. When Toby and I are together, it's as if we're on a different plane, in a different reality. It's all so new and fresh. It's so *intense*. In a way, it doesn't even seem like adultery—no one else knows, we're not hurting anyone, and it's only happening in our own little world, the world inhabited by just the two of us."

"Where do you meet?" Carley had asked the right question. Maud beamed, eager to talk.

"At first, the time I think of as 'our' first real time, I mean when I knew we were in love, it was just in the Stop & Shop parking lot. He asked me how Spenser's been, I've been worried that he's hyperactive, and we talked about that for such a long time. I finally said, 'Oh, excuse me, you're busy, I mustn't keep you,' and he said, 'I wish you would keep me,' and wow!" Maud's face was crimson. "For a while I couldn't even speak, I just stared at him—"

"Stop." Carley held up her hand. Suddenly the truth hit her hard. "Have you been 'seeing' Toby this whole time when you're supposed to be at yoga?"

Maud dropped her eyes. "Well, at first I was going to yoga. And *sometimes* I'm at yoga . . ."

"Oh, Maud." Carley collapsed in a chair. She'd helped Maud sleep with Vanessa's husband! "This is a disaster."

"No!" Maud protested. "If you're worried that this will somehow hurt my children, listen, don't be. I'm much nicer to the kids than I've been for months! I like my life more, I have more energy, more creativity, more patience—"

"But in the *long run*," Carley interrupted. "You can't—"

"I don't care about the long run, I don't care about the future! This is my own thing, and I *want it,* Carley! I'm a damned good mother. I work hard. This isn't hurting anyone, and it's making me happier than I've ever been in my life."

"But it's hurting Vanessa," Carley insisted.

"No, it's not," Maud retorted. "She doesn't know. She'll never know. Besides, she told me sometimes when she and Toby are at it, she gets so bored she wishes she could prop up a book next to her."

"Yes, but that's *marriage,*" Carley insisted.

"Still, Toby has feelings, too. He has needs."

Carley almost exploded. "Yes, well, what about *Vanessa's needs?*" She was angry enough to hit something. She shoved back her chair and paced the kitchen. "Maud, I can't do it anymore, I won't do it. I won't have your boys here while you're at 'yoga class.' "

"But sometimes I *am* at yoga class," Maud protested sweetly, tilting her head.

"I don't care. I won't do it. Oh, Maud!" Carley wanted to throw all the china against the wall. "Maud, how can you do this?"

Maud sat very still. After a long moment of silence, she said, "I've never felt this way before, Carley. I loved John, in a sort of friendly way. I never felt this—this undeniable desire. Absolute *longing*. Followed by absolute bliss. Carley, come on. I'm a good person. I'm a good mother, a good wife. I'm not wicked, I'm not *evil*. We didn't choose for this to happen." Clasping her hands together, she pleaded, "Please don't hate me."

"I don't hate you, Maud." Carley sank back down into a chair. She was torn in two, and thinking furiously. Perhaps this was just sex, just something they both needed, and it wouldn't last long, so fiery, so hot, it would burn itself out like a supernova. "But I can't keep the boys for you, Maud. I can't collude with you."

Maud snorted. "*Collude*. You make it sound like a crime."

Carley let her silence speak.

"You can't tell Vanessa."

"No. I won't."

"I guess you want me to go."

"Yes." Carley looked at the clock. "It's time for me to start dinner, anyway."

It wasn't fair of Maud, Carley thought, for her to share her secret with Carley. It made Carley somehow seem to approve of the affair. Carley fretted about this, turning the problem around and around in her mind like a Rubik's Cube, as she cleaned and made up the bedroom and bathroom off the laundry room.

Reverend Salter's nephew was just her height, slender but muscular, with spiky brown hair, dreamy blue eyes, and a gorgeous smile.

Best of all, he was happy, and when he arrived in January, in his low-slung, faded jeans, his Aéropostale tee and hoodie, his braid necklace and his tattooed forearm, he brought fresh air into the Winsted household. Cisco and Margaret fell in love with him immediately. Carley's friends developed mad crushes on him, too, and when they came over to visit, they wore sexy little shirts and more makeup than they usually wore.

They didn't often get a chance to flirt with Kevin, though. He was almost always out at the historical association, doing research, or running or biking or ice skating, and, after only a matter of days on the island, he developed a wide group of friends, male and female, and spent all his free time with them.

She suspected he spent quite a few nights with one woman or another, but he never brought a woman back to his room, even though Carley hadn't said anything about having an overnight guest. She hadn't even thought about that sort of thing when she rented him the room.

Kevin used the bedroom at the side of the house, off the laundry room. It had its own bathroom and a good double bed and an almost private entrance leading from the side door through the mudroom. When she first offered the room to Kevin, over the telephone, she'd said that breakfast would be included with the room, just juice, coffee, muffins, cereal. He could fix it himself, she said, because she would be dealing with getting her daughters off to school. After she got acquainted with Kevin, she altered the arrangement: he was welcome to join them on Saturday and Sunday mornings, when she and the girls usually had what Margaret called a "fancy breakfast" of pancakes or French toast, eggs Benedict or cheesy soufflés, omelets stuffed with goat cheese and bacon. Kevin began to join them, occasionally. When he did, Margaret giggled through the entire meal while Cisco stared, smitten, at her plate.

He was twenty-seven. Carley was thirty-two. Yet she felt so much older than Kevin that she could be in his presence without feeling any kind of sexual attraction for him, even though she could appreciate how completely gorgeous he was. She felt relaxed and easy with him, as if he were her kid brother.

Most of all, she was very glad for the money he paid every month. It was enough to pay for Cisco's ballet lessons, with a nice chunk left over. Carley hadn't made any money herself since she waitressed back when she met Gus, and she liked the way it felt. She knew very well that she wasn't actually making the money herself— it was the house that made the money.

It was the house that made the money.

Suddenly, she thought, with a leap of her heart, maybe she and this grand old house could make even more money!

Carley wandered through the rooms, letting her imagination take her wherever it could. It *was* fun having Kevin around. She liked people. She liked cooking. She liked it when people stopped her on the street to ask where to go, which were the best shops and restaurants.

Maybe she could run a small B&B!

The thought glowed in her mind like the sun blazing out after a storm.

Margaret came down with a cold that sent her sniffling and whining to bed. Carley spent the weekend nursing her little girl, bringing her ginger ale and Popsicles to help her fever, filling and refilling the humidifier, reading to her, cuddling her. When Margaret fell asleep at night, Carley didn't have the energy to think about her plans. She took a long hot shower and crawled into bed with her own book, one Maud had passed on, with lots of unrealistic romance.

Monday she kept Margaret home to be certain she was better, and by Monday afternoon her daughter was well, and bored, almost bouncing off the walls. Carley was delighted to send her back to school Tuesday morning. She started making lists. Thinking about who could give her advice. She'd call her parents and her sister. Maud worked and made money, so she'd know some things, about taxes and so on, but her work was more solitary. Who else?

She thought of Lexi Laney. Lexi ran her own clothing store on the island, Moon Shell Beach, which was wildly successful. Lexi didn't actually run with Carley's crowd—Lexi was single, with no children, but she was close to Carley's age and whenever they met at parties, Carley had always liked talking to her. It just might work, asking Lexi about running a business. She picked up the phone.

"One thing's certain," Lexi said as she stood in Carley's kitchen looking at the cluttered desk piled with mail, the girls' schoolwork, and Carley's appointment book, "you can't run a business from here. Especially not a B&B."

"Why not?"

"It's not professional, for one thing. You want your guests to come up here for muffins and coffee and see that mess? You must have *some* place in this huge house for an office."

Carley chewed her fingernail. "Well . . . there's Gus's office."

Lexi followed Carley down the hall and into the room.

"This is perfect! You've got a desk and a computer here already. Clear off Gus's stuff and set up your office."

Carley gulped. Lexi intimidated Carley. Lexi was at least six feet tall, slender as a willow reed, with long white-blond hair and huge blue eyes. She was perfection itself. Today she wore black pants and a white tee shirt. She looked like a million dollars. Carley had always thought there was something a little hard about Lexi. She'd heard how, years ago when she was nineteen, Lexi had married a much older and very wealthy man, then divorced him after ten years and returned to the island. In that time, Lexi had acquired a kind of gloss, an *attitude*.

Carley screwed up her courage and confessed: "It doesn't feel right."

"Well, honey, he's not going to be using them anymore."

"Still . . . it might make my daughters sad."

"So you want to keep this as a shrine?"

"Well . . ."

"Fine." Lexi turned on her heel and walked out to the hall. "This is a big house. You have lots of rooms. Of course the placement of the office is perfect. It's near the kitchen and at the back of the hall, but it's your decision. We can turn any room into an office. You just need a desk, a computer, and some file cabinets."

"My computer's in the kitchen."

"Nope, can't use that. That's the household computer. You'll want to move it, though—into the den with the television. Your girls use it, right? You email your friends? That's what *that* computer's for. You need a computer dedicated to your business. For tax reasons as well as for organizational reasons."

"Lexi . . . listen, I'm having trouble thinking clearly. I do need to get organized. Do you think we could just sit in the kitchen for a while and you could tell me stuff and I could write down a list?"

"Sure, Carley. That will work."

Once settled in the kitchen with Diet Cokes, Carley picked up a pen and pad of paper. "Go."

"All right. Just off the top of my head. Signage."

"What?"

"You need to have some kind of sign to show people they've come to the right place. Signage is strictly controlled by the Historic District Commission. You may not even be able to have a sign up here in this residential area. Better have one of your lawyer relatives organize that for you. At a quick glance, I'm seeing lots of nice stuff that you won't want broken. Put it away. Especially anything that might be valuable or look valuable."

"You're kidding."

"Not kidding. You'd be surprised how many people just slip a little souvenir into their pockets. They think, since they're paying such high prices to stay, eat, and shop on the island, that they deserve it."

"Wow."

"You need to get a credit card machine. You need to decide what kind of record-keeping program you want, which one you can work with most easily. You can talk to Martha at Computer Solutions but you'll also need to run it by your accountant. You need to check to see if your guests can access the Internet in this house. Do you want them to have coffee/tea in their rooms? Do you have maids to help make the beds and clean the bathrooms every day?"

Carley shook her head. "Reverend Salter's nephew Kevin is here. We don't make his bed every day. He doesn't have afternoon tea, either. We don't change his sheets . . ."

"Right. He's just renting a room. That's quite different. Look, I don't run an inn. I'm just hitting some of the points. You've got to talk with an innkeeper."

Carley buried her face in her hands. "Lexi, I don't think I can do this."

"Maybe not," Lexi responded bluntly. "But maybe you can. And maybe it's just what you need. When I came back from New York, I was divorced and miserable and lost. My business saved my life, in more ways than one."

When the girls arrived home from school, Carley had them sit at the kitchen table with her. She'd set out snacks of fruit and cookies, and she asked them about school, and then she cleared her throat.

"Girls, I'm thinking of opening a bed-and-breakfast. An inn. We'll have guests staying with us."

"Like Kevin?" Margaret piped up hopefully.

"Well, sort of. Probably, they'll be older people. I've got a ton of work to do, and I'll be using Daddy's office as an office for the B&B. Which means that I'm moving a lot of Daddy's things out."

Margaret tugged on a lock of black hair. Cisco's face turned stubborn.

Carley continued, cheerfully, "I thought you girls might like to go through Daddy's office and find some things of his you'd like to keep in your room. The sailing trophies, maybe. Cis, you might like his desk set." She waited for a response, but the girls didn't speak. "I'm going to box up Daddy's legal books. Some of the others I'm putting in the living room for the guests to read on rainy days. Things are going to change here, girls. They have to. I need to find a way to make some money, and with this big old house, I think I can."

Cisco's face was set. "If we lived with Nana and Granddad, you wouldn't have to make money."

"Cisco, this is my home. This is your home. This is Margaret's home. We are not moving out of it."

"Well, I think you're stupid."

Carley hesitated, then let it go. "It's going to be fun! Every room will need some chairs, a little writing desk, a little table."

"Strange people in our house," Cisco muttered.

"Cisco, I need to find a way to make money. I'm doing what has to be done." Suddenly Carley was exhausted. She could see the strain on both her daughters' faces, too. "All right. It's a sunny day. Enough talking. Go play."

"I don't *play,*" Cisco snapped as she exploded from the table. With her hand on the door, she turned back to Carley and snapped, "Have you told Nana and Granddad about this?"

"Not yet." Carley forced herself to be calm. "I wanted to tell you girls first."

14

. . . . .

The next morning, as soon as the girls were off to school, Carley pulled on her dress coat and boots and walked down toward the Winsted legal offices on Centre Street. When she came to the distinguished brick building, she hesitated. All last night, she'd thought, made notes, plotted, and planned, finally deciding that she'd talk with Russell first, before she spoke with Annabel. Russell would know the legalities of opening a B&B, and perhaps he might be less emotional about Carley turning her home into a business.

She stood there in the bright cold light of day, fighting off fear. If Russell strongly objected, if he grew angry, Carley would fall apart, and so would her plans. Shoulders slumping, she turned back toward home.

"Carley!" Wyatt strode up the sidewalk from town, a newspaper in his hand. His camel coat and scarlet muffler gave him an impressive professional aura. "Were you going into the office?"

She hesitated, then admitted, "I was, but I changed my mind. Oh, Wyatt, I think I have a really good idea, a way to make money and keep the house and still be independent, but I'm pretty sure Russell and Annabel will hate the idea."

"Try me," Wyatt suggested.

"I want to run a B&B."

Wyatt stuck his hands in his pockets and rocked back on his heels, thinking. "Hm. Yes. I can see that. I think that could work."

"You *do?*" She almost burst into tears of relief.

"Let's go look at the house." Wyatt linked arms with her and ushered her briskly along the sidewalk. "It is a huge house for only three people. It's got spectacular water views. It's a short walk to town, that's always a plus. You wouldn't want people on the second floor, though, not on the same floor as the girls. Somehow that doesn't seem quite right. The attic? Perhaps too many stairs for older folk."

His enthusiasm was contagious. By the time they reached the house, Carley's mind was buzzing.

They hadn't even gone in the front door when Wyatt snapped his finger. "The basement! Let's check out the basement!"

Like many Nantucket houses, Carley's had what was called an English basement, the walls half in the ground, half above ground, with large windows letting in light. There was a private entrance from the side of the house, a few steps down. They went in.

Carley flicked on the light, exposing a large unfinished room. Over the years, all sorts of orphaned bits had ended up here—a centerboard and rudder from a sunfish, parts of bicycles and ice skates and skis, a pair of crutches from when Gus sprained his ankle, a few boxes of unnecessary junk bought at church auctions. Most of that had gone in the tag sale. The windows were covered with old roller blinds that had yellowed over the years. Carley tugged on them, trying to get them to snap up. Some worked, others tore.

"It's a great space," Wyatt told her. "The floor is dry. The walls are dry."

"We're high on the cliff. Rain never has been a problem."

"Good light from the windows. Solid construction." He ran his hand over a wall. "These old houses were built to last. The floors are wood, handsome wide pine. Antique lovers would appreciate them. The walls are plaster. This doesn't feel like a basement."

"True." Carley circled the room. "Look at all the sunlight."

Wyatt unlocked a window, raised it, shut it. "You've got one bathroom down here, right?"

"Right. Just with a stall shower. We could have another bedroom if we put in a private bath, but I can't imagine how much that would cost . . ."

He whipped a pad and pen out of his pocket. "Let's look at some numbers." He walked toe-to-toe, measuring with his feet. "A house like this, a location like this, you can make a big fat profit from a couple of posh rooms. You don't want college kids here and frankly they wouldn't want to stay up here on the cliff. It's an old residential area. You need to get some nice retired people in here. You could double the amount of money you make if you put in another bathroom."

"But first I'd have to pay for the bathroom," she reminded him.

"Maybe you could take out a short-term loan." Wyatt scratched numbers on his pad, showing her how the money would come and go; by July, she'd have the loan paid off and be making money free and clear.

Carley tapped her lip with her fingertip. "My father could loan me the money."

"I'd be glad to loan you the money, Carley."

Carley met his eyes. In this light, the green had deepened to emerald. He held her gaze, and something seemed to stretch between them, an invisible tug. His smile held such affection, such warmth.

"I, um—" She knew he was being kind but she didn't want to take his money if she weren't certain she could repay it. "I'm sure I can get the money from my father." She crossed the room and looked out the window. "What I would appreciate would be if you could help me convince Russell and Annabel that running a B&B would be the right thing for me to do."

Wyatt hesitated. "I have a feeling they might resist this, Carley. But I'll certainly do all I can to help you."

"In that case," Carley said with a grin, "I'll let you be the one to tell Annabel and Russell!"

Wyatt laughed. "I'm afraid you're going to have to drop that bomb yourself. But I will check out some contractors for you. I have a pretty good idea who's available, fast, and won't cheat you."

"Wyatt, that would be terrific!" Suddenly the idea seemed possible. She clapped her hands. "Oh, this is exciting!" Without thinking, she gave Wyatt a big tight hug. "Wyatt, thank you!"

Wyatt's body stiffened inside the circle of her arms.

Oh, no, he thinks I'm making a pass at him! Carley thought with a rush of humiliation. She practically ran out the door, into the open air. "I think I'll go talk with Annabel this minute, while I'm so determined!"

Wyatt came outside, too, pulling the door closed behind him. "I'll walk back toward town with you."

This time, he did not take her arm.

"I'm thinking about the room off the laundry room," Carley babbled. "The one Kevin's in now. He'll be leaving in March. It's a good size room, but not particularly charming."

"Take out the two small windows that face the garden and replace them with a half-moon window with casement windows at each end."

"Wyatt, you're a genius! Yes, I can just see it, with a long window seat. Charming." She restrained herself from hugging him again.

When they came to the law office, Wyatt said, "Okay, then, I'm off to work."

"And I'm off to Annabel's."

Wyatt paused, as if he had something more to say. Then he said simply, "Good luck, Carley," and gave her a mock salute before turning away.

15
· · · · ·

Carley often dropped by her in-laws' house without calling first. They had insisted over and over again when she first married Gus that they liked it that way, and after all, they were family. In return, they often dropped in at Carley's without calling first. But so did Carley's friends and her children's friends.

She knocked on the door of her mother-in-law's house. Annabel was in old chinos and a cashmere sweater with a scarf around her neck. She accepted Carley's kiss on the cheek without a smile. "This is a surprise."

"I hope you don't mind . . ."

"Of course not."

"That's a lovely scarf."

Annabel grimaced. "Arthritis. Keeps my neck warm."

"Annabel, could I talk to you a minute?"

"Of course. Come back to the kitchen and we'll have tea. How are the girls?"

"They're well. Cisco's new friend, Polo, is *not* obsessed with ballet. I'm delighted about that. Cisco's hardly eating anything these days. I'm worried about her."

"I'm keeping an eye on her, too. Sooner or later, someone has to tell her that she's too tall, too broad-shouldered, to be a classical ballerina."

Carley winced. "You're right. Annabel, I'm afraid it will crush her."

Her mother-in-law leaned over and patted Carley's arm. "I don't think your daughter is so very crushable."

"Good. That makes me feel better. I don't think she's smoking, either."

"I agree. I haven't smelled it on her clothing or hair." Annabel tilted her head. "Is that what you wanted to talk with me about?"

"No . . ." Carley took a deep breath. "Annabel, I've decided to run a B&B here this summer."

Her mother-in-law was at the stove, pouring boiling water into a teapot. Her back stiffened, but she didn't speak.

"I'm going to have two bedrooms with private bathrooms added in the basement. I'd like to start having guests in June."

"*Guests.*" Annabel brought the pot to the table and sat down. Her mouth had tightened into a thin line.

"Annabel, I need a way to make money and stay home with the children, and this is the perfect way to do it."

"The house is not a hotel."

"Well, it's big enough to be one." Carley bit her tongue and counted to ten. It would not help if she became confrontational.

"Carley, it's always been a *home*, not a place of business."

"Renting out three rooms isn't really turning it into a *business*. It's not like I'm setting up shop, tearing down walls and installing windows full of mannequins in girdles and bras—"

"I doubt that the zoning laws would allow you to do that."

"The point is, the people who stay here will be tourists on short-term stays. They'll come because of the beauty of the island."

Annabel folded her hands on the table and drew herself up as straight as a judge. "I strongly oppose this, Carley. This house has been a private family home for decades. It has weathered the Great Depression and any number of family problems without being opened to the public."

"I understand how you feel, Annabel. It kills me to disagree with you. But it's necessary."

"Russell and I have offered to help you financially. We've asked you to move in with us."

"Yes. I do appreciate your kindness. Of course in an emergency, I'd be grateful to have to rely on you both. But we've got our whole lives ahead of us. I have to find a way to work, to support myself and the children. Besides, Annabel, this is something that appeals to me. I think I might really enjoy it! I love people, I love cooking—"

"The house is hardly set up for guests."

"True. I'll need to have some work done. I've spoken with Wyatt. He's going to find a contractor for me."

"You've already spoken to Wyatt about this?" Annabel's tone was indignant.

"Well, yes," Carley answered, trying not to be apologetic. "We sort of ran into each other on Centre Street and I told him what I was planning, and he offered some advice." Her mother-in-law was beginning to tremble slightly and her face had gone pale. Annabel was heartily furious, but holding back her fury. "I'm sorry to upset you, Annabel. Please understand I'm doing the best I can."

"I think we disagree on what 'the best' is," Annabel commented coldly. She rose without bothering to pour the tea she'd made. "This has come as a blow to me, Carley. I need to go lie down. Please excuse me."

Guilt thumped down in Carley's belly like a twenty-pound weight. Annabel had never been so adamant before, so bitterly disapproving. But they were, after all, family, Carley thought, and they would get past this, she was sure.

Head high, she let herself out the front door.

Carley walked home without noticing the snowmen smiling in the yards or the birds swooping down to the feeders on the neighbors' lawns. She was sad about Annabel's disapproval, excited about Wyatt's positive reaction, hopeful about running a B&B, worried about Cisco's extreme thinness, frustrated because she couldn't talk to her parents or Sarah or Sue because they were at work, and generally confused and overwhelmed.

This much was clear: Her future, at least the immediate future, was simply this: She was alone. She was widowed. She needed to make money. She needed to protect her daughters. The B&B might not be what Annabel wanted, but Carley was convinced it was the only option that made sense for her.

She'd just entered her house, hung up her coat, and kicked off her boots when a knock sounded at the door and Vanessa came in, wrapped in a glamorous faux fur.

"Hi, Carley!"

"Oh! Vanessa. Hi!" Guilt slammed Carley hard. She had *promised* not to tell Vanessa that Maud was "seeing" Toby. A headache tapped at her temples. "Umm, want some tea?"

"I'd kill for some. I've spent all morning in a committee meeting, and I've got another one this afternoon." As she talked, she pulled off her handsome leather high-heeled boots and thudded her feet up on another chair. "I don't know how I let it happen, but I'm chair of the hospital summer fund-raiser, and you know that's insane, plus I'm co-chair for the library's fund-raiser."

"You're a saint."

"I'm a sucker." Vanessa looked around. "I thought Maud's boys would be here . . ."

Carley headed toward the stove, hiding her face from Vanessa. "No, I'm not babysitting for them much anymore. I think Maud's made other arrangements."

"Carley. Have I offended you?"

Carley turned, startled. "Oh, Vanessa! Of course not! How can you ask?"

"You haven't phoned me for ages. We haven't been getting together like we always do." Vanessa slipped off her coat and hung it over the back of a chair. "What's going on?"

Carley closed her eyes, wondering how to have an intimate conversation with this beloved friend and still keep Maud's secret, which she wasn't even sure she should keep. "Oh, hell, I don't care about calories, I'm going to make some Godiva hot chocolate with whole milk. Want some?"

"I'd love some."

Carley bustled around, searching out the container from the high cupboard where she'd hidden it from herself, pouring the milk, stirring steadily.

"There's a flu bug going around," Carley said. "Toby must be crazy busy." *Oops*, she ordered herself. *No talking about Toby.*

"He is," Vanessa agreed. Automatically she got out the little rose-covered tray Carley kept next to the stove and set it with napkins and spoons and Carley's prettiest mugs. "Cookies?"

"Sure. There's shortbread in the tin." How pleasant this could be, just like always, except that Carley's heart raced around inside her, up to her throat, down to her stomach, skipping and thudding with nerves. She *hated* this. Maud had put her in an indefensible position; she was betraying Vanessa with every moment that she didn't tell her the truth.

"Your hands are shaking," Vanessa observed as Carley poured the hot chocolate into the mugs.

Carley sighed. Vanessa took the pan away from Carley and finished pouring the steaming fragrant dark liquid.

"Do you want to talk about it?"

Carley sank into a chair. "It's just—it's just that I've decided to open a B&B. I'm sure I can make a good amount of money. I've talked with Wyatt about it, and he agrees. But I just told Annabel my idea, and she's completely against it. She's offended by the very thought."

Carley couldn't help it, she began to cry, but she wasn't crying about Annabel, she was crying because she was such a traitor, such a *shit*, aware that Vanessa's husband was sleeping with Maud and not telling her. She *hated* this situation!

She felt even worse when she felt Vanessa's arms fold around her in a consoling embrace. "Oh, hon, I didn't realize. I knew Gus made some bad investments. Toby did, too. I think everyone has."

Vanessa grabbed a handful of tissues and wiped Carley's tears. "Carley, you should have told me. I can loan you some money."

Carley was speechless with misery. Oh, God, this was horrible, she couldn't do this, she had to tell Vanessa, it would break Vanessa's heart, but at least then only her *husband* would be betraying her, not her husband and both of her close friends!

"Oh, Vanessa. You're so generous. I've got to tell you something—"

"Mommy?" Margaret came in the door, her cheeks red from the cold. Carley blew her nose heartily but she couldn't speak. Margaret stood stock still, staring at her. "Mommy, you're crying!"

Vanessa picked Margaret up and held her on her lap. Her black hair was held back with a blue headband that matched her blue and white snowflake sweater. Vanessa's hair was as dark. They could be mother and daughter. "Hi, cutie-pie. Don't worry about your mommy. She burned her tongue on her hot chocolate. Would you like some hot chocolate?"

Margaret drew back. "I don't want to burn my tongue."

"Oh," Vanessa laughed, "aren't I silly? It's not hot *now*, honey. Look, here's my cup. I'm going to dip my spoon in, and you can dip your fingertip in the spoon and see how warm it is, *not* hot, but nice and warm."

Carefully, Margaret touched the liquid. "It's warm, not hot."

"Want to taste some of mine?" Vanessa held out her cup.

Margaret took it warily and brought it slowly to her lips. She took a sip. "It's *good*. Thank you, Vanessa."

"Your mommy made it. How's your hot chocolate, Carley?"

Carley took a drink. "Perfect." She sent Vanessa a smile of thanks.

Vanessa gave Carley an affectionate smile. "Listen, I think a B&B is a fabulous idea! You love to bake, you make delicious bread, you love people, you have all these rooms, and you've got a dynamite view. You could make quite the tidy sum."

"Oh, Vanessa, I'm so glad you think so."

With Margaret nestled on Vanessa's lap, Carley couldn't tell

Vanessa about Maud and Toby. Perhaps this was good, Carley decided, as she and Vanessa began to talk about other things, town
scandals, school events. After all, it was possible that Maud's affair
would end. Married people sometimes needed a *fling*, and perhaps
that was all it was for Maud. Perhaps it would be better for Vanessa
if she never knew about it.

Besides, it was really between Toby and Vanessa. It was Toby who
should tell her if anyone did.

Wyatt recommended a contractor named Hugo Pineda, and Russell grudgingly admitted that if Carley was going to go ahead with the B&B plan, Pineda was as good as any to do the work. Both Russell and Wyatt went through the basement with Carley and the contractor, specifications were drawn up, and the Historic District Commission approved the plans. A contract was signed, and in the middle of February, the renovations began. It was a slow time for builders, and Hugo was glad for the work.

While Hugo hammered away in the basement, Carley ordered new beds and mattresses for the bedrooms. She dug through the trunks in the attic for hand-embroidered bed linen and hand-sewn quilts. She talked with other innkeepers, got her certification of registration with the state, bought a date book and register, and paid a local computer guru to put up an attractive website. She brainstormed with her daughters and they officially named the B&B: Seashell Inn. She got a credit card machine and learned how to use it, and just in time, for reservations began to come in for June, July, and August. The first time she saw the reservation blinking on her website, she nearly had a panic attack. This was real. This was happening!

When Hugo had finished the major renovations on one basement room, Carley whizzed in with her paints and brushes and curtain fabrics. Years ago, when she and Gus had first moved into this house, they had worked together to repair and refresh various rooms of the big old house. They'd wallpapered and painted and hammered and caulked. Soon they had two guest rooms ready on the second floor, for Carley's parents and her sister and Sue, or Gus or Carley's college friends, to stay in when they came to visit. Annabel had gladly babysat Cisco while they worked. Carley carefully drew her brush across the new molding on the sunny little ground floor bedroom, remembering those days with satisfaction. Gus would approve of this, she was sure. He would want her to do whatever she could to keep the house.

The renovations kept her so busy she didn't have much time to visit with Maud or Vanessa—not that Maud ever had time to stop by these days. Not that Carley had any desire to hear the latest lovers' update from Maud. Perhaps that little fling was over and done with. She hoped so. Her mother-in-law didn't stop by as often, either, and when Annabel did see Carley, she held herself aloof. *Fine*, Carley thought. *Can't be bothered.* But she missed Annabel's warmth and humor; she was sorry to upset her mother-in-law. At least both Annabel and Russell were still involved with their granddaughters, taking them out for pizza, attending Cisco's recitals and Margaret's kindergarten play.

Kevin moved out, much to the girls' disappointment, in March. Hugo began work on the window at once. A few days later, he called to Carley, "Come see!"

The room was a glowing jewel. The half-moon window gave the space the air of a medieval chamber. Its mullioned windows divided the garden into a dozen small oil paintings of flowers, sunshine, green grass, and the room was dazzling with light.

"Hugo, you're a genius!" she cried.

"It's true," he agreed. "I am."

. . .

The basement rooms were ready. All Carley had to do was organize the furniture. She had to go to the Cape to buy accessories and necessities—fresh bath and beach towels, lamps, soaps, tissues, bed linens. She was looking forward to that shopping trip, eager to turn all three rooms into perfect retreats of peace.

She was just checking her calendar to see which day she should go off-island when Cisco exploded into the kitchen.

"I hate you!" Cisco screamed.

Startled, Carley stared at her older daughter, quickly checking for signs of injury. Cisco was in a full-blown tantrum, her face splotched with anger, her eyes streaming with tears.

"Cisco, honey." Carley went toward her child. "Cis, what on earth has happened?"

"*You* have happened!" Cisco screamed. "You with your great big enormous bones! Your monster swimmer's shoulders! You've ruined me! Why did you ever have to give birth to me?"

Madame Fourier must finally have told Cisco the terrible truth: Cisco could never have a career as a ballerina. Like Carley, she was tall, with wide shoulders and, increasingly, a real bosom.

"Cisco." Carley tried to embrace her daughter but Cisco shoved her off. "You need to calm down, Cisco. You're working yourself into a state."

"Into a state? You want me to calm down? My life is over and you want me to calm down!"

"Cisco, your life is not over."

"The life I want is over. My dreams are over."

"You'll have new dreams. I promise you, you'll have new dreams—"

Cisco dropped to her knees. Her shoulders shook. "I don't want new dreams. Oh, Mommy, why didn't you tell me? Why did you let me take ballet? Why did you let me go on believing I could be a ballerina?"

"Darling, when you started ballet, you were just a kid, like Margaret. Neither of us could guess you'd come to love it so much."

"You could *guess* I'd look like *you*."

Carley knelt next to her daughter. Reaching out, she took Cisco's hand. "You look like me, true, but not *exactly* like me, Cisco. You've got a lot of genes mixed up inside you, we all do. You have your father's black hair and eyes. For all I knew, you'd end up with narrow shoulders like Auntie Sarah. The point is, you may be too broad-shouldered for ballet, but you can still dance—"

Cisco shook her head violently. "I'll never dance again."

"Oh, honey, that would be terrible. You love to dance. Didn't Madame Fourier suggest something else—modern dance, for example?"

"No, she didn't! Because the truth is, I'm an Amazon, I'm an ostrich, I'm a giraffe!"

"Cisco," Carley laughed. "Come on. You're hardly—"

Cisco pushed up off the floor. She seethed with anger. "Go on, laugh at me. Laugh at me because I'm too hulking to ever be a ballerina. You must have been making fun of me all along! *Everyone* must have been laughing at me to think that great big huge Cisco could be a ballerina! I wish I'd never been born!"

Carley reached out for her daughter. "Cisco, my darling—"

"Don't touch me! I hate you! You've ruined my life!" Cisco ran from the room.

Carley's heart ached. But what could she do? Everyone saw dreams die, that was part of what growing up was about. When Carley was very young, she wanted to grow up to be a horse, not a cowgirl, but a horse. When Sarah was Cisco's age, she'd wanted to be a NASCAR driver. It was heartbreaking, but Cisco would survive. She would find other dreams. And Carley was glad this particular dream had met its end. Maybe now her daughter would eat.

Carley would have spent more time fretting about Cisco's broken heart if she hadn't been so overwhelmed with the way summer was spinning toward her.

Finally the day came to set up the rooms. One Sunday in April, she invited Lauren and her husband Frame and their three children, and Wyatt and his girlfriend Angie over to move furniture and, in return, enjoy a luncheon feast. The men carried chairs, end tables, antique writing desks, old paintings, and framed maps of the island down to the guest rooms. They screwed in curtain rods and hung draperies. They set up the new bed frames and mattresses. Carley and Lauren sailed crisp white cotton sheets over the beds, and Margaret tenderly unwrapped the exquisite new soaps. Even Cisco, still furious with her mother, found herself unable to resist the excitement and joined in to help. They hung thick new towels on the racks, arranged seashell-shaped soaps in the azure soap dishes, folded feather-soft afghans over the arms of the chairs.

When they were finished, Lauren stepped back, folded her arms, and asked, "When can I move in?"

Carley laughed. The rooms were gorgeous, tranquil and dreamy. "They do look inviting, don't they?"

"You have a gift for this," Lauren told her.

With a lift of her heart, Carley thought: *maybe I do!*

. . .

When the work was done, Carley and the others brought lunch to the table beneath the grape arbor. It was the first day warm enough for eating outside, and she'd spent last night preparing picnic food: cold pesto-rolled chicken cutlets, Parmesan potato salad, macaroni salad—the children's favorite—arugula and spinach, sliced tomatoes, the first early sweet ones of the season, and four different kinds of cookies for dessert. The children ate fast and raced off into the yard, leaving the adults to enjoy their conversation.

"Wyatt," Lauren asked, taking a second helping of potato salad, "where's Angie? I thought she was coming."

Wyatt shrugged. "Angie's not big on physical labor. I think she went over to the Cape."

"You think?" Lauren cocked an eye at him. "Is there trouble in Paradise?"

"Lauren." Wyatt lowered his head and gave her a level glare. "No one ever said it was Paradise. We're just friends."

"Leave the man alone, for Pete's sake!" Frame bellowed. "You women."

Carley refrained from pointing out that she hadn't said a thing.

"—do you, Carley?"

"Oh, sorry, Frame, what did you say?" Fortunately just at that moment a soccer ball rolled under her feet. She tossed it back to the kids.

"I said it seems to me your kids are doing fine," Frame repeated.

Carley looked out at the yard. Fourteen-year-old Nicholas, nine-year-old Rosalind, and five-year-old Will were playing against twelve-year-old Cisco and five-year-old Margaret in a nonsense game they'd named "Kick-Steal," which was basically a free-for-all with the big kids protecting the little kids from getting tackled.

"They're having a good time now." Carley lowered her voice. "Cisco's had a rough week. Madame Fourier told her that her shoulders are too wide for her to become a classical ballerina. She's devastated, and furious at me."

"Why is she mad at you?" Wyatt asked.

"Because she got her big shoulders from me."

"Your shoulders aren't *big*," Wyatt objected. "They're perfectly—" All at once he looked embarrassed. "Fine," he muttered. "Perfectly fine." He crammed another cookie into his mouth.

Across the table, Lauren said, "I have an idea. Has Cisco ever ridden? Why don't you bring her over and let's put her on one of our horses and see if she likes it."

"Your horses are twelve feet tall," Carley gulped.

"They only look that tall. They're all loves. I'll bet Cisco would take to it. She's just the right age."

"All right," Carley agreed. "We'll try it." She was ready to try anything to make her older daughter smile.

At the end of the day, Lauren and Frame rounded up their three children and went home. Wyatt helped Carley bring the food into the kitchen. It was only natural for Carley to offer him some wine. Cisco went up to her room to tap on her computer, and Margaret settled in her own room with her dolls. The evening was still bright with early spring sunshine, but the air was chilly.

"Let's sit in the living room," Carley told Wyatt. "I could use a soft cushion after working all day."

For a few moments, they sipped their wine in silence. Carley allowed herself to look at Wyatt, really *look* at him. He was as handsome as always, even in his old stained work shirt, but his eyes were weary and silver sparkled in his glossy brown hair. Surely Wyatt was too young for silver hair.

"Wyatt, how are you doing?"

"Oh, I'm all right."

"No, seriously, Wyatt. Tell me." When he didn't reply, she prompted, "Do you miss Gus?"

"Of course I do. I miss him like hell." Wyatt's face creased. He rubbed his hand over his forehead. "I feel so damned guilty."

"You! Wyatt, why should you feel guilty?"

Wyatt looked down into his wineglass. "I knew Gus was unhappy with the law. I knew he wanted to make more money. He was investing heavily, and not always wisely. When he lost it all, I loaned him some money, but it wasn't enough. He wanted more. I couldn't give it to him."

"I didn't know that. I was aware that he was playing the stock markets but I certainly had no idea he'd borrowed money from you. How much?"

"That's not the point, Carley. The point is I wish I'd been a better friend to him."

"Wyatt, remember, Gus didn't die because he was worried about money. He died because of a faulty heart valve no one knew he had." Softly, she said, "Wyatt, Gus was your best friend."

Wyatt's voice was hoarse. "Yes." Wyatt bent over, elbows on knees, head in hands, and his shoulders shook.

Carley sat very still. She could feel Wyatt's grief rising off him like a mist, a fog of misery and guilt and sorrow. Her heart ached for Wyatt, for Gus, for herself. She wanted to pat his back like a mother consoling a child, but she didn't reach to touch him.

"Sorry, Carley." He stood up suddenly, setting his glass on the coffee table. "I'd better get out of here. I'm tired and sounding downright maudlin."

She followed him to the door. "Wyatt, I want to pay you back the money Gus borrowed. How much is it?"

Wyatt shook his head. "Carley, don't even think about it. It was nothing."

"But—"

"Really."

"Oh, Wyatt, that's unnecessary. But thank you. Thank you for helping today, too."

Wyatt smiled down at Carley. "I'm always glad to be here." He kissed her cheek lightly.

Then he was gone.

· · ·

Sunday night, after Carley had Margaret tucked away in bed, she knocked on Cisco's door.

Cisco looked up. She was in her pajamas, lounging on her bed with her laptop open. She just stared at her mother.

Carley sat on the end of Cisco's bed. "Can we talk a little?"

Cisco didn't look at Carley. "Like I have an option?"

"Well, I guess that's right. No, you don't have an option." She considered her words. "You spent last night with Granddad and Nana. How was it?"

Cisco picked at the skin around her thumbnail. "Okay."

"Did Nana help you feel better about not being a ballerina?"

Cisco hunched her shoulders. "I guess. She said life is a process of losing what we love."

"But Cisco!" Carley grasped her daughter's hands. "That's so sad. That's not the way Nana thinks when she's her normal self. Goodness! Life isn't just about loss."

After a moment, Cisco whispered, "Nana cried."

"Honey, we all cry about losing Daddy."

Cisco peeked up at her mother. "Nana lost her *son*. Her only child. She'll never be able to replace him, just like I'll never be able to replace my father. But *you* . . . "

Carley sat very still. When Cisco didn't continue, she prompted, "Go on."

Cisco didn't speak.

"You mean that I'll be able to replace my husband?"

Cisco shuddered and hugged herself tight, but couldn't keep it in. "Isn't that the truth? You're young, Nana says! You're pretty, Nana says. Men will be coming around to help you . . . "

"Cisco, no man will ever be able to replace your father. Gus and I had a life together for thirteen years. We *made* you. We *made* Margaret. We were a happy family. You *know* that, Cisco. Your father loved me and I loved him."

Reaching out, she took her daughter's foot in her hands. Cisco didn't pull it away.

Carley continued, "Annabel and Russell could never doubt that Gus and I loved each other."

"Nana wants me to go live with her." Cisco chewed her lip.

"Cisco, I am fully aware they want us to live with them, but that's not even practical. You're too young to have to hear about all the financial aspects of owning a house, but . . ."

"I said, *I* should go live with her. Just me."

Carley was appalled. "Oh, Cisco! What about Margaret?"

"She said Margaret could stay with you."

"But it would break Margaret's heart if you didn't live with her, Cisco! She's your little sister! My God, what is Annabel *thinking*!" Distraught, Carley pushed off the bed and paced the room. Anger and desperation made her voice shake. She dropped to her knees and gripped Cisco by the arms. "You are *my* daughter. *Mine*. You might not like that, but you can't change it. Nothing can change it. I take care of you. I always have and I always will. If I want to sell this house and move to Australia with you and Margaret, that's my right and no one can stop me!"

"Mom, you're hurting my arms."

"Well, you're hurting my *heart*!" But Carley released her hold.

Cisco whispered, "I don't want Nana to die."

"What?" Carley moved up Cisco's bed, sitting next to her. Cisco scooted over, making room. They sat side by side, leaning against the pillows. Carley could feel the tension in her daughter's body. "Cisco, Nana's not going to die, honey."

"If Daddy had a weak heart, he might have gotten it from Nana's side of the family. Nana's heart . . ."

"Nonsense," Carley stoutly objected. "Look how healthy Nana is. She eats well. She exercises. She's not overweight. She takes care of herself. And she's got Granddad to love her and watch over her. And she's got us, but we don't have to *live* with her for her to have us."

Cisco wasn't reassured. Studying her daughter, Carley thought: this isn't about how Cisco feels about me. *It's how she feels about her grandmother. Cisco wants to do something. She wants some control of something in a world where all control has been wrenched away.* After a moment, Carley offered, "What if you spent every Saturday night with Nana?"

"Why not more? Why not three nights a week? Nana says—"

"I couldn't stand to have you away so often. Margaret would be miserable. And I am the official keeper of your schedule! This is your *home*."

"What about Friday and Saturday nights?" Cisco pleaded.

"Oh, Cisco."

"I think Nana would like that, Mom. I think it would help her."

"Oh, Cisco. All right, then. Do you know how much I love you?"

"I know, Mom."

Cisco leaned in to Carley's embrace. They sat together, hugging tightly, too tired to cry.

18

· · · · ·

Carley had had Hugo build a row of cubicles in the back hall leading into the kitchen. She was folding and carefully putting away brand-new, newly washed hand towels, bath towels, washcloths, and beach towels, stacks and stacks of them so that Maria, who was going to help her clean the rooms, would always have plenty on hand.

She stood back to admire her organization. Each room would have its own summery color—sea blue, navy blue, or leaf green. The beach towels were in stripes of all three colors. Everyone could use those. At an amazingly inexpensive outlet shop, she'd found beach bags and umbrellas covered in polka dots in similar colors, dark and light blue and green. Next, she'd take the hair dryers around to each room, and the shampoos and conditioners and the clever little radio alarm clocks—

Maud pounded on the kitchen door and then burst into the house.

"Carley, Toby's going to leave Vanessa!" Maud's eyes were shining. She'd never looked so glorious.

Quickly, Carley took stock. Margaret was in her room, playing with a neighborhood friend. Cisco was out with Polo. And there went Maud's boys, kicking a soccer ball around the yard.

"I told the boys to stay in the backyard. " Maud hugged herself, grinning from ear to ear. "Toby's going to do it. He's telling Vanessa tonight."

Carley's fists clenched. "Maud, come on! You can't do that to Vanessa. It's so wrong! You should be ashamed of yourself for even—"

"*Ashamed*? There's nothing shameful about love. When have you become so frigid?"

Carley stared at Maud, inarticulate with anger and misery. Maud glared back, determined.

"You don't know what you're saying, Maud." Carley let her voice go soft as she sank into a chair. "You don't know what you're doing." She felt ill. "My God, Maud. This will change everything."

"Well, *duh*! I'm *dreading* it." Maud paced around the kitchen table. "But it will be all right, Carley, really it will! I mean everyone on the island adores Vanessa. Toby won't be out of the house two seconds before half the men on the island show up to take care of her!"

"I hope you're right." Carley put her head in her hands. She could think of no way out of this.

Maud was irrepressible. "Carley. Toby loves me and I love him."

"And Vanessa?"

"Toby will take care of Vanessa financially."

"Oh, good. Because money's all that matters."

"I'm not saying that. But it is important. Vanessa will be fine, Carley. To start with, she's totally beautiful. She's a strong woman, and she's so active on all those boards. She won't even realize Toby's gone." Seeing Carley's face, Maud sagged. "Oh, Carley, of course I'm concerned about Vanessa. I don't want to hurt her. I don't want to hurt anyone. But it's possible, isn't it, that after all the dust settles, Vanessa could be happier?"

"I don't know. It's not like it's her choice."

"Come on, Carley. Her marriage with Toby is *over*, it was over before he and I started sleeping together, we wouldn't have gotten involved if there had still been even a *spark* between him and Vanessa. You have to trust that Toby and I care about Vanessa. We've gone over and over this, looking at it from every possible angle."

"Especially from lying on the bed," Carley shot back.

"All right, yes, and what's so terrible about that? Life is short. Life is fragile. Life is hard. Toby and I are *passionately* in love, and it just seems right for us to be together."

Looking at her friend's shining face, Carley sighed. She knew she couldn't change anything. Perhaps she should have done something when Maud first told her, but she hadn't, and things had gone so far, it was too late now.

"Okay, Maud. Talk it through for me."

"Okay. First, my boys will not have to go through any major upheaval. Of course they already think Toby's cool; he's their doctor. I'll need to introduce them to the idea of Toby being in my house and in my life. Second, Toby's going to talk with Vanessa tonight." She shivered with happiness. "He's going to come to my house tonight. He's going to spend the night."

"Who's going to be with Vanessa?" Carley asked.

"Don't be so judgmental."

"I'm just asking the question. If Toby leaves her, she'll be all alone. It seems only decent to arrange for a friend to be on call."

"Fine. You can be on call."

Carley spit out the word. "*Fine.*"

Maud put her hand on Carley's arm. "Please don't be angry with me. I've been so lonely for so long, Carley. You've lost your husband, you should understand the kind of loneliness I've gone through, except I've been going through it for *years*. John left me when Percy was just a baby." Tears flooded her round blue eyes. "Carley, *now* my boys will have a father living with them! Vanessa doesn't have any children, so we won't be hurting any, don't you see?"

"Yes," Carley agreed, reluctantly. "Yes, I do see that. Of course it's been hard for you, raising the boys alone. But you've done a good job, Maud, remember that."

"Thanks for saying that, but I do worry. Sometimes the boys seem so wild. And as hard as I try, I can't show them how to hit a ball or catch a Frisbee."

"That's true," Carley agreed; Maud was spectacularly uncoordinated.

"But that's not why I'm in love with Toby," Maud insisted. "Give me a break, if I'd just wanted to get a father for my boys, I could have found *someone*."

Carley nodded. This was true. Not only was Maud lovely to look at, she could be staggeringly funny and great fun to be with. She was often almost eerily insightful about people. She'd predicted that the high school principal's son would join the military, that the Grossfelds would get divorced, that Sonya Elliston would go to New York and make it in the theater. When Vanessa and Carley asked Maud how she got to be so psychic, Maud had replied simply that she just looked and listened, and she did have an innate talent for paying attention. She worked hard on her books, which were favorites in children's libraries and bookstores across the country, but she was modest about her success, never flashing herself around like a star.

Carley looked hopelessly at Maud. "But how can I wish you happiness when I'm sure it's going to cause Vanessa misery?"

"Because it's not." Maud drew herself up straight. "Do this: remember all the times Vanessa complained about Toby."

"I complained about Gus just as much," Carley retorted dryly.

"Yes, and that's something you ought to think about, but that's not what we're talking about right now. We're talking about Vanessa and Toby. She thought he was boring sexually, right?"

Carley ducked her head. A kind of sadness slid through her, like the guilt of a child who tattled on her sibling, or stole someone's doll. An intimate, deep, even primitive regret settled in her heart and fogged her mind. She *had* loved Gus, but never passionately. She'd never told her friends that. She probably never would. It seemed wrong, now that he was gone.

"Do you agree?" Maud prompted. "Vanessa found Toby boring?"

Quietly Carley agreed, "Yes. Of course I remember." Lifting her head, she met Maud's bright gaze. "Maudie, to be honest, I think I'm sad for myself, too."

"Because I found someone and you're alone?"

"No. Not that. No, because our threesome has been so important to me. It's held me together, in a way. I'll miss it."

"Look, you can still be my friend. And Vanessa's friend, too."

"But not the three of us together. Las Tres Enchiladas! Won't you miss that?"

"Of course I will. I love Vanessa. I know how remarkable our threesome was, but it wasn't enough, it wasn't everything." Maud stood up. "Carley, the whole wide world is before each of us. Maybe *now* Vanessa will meet a man who really rings her chimes. Maybe in a year she'll be in love and the three of us will be back in our trio again."

"Maybe pigs will fly."

"Don't be so negative!"

"I'm not trying to be negative, I'm just trying to think this through. Look, Maud, be sensible. I can't be your friend and Vanessa's, too. In divorces people always have to make choices, and this is really hard, because I love you both. But someone has to be on Vanessa's side. Someone has to help her through the next few months."

"Well, you'll have to see me sometime because our kids play together."

"It's almost summer. Margaret will be at day camp."

"So will Percy and Spenser!"

"So they can see one another then."

"Fine." Maud turned to leave, then stopped and faced Carley. "I love you, Carley."

"I love you, too."

"I love Vanessa, too."

"Strange way of showing it."

"I'm happy for the first time in my life. Can't you be glad for me?"

"Honestly, Maud, it's a challenge."

"Well, I think you're being a pill."

"Well, I think you're being selfish, greedy, and spoiled, wanting everything your way immediately."

Maud opened her mouth, then shut it. After a moment, she shrugged and grinned ruefully. "You know, Carley, perhaps you're right. I apologize. But I won't stop being happy." She went out the door, into the yard, calling her boys.

That evening as she prepared dinner and ate it with her daughters, discussing the day, Carley was tense with anticipation, expecting the phone to ring at any moment, expecting to hear Vanessa in tears. But the phone was silent.

She got the girls tucked into bed and finished cleaning the kitchen, then went into her office and spent some time organizing her B&B files and tax-deductible expenses—the amenities she'd bought at the Cape the day before. The phone didn't ring.

By eleven, she decided Vanessa wasn't going to phone her for help and consolation. Despair and self-anger plunged through her. What kind of friend had she been to Vanessa? Both Vanessa and Maud had been so good to her when Gus died, bringing over dinners, taking the girls out for a fun afternoon, helping with the myriad details of the funeral, and most of all listening endlessly while Carley wept and ranted. They had both wept with her. They had spent hours sharing their special memories of Gus, how blissed-out he'd been when his daughters were born, how many people loved him because he'd coached Little League baseball, what dazzling hours they'd enjoyed when he took them sailing. Their friendship, their words, their embraces, and most of all, their *listening* had woven a kind of cocoon around Carley, a soft protected world in which she could curl up and mourn, and eventually recover and reenter the real world.

It pierced her heart that she couldn't do the same for Vanessa. Maud didn't need her tonight. Maud had Toby coming to live with her. If all went as Maud had planned, by now Vanessa was *alone*. Should she phone Vanessa, ask her to come here?

By midnight, Carley couldn't stand it any longer. She dialed Vanessa's number. The line was busy.

19

.....

Carley drove Cisco out to Lauren's farm to spend Saturday morning. She dropped Margaret at Annabel's for a special day with her grandmother. Then she drove to Vanessa's house.

Vanessa's phone had been busy all morning, which made Carley sure Vanessa had taken it off the hook. She was determined to help Vanessa somehow, to be there for her, and when she turned onto Duck Pond Lane and saw only one car—Vanessa's Saab—in the driveway, she was glad she'd come. Toby's Volvo was gone.

The front garden was in full, luscious bloom. Vanessa spent hours planting, weeding, nurturing her flowers—Carley could only imagine what a fabulous mother she could have been. It was too cruel, Carley thought, that Vanessa was left, after years of marriage, with nothing.

Carley parked behind Vanessa's car, went up the walk, rapped the brass whale knocker. After a moment, the door opened, and Vanessa was there, her face swollen from crying.

"Vanessa, can I come in?"

Fury tightened Vanessa's face into an ugly mask. "Why would I *ever* want *you* in my house again?"

"Vanessa, please. I'm so sorry. Let me come in. Let me explain."

"Explain? Really?" Sometimes Vanessa could be sarcastic in a humorous way, but today there was only misery in her voice and he eyes and her posture. "You can explain why you helped Maud have an affair with my husband."

"I didn't help—" But Carley broke off. Because, of course, in a way, she had helped.

"Oh, come in." Vanessa yanked the door open. "Otherwise the neighbors will hear me yelling like a fishwife and they'll think *poor Dr. Hutchinson, no wonder he left her!*"

"No one will think that," Carley protested. She shut the door behind her and waited for Vanessa to lead her into the kitchen or living room, but Vanessa only stood in the hall, arms crossed defensively over her bosom. "Look, Vanessa, can't we talk?"

"Oh, *now* you want to talk." Vanessa was barefoot, her lavender dress creased with wrinkles, as if she'd slept in it, her black curls savagely pulled back in a band.

"Vanessa—"

"You didn't tell me! How could you not have told me? All those days and nights and weeks when we saw each other, Carley, you *knew! You knew!* I trusted you and you lied to me, you sided with Maud, you chose Maud over me, you let Maud steal my husband, you let her take away my entire life! What kind of woman *are* you?"

"Vanessa, I promised Maud—"

"What, and you've never broken a promise? Come on, Carley, you have to admit you made a choice. You chose Maud."

Carley's stomach cramped with guilt. "Vanessa, I'm just sick about it. I was *wrong*. I made a terrible mistake. I should have told you. I should have done *something*. But Maud told me it was a fling. That it would end. That it was like a vacation."

"You babysat for her so she could fuck my husband!"

"Vanessa, at first I had no idea! And when I found out, I refused to babysit for her anymore—"

"Well, that makes everything fine, then."

"I can't tell you how I regret what I did, Vanessa. I suppose I just hoped—and believed, I did believe it—that their affair would end. I never dreamed it would come to this."

Vanessa slumped against the wall, running her hands over her face. "I'm so tired. I've been awake all night, crying and packing."

"Packing?"

"I'm going to stay with a friend in Boston while I decide what to do next. I'll probably move to Boston."

"Oh, Vanessa, no. You can't leave the island. You love it here so much."

"I did love it here. Before."

"Vanessa—"

"You know," Vanessa suddenly laughed, a tight, harsh laugh. "This is like some kind of bizarre TV ad. 'Your husband has just left you for another woman. But wait! There's more! The other woman is one of your best friends! So you've lost her, too. But wait! There's more! Your other best friend helped them have their affair!' "

Vanessa was trembling all over. She seemed close to collapsing onto the floor, in spite of her manic speech. Carley knew about this kind of craziness. She'd been there herself, when they told her Gus had died.

"Vanny, when did you last eat?"

"When did I eat? When did I *eat*?" Vanessa was laughing, and crying, too. "Because that will solve everything, if I eat."

"It will help." Carley reached out and fully expecting Vanessa to hit her or push her away, she put her arm around Vanessa. Vanessa was shuddering. "Come on," Carley coaxed, and ushered her into the kitchen. She settled her friend in a chair and set a box of tissues in front of her. "I'll scramble some eggs."

It was just what she needed to do, to move around in a space she loved, doing what she loved, melting butter in Vanessa's shining skillet, cracking open the perfect shells, whisking the eggs with a sprinkle of Parmesan cheese, spilling the healthy golden liquid into the pan. She toasted rye bread and set out jars of beach plum jam and blueberry jam.

The familiar movements calmed her. The aroma of butter soothed her. It seemed to soothe Vanessa, too. She wept while Carley worked, and when Carley set her plate in front of her, Vanessa stared at it for a moment as if she had no idea what it was.

"Eat," Carley ordered.

Vanessa lifted a forkful of eggs to her mouth. "Oh," she said after she'd swallowed. "Good."

Carley put her own plate next to Vanessa's and sat eating alongside her. They ate together companionably, as if tamping down their misery with this reliable comfort.

When she was finished, Vanessa murmured, "Thank you."

"You're welcome."

"Isn't it odd, how food can taste good at a time like this?"

"It's got to be some basic animal need. When Gus died, I had this thought, not right away, but a few days later, I thought: *Oh, dear, what if I won't be able to enjoy chocolate anymore?* Terrible of me, wasn't it?"

"Normal, I'd say. The completely weird thing is, in a way, I'm sadder about Maud and you than about Toby." Vanessa dragged her fork around the surface of her plate, looking at the squiggles she made. "I mean, men are genetically programmed to be unfaithful, they want to sleep with every woman in the world. But friends, *women* friends—"

"We were *such* a good little clique."

"Do you think we were ever snotty? Maybe that's why this happened to me, maybe I was too arrogant."

"You're the least arrogant person in the world, Vanessa. Are you saying I was widowed because I was arrogant?"

"Heavens, no, I'd never think that."

"Well, then." Carley reached over and put her hand on Vanessa's. "I don't think there are reasons for a lot of things. Or at least not reasons we can figure out the moment they happen. It may be that the love of your life is just around the corner and you need to be free for him."

Vanessa snorted. "How could I ever trust another man?" She pulled her hand away from Carley's. "For that matter, how can I ever trust another woman?"

"Vanessa—"

"Look," Vanessa said, and suddenly she seemed weary. "I'm grateful for the food. It's calmed me down and I needed to get grounded. And okay, you feel terrible, Carley, that sucks for you. But I'm really pissed off at you, and I think I deserve to be. And"—She held her hand up to stop Carley from speaking—"and I've got to get off this island as soon as I can. It's hard enough to have Toby leaving me for Maud, but I can't stand the thought of being around for the breaking news on the island gossip channel. All those people rushing up to me, cooing, oh, poor Vanessa, we just heard, it's so terrible, so sad. Oh, man, suddenly I have the greatest sympathy for Jennifer Aniston."

"Well, you look more like Angelina Jolie."

"Yes, and that's helped me a lot, right?" Tears glittered in her eyes. "I should do what Jolie did. I should just get my own babies." Vanessa shoved back her chair and stood up. "Look, Carley, do me a favor and leave, will you?"

"Let me just clean up the dishes—"

"Oh for heaven's sake, leave the fucking dishes!" Vanessa commanded. "Do you think if you do my dishes you'll make everything all right? I'm about to go into another fit of weeping again and I don't want you here to witness it."

"I want to help you—"

"Your time to help me was when you learned that Toby was sleeping with Maud."

Carley winced. "I am so so sorry."

"Maybe that will mean something to me someday," Vanessa said bitterly. "But right now, it means *nothing at all*. Now please, if you want to help me, just go."

Carley went.

20

. . . . .

The end of May was always an unsettling time on the island. Days that should have been sunny and warm were often windy and wet and as cold as February, shutting down the baseball games all the island kids were eager to play. School was almost out, so teachers and students alike seemed to lose interest and Carley's daughters came home restless and uninspired. Tourists were beginning to make their pilgrimages to the island, some to their own houses, others to inns or rented homes. The roads in front of grocery stores, pharmacies, and shops clustered with UPS trucks, and the sun sparkling on the sea glanced off more and more masts as boats sailed into the harbor.

Carley had had six months to become accustomed to her widowhood. She'd grown used to life without Gus. She'd learned how to repair the tricky pipe under the kitchen sink, how to pay the bills, how to cheer up her children. Now all she had to learn was how to live without her two best friends.

Vanessa left the island, locking up her house and refusing to communicate with anyone. Maud was MIA for Carley, too. She was too busy making her relationship with Toby clear to the public. Toby, Maud, and her boys ate dinner out at least three times a week, one big happy family. Maud dropped in at Toby's office at least once a day to bring his staff cookies or candy, and rumor had it that she'd hung a large picture of The Happy Family—Percy, Spenser, Maud, and Toby—on Toby's consulting room wall. They hosted a Memorial Day picnic at the house Maud publicized as "their" house—Toby had moved in with Maud, giving his former home to Vanessa. That house sat empty while Vanessa was in Boston. Maud left a message on Carley's answering machine, inviting her and the girls to the picnic, but Carley took the girls to her in-laws' instead.

Carley needed to spend time with her in-laws, because Cisco was agitating for more sleepovers with Annabel and Russell. Carley felt estranged from her older daughter, and secretly resentful of her mother-in-law. While it was true in one way that they would never recover from Gus's death, in another way, it seemed unfair for Annabel to use her grief to seduce Cisco over to her house. Carley had to admit to herself that after Cisco spent time at Annabel's, she was more pleasant. But how long would this go on? Didn't Annabel see that she was causing a break between Margaret and Cisco? The nights Cisco wasn't home, when only Carley and Margaret slept in the huge old house together, seemed so lonely, the house so empty.

It was *awesome* when the guests arrived.

The very first couple were Jenna and Harold Hooper from Oklahoma. They were in their fifties, both widowed and remarried, here on their honeymoon. He wore a belt with a silver and turquoise buckle and she dripped with gorgeous turquoise and silver jewelry. They were charmed by the house, the view of the water, their room, the island. Carly didn't want to hover, but she wanted to be available, helpful. She was so glad the early June day was full of blue sky and birdsong. June could be a windy, rainy month.

Later that afternoon, the Munsens arrived from Connecticut. They were ancient, genteel, hard-of-hearing, slow-moving. They were visiting grown grandchildren who picked them up and brought them back. The rest of the time, the Munsens sat in the living room or the garden, dozing. When Carley watched them creep around, she was glad the other innkeepers had advised her to install bathtub safety bars.

Brie and Candy arrived that afternoon, two young single women with appropriately delicious names. From New York, they were on the island looking for husband material—they'd heard that you had to be megarich to own a yacht. Carley tried to convince them that their very high heels, tied at the ankles with ribbons, would be uncomfortable if not dangerous for walking on Nantucket's brick sidewalks and down the wooden piers, but they wouldn't sacrifice their beauty. They set off to walk around town with their long hair— Brie's blond, Candy's brown—flowing and their short skirts flouncing, wearing more makeup than anyone wore even at the island galas.

They returned home several hours later, shoes in hand, limping. Bravely, they showered, changed into even more froufrou dresses and higher heels, and went off to an expensive restaurant for dinner. They returned before midnight, alone. Carley toured her house to be sure everyone was tucked in, all lights on or off, and went to bed herself, feeling oddly responsible for Brie and Candy's disappointment.

The next morning was the first day Carley was serving a real B&B breakfast to real guests. She'd dreamed of this for months, and felt as if she were presenting a play, arranging a little world, a brief and perfect moment, for her guests. She set the long kitchen table with her grandmother's blue-and-white Limoges china, the family's sterling silver utensils, thick, white cloth napkins, and centered it with a low bowl of blue-and-white pansies. She stirred up her own favorite recipe for pecan and apple muffins, drizzled them with cinnamon butter, and put them in the oven. She chopped up melon, apples, grapes, and bananas into fruit cups. When she heard water running downstairs in the Hoopers' room, she made coffee.

The Hoopers arrived fully dressed for the day in matching floral shirts and white cotton slacks and sneakers.

"Why, isn't this just the ticket!" Jenna Hooper exclaimed, actually clapping her hands at the sight of the kitchen table. "I swear, I want to take a picture. Harold, would you get the camera?"

Harold obligingly went back and fetched the camera. By the time he'd returned, taken some photos, and settled into a place at the table, the muffins were ready. Carley served them fruit cups, coffee, orange juice, and muffins, all the while chatting with them about the island and asking them about Oklahoma. Then the ancient Munsens came slowly toddling in, clad as if on their way to church, and Carley quickly moved to assist them as they wavered and wobbled and finally creakily subsided into chairs.

As Carley was serving them breakfast, Brie and Candy wandered in, still in their robes, which, since it was summer, were brief and diaphanous. *Oh, dear,* Carley thought. *Should I have established a dress code? Should I have put up a sign stating in no uncertain terms that guests were to come to the table dressed for the day?* Would her older guests take offense at the informality of her younger guests?

"Please introduce yourselves," Carley asked as she bustled about getting the young women's breakfasts.

To her relief, everyone spoke cordially and when the Hoopers said they were here on their honeymoon, Brie and Candy cooed like doves.

"Oh, your honeymoon, how romantic!"

"Look, you've got your camera, let me take a picture of the two of you here at the table," Candy offered.

Carley wished she'd thought to do that herself, and tucked the thought away for the future.

"Maybe we'll come here someday for our honeymoons," Brie said wistfully.

"Oh, are you engaged?" Jenna Hooper asked.

"I wish." Candy looked at her friend with despairing eyes. "We don't even have boyfriends. And we're *twenty-three!*"

To Carley's surprise, ancient Mrs. Munsen spoke up, telling the girls not to be in a hurry, it was better to marry late than early, and the Hoopers joined in, to regale them with stories about their disastrous early marriages, and old Mr. Munsen croaked with pride that he hadn't gotten married until he was thirty-seven, and they'd been married fifty-one years! Carley refilled the coffee cups, passed around the muffins again, and listened with wonder as her guests talked. They were all eating everything they could get their hands

on, and they seemed absolutely happy. Margaret came in for breakfast, and stayed to gaze at the resplendent young women in pastel.
Carley wished Cisco would wake and come down. She'd enjoy
watching Brie and Candy, too.

"I'll tell you what," Harold Hooper said. "You are two fine-
looking fillies. But you won't get a man's attention just by looking
good."

"That's right," Jenna Hooper agreed with a fervent nod of her
head.

"No, you have to *do* something," Harold continued. "Men might
like to look at you, but if you want them to find you of interest,
you've got to be doing something they like doing."

"Like what?" Brie asked.

"Well," Jenna informed them with a cunning smile, "I met
Harold when I was taking skeet-shooting lessons."

"Oh, that's terrible!" Candy looked horrified. "All those poor
little skeet! I could never do that."

A Vesuvian rumbling erupted from the Hoopers' end of the
table. For a moment Carley was ready to punch 911.

"Har-har-har!" Harold Hooper chortled and shook with laughter, his face turning red.

"He's all right," Jenna hastened to assure Carley. "That's just his
way." To Brie and Candy, she said soothingly, "Honey, skeets are just
clay targets. They're not live birds."

"Oh, okay. So is that where you met Mr. Hooper?"

"It is. Please understand, I wasn't out there trying to hook a
man. I grew up in Oklahoma; I possess a rifle and a revolver. I don't
shoot birds but in my time I have been known to shoot a rattler who
was aiming to bite my horse. But I got so busy in my first marriage,
raising my children and all, that when my first husband died, and
my kids had left home, I wanted to get back to my old self. Perhaps
get another horse. So I went out skeet shooting to get my aim back.
You have to aim right well the first time if you're trying to kill a rattler."

Brie and Candy were mesmerized. "And you met Mr. Hooper?" Brie repeated.

"I did." Jenna's eyes twinkled. "And he's got lots of *horses*."

The young women's heads whipped toward Carley. "Is there a skeet-shooting range on the island?"

"There is a target practice range somewhere around, but I don't think it's open to the public. Anyway, no one comes to the island to shoot. They come for the water sports."

"But we don't own a boat."

"Have you ever tried a kayak?" Carley pulled out some brochures. "Or you could go down to the wharves to see if you can join a charter going out to sport fish and learn to cast. Lots of men love fishing."

"Super!" Brie jumped up from the table, followed by Candy. "Thanks, you guys, you're the best!"

"Let us know what happens," Harold Hooper called as the young women ran out the door.

A few moments later, the Hoopers went off for the day and the Munsens left with their grandchildren. Carley was buzzed as she tidied up the kitchen. Everyone had gotten along so well! It had been like having a little party. And what if Brie or Candy met someone? The front garden with its sweeping view of the ocean would be the perfect place for a summer wedding . . .

Carley was dusting the living room when she heard a knock on the door and then Wyatt stuck his head in.

"Hey, Carley."

"Wyatt!"

He wore tennis whites and his wavy hair was damp, his face blazing with tan. "I don't want to interrupt—"

"You're not—"

"I just wondered how it's going. Your Seashell Inn."

"So far? It's *great!*" She tossed down her dust cloth. "Want some lemonade?"

"I could use a long cool glass of water."

She led him to the kitchen, got out a glass and ice, ran the faucet, and handed him the drink.

His fingers lingered on hers. His eyes lingered on her face. Confused, she said, "Want a cherry blackberry croissant? Made fresh today?"

"No thanks. I've got to go to the office."

"Like that?"

Wyatt laughed. "You know we've got a shower, and I always keep a set of fresh clothes at the office. I was just walking back from the court and thought I'd look in. So everything's going okay?"

"The guests are wonderful, so far. Actually, some of them are so much fun, or so *wise*. They all love their rooms and their breakfasts and teas."

"How do the girls like it?"

"Of course everyone adores Margaret, so she's in heaven. Cisco, not so much. I'm trying to convince her to do some housework in return for pay, and she's having a difficult time with it."

"I can understand that. She's an adolescent." Tilting back his head, he drank his water. "Maybe the girls would like to go out sailing someday."

"I'm sure they'd love it, Wyatt."

"You, too, I mean."

Was he blushing? Perhaps in this light, his tan glowed like a burn. "I don't have much free time."

"You need to give yourself a break, Carley. You can't work all the time."

"You're right. And I'd love to go sailing."

"Good. I'll call you when the weather looks cooperative."

He moved toward Carley, tall, tanned, so male, so athletic. Hot from playing in the sun, his body radiated heat as he neared Carley.

He set his glass on the counter next to her. Leaning forward, he kissed her cheek lightly. "Thanks for the water." His voice was strangely hoarse. "Tell the girls hello."

Then he turned and headed out the door, leaving Carley warmed and slightly flustered.

The days tumbled over her, guests arriving, guests leaving, guests asking for directions, more towels, more coffee, just one more muffin.

It was a custom at many of the charming Nantucket inns to give the guest rooms names instead of numbers. Some were historic names: Starbuck, Macy, Folger, Swain, Chase. Coffin was one of the most respected names, but understandably many guests didn't want to sleep in a room with that appellation. Some inns used nautical terms: Anchor, Mast, Sail, Bow.

Carley had consulted with her girls, and they had decided to use the names of shells: Scallop, Moon, and Angel's Wing. Carley had small, gilt-trimmed quarter boards made and nailed to the doors of the three rooms, an expensive but elegant touch, she thought. When she and Maria were together, cleaning the rooms, preparing them for new guests, Carley would call, "Scallop needs fresh hand soaps," or "The Carters phoned to ask whether they left their iPod in Moon." The names seemed mystical to her, as if the very words brought with them the wild salt and strange spice of the sea into the perfect chambers where her guests slept. At some moments, when she opened the door for a new guest, she'd hear them—always the woman—give a little gasp as she stepped into the room. "Oh," she'd say, "oh, look." And Carley would allow herself a smug smile. She had created a magical miniature universe for her guests, everything aquamarine and crisp white, scrolled like shells, as clean as if scoured by the waves. Here on the curtains and towels were mermaids and sea horses. Lamp bases were filled with sand and tiny starfish, sand dollars, sea glass. The sheets, expensive cotton, embroidered thickly and stretched taut beneath the palest blue blanket, welcomed the visitor to rest, to dream. In these three rooms, you could float anywhere.

Every morning Carley would rise at five, pull on shorts and a tee and flip-flops, and tiptoe down the back stairs to the kitchen. She'd been plotting, the night before, just which new recipe to use—cranberry-blueberry muffins, or beach plum–strawberry croissants. She always squeezed fresh oranges for the juice. Most days she slipped out to the garden to gather a few flowers for the center of the table. She loved seeing the faces of her guests when they entered the kitchen. The first morning, they looked surprised, curious. The second morning, they looked *eager*.

One day a middle-aged couple, the Awtreys from Indiana, checked in, both of them looking nearly desperate with weariness. They scarcely spoke to Carley. They didn't touch each other. They entered their room with slumped shoulders, as if their luggage was almost too heavy to bear. They didn't show for her complimentary afternoon tea.

The next morning, when they came up for breakfast, they were different. Lighter. Brighter. And very much *together*. They chatted with the other guests, ate Carley's food with gusto, and shot each other shy and affectionate glances, like a newly courting couple. Later, as Carley cleaned the kitchen, she hummed to herself. She thought: my sister might save lives, but I save *marriages*. And, she thought, laughing, perhaps I also save a few people's sanity.

Rain, Carley learned, was her enemy. And it rained a lot. If you were interested in Nantucket history, you could spend hours at the Whaling Museum or any of the other museums. You could shop in any of the fabulous shops on the island. You could relax in Carley's comfortable living room and read a book or play a board game. That was about it for wild entertainment on the island. Nantucket was at its best on sunny days.

Long stretches of sunny days could be busy, too. Everyone needed more towels, beach towels, towels for showering, for their hair. Did Carley have some sunblock they could borrow? They'd left the beach bag Carley had provided at the beach, could they have another one? Many of her guests had trouble reading the maps included in the Chamber of Commerce guides.

She sat down at the computer and typed out:

How to Get to the Whaling Museum from 9 1/2 Mitchell Avenue.

Turn left from our driveway. Walk two blocks until you come to the cobblestone lane going downhill. Go down the hill and turn right on South Beach Street. Walk five blocks. You will pass the Beachside Hotel. Continue walking three long blocks. You will be at Steamboat Wharf. Turn right. The Whaling Museum is a large brick building.

She wrote similar guides for the library, other museums, restaurants, the movie theater. She printed them out in a large font and put them in the guest rooms and living room. Still, she got phone calls: "We're in town. How do we get back?"

Margaret seemed to enjoy the guests. When she wasn't at day camp, she stuck by Carley as if glued to her, willingly ran little errands, helped Carley mix the batter for the tea scones, and rode out to Bartlett's to choose the best fresh fruit. Perhaps, Carley thought, Margaret spent too much time with her. She didn't run down to play at Molly's as often as she used to. But the B&B was a novelty; she thought Margaret would be bored with it by the end of the summer.

Cisco was more difficult. Carley had made a deal with Cisco: since Maria was busy keeping the guest rooms clean, Carley would pay Cisco to vacuum and dust her room and Margaret's. Many of her friends made money babysitting; when school started, Cisco would need money for clothes. Cisco had to work only one hour a week. Cisco agreed, but she *hated* cleaning. She didn't do a good job, and she became more and more sour about it.

What could she do? What should she do? Carley hardly had time to think about Cisco. She kept the accounts and paid bills and took reservations and answered phone calls and solved problems and bought groceries and made afternoon tea and scones or crumpets or tarts and went through the house late at night, being certain that everything was locked and secure, and fell into bed exhausted. She greeted the guests and anticipated their needs and answered their questions and enjoyed their pleasure in her home.

But she could understand how Cisco would be bored and unhappy.

One evening, Carley sat on Cisco's bed. "You're having a tough time."

Cisco cocked her head and retorted accusingly, "You're having fun."

"Well, Cisco, I'm running a business. I have to act pleasant."

"Yeah, but you like it."

"That's true. I'm enjoying it. That doesn't mean I don't think of Daddy all the time. That doesn't mean that I don't miss Daddy every minute. I do."

Cisco's chin wobbled. She pulled her knees up and buried her face between them, her black hair hanging down all around like a curtain. "I hate it here, Mom. Everything is way different. Everything is *wrong*."

"Cisco, I get how you feel. I understand. And it's true, I do enjoy running the B&B. But I'm doing it because our family needs money." She shifted position on the bed, a bit away from her daughter, to give her space. "Grieving is confusing. And you've got teenage hormones starting to flood into your body. You've got a lot to handle."

"Eeuw." Cisco winced.

Carley sighed. "Oh, Cisco, I wish I could help."

Cisco didn't respond but kept her face hidden.

"Well," Carley capitulated, too tired to continue. "Remember how much I love you." She kissed the top of her daughter's head gently and left the room.

She put a load of beach towels into the washer and bath towels into the dryer. She swept and mopped the kitchen floor. Upstairs, she folded her own laundry and tidied her room. Margaret was in her room, playing with her dollhouse. She looked melancholy, and on the spur of the moment, Carley announced, "Come on, Margaret. Let's go to town and get an ice cream cone!"

She held her daughter's hand as they walked, and after their long wait in line and the excitement of choosing an exotic flavor— which for Margaret was peppermint stick—they sat in the Atheneum garden. People-watching was always fun on the island in the summer. Carley enjoyed seeing all the gorgeous clothes. Margaret loved the dogs being walked and the babies pushed in strollers. When they finished their cones, they strolled down Main Street, stopping to listen to the boy playing a classical piece on the violin. He had curly black hair and a dramatic way of tossing his head, and he was only about ten years old. Carley thought Margaret was developing a crush on him; she could hardly tear Margaret away, and she was glad for this little thrill for her daughter.

Carley swung Margaret's hand. "How are you doing these days, my little flutterby?"

"I'm good. But I miss Daddy," Margaret continued, her mouth downturned, her long black lashes brushing her cheeks.

"I know, sweetie."

"When I wake up in the morning . . ." She frowned, searching for the words.

"You forget Daddy's dead? You think you'll run into our room and jump on the bed and wake him up?"

"I do, Mommy!"

"And you think he'll tickle you and lift you up in the air?"

Margaret's eyelashes sparkled with tears.

Carley said, "He was such a *good* daddy. He took good care of us and we had a lot of fun with him."

Margaret stopped walking and stared up at her mother. "Mommy, is Cisco mad at you?"

Carley started to deny it, but paused. This little child saw and understood a lot. "Yes. Yes, Cisco's mad at me. I think she's mad at the world, like we're all mad at the world because Daddy died. But you can't well, kick the world, can you?" She made her voice light, and her daughter relaxed a little. "Losing Daddy is really hard, Margaret. We're all sad. We all have to manage in our own way. Cisco still loves me, Margaret, and I still love her. Families are very complicated. Cisco is helping Nana, you see. It helps Nana to have someone young and cheerful around." *If only Cisco could be cheerful around me*, Carley thought, her heart hurting. She shook off her self-pity.

"I won't leave you, Mommy."

Carley dropped to her knees on the sidewalk and hugged her little daughter tight. "Oh, thank you, Margaret. I know you won't leave me. And I won't leave you."

Later, after Margaret was in bed, Carley worked at her computer for an hour, catching up on paperwork and reservations and bills. She folded the bath towels from the dryer and moved the beach towels from the washer. She showered quickly and fell into bed exhausted. These nights she was asleep before ten o'clock.

In the middle of the night, a soft hand touched her arm.

"Mommy. I wet the bed."

Like a sleepwalker, Carley rose, stripped her child of her wet pj's, stripped Margaret's bed, and dumped the wet things on the bathroom floor. She pulled a clean nightie over Margaret and brought her into her own bed. Someone, just after Gus's death, had warned Carley against letting Margaret sleep with her. Once you start that, it will be difficult to stop, they had predicted. But it was *comforting* to hold her child's warm little body against hers. It was much less lonely.

On a hot July evening, since Margaret and Cisco both went for a sleepover at their grandparents', Carley was free to take Lexi out to dinner. Ostensibly this was to thank Lexi for all her advice and support as Carley began her business, but also Carley just plain enjoyed hanging out with Lexi. They were close to the same age, but Lexi wasn't married—she was divorced, and she had no children. She didn't run in the married group Carley ran with; she didn't come with the same set of expectations.

They sat at a table in the corner at 56 Union, enjoying their wine and kicking back after a long day of work. It always took Carley a few minutes to get over Lexi's presence. The blond woman was exquisite. On the other hand, while Carley could never be as tall as Lexi, widowhood had quickly made her just as slender.

"Let's not talk about work anymore," Carley begged. "And not about Gus, either." She leaned her chin in her hand. "Tell me about your love life."

Lexi laughed and tossed her silver-blond hair. "The truth? It's *amazing*. Have you met Tris Chandler? He runs a boatyard out in Madaket."

"I don't know him. But obviously, you do."

Lexi's eyes twinkled. "You might have read about him a couple of years ago. He went missing. His boat was wrecked up near Nova Scotia, on Sable Island, which is uninhabited, but did have old fishing shacks for shelter. Some Newfoundland fisherman found him, saved him—it was all very dramatic."

"I did read about that, in the paper."

"*Chronicle* did a segment on it, too, on their evening program. But the amazing thing is, the whole time Tris was missing his daughter, Jewel—I think Jewel is just Cisco's age. I'll bet they run into each other in school. Jewel Chandler?"

"I don't recognize the name. But Cisco's been a ballet fanatic until recently."

"Well, anyway, Jewel used to hang out on the pier near my shop. She was waiting for her father to return. He was gone *three months* and she never gave up hope. I used to go sit with her. She's mature, complex, fathoms deep. I adore her. I think she's pretty fond of me, too."

"What about her mother?"

"Tris and Bonnie are divorced. Bonnie left Tris for a wealthy man, Ken Frost. They have a toddler. Jewel lives with her mother during the week and with Tris during the weekends. We're planning to get married, Tris and I, but we're not in any rush. We've both been married before, and we have Jewel's feelings to consider, but we've been together for almost two years. We don't live together actually, although I often spend the night at Tris's house or he comes to my apartment."

"And Jewel?"

"She seems happy that we're together. She often sleeps over at my apartment when Tris is there, or at Tris's when I'm there. Of course there's no hanky-panky the nights Jewel's around, but that's all right. I love Jewel. She's a very cool kid."

Carley ran her fingertip over the stem of her glass as she listened to Lexi talk. Her shoulders relaxed, her breath slowed, her heart warmed. It was therapeutic to hear about others' joys and troubles, old loves and new.

Lexi's face brightened. "My oldest best friend, Clare Hart, is married to my brother, Adam. They have the sweetest little baby boy, Alexander. Alex." She struck a pose. "Named after *me*, his auntie and his godmother! They let me babysit a lot, thank heavens, but as much as I love Jewel—and I do, we have a very special bond—I'm still longing for a baby of my own." She waved her hands. "Listen to me, Ms. Self-Absorbed, going on and on."

"Oh, but I'm fascinated! And you have no idea how sick I am of myself!"

Later, after the steamed mussels and the spicy Javanese rice with shrimp and chicken, they decided to split a crème brûlée.

"I can't believe how much I've eaten." Carley put her hand on her belly. "My stomach actually hurts."

"You could use a few pounds."

"You should talk." Carley leaned back in her chair. "I'm glad we're tucked in a corner. I'd hate for anyone to see me having such a good time."

"Just because you're widowed doesn't mean you're never allowed to smile again."

"It seems that way, though. When I'm in the grocery store and an acquaintance sees me, their faces drop and they kindly ask how I am. What if I said, 'Actually, today I'm having an okay day'? What if I *smiled*? It would be all over town in a flash. Carley's happy her husband's dead. She didn't love her husband."

"Did you love him?"

"How can you ask that? Yes, of course I loved him! He was the father of my children. He was my *husband*."

Lexi scooped the last of the silky cream from the little pot. She took her time tasting it, leaning back in her chair, savoring it. Tilting her head, she looked at Carley. "Anything you tell me is in confidence. I know what it's like to marry a man you think you love, only to discover you don't really love him at all."

"But I *did* love Gus," Carley insisted. "We had great times together. Perhaps we were more a family than a couple, maybe we never had that truly, madly, deeply kind of love going for us, but we did love each other. We never would have divorced."

"Because of the children."

"Right! And his parents. I mean, we had a *life*."

"And you're only thirty-two. Someday you'll be able to fall in love again," Lexi told her. "Perhaps you'll meet the love of your life. I did."

No one had ever suggested this to her before. Carley picked up her glass of water and downed the whole thing, fighting to get in control. "I'm such a wuss."

"Honey," Lexi said, "you're allowed."

Toward the end of July, the heat intensified so fiercely it became the main subject of conversation around Carley's breakfast table. Men kept tapping their BlackBerrys and iPhones, checking the Weather Channel, as if that would give them a better report. The entire Northeast coast was sweltering under a heavy layer of heat that would not move. Because Nantucket was thirty miles out at sea, it was a few degrees cooler, but the humidity was brutal. Most huge old houses on the island didn't have central air-conditioning. A hundred fifty years ago, when they were built, the weather was cooler in the summers. Installing central air was a major expense, involving lots of architectural renovations. Carley had had room air conditioners installed in the guest bedrooms, but nowhere else. Usually a cool sea breeze sufficed to keep things comfortable. But this was not usual weather.

Sunday morning, Carley had just put in a new load of wash when she heard voices, and then Wyatt and Cisco walked in to the laundry room. Wyatt wore a bathing suit, a ripped polo shirt, a scalloper's cap with a long bill for sun protection, and Docksiders. His arms and long muscular legs swirled with thick brown hair and when he moved, she could see a strip of white skin under the short sleeve of his shirt, shocking against the dark tan of the rest of his limbs. The healthy scent of fresh air and salt water accompanying him stirred Carley deeply, in a primitive, sexual way that made her turn away, embarrassed.

"Wyatt's taking us sailing!" Cisco announced happily.

"Oh, how nice." Carley shut the lid of the washing machine. "I'll get Margaret ready."

"Get yourself ready, too," Wyatt told her.

"Oh, Wyatt, I'd love to go, but I've got—"

"Just a few hours," Wyatt insisted. "It will be good for you. You're turning into a drudge."

"I am not!" Carley objected.

Cisco giggled, glancing at Wyatt with a conspiratorial smile. "Actually, Mom, you are."

Cisco was *smiling*. Cisco was teasing Carley. Cisco wanted Carley to join them sailing. How could Carley resist? Wyatt was working some kind of magic.

She flashed him a smile. "I'll get ready."

As they rode out to Madaket in Wyatt's convertible, the sun flashing down on them, the breeze fluttering their hair, Carley laid her head back against the seat and allowed the warmth and fresh air to ease into her bones. Wyatt had a Beach Boys CD playing, and for the first time this season, Carley was really *there* in the magic of summer. At Wyatt's house, everyone, even little Margaret, helped carry things out to the rowboat and lift them onto Wyatt's twenty-two-foot day sailer. Carley helped Wyatt rig the boat. She double-checked the life vests on her daughters, zipped one on her own body, then settled down to watch Wyatt steer them out of the harbor.

The wind was fresh and fickle, not too strong or steady. Wyatt's attentions stayed with the boat. Occasionally he gave an order to Cisco or Margaret, who scurried to obey.

"Open the cooler, Carley," Wyatt called when they were out in the open water. "I've got beer for me and Cava for you."

"What do you have for us?" Margaret asked.

Wyatt grinned. "Check it out."

Margaret lifted the lid and squealed. "Popsicles!"

In a terribly responsible voice, Wyatt said, "Made of fruit juice, Carley."

At that moment, Carley didn't think she would have cared if they were made of pure sugar. She poured the sparkling wine into a plastic cup and sipped it. Bliss. The hot July sun shone down and the playful breeze swept the boat along. The water leapt and hissed and sparkled all around them. She stripped off the life jacket and shirt she'd pulled on over her bikini and let the heat melt her. She closed her eyes.

When they neared Great Point, Wyatt dropped the sail. "Lunchtime, ladies. Carley, don't move. We'll bring you everything you need."

"I can deal with that," she murmured.

Wyatt had picked up several varieties of sandwiches and chips at Something Natural. Margaret handed them around. The girls sat on the bow, legs folded, to eat their lunch. Carley lounged, sipping her wine, enjoying her food, deeply content to see both her daughters eating hungrily, chatting together about the trucks on the beach, the other boats in the water, squealing when they saw someone catch a large bluefish.

"This is a sensational idea, Wyatt," Carley said gratefully.

"I'm glad you like it."

She studied Wyatt. He was deeply tanned, and more specks of silver glittered in his brown hair. He'd always been lean, but he'd lost some weight during the past year. They all had.

She lowered her voice. "How's it going, Wyatt?"

He thought for a moment. "To be honest, I'm a little concerned about Russell. He works constantly, more than he ever did."

"I can understand that," Carley said. "I'm finding it really helpful to *have* to hustle at the B&B. It keeps me from brooding. It gives me a purpose. And I suppose it gives me a sense of control. I don't feel quite so helpless."

Wyatt nodded thoughtfully. "Okay. I see that. At the office, we've got piles of Gus's work to take care of. Still . . . last summer Russell played a lot of golf. Went sailing. Played some tennis. But this summer, he isn't doing anything to relax. It's as if he thinks he doesn't deserve to enjoy life."

"I feel that way sometimes. When I catch myself feeling happy, suddenly I'll be overwhelmed with a sense of guilt. How can I be *happy* when Gus is dead?"

"Gus would want you to be happy. He'd want his girls to be happy, *all* his girls." Wyatt reached over and wrapped his arm around her, pulling her next to him. He smiled down at her, and his eyes were warm.

"And you," Carley reminded him. "Gus would want you to be happy, too."

She knew Wyatt meant to console her, so she was startled by her body's reaction to the touch of his skin on hers. Signals zipped through her body that had nothing to do with grief or sorrow and everything to do with the appetites of the flesh.

Carley was intensely aware of her near-nakedness, here in the sun in her bikini. She could see beads of sweat glisten on the brown hair on Wyatt's legs and arms and on his flat torso.

"Mom?" The girls were scrambling down from the bow. "We're getting hot."

Carley laughed in response to the inadvertent pun of their words. She flushed with embarrassment, and rose, stumbling as the wake of another boat rocked the sailboat.

"Right," she called. "We'll get the captain to give us some breeze."

She helped Wyatt with the sheet as he raised the sail, and in moments the boat was skipping over the water. The girls leaned out, hoping to glimpse something in the water—a whale, a fish, a mermaid.

Wyatt sailed them leisurely back to Madaket, taking time to show them where the ocean had shifted the shoals, creating sandbars in unexpected places. He demonstrated his GPS system and explained how he turned it off when he fished because he thought the fish finder option took the challenge from fishing. Margaret sat on his lap while he talked and Cisco leaned over his shoulder. The girls laughed, and for a moment, they looked like a family.

Immediately Carley shook herself. What the *hell* was she doing? How could she even think about Gus's best friend this way?

Cisco had her hand on Wyatt's bare shoulder to steady herself as she peered over to study the GPS. The line of Wyatt's neck and wide, strong back compelled Carley. She wanted to put her hand there, too.

She wanted to put her mouth there.

She wanted to lick the spot on his neck where sweat sparkled, just where his wavy brown hair ended.

Cisco turned. "Mom, you should come look at this!"

Carley flinched at her daughter's sudden gaze, as if Cisco could see her thoughts.

"Oh, okay," Carley answered, hoping her voice sounded normal. The boat wasn't moving, but she trembled as she stood up.

She crossed the few steps and, taking care not to touch Wyatt, leaned over to see the GPS. "Cool," she said, although her heart was fluttering in her chest and she could hardly see.

A fog drifted toward them from over the water as it often did at the end of the day.

"We'd better go on in," Wyatt told them.

Carley quickly resumed her seat.

They finished the sail, Wyatt concentrating on navigating through the sandbars and eelgrass into the harbor.

"Mom, look!" Cisco said, sitting next to Carley and pointing upward.

Carley looked. Long feathery cirrus clouds floated in the blue sky, their tips tinged pale pink by the sun.

"It looks like heaven up there, doesn't it?" Cisco asked.

Margaret scrambled onto Carley's lap. "Is Daddy up there, maybe?"

Carley nestled her chin into her daughter's hair. Margaret

smelled like sunblock, sunshine, and sugar. "I think he is, sweetheart."

Carley set her girls about various tasks, picking up any papers,
handing the coolers and beach bags down to the rowboat, unzipping
the life jackets and stowing them in the cabin. She was uncomfortably aware of Wyatt's every move. She pulled on her shirt and felt
less vulnerable to her raging thoughts. As they lugged their gear to
his convertible and dropped their beach bags into the trunk, Carley's arm brushed Wyatt's. Once again she experienced a flash of lust
so powerful it took her breath away. She couldn't help it. She looked
at Wyatt to see if he felt it, too.

Wyatt's sunglasses and cap shaded his face, but his jaw was
clenched and he averted his face quickly, pretending to search the
ground around them.

"Anything else for the trunk?" he asked. His voice was hoarse.

He feels it, too, Carley thought. At the same time, she thought,
Oh, stop this, you nutcase.

They drove home along Madaket Road, with music soaring over
them, making conversation impossible. At the house, she forced
herself to look at Wyatt, because she would naturally look at him.

"Wyatt, *thank you* for this fabulous day."

Wyatt was already out of the car. He reached in and lifted Margaret out.

"Yay, Wyatt, thank you!" Margaret said, hugging him.

Cisco climbed out. "Thank you, Wyatt."

They gathered around the trunk once more to collect their
beach bags.

"Wyatt," Carley heard herself say, as if she were a puppet being
operated by a maniac, "would you like to come in? Stay for dinner?"

Wyatt didn't look at her. "Thanks, Carley. Another time. I've
got plans for tonight."

Carley felt herself flush all over with humiliation. *Of course* he
had plans for tonight! He was dating Angie Matthews! A little sun
and fresh air had transformed Carley into a pathetic old widowed

slut! Here he had been innocently trying to give his best friend's daughters a pleasant day and Carley had turned it into some sick sex fantasy.

"Oh, right, well, have fun tonight, and tell Angie hello for me, and thanks again, Wyatt!" she babbled. "Come on, girls, into the shower first of all." She ushered her girls up the walk toward the house. She didn't look back. She heard Wyatt start the car and drive away.

24
. . . . .

Rain streamed down steadily for the second day in a row. The sky, the air, everything was gray, wet, and steaming in the early August heat. Making beds and laying out fresh towels in the guest rooms gave Carley a few moments' comfort in the air-conditioned rooms, though at the same time she fretted at the thought of her electric bill. She considered turning the air conditioners off—all the guests had left for the day—but decided against it. When they returned to their rooms, they would want instant relief from the humidity in the cool, dry air. And they were paying for it.

She lugged a basket of towels to the laundry room. She transferred a pile of soggy clothing to the dryer and filled the washing machine. She folded the dry clothes, sorting as she went through them. Tomorrow the girls were leaving for a week with their grandparents in New York. They were flying by themselves from Nantucket to New York, where Marilyn and Keith would meet them, and Carley was tied in knots of anxiety about the trip. Of course the girls would be okay. The flight was nonstop. In July, Cisco had had a birthday, and now she was *thirteen*, and she had vowed to be sweet as pie to her little sister. She would be, too, Carley was sure of that. They would be in the air less than an hour. Cisco had a cell phone. Marilyn and Keith had cell phones. The girls would be *fine*.

"Here you are!" a woman said.

Carley jumped. "Maud! You surprised me."

"I called your name. Where are the girls?"

"With Annabel and Russell. They spent the night over there because tomorrow they're going to fly down to visit their other grandparents."

"Good. I haven't had a good long chat with you in forever! Carley, how are you?"

Carley stared at Maud, who wore shorts, a sequined little peasant shirt, and rhinestone-adorned sandals. Carley was suddenly aware of her limp hair, sweaty work clothes, and especially of the sneakers she wore because they gave her support when she was doing housework. More than that, Maud looked so damned happy and healthy, *glowing,* as if her body was radiating some kind of aura that only happened when one was madly in love.

When one was madly loved.

"*Busy.*" Carley knew she sounded petulant.

Maud tsked. "You can stop for a cup of coffee. Sit down. I'll make it. With ice and cream and some chocolate sprinkled on top."

"Mmm." Carley had to admit she could use some of that. She followed Maud into the kitchen, which Maud knew as well as her own.

"Put your feet up," Maud ordered.

"There's some fairly fresh coffee in the—"

"And ice in the freezer, right? I think I can figure it out."

Carley grinned. Relaxing, she stretched. "How are you, Maud?"

"Happy. Crazy busy." Maud took down two tall glasses. She fished cubes out of the ice container in the freezer and dropped them into the glasses. "Honestly, I'd forgotten how much I hate August. The traffic is a snarl, the grocery store parking lot is *impossible,* and the boys are wild with energy. And I've got a ton of book stuff to do."

"How's Toby?"

"Don't ask." Maud poured coffee over the ice cubes. Returning to the refrigerator, she searched out the cream and added it to the coffee, then added sugar, real sugar.

"Why not?"

"Well, because there are about a million more people here in August and the hospital's crowded and his practice is overloaded. He comes home exhausted." Stretching to find the chocolate in Carley's cupboard, she continued, dreamily, "Well, not *too* exhausted. We have to wait until the boys are in bed, of course, and then we have to be quiet, even though we're in a wing at the other end of the house." She took the grater out of a drawer, shaved off tiny flakes of chocolate, and sprinkled them on top of the coffee. "There." She set a glass in front of Carley and sank into a chair.

"This is delicious. Just what I need. Thanks." Carley held the cold glass to her forehead for a moment. It was weird to hear about Vanessa's ex-husband with Maud.

"You're welcome. But it's not just sex, Carley, it's everything. He's so helpful. He *fixes* things, he owns his own hammer! You should see our garage, it's turning into a workshop, and he has the boys 'help' him. He's made one wall into a tool area. 'Hand me the wrench,' he'll say to Spenser, and Spenser will find it in the big box of tools Toby brought over, and he'll hold it steady while Percy draws the outline around it. So the boys are learning *guy* things, like the names of tools." Maud was radiant.

"I'm so glad, Maud," Carley said, and she really was. Spenser and Percy needed a man in their lives.

"Last week? The boys had taken their showers, and they came into the living room to say good night and Percy said, 'Mommy, the end of my penis hurts,' and I almost collapsed with fright. I thought he had some rare horrible penis disease." Seeing Carley's face, she held up her hand. "Don't laugh! Do I have a penis? Before I could freak out, Toby said, 'Percy, go to the bathroom and pee. Sometimes soap gets up inside and irritates your skin.' And Percy peed, and everything was okay! *How* even with my genius imagination, could I have ever known about *that*?"

"Good for you, Maud. Good for the boys."

"Good for Toby, too. He loves the boys. Seriously. He gives them piggyback rides to bed, and roughhouses with them and reads them stories at night. He loves being a father. We're all so truly happy together." Maud sipped her coffee. "Okay. Enough about me. Tell me about you. How are you doing?"

The concern in Maud's voice was a balm. "I think I'm okay. August is overwhelming me, too. I had no idea how much work it would be to run a little B&B. Not just the physical stuff of cleaning and cooking, but the paperwork. Tax forms and credit card rules and keeping records. Oh, it makes my head hurt. But it keeps me from fretting about Gus. I mean, I think of him all the time, but I can't *mope*."

"And the girls?"

"They're doing all right, I think. Cisco's seeing a counselor, not that she ever tells me about her sessions. Lauren is teaching her to ride, and Cis loves it. She seems to be transferring her ballet obsession over to horses. She's even hinting about having her own horse. Lauren would board it—"

"Oh, God, Carley, *I* should do that!"

"Do what? Board horses?"

"No, help with your kids. Look, whenever Cisco goes out to Lauren's to ride, drop Margaret over at my house. She can play with the boys. Maybe she'll even civilize them."

"That would be great, Maud. Thanks. The girls will be gone for a week, but when they get back, I'll do it."

"Good." Maud cocked her head. "Do you ever think about men, Carley?"

"Gus hasn't been dead for even a year, Maud."

"It's been eight months. Plus, you thought about men when he was alive. We all did."

"We fantasized about movie stars. That's different from 'thinking about men.' " Carley lifted her glass to her lips, hoping to hide the flush she felt stain her cheeks. "I don't have time to think about men or sex or dating or anything like that."

"You're going to have an empty house for a week."

"Hardly. I have all three rooms solidly booked."

"I mean your girls will be gone. You'll have privacy."

"You think I should wander down to a bar and pick up a stranger and bring him home?"

"Might not be the worst thing you could do for yourself." Maud leaned forward. "Carley, you used to be *different*."

"Of course I was!" Carley shot back. "I wasn't a widow!"

"No, even before Gus died, you had kind of *lost* something. A sparkle. An exuberance."

Defensively, Carley snapped, "Not everyone can vamp around like Angelina Jolie, stealing another woman's man!"

Maud recoiled. "Vanessa's the one who looks like Angelina Jolie."

For a while they sat in silence.

Carley gave in first. "I didn't mean to insult you."

"I'm sure you didn't," Maud told her. "You were only reacting. Still, I think I hit a nerve."

Carley squirmed. "Maud, of course I 'lost my sparkle.' Gus was depressed. He was totally fixated on money. He'd made bad investments, and then he made *more* bad investments. He gambled and lost the girls' college funds. Our savings are gone. He even borrowed money from Wyatt."

"Oh, honey, what a mess. Listen, I didn't mean to be criticizing you." Maud leaned forward and took Carley's hand. "Carley, listen. Gus is dead. You are not. You are still young. You are a *babe*. You've been working like a trouper for months, getting the B&B ready and running it. That's all good. But you need to think about yourself. You're developing these *lines* around your mouth—"

"Oh, thank you very much!" Carley pulled her hand away.

"*Someone* should tell you," Maud insisted. "This is how you look these days." She pressed her lips together tightly. "Like an old farm woman who has to plow with a mule."

Carley didn't know whether to laugh or cry at the image. "Well, that's just awful!"

"I'm telling you because it's totally *not* the Carley we know and love!" Maud's blue eyes were earnest. "You can change! Sweetie, you deserve to be *happy*. You deserve all the good things in life. Lots and lots of delicious sex, too. You don't have to be a saint."

"Maud, I'm glad you're concerned. I hear what you're saying. I don't want to look like an old farm woman, but at this point in my life I don't feel—emotionally open. I think I'm actually doing fairly well, all things considered."

"You are, you really are. I'm proud of you. It's just time you got on with your life."

Carley bowed her head. "I don't want to do anything wrong."

Maud squinted at Carley. "Are you worried about the girls? They might freak if you dated some man?"

Carley squirmed. "I think Cisco might. We're going through a tough phase these days."

"Cisco is a teenager. She blamed you because she couldn't be a ballerina. She's going to spend the next five years blaming you for everything that goes wrong with her. That's what kids do. But think about this, Carley, you need to be a role model to your girls."

"I know that! I'm certainly trying my best!"

"No one could be better. But a role model successfully takes care of her own needs, too. You get to have a life of your own."

"I have a life of my own," Carley argued.

"Listen, Carley, one of the seven deadly sins is called sloth, but it's really acedia. It's a failure to love God and his works. It's a failure to love *life*. And you still have life, Carley. And part of life, especially while you're young, is sex, sensuality."

Carley started to disagree, then subsided. After all, Maud was right. "I see what you're saying, Maud. I do. But you've got to remember, it's not just the girls I have to think about. Annabel and Russell will be terribly hurt if I ever do start dating again."

"Why do they get to have a vote? I'm not saying it's time to get *married* again. It's too soon for that. But it's not too soon to have a little sugar on the side."

Carley laughed helplessly. "Since when have you started writing the rules of life?"

Maud aimed the full Bunsen burner force of her big blue eyes at Carley. "Since I started living with a man who makes my pulse race and my heart sing. I used to feel that life was *boring*, Carley. Now that I've had what I've had with Toby, I could die tomorrow knowing I haven't missed anything. You can't go back in time, Carley. You can only go forward." In a milder voice, she said, "I know I say the hard things. But I'm right."

"Maybe you are," Carley agreed thoughtfully. Looking up at her friend, she said, "I do love running the Seashell Inn."

"Yes, of course you would."

"What does that mean?"

"It means the B&B is work. Making other people happy. When are you going to take care of yourself? Do Annabel and Russell intimidate you?"

Carley took a moment to think about the question, but it bothered her, it made her uncomfortable. Finally, she answered, "I don't think so, Maud. Annabel and Russell didn't want me to run a guest house. They wanted me and the girls to move in with them. I went against their wishes. We stayed here, and I'm running the B&B. So I don't think I'm afraid of them. I love them. I respect them. But I can't help but think how absolutely crushed they would be if I brought another man into Annabel's house."

"What about your girls? Do you think it would be better for your girls to *not* have a man in their lives?"

"I hadn't thought of it that way, Maud. I can't really think about it now. Not in the summer, when everything's so busy. Not in this terrible heat." Carley wiped her forehead. "The heat just *drains* me."

"Me, too. I take about ten showers a day. Look, Carley, I'm not trying to pressure you. It's just that I love you, and I want you to be happy."

"Thanks, Maud." Carley knocked back the last of her iced coffee, her movements obscuring the tears that sprang to her eyes. It had been a while since anyone had said they loved her. "Gosh," she admitted in a sudden rush of emotion, "I've really missed spending time with you, Maud."

"We'll get together more when the summer's over. Until then, will you think about what I've said?"

Carley nodded. "I will."

"Good-bye, good-bye!" Carley reached out, trying to corral both daughters before they boarded the plane to their grandparents. Margaret was wiggly and giggly with excitement, while Cisco had gone stiff in her attempt to appear sophisticated.

"Cisco," Carley put her hand on her daughter's chin, forcing her to meet her eyes. "If Margaret needs you to hold her hand, you will, right?"

"Gosh, Mom, I'm not a *sadist*," Cisco retorted, rolling her eyes.

At thirteen, Cisco had a whole new vocabulary. "And you have tissues in your purse for both of you."

"Yes, Mom."

"And you'll call me when you land."

"Yes, Mom."

She turned to her younger daughter, who looked peppermint candy sweet in pink. "Margaret, you hold Cisco's hand when she tells you to, right?"

"Yes, Mommy."

"And you don't talk to strangers."

"Yes, Mommy."

"Can she talk to the flight attendant?" Cisco asked archly.

"*Cisco.*" Carley used her "don't push your luck" voice.

"They're *boarding*," Cisco reported, and excitement made her voice quaver. The girls had never gone off anywhere alone together for an entire week.

"One more hug." Carley clutched her daughters hard against her. She smacked kisses on top of their heads, then let them go. What had she forgotten? She had checked and double-checked that they had enough money and enough change in case of emergency. She'd written her phone number and her parents' and Sarah's on paper and made each girl carry one. Cisco had her cell phone, freshly charged. "Do you have your boarding passes?"

Both girls held up the rectangle of red plastic. They waved them at Carley, then hurried to get into the line of people walking through the gate behind the flight attendant to the plane. They were the only children on board. Immediately their shorter heads were hidden by those of adults. She glimpsed their shining black hair as they climbed up the stairs and ducked into the plane. The stairs, which were attached to the door, rose. The door was latched into place. The engines started. The plane taxied away from the terminal.

Carley bit her lip to keep from crying. She kept her sunglasses on as she fled the building. All around her, people were rushing up to greet family and friends, shrieking with joy, hugging so hard they almost fell over. Reaching her SUV, she crawled into it, slamming the door tight, locking it, putting on her seat belt, pretending it was an ordinary day. But her hands were shaking so hard she couldn't get the key into the ignition. She was absolutely *slammed* with loneliness. This hadn't hit her before, not when the girls spent the night at Annabel and Russell's or at their friends'. Why should it hit her here? She could only surrender.

She sat in her car and let it come, here where no one could see her. She bawled like a calf until her throat ached and her eyes were sore.

Finally she pulled herself together. She dug tissues out of her purse—she always had tissues at hand these days—and blew her nose and dried her eyes. She flipped down the visor and studied herself in the mirror. Ugh. Swollen nose, pouchy eyes, no lipstick. She dug out her eyeliner and lipstick and tried to create a semblance of normality on her face. Did she *really* have lines on either side of her mouth? She was only thirty-two!

Next to her four college-age women were tossing luggage into a convertible, shouting out all the fabulous things they were going to do this week: the beach, the parties, the mojitos, the shopping . . .

The *shopping*. When had she last bought a new dress? Or even a new shirt? It had to be almost a year. When Gus died, she immediately went into what she called her austerity mode, and the first thing she'd cut out was clothes for herself. The girls had to have new clothes all the time, they were growing, they had school and parties and events. It didn't really matter what Carley wore as an innkeeper.

When had she last worn a red dress?

When had she last worn a black dress?

She'd last worn a black dress at Gus's funeral.

Right.

Well, still, she hadn't been thinking of *that* kind of black dress.

She put the key into the ignition and drove to Lexi's shop, Moon Shell Beach.

It was early in the day. While lots of cars were parked on Main Street, most shoppers were out to buy the morning newspapers and fresh produce from the farm trucks.

Carley walked down the cobblestoned wharf to the small shingled shop and stood for a moment gazing in the window at the clothing displayed there. The garments were silky, fluid, drapey. She hadn't bought anything like that for months. Possibly, for years. She and Gus had been hardworking and deliberate, renovating their home, raising the girls, taking part in the town activities, spending plenty of time with his parents. Not every woman at thirty-two was as conscientious as Carley had been. As Carley still was. Some women weren't even married. Some women of thirty-two were sauntering along the beach in clingy pareos, slanting sexy eyes toward any man who caught their fancy. Some women wore necklaces like that shimmer of silver that spilled over the mannequin's breasts . . .

Lexi appeared in the doorway, smirking at Carley. "You're drooling. Most becoming."

"Oh, Lexi, everything is so—not just gorgeous. *Sensual.*"

"Come in." Lexi stepped out, wrapped her arm around Carley's shoulders, and ushered her into the shop. No one else was there. "It's always quiet in the mornings," she explained.

Carley pouted. "Maud told me I look like an old farm woman who has to plow with a mule."

Lexi laughed a come-hither laugh. "Then let's transform you."

"I don't have much money," Carley confessed.

"That's okay. I happen to have an in with the owner."

She pulled Carley into a little paradise. Summer colors—azure, lime, coral, crimson—undulated in satin waterfalls from hangers and hooks. Pashminas and shirts as light as flower petals layered the shelves. A pirate's trove of jewelry glittered from the display case. A spicy fragrance drifted through the air along with dreamy, creamy music, like waves lolling up to the shore.

"Try these." While Carley had been gaping, Lexi had gathered up several garments. She hung them on hooks in the dressing room at the back of the shop and ushered Carley in. "I'll bring you other things."

Carley tugged off her Capris and tee shirt. She slipped on a chiffon sarong in muted blues, shivering as the material slid over her skin. She stood gawking at her reflection in the mirror.

Lexi pulled open the curtain. "Better, right? We've got you away from the farm."

A kind of greed rushed through Carley's blood, a kind of lust. Whatever Lexi brought her, she tried on, shimmery skirts, loose tops with heavily beaded plunging necklines, exotic tunics richly embroidered, tops accentuated with cutwork and lace. Everything had tassels or beads or crocheted openwork.

"Put these on." Lexi handed Carley a pair of gold filigree earrings. They had a vaguely Egyptian look about them, they were large and ornate, and they were as light as air.

"Oh, I can't wear these!" Carley almost ripped them out of her earlobes. "I look too—too exotic."

"Sexy is the word you want," Lexi told her.

"All right, then, they're too sexy. I can't go around looking sexy. I'm a widow."

Lexi didn't argue. Carley pulled back on her favorite, a halter-top dress, the bodice accentuated with coins and needlework and beads.

"You have marvelous shoulders," Lexi told her.

"Cisco thinks they're too wide. We can't be ballerinas."

"And thank heavens for that."

Carley twirled in front of the mirror. She looked different. She looked young. She *felt* young.

"You should take that," Lexi advised her. "And the blue sarong."

"I don't have anywhere to wear them."

"Wear them and you will."

Carley chuckled. Lifting her arms, she pulled her hair up into a loose twist. She did look good. "But what will my in-laws think if they see me?"

"Could they possibly think you're a young woman wearing a cool dress on a hot day?"

"I don't want to dishonor Gus's memory."

"Let me show you something." Lexi turned Carley away from the mirror and swiftly dressed her in a filmy skirt that started just at Carley's hipbones and a tiny little triangle of silk that tied like kite strings around her neck and back and ended far above her belly button. She rotated Carley back to face the mirror. "What do you see?"

"Wow." Carley shifted uncomfortably on her bare feet as she gazed at her image. She was slim enough to wear this well, to allow her flat belly to be exposed, to carry her breasts braless, poking seductively through the silk. "This shows more than it covers."

"Go out in the shop. Walk toward the mirror."

Carley obeyed. She went almost breathless at the sight. There was a slender, willowy woman, her belly taut, her breasts high and pert, her hips as they moved an invitation.

"You look amazing in that," Lexi said, "and I wouldn't let you wear it out of the store. *That* might stress out your in-laws, and Maud would think you've moved way too fast from the farm to the bordello. That might make you seem to be, well, not dishonoring Gus, but perhaps forgetting him. But these other things, Carley, they're not seductive or wanton. They're just *pretty*. It wouldn't be such a terrible crime if you looked pretty, would it?"

Carley smiled. She returned to the halter dress and put it on. She did look good in it, and she felt free. She felt like it was summer. Even if she was a widow, it was summer.

Driving home, her cell rang. She glanced at her caller ID. Cisco.

"Hi, Mom!" she shouted. "We're here! In Grandpa and Grandma's car. The plane ride was a blast!" Muffled noises filled the background. "Margaret wants to say hello."

"Mommy! We didn't get lost! We got peanuts! Cisco showed me how to play tic-tac-toe and I won! The plane *roared*! It shook!"

"It didn't shake, Margaret, don't freak Mom out." Cisco commandeered the phone. "The plane didn't shake. Or just a little. Margaret was scared and I held her hand."

Margaret was on again. "Cisco had the window seat. I didn't want it, I thought I might fall out if I leaned against the wall. Cisco says I'm silly . . ."

"Margaret, honey, let me talk to your mother." Carley's mother came on the line. "As you can tell, your children have landed. They're quite thrilled with themselves."

Carley laughed, delighted to hear her girls bubbling with excitement. "Thanks for letting me know they arrived safely."

Her father's voice rumbled in the background.

"Keith says he already needs a nap. Oh! We're pulling into the driveway. "We phoned earlier but you didn't pick up."

"I had, um, errands to run. I guess I didn't hear my phone."

"We're home. Must unload. We've got a full week planned. I hope you get a good rest, dear. Whoops, must go, bye!"

"Bye," both girls chimed before clicking off.

Carley thought about her mother's words as she went into her house and climbed the stairs to her bedroom.

A good rest.

Was that what she needed? True, without the girls around, her schedule was freed up a bit, but the Seashell Inn was full this week. She had to bake every morning, help Maria clean, and manage the bookings and billings. Her evenings would be free, though, and summer evenings were long. She wondered whether, as a widow, she should be too sad to enjoy life. If she bought herself a nice new hard-back mystery and ordered a pizza and opened a bottle of wine all for herself this evening—would that be wrong?

The phone rang again. Annabel, her voice slow, even weary. "Carley. Do you have a moment?"

"Of course, Annabel. How are you?" She lay her shopping bag gently over a chair and flopped down on her bed, kicking off her sandals.

"I am *miserable* with this heat. I know Russell and I have been rigidly puritanical about not having air-conditioning on the island. Now I must admit I don't know why we considered it a point of pride to endure this heat and humidity."

Carley had cooled off in the air-conditioned SUV, but the heat of the second floor bedroom made her drowsy. Lazily, she consoled Annabel. "It only lasts for a couple of weeks."

"That's what we always say, but really, summers seem to be hotter every year. Russell blames it on global warming."

Carley was pleased to be having a conversation with her mother-in-law on a neutral topic. Helpfully, she suggested, "You could buy air-conditioning."

"Too expensive and complicated for this old ark. Anyway, we've made another plan. We're going up to Boston for the week, to stay at the Ritz, where the rooms are posh and air-conditioned and we can go to air-conditioned museums and restaurants or just lie and stare at the ceilings and cool off."

"What a good idea."

"The only thing I worry about—I don't want you to feel we're deserting you, Carley. We just thought, since the girls are with your parents, you won't need us for a week . . ."

The strain in Annabel's voice touched Carley. "Annabel, you're absolutely right. I just spoke with the girls and my parents. Cisco and Margaret arrived at the airport. Mom and Dad have lots of plans. I feel like I'm on vacation! I won't have to fix dinner or do laundry for a week." Except for the guests, she added silently. "Please, go to Boston and enjoy yourselves."

When Carley clicked off the phone, she sat for a moment in a kind of suspended animation, like someone struck by lightning or caught in amber.

Annabel and Russell were going to Boston. To museums and restaurants. To a posh hotel with air-conditioning. Cisco and Margaret were with people who adored them, they were all laughing, they were having fun.

That night, Carley curled up with a fat new mystery and a deluxe pizza and a box of expensive chocolates. It was pleasant for a while, but not as satisfying as she'd expected.

She was bored. She was lonely.

She wanted to wear the halter dress she'd bought at Moon Shell Beach.

She opened the island newspaper and studied it. She picked up the phone.

"Lexi? How would you like to go see *Our Town* tomorrow night, and then stop afterward somewhere for a drink?"

Lexi laughed. "I'd love to."

Next, she phoned Maria, who helped her clean the rooms. "Could you come over tomorrow night and just be around in case any of the guests need something? I'd pay you, of course."

"I'd love to!" Maria chuckled. "And it will be good for you to get out!"

In the off-season, it seemed as if every single person on the island knew Carley, or knew who she was and was capable of reporting her every word and move to the rest of the town. Gossip was one of the few off-season island activities.

But in the three months when the summer people flooded the island, a restful anonymity curtained Carley from the world. The play was held in Bennett Hall on Centre Street, a small auditorium next to the Congregational church. It contained a small stage and only about one hundred twenty-five seats. There were, as she'd expected, acquaintances in the audience who waved at her or kissed the air next to her cheeks and told her how glad they were to see her out, and half of these people would phone Annabel and Russell as soon as possible to inform them that they'd seen Carley at the play, while the other half would privately discuss what Carley was wearing, how suitable it was, how sad or inappropriately happy she looked, and how interesting it was that she was with Lexi Laney, who was wealthy and divorced and involved with Tris and Jewel Chandler.

Most of the people at the theater that night were strangers. Many of them cast admiring eyes over Lexi and Carley in their chic dresses and high heels. The play was a complete success, commanding a standing ovation, and afterward, as they filed out into the hot

summer night, Carley's body felt different. Smoother. Supple. She
was fluid, she was comfortable, she was young.

They strolled beneath the high leafy trees down to the outdoor
patio at the Boarding House. They ordered cold Prosecco and sake
cockles and spicy shrimp rolls to share and leaned back in their
chairs to gaze at the high indigo sky. Lexi talked about her past in a
self-deprecating, amusing way, and Carley listened and found herself
laughing. She was aware of men admiring them. Mostly, she knew,
they were gawking at tall, blond, stunning Lexi, but occasionally she
glanced up to see a man's eyes on her, and she allowed herself a
Mona Lisa quirk of her lips.

The waiter appeared at their table with two more glasses of wine
on his tray. "Compliments of the gentlemen in the corner."

Lexi looked across the patio, then laughed. "Thank you," she
told the waiter. To Carley she said, "It's Tris and Wyatt."

Carley frowned. "Who?"

"Tris and Wyatt. My Tris, remember? I'm practically living with
him. I told him we were going out tonight. Wyatt's one of his buddies. Oh, come on." Lexi frowned. "Don't tell me you're going to be
inhibited because Gus's best friend is here. I mean, *he's* here, isn't
he? Do you think Wyatt shouldn't enjoy himself because he lost his
best friend?"

Before Carley could answer, the men were at their table.

"May we join you?"

"Of course," Lexi said.

As the men pulled out their chairs, Carley picked up her water
glass and chugged it down. She needed a clear head if she was going
to be around Wyatt on this soft summer night.

"We went to see *Our Town*," Lexi told the men.

"I saw it last night," Wyatt said. "Wasn't Riley Wynn amazing?"

Carley relaxed, listening to the conversation, loving the way
Wyatt knew the actors, the director, the set designer. This was his
community, and hers, too. She felt easy, at home. Leaning forward,
she joined in the conversation. They talked about everything, how

well the island economy seemed to be doing, and the Red Sox, whom they all loved and followed, and the Swedish writer Stieg Larsson. They ordered more food, tuna tartare and duck spring rolls and a rich appetizer combining sirloin and lobster, and they all shared the food, licking the sauce off their lips and groaning with satisfaction. Carley was careful not to touch her wine. She stuck to water, wanting to stay sober and restrained. Wanting to keep herself from blurting out something she'd regret.

Wanting to stop herself from simply touching Wyatt's tanned, muscular arm.

They were surprised when the waiter arrived to tell them the restaurant was closing. It was after one in the morning.

"I can't remember when I've been out this late." Anxiously, Carley grabbed her cell phone from her bag and punched in the guest house number. When Maria answered, she told her she could leave now; Carley was on her way home. Maria assured her the evening had been quiet. She'd see her tomorrow. Clicking off the phone, Carley pushed her chair back from the table. "I've got to get back."

"Hey," Lexi said. "It's okay. Your girls are with their grandparents, remember? No one's going to give you a demerit for signing in late at the dorm."

"Still." She gathered up her purse. "I'd better go."

"I'll walk you home," Wyatt said.

Surprised, she glanced at him quickly, then looked down at the table, flustered. "Oh, it's only a few blocks away."

"Nevertheless." Wyatt reached over and took her arm.

Her knees went weak. She wasn't sure she could stand up.

Lexi leaned over and kissed Carley's cheek. "Tonight was fun, Carley. Let's do it again. You and I both work hard in the summer; we need a little entertainment."

Carley knew the subtext of Lexi's little speech. She wanted to confess: *This might be more than entertainment for me. This might be more than I can handle.*

She rose on shaking legs. What was wrong with her? The man had only offered to escort her home safely at this late hour.

He was a *friend*.

Tris had his arm around Lexi. "We're walking this way."

"We're this way," Wyatt said.

"Good night!" Carley called, trying to sound normal.

The streets were quiet. The shops were closed. As they strolled down residential lanes, few houses burned lights in the windows. The town was sleeping. The sidewalks were famous for the uneven brickwork that could make anyone stumble on the brightest day. Wyatt put his arm around Carley in a natural, protective manner, drawing her close to his side.

They turned down a narrow lane darkened by high hedges. The heavy perfume of lilies drifted around them. The heat, which had been tormenting during the day, seemed like a caress against her skin. She was afraid Wyatt could sense how her heart was racing.

Proud that her voice sounded natural, Carley said, "It's kind of fun, being the only people awake, isn't it?"

"Very cool," Wyatt agreed. "It's like we know secrets."

"Well," Carley said, her pulse fluttering, "everyone knows secrets."

"I know a secret," Wyatt told her.

"Do you? Tell me."

"Okay." Wyatt stopped her next to a privet hedge. A streetlamp a few houses down illuminated his face. "Here it is."

He leaned toward her, and Carley lifted her head, turning it slightly, thinking he would whisper into her ear, but he gently took her chin in his hand and tilted his face toward hers and brought his mouth down to kiss her on the lips. It was a long, deliberate, searching, sexual kiss.

When finally he drew back, she saw the question on his face.

Her heart was quivering away in her chest like a frightened rabbit, but desire created its own courage and she heard herself murmur, "And here's my secret."

She raised her arms, folded them around his neck, went up on tiptoe to press herself against him, and kissed him back.

The hardness of his erection against her gave her an unexpected sense of triumph.

"Let's go to your house while I can still walk," Wyatt joked, gently pushing her away from him.

They had only two more blocks. They walked quickly, in silence. Above them, a half moon rode the sky, joining with the stars to sprinkle the earth with silver light and darker shadows. SUVs sat in driveways like giant primeval sleeping monsters. No wind stirred the trees, no dog barked, no bird chirped. Carley felt as if she were on another planet, a fantasy world separate from reality.

They were holding hands. As they came to her house, their pace increased. She fumbled with the keys and then they were inside. Wyatt pushed her against the door and pressed himself against her.

After a long kiss, she tore herself away. "Wyatt—I'm a little nervous."

To her surprise, he said, "Me, too. We'll go slow. We'll stop whenever you want."

She took his hand and pulled him up the stairs to the second floor, which was off limits to the B&B guests. She led him down the hall past the master bedroom to one of the extra bedrooms, where her parents or Sarah and Sue stayed when they came to visit. She shut and locked the door. She turned to face him and Wyatt came at her, tall, lean, hard, almost desperate, wrapping his arms around her and half walking, half carrying her to the bed. They fell on it, and as she ground her body against his, her lips against his, all nervousness vanished. All restraint was gone. This was primitive, unstoppable, basic. They moved apart only for Wyatt to unzip and lower his jeans, for Carley to raise her dress and remove her panties, and then his naked skin was against hers, she felt the brush and bristle of his hair against her abdomen and thighs, she twisted beneath him, she raised her hips, and with a low moan, he entered her.

"Oh," she said. Every cell of her body was alive. Anticipation rippled through her like starlight on water, possessing her very depths.

"Don't move," he said. He raised himself on his elbows and looked down at her. "I want this to last."

But she was on fire. She was on the verge of something, she was somewhere she'd never been before in her life.

"You've got to be kidding," she told him, and she moved her hips, and he thrust deeper, and a wild sensation shuddered through her, like the sun rising in the morning, expanding its warm light everywhere, illuminating the world.

He put his hand over her mouth to stifle her cries. She licked the palm of his hand, and he groaned deeply and came.

She didn't want to let him go. He didn't want to move. For a long time he supported himself on his arms, while their torsos grew moist with sweat, but finally she unclenched her legs from around him and he rolled on his back. As he moved, he kept his hand on her body, not wanting to break the connection.

She rolled on her side and nuzzled against him. She drew her hand over his long abdomen, curled her fingers in his thick brown pubic hair, stroked his thigh.

"You're created from marble and satin," she murmured.

"You're created from honey," he replied. He rolled onto his side and gazed into her eyes. "Carley, I've wanted to do that ever since the first time I saw you."

She touched his face with her fingertips. "Are we very bad?"

He captured her hand in his and kissed her palm. She shivered.

"Just for this week," he said slowly, "let's not think about anyone else. Let's just be ourselves, together." When she hesitated, he said, "The answer is no, Carley, I don't think we're being bad. If I did, I wouldn't be here. But this week has fallen out of the sky like some kind of miracle, and I don't want to lose a minute of it."

"Okay." She ran her free hand down his belly to his groin. "What should we do?"

He answered by rolling back on top of her, and this time they made love together with a slowness that left her breathless.

The smell of coffee woke her.

"What?" She sat up in bed, dazed. She still wore her watch. It was after eight. Next to her, Wyatt slept heavily, snoring, naked, the sheet crumpled around his legs.

"My guests," she whispered to herself and jumped from the bed. No time for a shower. She raced down the hall, pulled on shorts and a shirt and sandals, and hurried down the stairs.

Maxine and Karl Yoder from Philadelphia sat at the kitchen table drinking coffee.

"I'm *so* sorry!" Carley apologized. "I overslept. I *never* oversleep. My daughters are away, and I didn't set my alarm—"

Mrs. Yoder was a plump motherly woman in her fifties. "Honey, I'm an old hand at brewing up coffee. The sweet rolls and muffins under the dome were as good as they were yesterday. The couple from Moon Shell went off to meet friends for breakfast at Arno's and I don't think the people in Angel's Wing are awake yet."

"Oh, good." Carley cast a longing look at the coffeepot. Should she drink the coffee Mrs. Yoder had made? If she did, should she give the couple a discount on their charge? God, she couldn't think straight and she knew she probably reeked of sex!

"You look very pretty this morning," Mrs. Yoder said. "And happy, too."

Carley dipped in a playful little curtsey. "Thank you. You look very pretty, too."

"This sunshine makes us all look good," Mr. Yoder said. Pushing himself up, he said, "Come on, Maxie. Places to go. Things to do."

Carley waited until they'd left the kitchen, then made a beeline for the coffeepot.

"Good morning." Wyatt appeared in the kitchen doorway. He had dressed in last night's clothing, but he needed a shave and his hair stuck out in all directions. Still, he looked as sexy as hell.

She poured him a cup of coffee and brought it to him. "Mrs. Yoder made it. I overslept."

"God bless Mrs. Yoder," Wyatt said. With one hand, he took the cup. With the other, he pulled Carley against him so he could kiss her cheek. "Man needs sustenance."

Carley smiled. "Sweet rolls and fruit, too."

They sat companionably, eating, drinking juice, as normal as any couple.

Carley stared at Wyatt, wanting to absorb him through her eyes. Wanting more? Oh, yes. She asked, "Wyatt, do you think we made a mistake?"

"Do you?"

She tried to sort through her thoughts. "Last night was astonishing. But this morning I have to say I'm a little freaked out."

"Do you feel guilty?"

"No. I don't feel guilty. But I guess I wonder if I *should* feel guilty."

"It is sudden," Wyatt agreed. "But Carley, I've been wanting to—"

"Good morning!" Francine and Genevieve, who were staying in Angel's Wing, breezed into the room, bringing scents of perfumed soap and strawberry shampoo. "Isn't it a fab day?" Casting their eyes on Wyatt, who had suddenly stood up, they both batted their lashes. "Well, hello. Are you staying here?"

"Actually," Wyatt said, "I'm just leaving." Leaning over, he pecked a chaste kiss on Carley's cheek. "I'll call you later."

She was not a teenager. She couldn't go to her room and bite her pillow and indulge in remembering every moment of last night. She had work to do. She checked Angel's Wing out and sent Maria off to clean and prepare it for the next guests. She settled at her desk, turned on her computer, and ordered supplies to be shipped from off-island, the toilet paper, tissues, paper towels, soaps, and cleaning supplies she bought in bulk.

When the phone rang, she snatched it up.

27
·····

"Hi, Mommy!" Margaret's sweet voice rang clear as chimes over the distance. "Do you miss us? We miss you. We went to the zoo yesterday! I saw a lion, and a chimpanzee smiled at me, they have really big teeth, and—"

This is reality, Carley reminded herself as she listened to her younger daughter chattering away. This is what really matters.

Cisco came on, sounding relaxed and happy. "We're going into the city today," she informed Carley, "to see the Museum of Natural History, like in the movie with Ben Stiller!"

"Ooh, how fabulous, Cis. Wish I were with you."

"Grandpa and Grandma have central air-conditioning, too," Cisco said smugly.

"Oh, flip me with a spatula and call me done," Carley joked.

She spoke with her parents about the plans for the week. Her parents lived such responsible lives, but Carley had seen photos of them when they were young and clearly they'd been crazy about each other. In their own undemonstrative way, they still were.

Mom, Carley wanted to say, *I just had the most unexpected, amazing, off-the-charts sex in my life last night. I feel like I'm in love and I feel nearly sick with guilt. What should I do?*

But she said nothing. She knew what her mother would say: sex gets people into trouble. She saw the results all the time at her day care center.

After saying good-bye to them all, Carley put down the phone and flicked on her accounting program. The numbers swam before her eyes. She folded her arms and put her head down and allowed herself to drift on memories of the night before. The slide of Wyatt's body against hers. His touches, delicate, and then not delicate at all. His—the phone rang.

"Carley," Wyatt said. "Can you talk?"

"Yes. Everyone's gone."

"I can't stop thinking about you."

"Good." Her voice was throaty with desire.

"Listen, here's what I think. We've been given a gift with this week. We'd be fools not to take it. I want to be with you every moment I can, and we can figure out where to go from here. What do you think?"

"Oh, Wyatt. Yes." She laughed at herself. "I want to crawl right through the phone into your arms."

"It might be easier if I just walked back to your house," Wyatt said. "Now?"

"Now."

As they lay in bed together, Wyatt's eyes lazily lingered on Carley's breasts, while a light, unconscious smile lifted his mouth. He said, "You're so beautiful."

She took his hand, kissed it, and murmured, "You, too."

She could feel her chest dappling pink from shyness at his staring, and from pure animal satisfaction, and she thought how the heat pulsing through her, dilating her veins and arteries, pinking her skin, deepening her breathing, was like that of any flower on a warm summer day. She could understand how bulbs could survive the cold winter beneath the dark earth, how dry seeds could split open, shooting shafts of green stems up into the light, where buds swelled and unfolded and lay themselves open to the life-giving heat of the sun. She had been through her own winter. Now she was returning to full life.

This was what Wyatt had done, was doing, for her. She loved her daughters, of course, they were the miracle and center of her world. But in her own body and spirit, something had been dormant. When she had given birth to her daughters, she had felt as if she were gripped by the deep source of the universe. Here it was again, the great fierce force of life seizing her by the scruff of her neck, shaking her awake, igniting her into a glowing, radiant blossom thick with juice, nectar, and joy.

It wasn't just the sex. They had everything to tell each other. They sat up late into the night, talking about their childhoods, their families, their dreams. They made juicy lobster rolls at two in the morning and ate them, licking each other's fingers. Because they had always suspected they shared a slightly warped sense of humor, they had a marathon of DVDs of Robin Williams, Dane Cook, and Ben Stiller. One night after a day of rain, when the temperature had dropped and a cool breeze made the muggy air comfortable, they put on music and danced. Quiet music, because Carley didn't want to wake her guests. Romantic music. Slow music.

They talked to each other like college students just learning about themselves. Wyatt asked Carley how it had been, having a sister who was gay. That hadn't been a problem, Carley told him. Sarah had been bright, witty, and a popular jock. She had been considered ultracool. The problem for Carley had been following in the steps of such a successful sister.

Wyatt remembered growing up with Gus, best friends and constant companions. Their parents were close friends who got together often to sail to Coatue or Tuckernuck for the day. Gus was an only child, but Wyatt had an older sister, Wendy, who treated Gus like her little brother. When their parents wouldn't take them to see *Ghostbusters* or *Indiana Jones* or *Batman*, Wendy took them. She was their hero. And she was their cheerleader. Gus had been quarterback of the high school football team, Wyatt had been running back. Gus had organized the beach cleanups and car washes for class trips. Wyatt was his first lieutenant. Both boys were fascinated by the law, and by the time they were in high school, they decided Wyatt would be a junior partner in the Winsted firm.

Carley said softly, "I wonder what Gus would think about us."

Wyatt made a face. "If he were alive, he'd kill me. As it is, I think he'd want you to be happy. Me, too."

Carley said, "I've thought about this a lot, when I'm not with you—when I'm capable of thought," she added with a smile. "I don't feel disrespectful to Gus. I don't have the sense that he's around somewhere, watching me angrily. People say things to widows, they say, 'Gus would want you to be happy.' "

"I think they're right. Gus *would* want you to be happy. He loved you and he cherished those girls. And his parents love you. That was important to him."

"I love his parents." Wryly, she added, "Sometimes."

"But do you know how unusual that is? How many people *love* their in-laws? Russell and Annabel appreciated everything you did with Gus. You fixed up this old wreck and made it a home. You came from off-island and made good friends in the community. We have to go on from this point. I think we need to worry about Cisco and Margaret and Gus's parents."

"I agree."

"I think we get to pay a bit of attention to ourselves, too. We matter, too, Carley."

The night before everyone returned, Carley and Wyatt sat in the kitchen, sharing a midnight snack of milk and scones and cookies and fruit. Carley, half-drugged from hours of intense sex, wasn't sure she wanted to get into a discussion. Yet perhaps they had to.

"I wonder whether anyone suspects about us," she said carefully. "About this week."

"I doubt it," Wyatt said. "We've been circumspect. I've walked here. My car hasn't been parked in front of your house. I've seen clients, talked to friends, you've gone grocery shopping. I think we've appeared absolutely normal."

"That's good." Carley looked down into her glass. "Wyatt. I don't want my girls to find any man in my bed, until—" She saw his face change, just a shadow crossing. "I'm not saying I don't want to be with you. It's just that once the girls are back, we just have to be more careful, okay?"

He nodded. "I agree."

For a moment, they were silent, caught in their own thoughts. Then Wyatt flashed his magic smile. "We should go to bed while we can."

So they did.

28
. . . . .

Saturday everyone arrived back on the island. Cisco spent about three and a half minutes with her mother before rushing off to phone her friends. Margaret curled up in Carley's lap and yapped away happily, recounting every detail of her trip. Later that day, Annabel phoned to say they were back, and Carley invited them to a big Sunday lunch the next day.

Annabel and Russell had brought gifts for everyone from Boston, and Cisco and Margaret had brought gifts for everyone from New York, which made Sunday afternoon a bit like Christmas.

The phone rang in the middle of the night, waking Carley from a deep sleep. Her heart went from its reliable thud to a panicked clatter as she sat up and turned on the light. Her girls were home, she'd tucked them in. Gus was dead. Who could it be? Her parents? Annabel?

"Mrs. Winsted? It's Melody Wiggins."

It was the woman who was staying in Scallop with her fiancé.

The woman was sobbing so hard she was almost incomprehensible. "F-f-f-forgive me for waking you, but I don't know who else to call. My fiancé and I had a fight and he left me out here and I've been trying to walk home, but I'm totally *lost!* I don't think I should call the police, I don't have any money for a cab, I'm in my bathing suit and flip-flops, and Jack took the car! It's *dark* out here!"

Carley looked at the clock. It was a bit after midnight. Tossing back the covers, she went to the window and looked down at the street. She didn't see the Jeep the couple had rented. She'd noticed during the four days they'd been in Scallop that Jack enjoyed his liquor. Probably Jack was in one of the bars.

Melody Wiggins was young, Carley remembered, probably no older than eighteen. Cisco would be that old in five years. This would be beyond the duties of the owner of a B&B, but Carley hoped someday someone would do something just as nice for her daughters.

"I'll come pick you up, Melody. Take a deep breath and let's see if we can figure out where you are."

It turned out not to be difficult to find her. Jack had taken Melody for a picnic and evening swim at Gibb Pond out on the moors, a place where few tourists went. Carley pulled on shorts and a shirt, checked on her sleeping daughters, and swept her keys into her hands. She hadn't left the girls alone in the house before, but they weren't really alone. Both Angel's Wing and Moon Shell were occupied by older and saner couples who, Carley knew, were already in for the night.

She found Melody at the small beach by the pond, pacing back and forth and weeping. The young woman threw herself into the car and startled Carley with a fierce hug.

"Thank you! Thank you! I thought I would *die* out there! I thought a bear would get me."

"Honey, no bears live on Nantucket," Carley assured her. "You were safe." She patted Melody's back. "But it must have been terrifying to be alone out in the wild at night."

"I don't know what to do," Melody confessed as Carley drove over the rutted dirt paths crisscrossing through the moors. "Jack and I are going to get married. I love him, and he loves me, I *know* he does. But he has such a temper."

"How long have you been together?" She watched her headlights pierce a bright track through the dark.

"Almost a year." Melody dug in her purse, pulled out some tissue and noisily blew her nose. "He wants to get married this fall."

"Maybe you should wait awhile before getting married. Give him time to—"

"Oh, no, he'd be really angry then. He's got an important job with a bank and they're transferring him to their British branch before Christmas."

The SUV bounced and waddled as it went through puddles and over bumps. Carley considered her words carefully. "What do your parents think of Jack?"

Melody was silent. "They did like him, at first. I mean, you've met him. He's so handsome, and charming, and smart, and he makes a ton of money. He just sometimes . . . he's just under so much pressure."

They arrived at the main road. Carley turned onto the pavement and their ride smoothed out. "You see," she pointed out, "now we're on the Polpis Road. You weren't far from town. Did you plan to go to college, Melody?"

"Yes, but I just wanted to be an elementary-school teacher."

"*Just?* Teaching's the most important job in the world. I'll bet you'd be good at it, too."

Melody was silent for a few moments. They came to the turnoff onto the 'Sconset road toward the rotary and town. Headlights from other cars flashed past.

"I *would* be good at it," Melody said at last, her voice a little stronger.

Carley thought of what Melody's parents must have said to her: *You're only eighteen, so young, how can you know what you want?* She didn't want to repeat that warning. "Moving to another town is always stressful," Carley continued, keeping her voice easy, chatty. "Moving to another country must be very difficult. In fact, someone made a chart of the top ten most stressful events in life, and moving is way up there with divorce and having a spouse die."

Melody looked at Carley. "I didn't know that."

"It's certainly something to think about. You might want to let Jack move first and see how he handles that pressure."

"Oh, but he *needs* me," Melody protested.

"You might want to think about what *you* need. That's what I'd tell my daughters."

Melody was silent, her face creased with worry.

They pulled into the driveway. They were home.

Carley whispered, "Shut your door quietly, if you can. I don't want to wake anyone." They walked up to the house, which rose so safe and welcoming before them, the outside light glowing like a beacon.

At the door, Melody said, "Thank you so much for rescuing me. I don't know how to thank you, but I'm so grateful."

Carley hugged the girl. "I'm glad to do it. Take care of yourself."

Melody nodded soberly. "I will."

The next morning, Melody and Jack appeared in the kitchen for their coffee and breakfast. They shoveled in the cheese croissants and fresh-cut fruit without tasting it. Without looking at each other. Immediately after that, they checked out. Jack's face was wooden. Melody's face was white, but her head was high, and before she went out the door, she turned to Carley, stuck out her hand, and gave her a very grown-up handshake.

School started the last week of August. Carley's parents had taken the girls shopping for clothes and school supplies and sent them home with so much new stuff they'd had to buy two new duffel bags. After Labor Day weekend, most of the tourists had left, especially all the ones with children. This was the season, Carley's innkeeper friends had told her, for the "Newly Wed or Nearly Dead" tourists to flock to the island, when the prices dropped just a bit and the beaches were not as crowded. Carley became a chauffeur once more, rushing the girls to riding lessons, softball and soccer practice, school picnics, social events. To her great relief, Margaret had no desire to take ballet or riding lessons. Cisco didn't ask to stay at her grandparents' house, although they all still got together for dinner once a week.

With summer over and a routine established, Carley took the girls to the MSPCA and let them each choose a kitten. Cisco picked out an orange striped boy cat she named, not surprisingly, Tiger, while Margaret chose a dainty calico she named Mimi. The kittens filled an enormous amount of time and emotional space. They were allowed to sleep with the girls. Their litter boxes were just outside the bedroom doors in the hall. They were fed in the girls' bathroom because the house was big and the kittens small. Plus, Carley didn't want to worry about a guest being allergic or phobic. She took the girls to Geronimo's and let them buy soft, round little cat beds, toys, and treats. The girls invited all their friends over to admire the new pets.

When she knew the girls were at school, Wyatt walked up to her house for a quick morning or early afternoon liaison. The rush and secrecy made the moments together even more exciting. She talked with Wyatt on the phone several times during the day, and always last thing at night before she fell asleep. Often Wyatt came, separately, like many of the islanders, to watch the girls' soccer and baseball games, and sometimes he sat next to Carley, but usually he joined other friends. Carley felt a subversive thrill to have him just a few seats away on the bleachers, not looking at her, but connected to her.

With the press and fluster of summer business over, everyone on the island calmed down. Here was the good season, the mellow season. The skies were sunny but the humidity had dropped, the water was still warm enough for swimming, and bank accounts, for this year at least, had been replenished by the tourists. Families had low-key parties to catch up on all the news and plan for the off-season.

Lauren and Frame held a cookout one Sunday afternoon for their three children's friends and their friends' parents. Wyatt wasn't there, probably, Carley assumed, because this was a family group.

Margaret and Cisco joined the other kids in a wild game of tag. Carley wandered through the crowd, chatting with friends, aware that she was the single female without a husband.

She took her glass of wine to the steps leading down from the wide deck and settled down, leaning her back against a post, just gazing out over the wide green stretch of lawn. It was almost a year since Gus died, and there were her daughters, running around with the other kids, shrieking with laughter, tanned, healthy, absolutely *fine*. She had been so frightened when she lost Gus. Their marriage, their family, had been her world. She'd been worried about raising her daughters alone, terrified about finances, unsure of how to get through each day. Somehow she had started a successful business running a B&B she enjoyed, kept them afloat financially, and kept their little family on track.

Lauren approached her. "What are you doing sitting on the steps? That post must be digging into your back. We do possess such things as deck chairs, you know. Don't you want to come sit in a chair?"

"In a while," Carley told her friend. "Right now I'm content right where I am."

One foggy September morning while the girls were at school, Carley was in Scallop, with the door and windows wide open. The last guest had worn a powerful perfume vaguely reminiscent of cat pee, and it had permeated the room. Carley was dropping sheets and towels into her wicker basket to take up to the laundry room when her cell rang. Her personal cell—she let the machine take calls for the B&B when she was busy.

"Carley? It's Vanessa."

"Vanessa!" Carley's legs almost went out from under her. She sat on the stripped bed, clamping the phone to her ear. "Honey! How are you?"

"Actually," Vanessa replied with a lilt in her voice, "I guess I could say I'm amazing."

"Amazing? Vanessa, have you met someone?"

Vanessa laughed. "You could say that."

"Where are you?"

"At home."

"At *home*? Do you mean on the island?"

"I do. I arrived yesterday. I've been unpacking and getting groceries, that sort of thing."

"Does that mean you're moving back?"

"Oh, yes. And not alone!"

"*What?*"

"Why don't I come over and show you?"

"Show me? Do you have him with you?"

"In a manner of speaking."

"Stop talking in riddles! You're infuriating!"

More laughter. "I'm coming over."

Carley raced up the stairs to the laundry room and dropped the basket on the floor. She hurried up to her bedroom, stripped off her drab work tee shirt and pulled on a clean peach tee. She ran a comb through her hair, lined her eyes and lightly dabbed on mascara and lipstick, although she was smiling so much she could hardly get the lipstick on straight. Vanessa had met a man! Maybe she was going to marry him! She sounded so buoyant, so happy! Carley almost skipped back down the stairs.

She glanced around the first floor. It looked great. It always did. She was forever dusting, straightening, bringing in fresh flowers, brightening the rooms for her guests. Besides, Vanessa wouldn't care what the house looked like, they had so much to talk about!

The knock came at the door. Carley pulled it open.

The first thing she noticed was that Vanessa was alone. No man stood next to her. Then she focused on Vanessa's familiar, lovely, beloved face, her full lips, her wavy hair, and her huge brown eyes full of emotion.

She wore a loose cotton tunic over loose linen trousers. She looked, in general, thinner than she used to look, except that her breasts were larger.

And she had a definite bump in her belly.

Carley swayed with shock. "Vanessa, are you *pregnant?*"

"I am." Vanessa threw her arms around Carley and hugged her close for a long time. "Oh, man, I missed you so much, I'm so glad to be back."

"I missed you, too. So much! It's been awful without you." Carley ushered her friend into the living room. "Sit down. Want some coffee? Tea? Lemonade? A sweet roll?"

"Nothing, will you stop it! Sit down!"

They settled at opposite ends of the sofa, for a long moment silently gazing at each other.

"You are so tanned," Vanessa remarked. "And you look fabulous. What's going on?"

Carley waved her hands dismissively. "The B&B, I guess. I really like running it, Vanny, and it's keeping us afloat financially. I mean, I'll never be rich, but we'll be okay. But tell me about you! About this!" She gestured toward Vanessa's bump. "Where's the father? Who is he?"

Vanessa hesitated. She folded her hands protectively over her belly. "Okay. You have to promise not to scream."

"What?" Carley demanded, almost screaming. "What's wrong with the father?"

"Carley."

"All right. I'll be good." She made a zipper-closed motion across her lips.

"Just listen, okay?"

Carley nodded without speaking.

"After the—what I call the *explosion*—I went to Boston to stay with Diane Wells, an old college friend of mine. She has a fabulous apartment on Beacon Hill. She runs an art gallery. She went to work every day. I mostly lay on the sofa and watched stupid television. I did go for walks. I did see the city. I didn't totally stay inside and lick my wounds, but I was devastated by Toby leaving me for Maud. I was kind of paralyzed. You understand, I think you went through something like that when Gus died."

"You're right. I did."

"Well . . . Diana likes the night life. She's never married, she's very chic, and she loves getting dressed up and going out. We went to lots of plays and movies. We went to concerts in the band shell on the Charles; I'd always wanted to do that. We went to lots of fabulous cocktail parties. Actually, I couldn't have stayed with a more perfect person, I met so many people, some really nice people, and important, too—"

Cut to the chase, tell me about the man, Carley wanted to demand, but she confined her impatience to wiggling her foot.

"—and it was fun to get dressed in city clothes again, and Diana loves being single and I began to see a way of life I thought I might like."

"Oh, no." Carley couldn't stop herself from saying, "don't tell me you're selling your house and moving to Boston."

"Don't interrupt. My point is, how can I phrase this, I wasn't perhaps in what people would call my 'right mind.' I was sort of mentally all over the place. I was getting divorced, and I'd lost Maud and you. I wasn't *grounded*. I *had* to go out with Diana, she wanted me to, she was only trying to cheer me up, so I went to parties, and then I, um . . ." Vanessa hesitated, frowning. She squeezed up her eyes and her shoulders, as if preparing to be hit.

"Vanessa, what? You met a man?"

"I met some men." Vanessa peeked through her eyelashes like a child.

"You met some men."

"Well, not all at once, of course."

"What are you even saying?" Carley demanded.

"I mean, I had a fling."

"A fling?"

"Well, two, actually. Listen. I met two different men. I don't mean at the same time. I mean I had dates, and dinner, and I liked the guys, but not enough to get serious, not that I'm in any state of mind to get serious. But I wanted to feel attractive. I wanted to feel *wanted*. So . . . I slept with them. Once each. And to my surprise . . ."

"Wait. Slow down. Did you see either man more than once?"

"No. By the time I discovered I was pregnant, they were long out of my life. Not that they'd ever really been part of it." She hugged herself. "I've always wanted to have a baby."

"Honey, I'm happy for you. But Vanessa, come on, which man is the father?"

"Don't know."

"Oh, good grief."

"Don't be a prude. It wasn't like there was a cast of thousands. It was two different men over a two-week period. The last thing in the world I expected was to get pregnant. I don't *get* pregnant. I never did with Toby."

"Yes, but Vanessa, it's important to have information about the father's genetic history—"

"Look. I liked the men. They were nice. They were diverting."

"Diverting!"

"Hey, don't think that's insignificant. My husband had left me for one of my best friends. I deserved to be diverted. And anyone who could divert me was pretty special." Vanessa clasped her hands together. "Just listen for a minute, will you? I slept with two different men. They had all their teeth and they wore suits and spoke well and ran with a civilized crowd. They were nice guys. Afterward, they didn't call me and I didn't call them. I wasn't hurt or mystified or anything. I kept going out with Diana at night and lying on the couch in the day, wondering what to do with my life." Vanessa paused. "Then I started throwing up." She crossed her arms over her belly. "But I thought—I thought it would end. I was horrified, but I was also a little bit hopeful."

"Oh, Vanessa."

"I didn't think I could carry a child. It seemed all I could do was wait. I stopped going out so much. I bought groceries and cooked for Diana and we watched old movies together. It was a good place to wait. A good way to wait."

"Did you see a doctor?"

"Not right away, no. I didn't even take a pregnancy test. Not at first. I was so sure it would end."

"How long has it been?"

"Eighteen weeks. I went to an ob-gyn two days ago. The baby's healthy."

"When's the due date?"

"February ninth." Vanessa's eyes misted over. "Oh, Carley, I want this baby so much."

Carley reached over and took Vanessa's hand. "I'll do anything I can to help you."

"Really? Then don't give me grief about the father, okay? I didn't give either man an opportunity to make a decision to be in my life. In this baby's life. I don't want either man in my life. One— don't you judge me!—was too young." A mischievous smile lit up her face. "The other was so sweet and lonely, like me. He was separated from his wife, hoping to go back to her. I hope he gets to. He was a good guy."

"But Vanessa, how can you raise a child alone?"

"Lots of women do it. Some men, too. When my mother died, she left me some money, not a fortune, but almost. So I've got money. I got the house in the divorce." Vanessa readjusted herself on the sofa so that she was almost kneeling toward Carley. "But the main thing, Carley, the important thing is—I won't be *alone*. I realized that when I was in Boston. I've got you, and I've got so many other friends, not as close as you and Maud were, but still good friends. Like Lauren. And the teenager who lives next door to me, Jenny, she will make the best babysitter. I have always loved Jenny and her parents and her mother knows *everything* about children. Plus, I'm on so many boards on the island, and no one has said, 'Oh, well! If your husband's left you for another woman, you can't play with us.' Instead, they've been very supportive, asking me over to dinner, that sort of thing. I haven't been raising children on the island, but I have been *doing* good work that has helped the town. People *like* me, Carley. I may not have a husband any longer, and I never had a sibling, and my parents are both gone, but I still have a home. I *belong* here." Vanessa's face was childlike with radiance.

"It's true," Carley agreed. "You *do* belong here, Vanessa."

"Oh, Carley." Vanessa pulled her hand away from Carley's and dug in her purse for a tissue to wipe her eyes. "Thank you. That means so much to me." She blew her nose, then lifted her chin, somehow seeming both sweet and defiant. "It may be selfish of me to want this baby for myself. But I've never wanted anything more. Nothing has ever felt so right."

"I'm glad for you, Vanny." Carley was tearing up, too. "I'll help you every step of the way."

"I'm going to have a baby," Vanessa whispered in awe, and for a few seconds while time glowed around them, the two friends sat smiling at each other.

"Oh, I'm really happy." Vanessa gave herself a little shake. "I have a board meeting this afternoon. It will be my first official public appearance as a divorced, pregnant woman."

"Have you told Toby?"

"Gosh, no, why should I? He's absolutely one place where I don't belong. Look, Carley, I have tons to do, but would you come over soon and help me organize a nursery? I need to go slow, something could still go wrong, but it has been four months."

"I'd love to," Carley assured her. "And when the time gets closer, I'll give you the *best* baby shower."

"Oh, a *baby* shower for *me!*" Vanessa burst into tears again. "Sorry, sorry. I think I'm a little hormonally swamped these days." She stood up. "I'll call you tonight, okay?"

"Absolutely. Congratulations, Vanessa."

30
·····

A baby.

After Vanessa left, Carley returned to Scallop to finish her work, but her mind floated with memories of baby bliss: the soft, fragile head, the wide trusting gaze, the warm snuggly little body. The smell of perfect sweetness. The little fist waving, the soft squeaking sounds during nursing. The dawning recognition, the first miraculous smile.

A baby. She'd always wanted another baby. Seeing anyone else's baby sent her into a cooing fit of baby greed. Was there possibly another baby waiting for her in her future? A baby with Wyatt? The thought was too important to go near. And the timing was wrong.

At the moment, she had two daughters who needed her attention, not to mention guests arriving early this evening.

The girls came home from school, full of their own gossip and concerns, craving bananas and juice. They piled into the car so Carley could drive Cisco out to Lauren's for her riding lesson.

"I'm staying longer today," Cisco informed Carley. "Lauren told me she's going to show me how to muck out the stalls."

"There's a thrill," Carley murmured.

"It is! If I can learn to do things right, Lauren says I won't have to pay for lessons. I can work instead. I'll be able to spend more time riding. Also, I'm getting good enough and some of the horses know me well enough, I'll be able to help the youngest novices by leading them around the ring."

"That's impressive, Cisco. I didn't realize you've become an expert."

"Oh, Mom, I'm not an *expert*," Cisco laughed, happily. "But I am becoming capable. The cool thing is that I'm not afraid of the big horses, like other girls. See, it's easy to think the ponies are safer because they're small, but ponies really are the troublemakers. They love to nip and buck and tear around, they're like yappy little dogs. The big horses, like Blue, have a more mellow personality."

Carley had never learned to ride, and she was a little wary of the big beasts Lauren hauled around like giant puppies. But she was glad Cisco had found something else to give her heart to.

When they arrived, Lauren strode out of the barn, an equestrian goddess in jodhpurs and riding boots. She led a huge gray horse that looked to Carley to be about ten feet tall.

"I thought you might like to see Cisco ride Blue awhile," Lauren said. "She's really coming along."

Margaret slipped her hand into Carley's and squeezed next to her, eyes wide at the sight of the big horse.

Cisco followed Lauren and the horse into the ring. She stroked the horse's neck and talked to it, then Lauren gave her a leg up, and Cisco was in the saddle, straddling the enormous beast. With a slight squeeze of her legs and a click of her tongue, she urged the animal to a brisk walk around the ring.

"Cisco's a natural," Lauren told Carley as they leaned against the fence. She noticed Carley's face. "Don't be afraid. Blue hasn't ever bucked or thrown anyone."

"He's huge," Margaret whispered.

"Yes, he is," Lauren agreed. "But he's eleven years old and the sweetest old guy on the planet." To Carley, she said, "Did Cisco tell you I'm considering having her work for me?"

"She's going to yuck out the stalls!" Margaret said.

Both women laughed.

"The thing is," Lauren said, "I hate charging you for Cisco's lessons, but it costs a fortune, keeping this place going. Not just feed and vet bills and maintenance, but keeping the tack cleaned and grooming the horses. If Cisco really gets into riding, it's something that could last her a lifetime, and she needs to learn everything. She could be helpful to me at the same time."

"I have to tell you," Carley admitted, "Cisco's not the biggest fan of cleaning house."

"That's different. That's her home. Here she's made herself very useful. Let's at least give it a try, what do you say?"

"I say a big fat thank you! Lauren, I'm awfully grateful to you for introducing her to riding. It's filled the void of ballet, and it's helped her move on"—she glanced down at Margaret—"in other ways."

"You and I have to agree that if it doesn't work out, our friendship will remain intact."

Friendships! What a minefield they'd become. "Of course."

Cisco had the horse trotting, and Lauren called out, "Thighs! Hands down!" To Carley she said, "Look how well she's posting already."

"Thanks, Lauren." She gave Cisco a thumbs-up. "What time shall I pick her up?"

Lauren checked her watch. "Give her three hours."

"Fine." Carley smiled down at Margaret. "Let's go to the grocery store." They headed back toward their car.

Some days Margaret eagerly went to The Boys and Girls Club or to a friend's house, but some days, for no obvious reason, she clung to Carley, sticking by her side no matter what odious task Carley had to perform. The counselor had advised Carley to go with this, not to make a fuss, not to urge Margaret to show up for T-ball practice, to act as if all were perfectly fine.

She picked up a glowing Cisco from riding, served her girls a healthy meal, pretended to eat something herself, and organized them for school the next day. She gave Margaret a bath and read her a story. She was actually invited to sit on Cisco's bed, listening to her daughter recount every clop and clip of Blue's adorable hooves.

She was thrilled by Cisco's happiness, but her mind kept returning to thoughts of Vanessa. And her body burned to be with Wyatt.

Russell and Annabel invited Carley and her girls to dinner every Sunday, but they sometimes gently refused to come to her house.

"I don't want you to take this personally," Annabel told Carley one rainy October afternoon when Carley picked up the girls after an overnight. "But when we come to your house, we feel the loss of Gus more intensely. It was where he lived, after all. It was his home. You've turned it into a place where *anyone* can live."

Keeping her voice polite, Carley reminded her, "The B&B is keeping us afloat financially. I could sell the house, of course, and buy a smaller place on the island, and then I wouldn't have to worry about money, but I don't want to do that. We all want the girls to have this house eventually."

Annabel sighed. Since Gus's death, she'd become even thinner, which made her look almost forbiddingly elegant. "I'm not sure about that anymore, Carley. Russell and I have been talking . . . perhaps we've put too much importance on being a Winsted. Certainly it seemed to cause Gus more pressure than anything else."

"Oh, I don't think—"

Annabel rose. "Let's continue this conversation on Sunday, shall we?" She seemed evasive and eager to have Carley leave.

What's going on? Carley wondered.

Sunday it was just the five of them around the table. Russell grilled out one last time, barbequing chicken. Annabel stirred up the girls' favorite casserole of macaroni and cheese. Carley tossed the salad and brought it with the bread into the dining room.

For a while the conversation was normal, centering on the girls' activities. Cisco sang the praises of Blue and the joys of mucking out stables. Margaret talked about her first-grade teacher, who looked like a fairy princess.

When dessert was served—an apple pie Carley had baked—
Annabel and Russell exchanged a glance laden with import.

Then Annabel steepled her hands and announced, "Russell and
I have an announcement. We're going to Guatemala this winter
with the church group. For six months. To help run their free clinic
and build houses."

Carley put her hand to her chest. "I'm stunned."

Annabel raised an eyebrow. "We're old, but still functioning."

"Annabel, don't be silly, that's not why I'm surprised. You and
Russell have always been such homebodies."

Russell spoke up. "That's why we want to go somewhere else.
We've been told that one way to deal with grief is to help those in
need."

"But the girls—"

"I think the girls will understand." Annabel looked at her
granddaughters.

"I understand," Cisco agreed with quiet dignity, sitting up very
straight. "When we were at Grandma's day care center, we met kids
with terrible lives. It's true, isn't it, Margaret?" Cisco turned to her
sister for confirmation.

In her high clear voice, Margaret added, "Some little kids didn't
have daddies. Some didn't even have mommies! Some didn't have
very many clothes—"

"Mom, we saw little children with really sad illnesses. And
Grandma and Bernice took care of them."

"You didn't tell me this," Carley said faintly.

Margaret hurried to explain. "We didn't want to make you cry."

"Oh, honey," Carley said, nearly crying.

"When do you leave, Nana?" Cisco inquired, sounding quite
grown-up.

"After Thanksgiving. We come home in May."

"Will you ride on a donkey in Guatemala?" Margaret's question,
and her mangling of the pronunciation of the country, made them
smile.

"We'll take our laptop, and I'll email you photos every week," Russell told them. "We can even talk live on Skype."

"Granddad, you are awesome," Cisco told him, and gave him a high five.

"Carley?"

"Hey, Maud." She'd been anticipating this phone call.

"I hear Vanessa's back on the island."

"She is. She came over last week."

"To your house?"

"Yes, to my house. She looks great."

"Someone saw her on the street and says she looks, um, like she's gained weight."

"She looks like she's pregnant, because she is."

"She's pregnant?" Maud's voice lifted with delight, and in that moment Carley forgave Maud everything on Vanessa's behalf, because Maud was so purely, spontaneously happy for Vanessa. "Who's the father? When's the baby due? Will she live here? Oh, how amazing!"

Carley laughed. "Listen, you could take a moment to ask me how I'm doing."

"Why? Good Lord, are you pregnant, too?"

"Very funny. I only meant it's been weeks since I've seen you. We haven't even spoken on the phone."

"Give me a break. I had book tours all summer, then Toby needed a vacation so we all went to the Adirondacks, then I had to get the kids ready for school. Would you come over for coffee tomorrow?"

"That would be great, Maud."

Wyatt arrived at Carley's at ten o'clock at night, when the girls were asleep. The moment he stepped in the door, he pulled Carley to him.

"God, I missed you." He kissed her fiercely.

She curled herself around him tightly, breathing in his warm male aroma, loving the swell of his masculine muscles, the length of his bones, the hardness of his body. She wanted to burrow right under his clothes.

"I guess you missed me, too," he whispered.

"Can we just go to bed?" she pleaded. "No, wait, I can't even make it up the stairs. Come into the den." She pulled him by the hand. "Don't worry. The door locks."

She pushed him down on the leather sofa and straddled him, running her hands over his cheeks, shivering at the prickles of his evening beard against her soft palms. She kissed his eyes, his forehead, his nose, cheeks. She brushed, then bruised his mouth with kisses. She nudged under his neck and down into the V of his button-down shirt. She was crazy for him, shoving herself against him, the cold metal of his belt buckle catching on her panties.

"Hey." Wyatt was smiling. "Slow down."

She couldn't. She unbuttoned his shirt, almost ripping off the buttons. She yanked her tee off over her head, and she'd purposely worn no bra. She unbuckled Wyatt's belt and unzipped his trousers, and then Wyatt wasn't smiling anymore, he moaned deep in his throat and rolled her over so that her back was on the sofa. He shoved into her. She held on to him as if she could never let him go. They were burning, sweating, panting, holding back, trying to hold back, needing to be this way together, locked together, joined, two beasts, two animals, two spirits, fused into one.

Later, curled together on the sofa, they caught their breath. After a moment, Wyatt said simply, "Wow."

Carley's face was pressed against his chest. "I want to have sex with you all the time. I hardly know what to do with myself."

His laugh was full and hearty. "I think you know exactly what to do with yourself," he told her.

They dressed and went into the kitchen to finish off the apple crisp Carley had made.

"How do you feel about Russell and Annabel going to Guatemala after Thanksgiving?" Wyatt asked.

Carley nodded. "Truly? I'm shocked. They've never done anything like this before. Will you be alone in the office?"

"Yes, but I can handle it. Winter's usually quiet. Although Russell and I have broached the subject of taking on a new partner. I think that's one reason they want to go away, far away. Without Gus, Russell has no one to leave the firm to. He's ready to retire. Ready to change his life."

"You're a partner in the firm," Carley reminded him.

Wyatt said, "Yes, that's true." He put down his fork and crossed his arms on the table. "It's complicated. Russell might retire, but he's active, vital. I can't see him not wanting to look over my shoulder. Can I carry the burden of Russell's expectations?"

Carley nodded. "I can sympathize."

"I could do it if I had you on my side."

Lightly, Carley responded, "You can have me on many parts of your body."

"Carley." His voice deepened.

She looked up, surprised by the tone in his voice. She pulled the neck of her robe tight.

"Carley, I've kept myself reined in for years. I loved Gus, he was my best friend, I would never disrespect him. You know I never came on to you. But Gus is gone. I'm thirty-eight years old. I want a life with you."

Carley didn't know how a person could be this happy and this sad at the same time without breaking apart. "Wyatt . . . it's so soon. *Too* soon. Gus hasn't been dead even a year. I can't get my head around this."

"I understand that. Although I was hoping you felt the same way . . ."

"I don't know how I feel." She shook her head to clear it. "The girls come first. Always. I have to consider their feelings."

"Of course. I love your daughters, too. I don't want to do anything to hurt them. But Carley, I want to *be with you*."

"Do you mean going out together?"

"First, of course. And staying in together, too. For the girls' sake, to let them get used to the idea. Marriage, eventually."

"Marriage." She took a deep breath. His gaze was intense. She slid off her chair, crossed her arms over her chest, and paced around the kitchen. "Annabel and Russell."

"We can't live our lives trying to please them."

"The girls . . ."

"I think the girls like me. I care for them. If we go slowly, they'll get used to the idea of us together." Wyatt came close to Carley, put his arms around her, and held her against him. "I've frightened you, and I don't want that. I don't want to pressure you. But you have to admit," he continued, confidently, "you and I have something pretty special together."

"True." She spoke against his flannel shirt. It was so soft and smelled so good, so clean. "But sex, well, it makes me think of Maud and Toby."

"We aren't hurting anyone."

She nodded, but her thoughts were in turmoil. She pushed

away. She walked away, the length of the kitchen. "This is so much, Wyatt. I do need to think. I do need some time."

He looked disappointed, but not defeated. "Yes, I thought as much. Carley, I'm going away for a few weeks."

"Where?"

"A friend's asked me to join him hiking down in North Carolina. I'm going to be really tied to the office when Russell leaves. I've got to take this opportunity to take a break. And to give you some time to think. That's why I planned this trip. Although I'll admit part of me was hoping not to take it."

A kind of pain sliced through her at the sight of this lovely man making himself vulnerable to her. On the refrigerator a picture Margaret had drawn in school depicted a family of three females, clearly Carley and her daughters, bright in colorful clothing, dancing in the flowers. It was two months old, but Carley didn't want to take it down. It was pretty, cheerful, and it gave her hope, this illustration of a widow and her fatherless daughters dancing, happy, enjoying life. Carley's heart felt torn in so many ways.

"When do you leave?" she asked.

"Not till the end of October. I'll go for a month. I need to be back before Russell leaves for Guatemala just after Thanksgiving. I'd like to be with you—and the girls—at Christmas."

"Christmas?" She put her hand on her forehead. "That seems so far away." She saw that response had disappointed him.

His eyes were solemn. "Life goes by fast, Carley." He approached her carefully, as if she were a wary animal. He kissed her lightly on the lips. "I'd better go home. It's late."

Carley walked him to the door, embraced him one last time, stood in the open doorway to wave good-bye as he drove away. She closed the door and her legs went right out from under her. Sliding down to the floor, she leaned against the door and hugged her knees. She was crying; she wasn't sure why.

She'd almost forgotten how much she loved Maud's house. It had begun as a basic ranch house, but over the years as Maud's books made money, she'd added wings and skylights and bay windows and nooks. Long shelves ranged throughout the house, holding all the treasures she'd bought whenever and wherever she found them to inspire her in her writing. Gargoyles, griffins, and ogres grimaced down next to fanciful fairies and angels. Of course there were mermaids everywhere—it was almost a mermaid museum. Shelves and walls held replicas of seals, sea lions, octopi, whales, sharks, fish, in addition to bowls and glass jars of every imaginable kind of shell. Wind chimes and small glass balls in swirls of color hung from the ceiling. Sun catchers turned the light into rainbows on the living room furniture.

Maud hugged Carley when she arrived. "I haven't seen you in forever."

"The summer just whipped past." The front door opened directly into the long living room. "Maud, let me just walk around first and look."

"Shall I make coffee?"

"I've had enough caffeine. Maybe some juice. Wait. You've changed your kitchen." She followed Maud.

Maud swept her arm around the spacious open room. "The boys are getting old enough to be interested in what I do, and Spenser especially likes art, so I've made a kind of arts and crafts area for them. It's a mess, that's why we never have people to dinner, but since Spenser's having trouble with school, I'm trying to open up new possibilities for him."

"I had no idea Spenser was having trouble with school."

"We thought it was dyslexia, but it's not that. It might be emotional, because Toby's moved in. He's stopped talking as much, he's sulky, he won't commit any time to school work, he won't *focus* on it. But when I get the boys going on art work, he zeroes right in."

Maud crossed the room and held up several large sheets of construction paper. Some were covered with colored pencil, some with glued papers and pieces cut out of magazines.

"Bizarre, right?" Maud shook her head. "It looks chaotic. Makes no sense to me. But it means something to Spenser and he freaks if I try to throw any of it out. When they were small, I did art work with the boys. I helped them 'write' their own 'books.' Perhaps this is kind of an extension of that."

"What do his teachers say?"

"They're working with us. They're good. He's got Anna Jane Krebs this year, and she's dynamite with boys." Maud crossed to her refrigerator and took out a bottle of juice. "Cranberry okay?"

"Fine."

Maud giggled. "I have to drink it since Toby. It helps prevent urinary tract infections."

"Are you having those?"

"Um, I didn't use to, back when I never had sex."

"Get out. Sex causes urinary tract infections?"

"It does in me. At least too much of it does."

"Too much sex?" Carley held up her hand. "Never mind. Don't tell me, please. Too much information."

"Poor baby," Maud cooed. "You'll have sex again someday, I'm sure."

Carley opened her mouth, then clamped it shut. Not until after Thanksgiving, she reminded herself.

They sat in the living room, talking about the children: Cisco and her newfound love of riding, Margaret and first grade, Percy and first grade, and at length about Spenser and his trouble at school.

Carley asked, "Does it help to be living with a pediatrician?"

"Not for this. This is emotional, we're pretty sure. I mean, we've had his eyes checked, and his hearing. He's not sick. The therapist thinks he's depressed and angry because it's really hitting home that his real father left and a substitute father has moved in."

"How does Percy get along with Toby?"

"He adores him. Loves playing with him, roughhousing with him, wants Toby to read him his nighttime story and tuck him in at night. But Percy never really knew his birth father."

"Families," Carley groaned. "They're like daily triathlons." Her eye fell on a captivating crystal statue of a child reading. It was placed in the center of the coffee table and had writing on it. She leaned forward. "Maud, what's this?"

"Oh, it's an award I won." Maud ducked her head shyly. "From the National Children's Library Association for best illustrated and written children's book."

"When did you receive it?"

"In August."

"Why didn't you tell me?"

"You were busy, I was busy . . ."

"You are such a dork! You should have told me! Congratulations! We need to celebrate. We need to have some champagne!" Her hand flew to her mouth. "Oh, you probably already celebrated with Toby."

Maud shifted uncomfortably on the sofa. Reaching out, she stroked the crystal statue, with affection, as if for courage. "Of course I did. I wasn't sure you'd even want to celebrate with me. Because of Vanessa, I mean. Would you have wanted to come over and celebrate with me and Toby . . ." She let her voice trail off.

Carley sighed, "I'd have to think about that. It's going to feel awkward seeing you and Toby together socially, but I guess I'll get used to it."

"You'll have to. We're getting married next summer. We've

booked the church." Maud stood up and paced around the room. "It will be a small wedding, a large one wouldn't be appropriate, but I would love for you to be my matron of honor, except how can you be, when you're Vanessa's friend, too?" Before Carley could answer, Maud asked, "How *is* Vanessa? Tell me everything."

Carley caught her breath. On the drive over, she'd contemplated how much she should share with Maud about what Vanessa had told her. "Vanessa's good," she slowly confided. "She's pregnant. She's happy." She paused. "She's going to stay on the island. She realized when she was in Boston that she loves it here, and she has a community here, and friends."

"Do you think she'll ever forgive me? Do you think she'll ever let me be her friend again?"

"That's asking an awful lot of her, don't you think, Maud?"

"Yeah, I guess, but Carley, I *miss* her!" Tears shot into Maud's big blue eyes. "I miss *us*, Las Tres Enchiladas! We had such fun."

"Instead," Carley reminded her, "you have Toby."

Maud chewed a fingernail. "Carley, who's the father of Vanessa's baby?"

"I don't know. Not Toby."

"Please. I can count."

"Whoever the father is, he won't be involved."

"She'll need friends," Maud mused. "And think about this. When Vanessa has her baby, who's going to be her pediatrician? Toby's the only one on the island."

"I hadn't thought of that. Well, then, once she has her baby, Maud, she'll be so happy, her life will be completely turned around, the way it is when you have your first child. She'll probably be ready to forgive you by then."

"Especially," Maud grinned, "if she has a boy. I know all about boys, and you don't."

33
.....

Carley woke to the sound of rain spattering against her window. An autumnal chill had crept in overnight, and a wicked early October breeze batted bushes against the side of the house. Today would be a good day to bake cookies in addition to her breakfast sweet rolls. All three rooms had guests who very well might want to stay in the living room, reading, playing board games, and munching. She'd light a fire in the fireplace, too.

With cookies and muffins in the oven, she pulled on her raincoat and slipped outside. She'd set pots of geraniums and begonias around the edge of the garden to add bits of color. It was almost time to bring them in. On a gray day like this, the bright blaze of scarlet and coral would be welcome in the house.

She took shelter on her porch and stood for a moment, looking across the rain-drenched lawn to the waters of Nantucket Sound expanding into what seemed infinity, but which she knew ended at Cape Cod. She had always been reassured by that certainty, that even though she looked out at an endless horizon, a limitless ocean, there in fact waited for her the reliable southern shore of the Cape and the solid mass of the continent, a harbor, a shelter, a place with restaurants, libraries, hospitals, shops, and thousands of other people going on with their lives.

The wind swept the water into rippling waves. October would

be busy for the B&B, but November would be quiet, except for a little rush around Thanksgiving, and another around New Year's Eve,
and no one for all of January, February, or March. Many innkeepers
took this time for their own vacations, fleeing to Florida or the
Caribbean for the sunshine. She had made no plans for a vacation
for herself and the girls except to take them down to her parents for
Christmas. She didn't have the money for anything extravagant, although she could take them to Boston for a few days of museums
and movies on the big screen.

Carrying the plants into the house, she set them on the sink,
hung up her raincoat, and dried off the containers. Such clever
things people created: these pots looked like blue-and-white Delft
china but in fact were plastic, or vinyl, lightweight and durable. She
spent a while deciding just where to place them in the living room.

She woke Cisco and Margaret and got them organized for the
school bus. She drank a cup of fresh coffee while watching her girls
eat breakfast. Now that Cisco was riding, she ate well and looked
healthy. Carley not only promised her daughters to save some cookies for them for after school, she took the first batch off the sheet
and tucked them into their old beehive cookie jar to prove it. She
walked them down the drive to the school bus.

By the time she got back to the house, her first guests were up.
They were a young couple, serious birders, completely prepared for
the rain with all sorts of waterproof gear. From the Midwest, they
were excited about seeing shore birds, especially the oystercatchers
with their cute carrot-orange bills, legs, and feet. They talked about
terns, eider ducks, various gulls, including the delicate black-
hooded Bonaparte's gulls that Carley had never heard of and suddenly longed to see. It was fascinating to be around people who were
on this island not because of the sandy beaches and sparkling seas
but because of the bird population, and she felt so enlightened by
listening to them that she packed up thermoses of coffee and bags of
warm cookies for them to take out into the rainy day.

The birders left. Four other guests came chattering into the kitchen. They were all women, friends from college who'd decided to get away from it all for a few days. They were in their early fifties, Carley thought, good-looking, educated, active women.

As Carley served them breakfast, they discussed their plans for the day. One woman, obviously the leader of the pack, consulted her iPhone for hourly weather predictions, times the museums were open, and menus at different restaurants. As Carley set her fruit bowl in front of her, she looked up at Carley and announced, "What you've got at your table is a perfect cross section of middle-aged American women."

"Really. Wow." Carley leaned against the kitchen counter, crossed her arms, and asked, "How so?"

"Four women." The leader, with silver hair cut short and chic, pointed to each woman at the table as she spoke. "Divorced. Widowed. Happily married. Unhappily married."

Carley burst out laughing at the final category.

"You left out a category," noted the plump, creamy-skinned blonde who was divorced.

"Oh? What?"

"Never married." She had her own little instrument in her hand and held it up triumphantly. "Twenty-eight point nine percent of all women in Massachusetts have never been married."

"Yes," Silver Chic argued, "but many of them are young and will get married."

The gray-haired woman with adorable dimples waved her hand at Carley. "Do you have a moment? Sit down. Join us. What are you?"

Carley pulled out a chair. "What am I?"

"Divorced, happily married . . ."

"Oh. Widowed."

Dimples's hand flew to her mouth. "Oh, dear, I'm so sorry."

All four women made regretful noises.

"It's okay. It was almost a year ago. And I have two wonderful daughters."

"You are so *young*," Creamy Skin said. "And gorgeous. I'm sure you'll get married again."

"Well, she *could*," Silver Chic cut in, "but should she?"

"Statistics show that the happiest people are married men and unmarried women." This was from the brunette with a true hourglass figure.

"General statistics have nothing to do with an individual life," Creamy Skin insisted.

Carley agreed. "I have a friend whose husband left her. She'd always wanted children so she went off and got pregnant. She's very happy."

"My point precisely!" Creamy Skin nodded. "Women never get over the Cinderella myth. Marry the prince equals the happy ending. But that myth is outdated. In the modern world, women make their own money, own their own property, and have their own children."

"But perhaps that's too hard on the children," Dimples argued.

It seemed that everyone talked at once. Carley joined in, enjoying the frank debate, the give-and-take, and especially the way the other women offered statistics and information from books they'd been reading. She found herself wishing Vanessa was there. And Maud, too.

"Wait a minute," she interrupted. "Do you all live in the same town?"

"Heavens no," Hourglass replied. "We all live in different states. We get together once a year for a sanity break. Of course we talk on the phone all the time, but this is different. This is special."

"And we always choose a part of the country we've never been in before," Silver Chic added. "So we learn something new while we're together. And by the way, if we're going to see anything of Nantucket, we'd better get our asses in gear."

They asked Carley if she wanted to join them. She thanked them but declined, saying she had so much work to do. Really, she knew they didn't want her with them. Later, after they'd cleaned up and gathered their things, they went chirping off down the driveway in their bright autumn sweaters, full of plans, bossiness, suggestions, and laughter.

It cheered Carley to watch them. She missed her own little group, Las Tres Enchiladas. The mysterious chemistry that bonded friendship was not much different from that bonding lovers, she thought. It worked only with certain elements, certain people. Would she, Vanessa, and Maud ever get together again?

She cleaned the kitchen and put a load of towels into the wash. Cisco had transitioned between friends naturally, she thought. She was still friendly with Delphine from ballet, but they seldom if ever got together. She seldom saw Polo except at school, for which Carley gave thanks. Carley had seen the boy Polo was dating, a senior with a car and a reputation for getting drunk. Polo's crowd was what Carley's own mother would call "fast." Cisco's current obsession was with horses, so she saw all ages out at Lauren's. But recently she'd been spending some time with Jewel, the daughter of the man Lexi was dating. Carley was pleased about that. Jewel was a darling girl, well-liked, much-admired, smart, and for some reason, she preferred to be alone much of the time. But she seemed to enjoy Cisco's company, perhaps because Cisco liked to read, too.

Margaret's best friend was still Molly from down the street. Since preschool, the two little girls had been inseparable. Carley had tried to bond with Molly's mother, Millie, but while Millie was nice, she was staggeringly boring. She could talk for hours about which detergent or toilet paper to use; the first time they'd gotten together, Carley had almost believed Millie was pulling her leg.

It was different, finding a "best friend" as an adult, Carley thought. Life changes were so dramatic, some purely geographical— she'd lost touch with her best friend from high school back in East Laurence. Her sister, Sarah, would always, in a way, be her best friend, even though their lives were so very different, because Sarah had seen Carley grow up. She'd seen Carley at her most spoiled, tantrum-throwing, thumb-sucking, worst, and never had there been a moment when Sarah wouldn't put her arms around her and hug her tight. She rejoiced for Carley's happiness, too; she adored Cisco and Margaret. She was proud of Carley's persistence with the B&B.

Once, Maud and Vanessa had been as close to Carley as Sarah. Alone, Carley felt muddled in her thoughts. During past evenings with Maud and Vanessa, when they all tossed out their problems and brainstormed solutions, Carley had believed she was one of a trio of wise women. Back in the days of Las Tres Enchiladas, there had been no problem she couldn't solve or at least cope with.

Lexi was certainly becoming a close friend and their bond was strengthened by Cisco's friendship with Jewel. But it took time to learn to trust someone.

Carley sat at the kitchen table eating dinner with her daughters and feeling unpleasantly gloomy. Perhaps it was the chili and cornbread she'd made that was darkening her mood as much as the early twilight and the shorter, colder days.

In the past, she and Gus held a Halloween evening party for children and adults. Their huge old house was made for just such an event. They started off with chili, cornbread, hot apple cider, and pumpkin cake, served in rooms decorated with jack-o'-lanterns and ghosts. Each year, the party became more elaborate. The girls dreamed up all kinds of creatures to add to the atmosphere. They made spiders in cobwebs and bats with fangs to hang from the ceiling. They instituted a best adult costume and best child costume prize. Friends and relatives gave them creepy store-bought ghouls, monsters, and battery-operated demons with low maniacal laughs.

Carley wasn't sure she had the energy to organize such a party this year. But would it hurt her daughters if she didn't have it? Or would it seem disrespectful to Gus if they did have it?

She decided to ask them. "Girls, I have a question. Should we have our Halloween party this year?"

Cisco and Margaret exchanged glances.

Delicately, Cisco inquired, as if Carley were a little child, "Would you like to hold it?"

It was sweet of Cisco to be protective of her, Carley thought, and a little sad.

"Honestly, I'm not sure." She toyed with her napkin, thinking aloud. "Daddy's been gone for almost a year, and I don't think it would be *wrong* for us to have the party. I believe Daddy would want us to be happy, to enjoy life. Daddy always loved the party."

Cisco began to tear at a fingernail. Margaret bit her lip and rocked sideways.

"It used to be, not long ago," Carley told her girls, "that societies had strict rules for mourning. That's what we're doing, you know. We're mourning Daddy. Missing him. Being sad. A hundred years ago, we might have had to wear black clothes, and only black clothes, for an entire year."

"Ick!" Margaret exclaimed.

"There were other rules, like no laughing or running in public, that sort of thing. The mourning family had to be *decorous,* that means very dignified, Margaret."

"Why?" Margaret asked.

"I suppose to prove to the world that you were honoring the person who had died. That you were suffering his loss."

Cisco spoke up. "My counselor says that some groups don't get all weepy when someone dies. They have a party, they sing. They dance. They celebrate the life of the person who died. They give thanks because that person lived."

"That's true," Carley agreed. "I like that way of honoring the person who died." She was silent for a moment, gathering her thoughts. "Still, Halloween is such a strange kind of time."

"It's when the dead can cross through the curtain between death and life," Cisco offered. "We studied that in school."

Margaret's eyes went wide. "Will Daddy come see us?"

"It doesn't work like that," Cisco snorted.

"Those are silly ghost stories," Carley reassured Margaret, who was too young for a talk about All Hallows' Eve and All Saints' Day. She didn't want her younger daughter confusing thoughts of her father's death with creepy skeletons, ghosts, and things that went bump in the night. For that matter, Cisco, for all her sophistication at thirteen, was just as impressionable.

Carley changed tack. "We've always been so busy getting ready for our party that we've never had time to go to the parade on Main Street and the party at the Fire Station afterward. That might be more fun this year."

Margaret perked up. "I'd get more candy!"

Cisco brightened, too. "Could I go with my friends? Polo and Kyla and Holly and I thought we might go as rock stars. We all want to be Lady Gaga, she's the most fun, but Polo said she'd be Madonna, the young one, not the old one, and Holly could be Taylor Swift."

"Just don't tell me you want to go as Shakira," Carley teased.

Cisco rolled her eyes.

"But what about you, Mommy," Margaret asked. "Will you be sad if we don't have the party?"

"Oh, sweetie." Carley picked up her daughter and cuddled her on her lap. "I'll be happy, if you want me to be honest. I've got such a lot to do, it might make me crazy, trying to get things ready for a big party."

"I'm going to call Kyla and tell her!" Cisco escaped from the room, glowing with excitement.

"You and I can have coordinating costumes," Carley told Margaret. "Like you can be Sleeping Beauty and I can be the Witch."

"Oh, Mommy, you're not a witch!" Margaret protested.

"Well, then, what should we be?"

Margaret lit up. "I'll be the Good Witch of the East and you can be Dorothy!"

"Shouldn't it be the other way around? I mean, Dorothy is shorter than the Good Witch."

Margaret's face fell. "But I want to wear the pink sparkle dress and carry a wand."

"Oh, I see. It's decided then. I'll be Dorothy."

34
. . . . .

Her girls were in bed, sound asleep. Tomorrow Wyatt would leave on his hiking trip. Tonight he was here, looking disheveled and distracted.

"I only just finished the work Russell needed help with," he said, giving Carley an absentminded hug. "I hope he's going to do all right without me."

"Of course he will. He always has before." Carley led Wyatt into the kitchen. He wore a suit but his tie was undone, his shirt was rumpled, his hair mussed. "It's his business, after all, Wyatt."

"True. But Russell's in his sixties. He's lost his only son. He's excited about going to Guatemala, but I think he's really going because it's what Annabel wants to do. I've seen him have spells of shortness of breath. He has high blood pressure." Wyatt paced, running his hands through his hair. "I hope I'm not doing the wrong thing by leaving him alone for a few weeks."

"Would you like some coffee? Or a sandwich? Have you eaten tonight?"

"What? Oh, no thanks, Carley. We ordered in a pizza. I wouldn't mind a beer."

She took one out of the refrigerator, uncapped it, and handed it to him. Leaning against the sink, Wyatt took a long thirsty sip. She looked at the movement of his elegant throat. Everything he did turned her on. Just looking at him made her blood flame. This was terrible, insane, it was like being thirteen again and having a crush on a rock star, so reduced by emotions into a trembling mass of nerves and desire she was always on the verge of hysterical tears. But should she build a life on passion?

"Thanks, Carley. Wow. I needed that." He slumped into a kitchen chair and stretched. "I suppose I feel responsible for Russell and Annabel. I feel Gus would want me to watch over them."

Carley sat down at the other end of the table from Wyatt. "Wyatt, I love them, too. I'll watch over them while you're gone."

"Great. I'm glad they have you and the girls." Wyatt shrugged. "The funny thing is, I don't worry about my own parents at all. They're the same age, but they're both busy, happy, healthy—"

"They didn't lose a son."

"True. And they've got my sister and her kids. They're crazy about the new baby."

"Yes." Carley's thoughts turned inward. "Babies are pretty special."

"They kind of terrify me," Wyatt admitted. "Wendy's little girl is either screaming or sleeping."

"She's what, four months old? She'll change."

"Her face gets so red when she's mad. Almost purple. And the way she squirms—when I hold her, I'm afraid I'll drop her."

Carley said, teasingly, "Somehow, centuries of babies have survived men holding them."

Wyatt looked across the table at her and all at once, he was really seeing *her*. His smile faded and his eyes grew warm and solemn. He said, "Carley."

His look was like a magnet, pulling her to him. His gaze was eloquent, luminous with desire.

"I'm a dope," Wyatt said softly. "Rambling on about babies and work when I could be in bed with you." He stood up, walked around the table, and held out his hand. "Let me take you to bed."

For a while, it was like heaven. For a while, Carley's skin was like new spring leaves and Wyatt's breath and touch was the sun. Everything disappeared, all worries, all fears, all the niggling complications of daily life. She was lifted up out of the normal world into a warm, golden realm of ecstatic connection. They were the flame, heat, and blaze of a fire in winter. They were incandescent.

When they fell apart, they were both slicked with sweat. They lay beside each other, breathing deeply, and the afterglow of sated desire flowed through Carley like a drug. *I do love him,* she thought. *I must tell him, before he goes, that I love him.*

She glanced over. His eyes were closed. As she watched, he began to snore. He's asleep, she realized, and closed her eyes, and she, too, fell asleep.

In her dreams, her boat was rocking on a tossing sea. She came awake to see Wyatt scrambling out of bed.

"Carley, it's almost five in the morning." Wyatt reached for the clothes he'd left scattered on the floor.

Carley sat up, dazed. They'd never done this before, fallen so soundly asleep after sex. She'd always asked him to go home so the girls wouldn't see them in bed together. Margaret still often woke in the night.

She looked admiringly at Wyatt's long stretch of naked back. The bed smelled warm and sexy. She didn't want anything to change.

"I can't believe we fell asleep." Wyatt yanked on his boxer shorts, his suit pants, his shirt. Without buttoning it, he snatched up his shoes and socks and sat on a chair, putting them on, tying his shoelaces.

"Hey," she whispered. "Don't panic. Your plane isn't until this afternoon and you said you were pretty much packed." Yawning, she got out of bed and pulled on her robe.

"I'm worried about your daughters seeing us," Wyatt said. He stood up and pulled on his suit jacket.

She pointed. "You need to button your shirt."

She ran her fingers through her tangled hair and followed Wyatt as he hurried out into the hall and down the stairs. He felt in his suit pocket for his car keys and patted the breast pocket for his wallet, then nodded to himself. Clearly his mind was on the day ahead.

"Good to go?" she asked.

"I think I've got it all. I'll call you before I leave, Carley. I'm going to call you a lot. I doubt if I can call you every day, the cell reception is probably iffy out in the woods. But I'll try. You call me anytime, if you need to talk, if Annabel's driving you crazy, anything." He was less romantic and more practical, as if running down a checklist in his mind.

"Got it."

He put his hands on her shoulders. "Look, I'm sorry to rush off like this. I'll be back before you know it." He hugged her to him tightly.

Then he left.

Carley stood stunned. She felt more than alone, she felt wrenched in half. *Don't be ridiculous*, she told herself. *You just need coffee*.

She hurried upstairs to shower and dress, then went to the kitchen. As she started a new pot of coffee brewing, she organized her thoughts. She had three rooms full of guests and her own recipe for pumpkin-cranberry-almond bread to stir up and bake. As she set to work, she felt a flush of satisfaction. She was taking control of her day. Of her life.

35
·····

At first, Wyatt phoned Carley every evening, to ask how her day was, to describe the challenging trails of the forested mountains. Before he hung up, he always said, "I miss you." But as the October days briskly disappeared into November, things changed. He and his friend were roughing it with tents, backpacks, and heavy hiking gear. His phone calls became less frequent, briefer, and more casual.

Carley kept busy. It was easy enough to do, with her daughters' activities, helping Annabel and Russell get ready to leave, and running the B&B. She was planning for Christmas, too. She was doing everything she could to distract herself from thinking about Wyatt.

This Saturday morning, her guests were a beautiful blond German woman named Christine and her boyfriend Andre, and two eager-beaver married couples from Boston who had come down to do *everything* the Cranberry Festival offered. Carley served cranberry-raspberry muffins and pumpkin-nut bread. The Boston couples ate fast and raced away, but the Germans ate leisurely, appreciating the food.

"I like the way you talk," Margaret shyly complimented the woman.

"Do you? Would you like to hear us talk to each other in German?"

Margaret's eyes went wide. "Yes, please."

For a few minutes the couple spoke in German while Margaret watched in wonder, giggling, entranced. "When I grow up, I'm going to speak German!" she exclaimed.

"Would you like to learn some German words?" Christine asked.

"Yes, please."

"Here is how you say 'hello.' *Guten Tag*. It means 'good day'!"

Margaret tried to say it, mangling the pronunciation only slightly. While she spoke with the Germans, Carley watched Cisco, who was eating hurriedly, eager to get out to the farm.

Carley suggested idly, "Perhaps Lexi and Jewel could join us for dinner tonight. Or sometime."

"Cool," Cisco said, which was about as excited as she got over something that wasn't a horse.

For years Carley had simply dropped by Annabel's house without phoning. If she was there, Annabel was always ready to drop what she was doing and have tea or a drink and a nice long chat with Carley. On Main Street, Carley slowed in front of the other Winsted house. Annabel's Saab was in the drive. Should she go in?

She shut off her engine, climbed out of the car, and went up to the house. As she always did, she just opened the front door and stepped inside, calling, "Annabel? It's me, Carley."

No response.

For a paranoid moment, Carley wondered whether Annabel wasn't answering because she didn't want to deal with Carley.

"Hello, dear." Annabel appeared at the top of the stairs. She was still in her robe, and her hair hadn't yet been combed. "I've been lying down."

"I didn't mean to disturb you." She put her hand on the doorknob. "I'll go."

Annabel came down the stairs, slowly, holding on to the banister, like someone older than her years. "Stay, please. I'm glad you came. Goodness, it's after noon." At the bottom of the stairs, she just stood there, blank.

"Let's have some tea," Carley suggested.

"Good. Right." Annabel drew herself up straight but didn't move.

Carley went down the hall and into the kitchen. She put the kettle on, set out the teapot and cups, and checked for bread for toast.

Annabel sat down at the kitchen table. "I haven't been to the grocery store recently." A wry smile crossed her face. "A fat lot of good I'll be in Guatemala. Can't even feed myself."

"Give yourself a break," Carley suggested mildly. "I certainly spend a lot of time in bed these days." She found a box of shortbread cookies, set them on a plate near Annabel, and sat down in the chair closest to her mother-in-law.

"I don't have anything to offer you as delicious as your muffins," Annabel said. "I don't even bake anymore. I can't imagine how you do it all, take care of the children, bake homemade treats, and run a business. These days I don't seem to do anything worthwhile."

Shocked, Carley could see that Annabel was struggling to keep her dignity. Carley busied herself with the milk pitcher and spoons. The kettle whistled and she poured the water into the teapot. Bringing it all to the table, she was stunned to see the expression on Annabel's face. It was a terrible regret, and something about it made Carley say, "Oh, Annabel, you've always done so much. You're the best."

Annabel huffed. "Hardly."

"But it's true. You are." She sat down, reached out, and took Annabel's hand. "You are the best at everything, the best grandmother, wife, mother—"

Annabel withdrew her hand gently, but when she looked at Carley, her gaze was tender. "I haven't been a very good mother-in-law these past few months."

Carley didn't object. She waited.

"I allowed myself to care too much about the past. How things were in the past. I suppose I was too caught up in what it meant to be a Winsted." She looked at Carley and her eyes were weary. "I apologize, Carley."

"Thank you, Annabel. Your opinion means a great deal to me. And as it happens, the B&B's turning out to be a financial lifesaver."

"That's good," Annabel replied automatically, listlessly.

_____ took a moment to gather her thoughts. She wanted to so_____ mpliment the older woman without opening herself to mo_____ m. Carefully, she said, "It's true that Cisco wasn't thri_____ the B&B at first. Margaret loved it from the start, but Cisc_____ ving strangers in the house. You were a godsend to Cisc_____ er in with you."

A_____ ce brightened at the mention of her granddaughter. "I thou_____ eded a place to escape to. I thought she needed to leave y_____ t really. I always knew she'd come back to you." Annabe_____ er hands together and touched her lips, then confessed in_____ m afraid I love my granddaughters too much. I want to ke_____ oth locked in my house and never let them out, never let t_____ e street, never let Cisco back up on one of those enormous stallions—"

"They're not *stallions*—"

"Well, they look like it to me! That's how I felt about my son. Especially when he was a teenager, when he learned to drive, when he started drinking and having sex. Oh, sometimes, Carley, it's all just too hard! Too frightening." She covered her eyes with her hand. "That Gus died of a genetic heart defect—I feel so responsible."

"You shouldn't—"

"I worry even more about the girls."

"I never knew you felt this way."

"I've always felt this way. Thank heavens you're such a great mother."

A lump rose in Carley's throat. "I'm glad you think that."

"Of course I think that." Annabel gave a rueful little laugh. "I'm sorry I've been such a bitch because you opened a B&B."

Annabel's language shocked Carley. "You weren't a bitch."

Annabel's mouth quirked. "Yeah, I was."

Neither of them had had a sip of tea yet. Carley poured both cups full, added milk and sugar, stirred, and sipped.

Annabel said, "Oh, I needed this. Thank you."

"I needed this, too," Carley replied.

Carley woke to see a flock of the most amazing scarlet and orange birds fly across the sky past her window. She thought: *I wish the birders were still here. They would flip out!*

More birds streaked past, and Carley blinked. They weren't birds. They were leaves. She could hear the muted roar of the November wind stirring the leaves, sending them spinning. She burrowed deeper into her pillows. It was Saturday. She was manning the baked goods table at the church fair and later she was taking Margaret and Molly on a hayride.

Cisco would spend the day at Lauren's, riding and helping with—

A strange and terrible thought struck Carley.

She no longer woke remembering exactly how many days it had been since Gus died. This was good, she supposed. A sign of healing. Still, it made her feel obscurely guilty.

Thanksgiving was held at Carley's house that year. Annabel and Russell had to concentrate on packing for Guatemala. Carley invited Vanessa, too, since she was alone. Vanessa had decided to tell everyone she'd gotten pregnant using a sperm bank, and after everyone got over their shock that sexy, gorgeous Vanessa would need to resort to something so impersonal, they accepted it. *Everyone* meant Vanessa's neighbors, the members of all the charitable organizations she was on, the minister, the mailman, and Annabel, Russell, Cisco, and Margaret, although when Carley told Margaret, she used creative metaphors.

Vanessa offered to help, but Carley ordered her to sit and put her feet up since she was in the seventh month. Annabel and Russell came late, preoccupied with their approaching adventure. As Carley listened to them talk, she secretly thought: only a few more days until they leave. Only three more days until Wyatt is back on the island.

36

. . . . .

Lauren and Frame always held a holiday party after Thanksgiving. Their basement rec room was set up for kids of all ages, with plenty of chips and eggnog and Christmas cookies, while the upstairs dining room table was laden with Lauren's family's special rum-plus eggnog, champagne punch, shrimp, spicy meatballs, and scallops in bacon. One of the kitchen sinks was stocked with ice and beer.

Wyatt was due back two days after the party. Carley was sorry he wasn't going to be there. She'd bought a dress on sale at Moon Shell Beach that made her look pretty great, even if she admitted it herself. It plunged a little in the front and a lot in the back. It clung to her when she walked, and it was scarlet. It was more than she'd ever paid for a dress, but she gave it to herself for her birthday. She'd made a resolution that she would do this every year. After all, *someone* had to spoil her.

She bought her daughters new outfits, too, to wear to the party. Margaret's was all pink, with beads and sequins. Cisco's was white with a little white crocheted sweater. Her figure was blossoming, Carley noticed with a plunge of sadness. Her little girl was turning into a teenager. Jewel arrived, went straight to Cisco's side, and started whispering and giggling with her.

The party was a crush. Food and drinks were set out in the living room and kitchen and even out on the porch, where some of the die-hard smokers sneaked out and stayed out in the cold to talk.

Carley leaned against the dining room buffet, chatting with anyone who squeezed through the crowd to get to the eggnog.

"Delicious, isn't it?" Beth Boxer asked. Beth was part of their general mommy group, a humorless woman, but a careful, loving mother. Beth wore a green silk dress completely unsuited for her olive skin, Carley noticed. Beth needed a fashion makeover. Actually, a personality makeover would help, too.

Carley licked her lips. "Yum. I always drink way too much of it, but it's the only time of year Lauren makes it."

"Don't drink too much," Beth cautioned. "If you gain a pound, you won't be able to fit in that dress anymore."

From anyone else, this would be funny, but Carley caught the undertone of bitchiness. Before she could reply, Beth lobster-pinched Carley's arm.

"Look! Maud and Toby!" She was squinty-eyed with malicious glee.

"I think Lauren invited Vanessa, too," Carley told her.

"What fun!" Beth snickered. "Maybe we'll get to watch some fireworks."

Carley couldn't help it. "Beth, if you want a catfight I think you're going to be disappointed. Maud and Toby are happy, and Vanessa's happy, too."

"Oh?" Beth's voice was suddenly sweet as sugar. "I'm so glad. So you've talked with Vanessa. Tell me, who's the father of Vanessa's baby?"

Carley dropped her head back and laughed. "Truthfully? I have no idea." She left the eggnog table to greet Maud and Toby.

"Happy holidays," she told Maud, kissing her cheek.

"Carley, what a dress! You look fabulous."

"So do you. Come get some eggnog."

Maud linked arms with Carley as they headed back to the dining room. Toby joined some men near the bar for a proper drink. More and more people were crowding into the room, so Carley had to shout to be heard and strain to hear what anyone else said. Dreadful Beth had gone into another room. Carley swooped down on a platter of smoked salmon and fixed herself a small plate. She navigated to a corner with a group of feisty older women who'd gone as a group to Europe and regaled her with hysterical anecdotes.

She felt a touch on her shoulder.

"Hey." Vanessa was there in a white dress that spread over her pregnancy, making her look like a sail in a full wind. "You missed our anticlimactic scene." She wore her grandmother's pearls. Her dark hair swooped up, showing off heavy pearl earrings and a swan's neck. As ever, she looked amazing, even at seven months' pregnant.

"Tell me." Carley took Vanessa's hand and led her to some chairs in the corner.

"Actually, I phoned Toby and Maud last night," Vanessa confided. "They each were on a phone, so I told them I wanted to go to this party, and I didn't want to create a scene or cause Lauren any discomfort, and besides, we all live on the island, so I wanted to be civilized."

"Good for you, Vanessa!"

"Well, not so very good." Vanessa chuckled. "Toby said fine, he would like to be civilized. Maud went all gooey. 'Oh, Vanny, I want to be more than civilized, I want to be friends again, blah blah blah.' I said, 'Up your ass.' "

Shocked, Carley said, "You didn't."

"I did. It felt *so* good. Maud went completely silent. Then I said, 'Anyway, now that I'm pregnant by a man with a penis long enough to get some sperm up inside me'—Toby's penis was perfectly fine, I just needed to get a dig in—I'm happy and willing to live in peace. So when I see you two at the party, I'm going to be pleasant, okay?" She looked back through the hall to the living room. "I just got here. I stopped and said hello to Toby, who went red when he said hello. I nodded to Maud, who crinkled her eyes up the way she does and kissed my cheek."

"Beth Boxer must be so depressed. She was hoping for a catfight."

"I'm sure she wasn't the only one." Vanessa readjusted her bulk on the chair. "I never can get comfortable these days."

"I remember how that was. You've always got a little foot sticking up into your rib cage."

"More like a big head pressing on my bladder." Vanessa chuckled, then held up her hand. "Don't make me laugh."

"What are you doing for Christmas?"

"Diane's coming down from Boston. She's never been on the island at Christmas, and she's alone, too, so we'll keep each other company and roast a turkey—and hit the sales after the twenty-fifth! Are you going down to your parents'?"

"Yes. The girls can't wait."

"What about your B&B?"

"It will close for a few days, then I've got it booked for New Year's Eve."

"New Year's Eve." Vanessa looked pensive. "Carley, do you ever think about other men?"

Carley smoothed her dress over her thighs, hiding her face from Vanessa. "Oh, I guess, if I'm truthful—"

"I need to sit down!" Rosy-cheeked and out of breath, Lauren threw herself into a chair next to Vanessa. "That's it. No more high heels for me." She kicked them off and rubbed her foot. "Women are so insane."

"This is a fabulous party, Lauren," Carley told her friend.

"Thanks. Secretly, I wish some people would leave. It's too crowded, and it's almost midnight."

Carley looked at her watch. "I had no idea it was so late." She stood up.

Lauren clutched her wrist. "Carley, don't go! I didn't mean *you*."

"I've got to get the girls home. Cisco has riding lessons tomorrow. She'll be a bear if she doesn't get eight hours of sleep." Bending down, she kissed Vanessa and Lauren on the cheek. "Thanks, Lauren. See you." She waggled her fingers at both her friends before slipping through the crowd toward the basement stairs.

Cisco was playing Ping-Pong with Delphine. Margaret was on the sofa, watching a video with the other little kids, her eyes drooping.

"Come on, love bug," Carley said. "Time to go home."

Margaret was drowsy, almost limp. Carley called Cisco, hefted her little girl in her arms, and they went up the stairs and out to the mudroom where Cisco dug through coats and helped Carley get Margaret into her fluffy white fleece jacket and hat.

At the house, she got Margaret mostly undressed before tucking her into bed. Cisco had climbed into bed with her clothes on and was snoring. Carley went into her own bedroom and stood for a moment looking at herself in the mirror. She really did look great in the dress. She hung it carefully on a padded hanger. She pulled on her comforting flannel pajamas. She brushed her hair and smoothed some moisturizer on her face. She was so tired, she almost didn't hear the knock on the front door.

Her heart thudded with alarm. She wiped her face, pulled her robe on over her pajamas, went down the stairs, and opened the door.

Wyatt. Wearing khakis, a blue button-down shirt, and an old leather bomber jacket with fleece cuffs that made him look so sexy she almost keeled over. His brown hair obviously hadn't been cut for weeks and curled over his ears and shirt collar. His skin was flushed with a healthy tan from a month outdoors, and his smile blazed.

"Wyatt! You're not due back for two days."

"I couldn't wait. I flew back early. I've called you four or five times. You never answered your cell."

She stared at him, stunned. She couldn't think. Her *cell?* She'd turned it off sometime in the afternoon and left it on her desk in her office when she went into party mode with her daughters.

"Look. Can I come in? It's cold out here. And I want to kiss you."

"Me, too." Smiling, she held the door open.

Wyatt stepped inside, shut the door, reached out, and drew Carley against him. He held her tight with both arms, stroking her hair, cupping her hip with one hand and her head with the other. She felt

the rise and fall of his strong chest against her cheek, the warm stir
of his breath against the top of her head, the firm muscles of his back
beneath her hands. They fit together perfectly.

He took her face in both hands, tilted her head back, and kissed
her for a long time.

He pulled back, looked at her, and said, "Carley. God, I missed
you."

She put her hands on his chest to steady herself. "I missed you,
too."

He said, "Could we go upstairs?"

She said, "Yes, please."

She cried when they made love.

Wyatt raised himself up on his elbows. "Am I hurting you?"

"No," she assured him. "I'm just so happy. This is so . . . rich."

Afterward, she lay on her side, Wyatt against her, his arm curled
around her waist, his hand resting on her abdomen.

"That was nice," he said.

She laughed deep in her throat. "Nice."

"But that's not all between us." He tugged the down comforter
up over her shoulder.

"Yes, I know that."

"We have fun together doing other things. Things not in bed."

She pressed her back against his chest, loving the warmth.
"That's true."

"And I like your daughters."

Her heart stopped beating. Here it was, time for a decision. She
wasn't sure she was ready to make it.

"I did a lot of thinking while I was hiking, Carley. I don't want
to move too fast for you. I don't want to upset or confuse your
daughters, but what would you think if you and I started openly dating?"

Dating. The word lowered the volume on her anxiety. This would help the girls get used to Wyatt's presence in their lives gradually.

"I think it's a good idea." Thinking it through aloud, she said, "People in town will gossip. What about Annabel and Russell?"

"They leave in three days for Guatemala," Wyatt reminded her. "What do you think?"

"They're pretty overwhelmed with getting ready. I think it would kind of pressure them or even panic them to make them deal with this so close to their departure. Let's wait until they've had some time in Guatemala. We can email them." She cocked her head. "Or does that seem cowardly?"

"No, it's good." Wyatt shifted, turning on his side, pressing against her. "What about Christmas?"

"Christmas?"

"I'd like to spend Christmas with you and your girls. I'd like to get your girls really nice presents."

"We always go to my parents' for Christmas, Wyatt. It's a family thing. We've made plans to go this year."

He was silent for a long while. He cleared this throat. He shifted on his back. "Okay. Well, a friend has invited me out to Hawaii for Christmas. I wasn't planning to go. I was hoping to be with you."

"We'll be home before New Year's Eve," Carley told him. She swiveled around, so that her head was on his arm, her hand on his chest. It was too soon to invite him to her parents'. Surely he must understand that. "Let's have a little Christmas for the four of us before we go to my parents and you to Hawaii, okay?" She felt his chest rise and fall as he sighed deeply.

"Okay." He took her hand in his. "You know I'd like to sleep with you all night, Carley. I'd like to wake up and have breakfast with you and the girls. I'd like to live with you. But I'll stick to your timeline."

"Oh, Wyatt, thank you for that." She nuzzled against him, kissing the side of his neck, and soon they forgot all about words and Christmas and plans.

In a flurry of lists, packing, good-bye parties, and last-minute visits
to the pharmacy, Annabel and Russell left for Guatemala. Carley
and the girls drove them to the airport and the small plane that
would fly them to Boston for the first leg of the trip. They all kissed
and hugged a thousand times. They waved and waved when the
Winsteds' flight taxied down the runway. It was a cloudy, windy day,
but Carley and her girls stood outside looking up at the sky, watching the little plane ascend, head to Boston, and disappear.

"Lexi, can you meet me for lunch?"

"I'd love to, but I've got to keep the store open. Here's an idea—
can you stop by Annye's and get some salads and sandwiches?"

"Absolutely!"

It cheered Carley, thinking of walking into Moon Shell Beach,
but when she entered the store with her bags of food, she was surprised to see how stripped down it was.

Lexi noticed her reaction. "End of season, honey. It's worth
keeping open until Christmas, because some people wander in looking for a present, but after the twenty-fifth, it's dead here." As she
talked, she cleared a space on her counter for the food and gestured
to a stool like the one she sat on.

Carley hung her coat and shoulder bag on a hook in a changing room. She climbed up onto the stool. "What will you do when you're closed?"

"Tris and I are leaving right after Christmas for Bali."

"Bali!"

"I love it there! The sun, the white-sand beaches, and the water is *amazing*. There are minerals in the sand that swirl, making these gorgeous free-form designs. I relax and get ideas for my shop. The silver work and the textiles—"

Carley forced a perky look of interest as Lexi raved on, but inside she felt melancholy. When Lexi stopped to catch her breath, she asked, trying to sound casual, "How long will you be gone?"

"Only three weeks. Back by the end of January. But then we're taking off again in February, during school vacation. We're taking Jewel to the Caribbean."

"Cool."

"Carley." Lexi put down her salad and straightened on her stool. "This is a shit time for you. You lost your husband and started a new business. You're raising two young children by yourself. You don't exactly have the most helpful friends in the world, and I lump myself in with Maud and Vanessa. But we all have times like that. Things will get better."

Carley tore off a bit of bread and chewed it thoughtfully. "Annabel and Russell are gone. It's the first time I've ever been on the island without them around."

"Do you feel a bit lost?"

"Not *lost*, no." Carley took a moment to consider her words. "But I'm beginning to think that, in a way, I've lived my life as if *performing* for Annabel and Russell. Certainly I kept their opinions in mind whenever I made a decision. Annabel was my role model. She was who I wanted to be."

"Annabel is charming."

"Yes. But more than that—I'm not sure how to express this. It was their conviction that *the meaning of life* resides within the home and family. I guess I just feel a bit daunted by this sudden change of theirs, this flight to Guatemala." She shrugged. "The truth is, it's kind of turned my world upside down."

"Carley, your world is already spinning like a snowball."

"Ha! You think?"

"I think it's great that your in-laws are gone. Good for them, first of all, and even better for you. This town is enough of a fishbowl without having your relatives watch your every move."

"That's true." Carley knew a crazy jack-o'-lantern grin was spreading all over her face. "Lexi, I want to tell you something. In fact, you're the first I'm telling. Wyatt and I are, well, seeing each other."

Lexi squealed. "Oh, Carley!" She hugged Carley, jumping up and down like a schoolgirl. "Oh, I was hoping that would happen, I *thought* that would happen. Wyatt's a truly good guy. When he looks at you, Carley, well, he seems absolutely smitten."

"We're both smitten," Carley admitted. "And I'm terrified."

"Of course you are. You've been on an emotional roller coaster. Don't look so worried. Enjoy this honeymoon period. It seems we're always rushing toward the next thing. Women think marriage means *the* happy ending, and believe me that's not true."

"You're right," Carley agreed solemnly. "The thing is, Lexi . . ." She took a deep breath. "What if I'm really in love with Wyatt?"

"Savor every minute of it," Lexi advised.

Carley and the girls were going down to New York to her parents'
for Christmas, but Carley still put up a Christmas tree and decora-
tions, still made sugar cookies shaped like snowmen and bells, still
filled the house with the music of choir boys' angelic voices and the
triumph of trumpets. She wrapped the banister to the second floor
in fresh greenery tied with red tartan bows and hung mistletoe
everywhere. She probably always would, even when she was eighty
years old.

After the Christmas Stroll this weekend, no guests were booked
for the B&B until New Year's Eve, but to her surprise, a number of
her summer guests sent her Christmas cards, wishing her happiness
and good health and thanking her for making their vacation on the
island extra-special. She even received a completely unexpected
present from Melody, the woman she'd driven out to rescue in the
middle of the night. Too curious to wait, Carley cheated and opened
the package—a silver link bracelet from Tiffany's! As Carley fastened it on her wrist, she thought: *I helped that young woman. I provided safety, comfort, and even wise advice.* A small sun of pride
bloomed in her chest. She allowed herself a moment to feel it there,
glowing.

Several of the guests mentioned in their cards that they'd love
to have the recipe for her cranberry muffins or blueberry tarts. *I*

could put together a cookbook to sell, Carley thought. Maud could il-lustrate it! What a fun project to work on during the winter. By sum-mer she could have it ready!

The weekend of the Christmas Stroll the B&B was full. Three cou-ples, friends from Connecticut, had come to enjoy the weekend and shop for presents. Carley prepared a delicious egg, cheese, cream, and veggie casserole for breakfast that she served with cinnamon coffee cake shaped like a wreath, decorated with cranberries and homemade green marzipan leaves. She set out bowls of candied wal-nuts and platters of decorated Christmas cookies—reindeer, Santa Clauses, bells, stars, snowmen, and Christmas trees—in the living room and in the middle of the kitchen table.

At breakfast, Cisco balked at joining her and Margaret for the Christmas Stroll. "It's not that exciting for me, Mom, to see Santa Claus arrive by boat."

"Oh!" The guests all lit up. "Santa arrives by boat?"

Margaret answered fervently. "Yes, and Mrs. Claus is with him! And there are Victorian carolers, and kids get to talk to Santa!"

Carley stared at Cisco, daring her to not join her little sister when Margaret was so thrilled about the day.

"Wyatt's going to walk down with us," Carley said casually. "He's going to Hawaii for Christmas, so he wants to get in as much old Nantucket holiday spirit as he can before he leaves."

"Yay!" Margaret bounced in her chair. "Maybe he'll carry me on his shoulders so I can see everything!"

"Maybe he will," Carley agreed.

The guests hurried off to get ready for the day. Carley tidied the kitchen quickly, then raced upstairs to pull on a red wool sweater. She dug out her special holiday earrings, shaped like Christmas or-naments, and while she was admiring herself in the mirror, Cisco sulked into her bedroom.

"You look pretty." It sounded like an accusation. Cisco wore a baggy sweatshirt to camouflage her changing body. An adolescent zit blemished her chin. But she'd braided a section of her black hair with festive red and white ribbon.

"Thank you. You look pretty, too. I like the ribbon." Carley braced herself. She guessed what was coming.

"So Wyatt's going to the Christmas Stroll with us?"

"That's right." Carley sat on the bed and patted a place near her. "Come sit down."

"I don't think so." Cisco folded her arms over her chest. "Are you going out with him?"

Carley hesitated. "Yes. Does that bother you?"

Cisco made a face and dug her foot into the rug. "It makes me feel kind of funny."

"He's been a really good friend to us, Cisco. He's a nice man."

"Do you kiss him?"

Carley hadn't been prepared for this level of questioning so soon. She equivocated. "I'd like to. But I won't kiss him in front of you and Margaret."

Cisco narrowed her eyes. "Did you wait till Grandpa and Nana were gone before you started dating him?"

Well, damn, Carley thought. *When you grow up, you can work for the CIA.*

"Cisco, we are only going to the Christmas Stroll together. In the broad daylight. You weren't upset when we all went sailing with him this summer. What's the problem?"

"Nothing." Sullenly, Cisco left the room.

Wyatt arrived, wearing his bomber jacket and a Santa Claus cap that made Margaret squeal with delight. Margaret was a picture-book child in a red velvet coat and hat her grandparents had given her. The day was perfect, cold but not uncomfortably so; the sky was blue and for once the wind behaved itself.

"Cisco," Carley called up the stairs. "We're leaving." She bit her lip, praying, *please don't make an ugly scene.*

Cisco came lumping down the stairs, expressionless. "I'm ready."

"Hello, Cisco," Wyatt said.

To Carley's relief, Cisco offered him a lukewarm smile. "Hi. Nice hat."

They walked into town and joined the crowds thronging down to the wharf where Santa and his crew would arrive. The air shimmered with excitement. Elves, angels, wise men, and sheep adorned the windows of the shops lining the cobblestone streets. Carolers in Victorian dress sang out all the holiday classics. People wore red coats and green scarves, opera capes and top hats dug out of the attic, hats shaped like reindeer antlers or snowmen or Christmas trees. Laughter rang out like bells.

"Hello!" someone yelled.

Carley looked over to see Lexi, Tris, and Jewel weaving their way through the crush. Oh, good, she thought, Cisco will cheer up.

"Carley!" another voice called out, and here came Maud. She held Spenser's hand. Percy rode on Toby's shoulders.

Wyatt hefted Margaret up onto his shoulders so that Margaret and Percy could give each other a high five. Maud hugged Carley and whispered in her ear, "*Well, well.*"

Wyatt's presence with her family at this event was better than taking out a full-page ad in the newspaper: *Wyatt Anderson and Carley Winsted are a couple*.

A cry went up. The Coast Guard patrol boat motored up to the dock, bringing Santa and Mrs. Claus and the elves who would all ride up Main Street in a horse-drawn carriage. Carley joined the crowd cheering and applauding. Both her daughters were cheering and clapping, too.

Christmas Stroll was always magical. Main Street was blocked to traffic so people could stroll down the wide avenue, greeting friends, pausing to hear holiday music spill out of shop windows. Whimsically decorated stores offered mulled cider and cookies, Joe Zito and his enormous puppet Grunge sent the girls into giggling fits, and

Margaret got to ride the Dreamland Train in the library garden, while everyone waved. So much excitement, such a surge, so much to see and taste and buy! She had to admit to herself that the richness was deepened by Wyatt's presence.

In the evening, Wyatt brought Carley and her girls home and with a grin and a wave left to catch up on work at the office. Carley served her daughters an easy meal of homemade pot pies and apples. Exhausted by their day, both girls curled up on the sofa to read. Carley stood in the doorway for a moment, just soaking in the satisfaction of seeing her daughters safe, quiet, and together—they lay with their bare feet touching, like a pair of bear cubs in their cave.

The B&B guests were all out at dinner and a concert. Wyatt was coming by later. Carley went into her office and listened one more time to the message Vanessa had left.

"You'd better call me, Ms. Sneaky Pete. Or I'll sic Beth Boxer on you. She's already called me three times today!"

Carley put her feet up on her desk and settled in as she called Vanessa.

"Carley! How could you not tell me about you and Wyatt? I had to hear it from Beth Boxer!"

"Vanessa, slow down. We only took the kids to the Christmas Stroll."

"Oh, so you're not romantically involved? You were just going along together as friends?"

Carley chuckled. This was delicious. "Well . . ." She confessed. That she and Wyatt were in love, but taking things slow, with the girls and Gus's parents in mind. That yes, she'd gone to bed with him, and it had been bliss beyond words. Vanessa shrieked like a teenager. Carley purred.

"Marriage?" Vanessa asked.

"Don't get excited. It's too early for that." She changed the subject. "How are you?"

"You know, I feel *generous* these days, with my own nice baby kicking away inside. I don't really miss Toby. The terrible truth? I'm having a ball fixing the house the way *I* like it. Setting my own schedule, not always waiting hand and foot on him like someone from the eighteenth century."

Carley said teasingly, "Well, honey, enjoy it, because in about two months you'll be waiting hand and foot on someone else."

Vanessa's laugh was full and smug. "Bring it on."

39
·····

It was almost eleven before Wyatt arrived, looking rumpled and weary. She led him into the den where he threw himself down on the sofa, kicked off his boots, and moaned, "Just cover me with a blanket, I'm done."

"Have you eaten?" she asked.

"Eggnog and gingerbread during the Stroll."

"I'll bring you something a little more substantial." She handed him the remote control. She knew how helpful TV could be for relaxing, changing moods. She heated a homemade chicken pot pie in the microwave. It was full of white and dark meat, onions, carrots, celery, peas, and gravy, and the pastry was flaky and rich with butter. She set it on a tray with a beer and carried it to him.

"What smells so good?" Wyatt sat up straight, looking with amazement at the food. "Where did you get all this?"

"I made it, silly. We had it for dinner. I just happened to have one left over in case you were hungry."

"Man, this is just what I need. Real food." He tucked in, eating like a starving man, not stopping to talk or watch TV.

She sat curled up in a chair across from him, surprised at how she enjoyed the sight of this big man assuaging his hunger with her food.

When he'd finished, he said, "Damn, that was good, Carley. I didn't even make a pot of coffee this evening at the office. Russell left things in a hell of a mess. Don't mention this to anyone, please. I'm sure after he's had some time off in Guatemala he'll be back to his old self. Still, I admit I'm a little concerned. He left some tax matters unfinished. Not like him at all. I'm going to have to scramble to get the year-end work completed before I leave for Hawaii." He looked at her almost shyly. "Did your girls enjoy the Stroll?"

"They loved it. It was extra-special because you were with us, Wyatt. Margaret was over the moon because you rode her on your shoulders." She'd put a few fresh carrots on his plate, and he'd left one, so she reached over, took it, and chewed on it. Such an easy, intimate thing to do.

"Carley, I'd like to give your girls Christmas presents."

She sensed how careful he was being with her, not to rush her. She was grateful. "That's nice, Wyatt."

"What would they like?"

"Books. They're crazy readers. I could give you a list."

"That would be great. Want to have our little Christmas before I leave?"

"Oh." She thought for a moment. "The twenty-first?" She hadn't bought him a present yet, but there was still time. "Yes, why not?"

"Good." He stretched and yawned. "Want to have a little Christmas right now?"

For a moment she was puzzled. Then she got it. The girls were asleep, and all her energies strained to be with this man. She held out her hand. "Yes, please," she said. They left the den and went, hand in hand, up the stairs to the bedroom.

The morning of December twenty-first, the first sight Carley saw when she woke was beads of snow, like pearls from a broken necklace, spinning past her window. The window itself was shuddering from the impact of the wind. Before she'd raised her head off the pillow, she knew what the day would bring.

A blizzard. A blizzard with gale-force wind was on its way. For anyone on Nantucket, that meant: if you have to be somewhere else in the next two days, get off the island ASAP. Soon all the planes and boats would be canceled. Nothing could cross the Sound in a gale force wind.

Wyatt phoned while she was fixing breakfast.

"Carley, I'm going to have to leave this morning. I'm going to fly to Hyannis while the planes are still going, take the bus up to Boston, and spent the day there so I can make my plane to Hawaii tomorrow morning."

"Are you sure the planes are still going?"

"Just checked. The fast ferries are canceled, but the slow boat's going. But I'd rather be bounced around for fifteen minutes in a plane than two hours on the boat. Look, I'm sorry, I'm going to miss our Christmas party this evening."

"Don't worry about it, Wyatt. We can trade presents when you get back. Just get yourself off the island while you can! Have a fabulous time." Deep inside her, another, passionate voice called: *Don't go, Wyatt! Stay with us!*

Wyatt was in a rush. "Thanks, Carley. I'd better go pack. Wow, listen to the wind. I'll call you."

Carley clicked off the phone and stood for a moment, shocked at how disappointed she was that she wouldn't see him tonight.

40
· · · · ·

Both girls, at different times, had emotional meltdowns during the Christmas season. They missed their father. They wanted to buy gifts for him, they wanted him to take them ice skating and sledding. Carley cried with them, held them, and said the most consoling words she could. Yet it was not consolation that staunched their weeping, it was, finally, sheer exhaustion. One night Carley slept in Margaret's bed, curled around her. One night she slept with Cisco, a rare and restless treat—Cisco kicked like a horse in her dreams.

At her parents' house over Christmas, most of the time was spent, as always, in a relaxed rambling around, but one afternoon Marilyn and Keith took Cisco and Margaret off to a movie, which allowed Carley time alone with her sister and Sue.

They made hot chocolate and curled up in the living room. Both women wore jeans and turtlenecks adorned with the Christmas necklaces, bracelets, and earrings Cisco and Margaret had created for them from kits. Sarah held her Yorkshire terrier, k.d., in her lap, and Sue held lang. Both dogs slept deeply—they'd enjoyed plenty of Christmas feasting.

"Well, kid," Sarah said to Carley, "how are you, really?"

Carley hesitated. "Mostly okay, I think. I worry about the girls missing their father. I worry about making decisions without another adult to help me." Carley stirred her hot chocolate with her finger. Suddenly she couldn't restrain herself. "Oh, Sarah, Sue, I really need to talk to someone, I think I'm losing my mind!"

"Why?" Sue asked.

"I think I'm in love with Wyatt Anderson!"

Sarah and Sue stared at her.

"For clarification," Sue calmly stated, "this is Gus's best friend?"

"Yes. I've been, um, seeing him. For a while. Since August, actually." Talking about it made something within her wake up, come alive. "Oh, Sarah, Sue, he is totally magnificent! He's smart and kind and funny. We have the same sense of humor. We talk for hours . . ."

"And sex?" Sarah asked.

Carley hugged herself. "Sex with Wyatt is like nothing I've ever experienced. It is absolutely earth shattering." She bit her lip. "Am I *awful*?"

Sarah asked, "Were you sleeping with Wyatt when Gus was still alive?"

"No!" Carley sat up straight. "Of course not!"

"Then why would you even wonder if you're awful? It's been over a year, Carley."

"Just barely. And it's complicated."

Sarah ordered, "Start from the beginning."

Carley told them about the week both her children and her in-laws were gone. The summer. The heat that made everyone want to lie around naked. The sense of loneliness and freedom. Maud telling her she looked like an old farm woman. The dress from Moon Shell Beach. The evening at the Boarding House, and Wyatt walking her home. It was *delicious*, talking about it, reliving it.

"All right," Sarah said calmly when Carley had finished. "Tell us why in the world you think it's wrong."

Carley squirmed. "It's happening too fast. It's too intense. It doesn't seem *right* for me to feel this way so soon."

"Carley." Sue's tone was mild, rich with affection and wisdom. "It seems to me that at our age, at your age, we've seen enough life

to know that if fate offers us a chance of happiness, we should take
it. Look," Sue pressed, leaning forward, "every day at the hospital,
Sarah and I see how life can change in a moment. Life is fragile.
Love is rare. Why would you deny it?"

"The girls. I worry about the girls."

Sarah spoke slowly, thoughtfully. "I see where you're coming
from. I love Cisco and Margaret as if they were my own. I'd never
want to see them hurt. They're certainly always going to have to
live with the loss of their father. But they like Wyatt, right?"

"They do."

"You didn't mess around with Wyatt while Gus was alive. Wyatt
didn't kill Gus in some deranged frenzy in order to be with you. I
think that if you refrained from any public display of affection, any
sexy touching or gooey kissing—"

"—which would freak the girls out if you did it with *any* man—"
Sue interjected.

"—then they might actually see it as a good thing. They're already comfortable with Wyatt. Maybe you could just sort of slowly
slide into it."

"I want to do it *right*."

"*Right*," Sue said, "is a difficult concept. Other people's defini-
tions of 'right' almost kept us from being together."

"What are you talking about?" Carley demanded. "I remember
when you first met—Mom and Dad loved you from the start."

"Not everyone's as enlightened as your parents." Sue toyed with
the beads on her bracelet before admitting, "My family still isn't
comfortable with the fact that I'm a lesbian. My grandparents
haven't even met Sarah, not after all the years we've been together."

"Sue, I didn't realize. I'm sorry."

Sarah said, "Carley, remember Freddie Matson?"

"Who could forget him?" She explained to Sue, "Freddie was
the high school quarterback. Handsomest guy in the school. In the
town. I was only a kid, but I remember gawking at him as if he were
a movie star."

"Freddie trapped me outside after the senior prom and told me he didn't like it that I was playing for the wrong side. He offered to help me out. He tried to 'show me how a man does it.' He was sure that one good fuck from him would bring me over to the home team."

"Oh, gross! What did you do?"

"First I tried to joke it off. I argued. I shoved. He was determined and he was drunk and he was rough. I finally kneed him in the balls. My dress was torn. I had to walk home."

Carley was stunned. "Sarah! I never knew!"

"No one did. I didn't even tell Mom and Dad. I sat outside in the backyard until after midnight so they'd think I was having fun with my friends at the dance."

"That's awful."

"It's not unusual," Sue said. "I can't tell you the number of times a guy has said to me, 'Honey, someone as good-looking as you ought to be able to get a man.' "

Sarah continued, "As if being lesbian is being second-place. Carley, I've lost friends because I'm with Sue. I've been turned down for jobs."

"And apartments," Sue recalled. "Remember, when we were in nursing school, we wanted to rent that cute little apartment on Oak Street, and the landlady asked, 'What do you girls want with a one-bedroom apartment?' She told us to get out. She said she wouldn't allow any of that *nasty* stuff in her place."

"I never knew that," Carley said.

"I didn't want you to get upset. You were younger, my little sweetie-pie sister."

"Yeah, because I would have gone out and slugged those people in the nose," Carley fiercely declared.

"We still get discriminated against," Sue continued. "Not as much as we used to."

"How about at work?" Carley asked.

"Oh, work's fine with it." Suddenly Sarah laughed. "Except some of the doctors, the ones with the biggest God complexes, often hit on us or make remarks. It's part of the territory."

"What we're trying to say, Carley, is that it's not always easy, choosing to be with someone who isn't 'right' according to whatever rules society has floating around in the atmosphere. When Sarah and I decided to be partners, my parents were horrified. They had thought, all along, that I was in some kind of phase I'd grow out of. They refused to meet Sarah for years. When I told them I loved Sarah, that I was going to commit my life to her, my mother wept and my father went ballistic. He drove his fist through the living room wall. I love my parents. It broke my heart to upset them like that. It also made me mad as hell that they wouldn't accept me for who I am and meet the woman I love!"

Sarah leaned over to pat Sue's hand. "Deep breaths." To Carley, she said, "The point is I love Sue. She loves me. We've made a happy life together. I guess we're trying to say that other peoples' concept of 'right' or 'wrong' doesn't matter when you're in love. What matters is the love."

"I hear you." Carley studied the faces of these two women who were as perfect a married couple as any she'd met. She cared for them with all her heart, and she didn't need to say it aloud. They knew it in the depths of their hearts. "I appreciate your advice."

"It's easy to give advice," Sarah said. "You and Wyatt have very big decisions to make."

41

. . . . .

With a whine of engines and a roar of backward thrust, the plane touched down on the runway. Carley and her girls were home. Along with the other passengers, they yelled, "Hooray!" People almost always did when the small planes landed safely after a bumpy flight over turbulent water.

They waited for their luggage—they'd had to borrow an extra suitcase from Carley's mother for all the clothing they'd bought in New York—then hurried out to the car. As they were all fastening their seat belts, Carley's cell rang.

"Carley?" It was Maud. "Listen, you need to go by Vanessa's. She fell."

"Oh, no! Is she okay?"

"Pretty much. Just shaken up. Sprained her left wrist, it's in a sling. Twisted her ankle."

"The baby—"

"The baby's fine. The doctor checked. I took her to the hospital—"

"*You* took her to the hospital?"

"Well, *you* were in New York. Lauren and her family are off-island. It was down to Beth Boxer or me. What a choice, right?" Maud chuckled. "She said she had to decide whom she hated less, me or Toby, and chose me. I went over, got her up off the floor, drove her to the emergency room. Drove her home. She's fine, a bit shaken up, and she'll probably need someone to cook her dinner or something for a few days."

"I'll bring her home," Carley decided. "We'll swing by Vanessa's now."

"No!" Margaret wailed. "I want to see Molly!"

"No!" Cisco echoed. "I want to go to Lauren's. I haven't ridden for days! Blue will be missing me!"

"Lauren's not here, remember?" Carley reminded her daughter. "Come on, it won't kill you to have a little Christmas spirit. Vanessa *fell*."

Vanessa's house was, like many island homes, a handsome old Greek Revival, narrow and long, with staircases to four floors of small rooms. When Carley opened the front door and went through the entrance hall, she found Vanessa collapsed on the sofa in the living room. A pair of crutches lay on the floor next to her.

"Vanessa, you poor thing!"

"I'm disgusted with myself." With difficulty, Vanessa shifted upright. She gestured toward the Christmas tree, surrounded by boxes half full of ornaments. "I thought I'd be efficient and take the tree down. It's so dry, the needles are falling all over. It's a fire hazard. So I was up on the ladder when I lost my balance. *Boom*. What an idiot I am."

From behind her, Cisco asked, wide-eyed, "Is your baby okay, Vanessa?"

"The doctor says it's fine. I'm only going to have a bruise on my bum. Good thing it's so big. It gave me a soft landing."

Margaret giggled.

"I can't use my wrist or ankle for a while," Vanessa continued. "How did you find out? Did Maud call you?"

"She did. We just got off the plane. Literally. We're going to take you to our house and pamper you."

"Not necessary. Really."

"But we *want* to, Vanessa!" Margaret insisted, patting Vanessa's arm. "We'll bring you hot chocolate and everything!"

Vanessa smiled. "Well, there's an offer I can't refuse." Slowly, pushing with her good arm, she sat up. "I'll go up and get a nightgown and my toothbrush."

"You stay here," Carley told her. "I'll get them."

On the way to her house, Carley considered just where to establish Vanessa's home base. Angel's Wing was empty, but it was a few steps too many from the rest of the house, it would seem they were sticking her out there on her own. Carley decided that since Vanessa couldn't climb stairs without difficulty, the den was the best place for her.

At home, her daughters raced up and down the stairs, bringing sheets, pillows, towels, and a down comforter into the den when Carley was setting up Vanessa's private lair. They moved the coffee table so that it served as a bedside table for water, books, and tissues, wheeled the TV around so she could watch it.

"You guys are so good," Vanessa praised, tears in her eyes. "I hate for you to go to all this trouble."

"Are you kidding?" Carley hugged her friend. "This is fun. Just prepare yourself for endless games of Chutes and Ladders!"

Margaret ran off to Molly's, Jewel arrived and secreted herself with Cisco in Cisco's bedroom, and Carley set about the business of unpacking and getting the house back to normal. Since Vanessa, an adult, even if an injured one, was in the house, she ran out to the store to stock up on groceries. And to phone Wyatt, who'd gotten back to the island the day before.

"We're back!"

"How was it?"

"Super. I'll tell you all about it tonight. Can you come over? I'm going to make chili, and we can have our little Christmas, oh, and guess what, Vanessa's staying here."

"What? Why?"

Carley explained about the fall and how they'd tucked Vanessa into the den.

Wyatt was quiet for a moment. "Um, then, should I get Vanessa a Christmas present, too?"

She was shocked to feel a childish twinge of jealousy. Ashamed of herself—how sad would it be, for everyone to exchange presents and poor Vanessa to get nothing, like a Dickens orphan?—she replied, "Wyatt, that's such a thoughtful suggestion. You really are sweet. Yes, get her something. A book would be perfect. Some nice juicy novel."

"Okay. What time shall I come over?"

"Six?"

"Great. See you then."

Wyatt walked in the door that evening, set a bag of presents on the floor, looked at Carley, and her heart absolutely melted.

"Come here." He pulled her into his arms.

"I missed you." Her words were muffled by his kisses.

He nuzzled her neck and pressed her body against his. "Do we have to eat? Can't we just go to bed?"

She pushed away lightly, laughing. "Sorry. We'll have to wait."

He picked up the bag. "Presents." Mischievously, he grinned. "I got a really nice one for Vanessa."

"Oh?"

"A kind of bribe, actually. Maybe while she's here, you can come out to my house with me for a few hours." He leaned close. "I want to make you moan."

She went weak in the knees. It was true, they were cautious, unnaturally quiet, making love with the girls at the other end of the hall. Breathlessly, she whispered, "What a good idea."

Margaret came shooting down the staircase, all long legs and tangled hair. "Wyatt!"

To Carley's delight, Wyatt caught Margaret up and swung her around. The evening had officially begun.

Over dinner, the girls entertained the adults with details of their holiday in New York. Cisco didn't act surly at Wyatt's presence, and Wyatt seemed happy enough to be around the children.

After dinner, as they gathered around the Christmas tree, Carley couldn't decide whether she was glad or unhappy to have Vanessa with them. It kept them from seeming like a family, but perhaps that made her daughters more comfortable. Certainly Vanessa seemed comfortable. She wore black maternity trousers and a red sweater that made her skin glow and her eyes and hair shine. Pregnant and hampered by her injuries, she moved slowly, shifting her voluptuous body like Cleopatra on her throne. She was so sensual! It was hard not to stare at her magnificent bosom. By comparison, Carley felt absolutely *chipper*, like Nancy Drew.

The girls gave Wyatt a book about sailing that Carley had suggested they choose. Wyatt gave them books, too. He gave Vanessa the newest Leslie Linsley book on Nantucket decorating.

Surprised, Vanessa said to Wyatt, "I don't have a present for you. When I'm healed, you'll have to come over and let me make you a gourmet dinner."

Hey! Carley almost shouted, but then Vanessa swept her soulful gaze over to Carley, "*Both* of you, I mean. To thank you. You, too, of course, girls. You're going to be my number one babysitters, after all."

Carley gave Wyatt a white silk muffler that made him look like Orlando Bloom. Wyatt handed her a small velvet box.

Carley paused, biting her lip.

"Open it!" her daughters yelled.

It was a pair of antique ruby earrings, small and twinkling. "Wyatt, they're exquisite." She put them on. She gave him a chaste kiss on his cheek, then held her hair back and leaned over for Vanessa to see.

"What beauties," Vanessa said.

Margaret and Cisco were both yawning. They'd had a long day with the excitement of flying back from New York and settling in at home.

"Girls," Carley said. "It's time to get ready for bed. I'll be up in a while to tuck you in."

"Mom, it's early," Cisco protested.

"No, it's not."

"For vacation it is!" Cisco argued.

"Look. Get in bed and I'll let you read late. You need to rest."

That satisfied both girls. They took their new books, kissed Wyatt and Vanessa on the cheeks, and skipped upstairs.

"Vanessa, we have a favor to ask you." Carley lowered her voice. "After I'm sure the girls are asleep, Wyatt and I thought we might run out to his house for a couple of hours, to, um, do some things. I'd be back before midnight. Would you mind?"

Vanessa glowed. "I'd be honored."

Carley felt like a teenager as she and Wyatt sneaked out of the house and into his car, and it was exhilarating, after so much devoted good mommy time. As they rode out to Madaket, Wyatt raved about his time in Hawaii. He'd swum, surfed, hiked, biked—and he'd missed Carley.

Wyatt's cottage was basically two big rooms with a galley kitchen and a bath with only a shower at the side. The living room had a stone fireplace, a recliner, a plasma TV, a small dining table and a few miscellaneous chairs, and a woven wool rug. The longest wall held shelves of books, CDs, and his sound system. In his bedroom was a queen-size bed covered with a down comforter, a dresser, and a chair with clothes tossed on it. A very clean, very expensive dirt bike leaned against one wall.

He wrapped his arms around her as she stood in the doorway of the bedroom. "All the neighbors are summer people, not back for months. You can make as much noise as you want."

She twisted in his arms and looked up at him. "And so can you." She rubbed her body against his like a cat. Wyatt moaned, picked her up in his arms, and threw her on the bed.

They were in such a hurry to get all their clothes off, they nearly ripped apart their underwear. Afterward, they lay in a heap of rumpled sweaters and slacks, Carley's bra hanging off one arm. They sprawled in each other's arms, deeply content.

"We can't fall asleep," Carley warned. "I can't spend the night here."

"I know." With a groan, Wyatt pushed himself up. "I'll make some coffee."

Carley kicked her clothes on the floor and crawled naked between the sheets, pulling the comforter up. Cozy. What a delicious feeling, to have someone else bring her coffee! She could get used to this.

She plumped up the pillows against the headboard, and folded back the bedcovers for Wyatt, who returned with a cup of coffee in each hand. They settled in together, sipping hot coffee, talking, laughing, and the dark night air was velvet against their skin.

Carley talked about the holiday with her family, exaggerating her parents' eccentricities to make him laugh. She told him about discussing him with Sarah and Sue.

"They're right, you know," Wyatt said. He set his coffee on the bedside table and angled toward Carley. "We shouldn't waste time."

"I know," Carley began, "and yet, I'm still afraid of rushing things."

"I'm not." Wyatt gently touched her earlobe. "I didn't want to tell you in front of everyone else, but these earrings belonged to my grandmother."

"Oh, Wyatt!" Her hands flew to her ears. "But why didn't you give them to Roxie?"

Wyatt smiled. "Not her style. She only liked great big diamonds. Never mind Roxie. These were meant for you."

Carley twisted the earrings out and held them in her palm. With only the kitchen light illuminating the room, the rubies still glowed warmly against her skin. "I don't know if I'm ready for this yet, Wyatt. A gift of such importance. A family heirloom."

"Why not?"

"I'm not sure I can explain. It's been only a little over a year since Gus's death."

"Carley, what we have between us—"

"You've got to understand, Wyatt, I don't want to make a mistake. My daughters and I have been through a terrible, frightening, unexpected time. We lost Gus, and I worry that we're still rocky. I know that I love being with you—that is clear to me. But something—I don't know what—is holding me back now."

Warily, Wyatt said, "Are you worried that what you feel for me is temporary?"

Carley hesitated. "Maybe."

"Does this mean you want to see other people?"

"No!" She shook her head. "Wyatt, no! I just want to go a little slower. I just need a little more time." She touched his arm. "Please understand."

"Well, hell. I can't pretend this isn't a long deep knife slice to my ego."

Wyatt made his voice wry, and he twisted his mouth in a smile, but Carley could see how she'd hurt him and her own heart sank. "Wyatt . . ."

"It's a good thing I like to travel," he said.

"I don't mean for you to go away," she protested.

"You don't mean for me to stay, either." Tossing back the covers, he rose, grabbing his clothes up off the floor.

"Wyatt, I don't have to go home yet."

"Yeah, Carley," he said, and his voice was hoarse, "I think you do."

42
.....

It was the worst winter New England had experienced in years. Blizzards followed storms, sleet covered snow, snow covered ice. The sky was perpetually gray, funeral gray, the sun hidden by a layer of ashy clouds, preventing the brilliant sparkle of light on snow. The girls had snow days, which they loved at first, then became bored with. They built an entire snow family, a snow fort, snow *castles*, they went sledding and ice skating and watched their favorite DVDs, but they missed their friends and the routine of school. They grumbled.

Carley trudged along, trying to be a good mother, a virtuous widow, and in January it was easy to do, because Wyatt went off on another trip. "To visit friends," he told her, but he didn't tell her who the friends were, if they were male or female, where they lived, when he would be back. She supposed he was trying to give her the space and time she'd asked for, but perversely she felt as if he were punishing her. She missed him so much it made her mad at him, and for a week or so her anger kept her from calling him.

And he didn't call her.

"Am I an idiot?" she asked Vanessa one day.

"Yes," Vanessa said. "Totally."

"Thanks so much." They were in the living room, a fire blazing in the fireplace, a pot of cinnamon spice tea on the coffee table, its fragrance drifting into the air. Carley changed the subject. "Tell me, how did you feel when Maud came to help you?"

Carley had helped Vanessa take a bath—a particularly humorous operation since Vanessa was pregnant and had to keep one wrist and one ankle out of the water. While Vanessa soaked, Carley had freshened Vanessa's lair in the den, changing the sheets, folding the comforter, bringing in a fresh glass and fresh water. She tossed Vanessa's clothes into the washing machine, helped Vanessa dress in a clean version of maternity sweat pants and loose top, and settled her back on the sofa.

"I felt grateful, of course." But Vanessa's eyes were sad. "I mean, there I was, on the floor like an overturned turtle. I dragged myself around to get hold of my cell phone. I didn't feel bad enough to call an ambulance. My ankle hurt like holy hell and my wrist wouldn't work, but I couldn't tell if they were broken or what. I worried most about the baby, so I just lay there, trying to be calm. You were gone, so I phoned Lauren, but she was gone. I really had to pee, so in desperation, I phoned Maud. She said she'd come right over. After a while, I heard a car in the driveway and I thought, oh, darn it, the front door's locked. Then I heard her shuffling around and remembered she knows where I hide my key."

"Behind the drainpipe."

"Right. She opened the door like always and came in, and looked *aghast*. She cried, 'Oh, Vanny!' " All at once, Vanessa's face split into a huge smile. "She had to sort of *haul* me up and wrestle me out to the bathroom and then out to the car. Really, we both got hysterical laughing. Maud's so tiny and I'm such a hippo. She drove me to the emergency room. That new carpenter from Rhode Island was there, the one who looks like Johnny Depp, he'd broken his shoulder falling off a roof, but the point is, he is so hot—Maud and I looked at each other and it was just like old times. That *connection*. Reading each other's minds."

Carley nodded. The tiniest bit of hope trickled through her at the thought that her two best friends might one day be friends again.

"Maud waited while the doctor saw me. She drove to the pharmacy and got my drugs, and drove me home and stayed with me until she got hold of you."

"Why would you call Maud but not Toby? He's a doctor."

"I can't explain. I suppose it's irrational. Part of it's vanity, I guess. Toby left me for another woman. I didn't want him to see me wounded, incapable, maybe peeing down my leg. I was feeling like such an *idiot*, falling like that, and Maud's so funny, I knew she'd turn it into a comic episode." Vanessa looked down into her tea. "The terrible thing is, I think I've missed Maud more than I've missed Toby. Maud is more thoughtful than Toby. At least with me."

"Do you think you can ever be friends with her again?"

"Like Las Tres Enchiladas? Please. She did sleep with my husband."

"Well, here's a question. I want to put together a B&B cookbook, and I want Maud to illustrate it. Plus she does come over with her boys sometimes so they can play with Margaret. Would you mind if she's here when you're here?"

"For heaven's sake, Carley, this is *your* house! You can do whatever you want. Besides, I hope I'm not going to be here too much longer. My ankle feels better already."

"Don't rush it," Carley advised her. "I like having a live-in babysitter."

"Much good it does when Wyatt's not even on the island."

"It's all right, Vanessa. I need time to think. We both need time to think."

But she couldn't seem to find the time to think about herself. She had to go through the girls' wardrobes with them—they were both growing out of their clothes, getting taller. She took care of Vanessa, ran errands, and worked on her cookbook, testing recipes out on her friends and children. She sat down with Maud and brainstormed about how the cookbook should look. She tried to balance her karma by helping at as many community and school events as possible. When the dismal weather allowed, she drove out to Lauren's several times a week, where she stood shivering outside the ring, watching Cisco ride. She joined Vanessa, whose ankle had healed, for patient, plodding walks—or waddles, as Vanessa called them—on the beach. She shoveled snow.

In the back of her mind, she was thinking, but nothing had come clear to her yet.

After two weeks, she phoned Wyatt. He answered immediately.

"How are you?" she asked, trying to keep her voice light.

"I'm great. I'm in Stowe, at the Gray Fox Inn, having a nice hot toddy with some friends."

Carley heard laughter in the background. Female laughter.

"Have you been skiing?"

"Yes. And snowshoeing. It's phenomenal up here. The air is so clear and clean. Everything sparkles."

He didn't ask how she was. She told him, anyway. "It's kind of gray here today. We've had more snow than usual. The girls have gone sledding a lot. I'm working on a B&B cookbook with Maud."

"How's Vanessa?"

"She's just about ready to go back to her house. She's got to get the nursery set up. Her ankle is pretty much healed."

"Half the people sitting around here are in casts," Wyatt laughed. "We all think we can ski better than we actually can."

More female laughter in the background.

"Wyatt, I miss you."

A moment of silence. Then, "I'm glad."

"Do you know when you're coming back?"

She could almost see him shrug. "Nope. I check in with the office every day and do some business online, but January's a slow month."

As if work were the only magnet pulling him to the island.

Confused, dissatisfied, even cranky all of a sudden, Carley kept her voice calm. "I'll phone you again in a few days, okay?"

"That would be great, Carley."

"You can call me, too, you know."

"I know." Now she could hear him smile. "But I like it when you call me."

Toward the middle of January, Vanessa decided she was well

enough to return to her own house. Carley and the girls helped her move back all the belongings they had been gradually shifting to Carley's house, and over the next few days, they went back to Vanessa's to help her set up the nursery. She'd ordered a crib, a changing table, mobiles, car seats, diapers, blankets, and tiny outfits. Carley washed and dried the clothing, and the girls helped her fold it.

"Oh, Mommy," Margaret cried, undone by the sight of a little white romper, "can't you have another baby?"

Carley laughed. "Not by myself, I can't."

"Then marry Wyatt," Margaret said in a sensible, even bossy tone.

"Maybe he doesn't want to marry Mom," Cisco told her little sister. "He likes to travel."

Astonished, Carley wanted to clutch her daughters by the shoulders and demand whether or not they truly meant what they said. But the girls were so casual about it, so nonchalant. She reminded herself that here, right now, they were focusing on Vanessa and her baby. It wasn't the time for a serious conversation about Carley and Wyatt and marriage and new babies. The girls were just caught up in a mood; they could change their minds in a flash.

"Look at this," she said, holding up a soft, white, fleecy, bunny-rabbit bunting. They all cooed together.

43

. . . . .

Snow fell all through that late January night. When Carley woke, she found the earth sheeted with a brilliant white, diamonds glinting where the sun touched. The temperature had dropped, the wind had died down, but ice glazed the land and streets.

It was a Saturday. Riding at Lauren's was canceled. Carley and her daughters were in the kitchen. Carley was serving them big helpings of French toast when the phone rang.

"Carley? I'm in labor!" Vanessa almost squeaked with eagerness.

"Oh, Vanessa!" Quickly she counted: this was early, but only about two weeks early. "This is so exciting! Should you call an ambulance?"

"Oh, heavens no. But maybe you should drive me to the hospital? Ouch. Let's time this one. Here it goes."

Carley watched the second hand on the kitchen clock tick around.

"Done," Vanessa said.

"Fifty-five seconds," Carley told her. "I'll come right over. Is everything ready at home? Suitcase packed?"

"Yes. Should I call my midwife?"

"Absolutely. And keep timing your contractions. I'm on my way."

She was almost dancing with excitement. "Vanny's having her

baby! I'm going to go be with her. Cisco, you're thirteen now. Can I leave you in charge?"

Cisco nodded soberly. "Yes, Mommy."

"And you won't torture Margaret, right?"

"I'll play dolls with her," Cisco said, full of sweetness and light.

"When can we see the baby?" Margaret asked, eyes bright with excitement.

"Honey, I have no idea. It's different every time. Maybe ten hours, maybe more. But if the baby isn't here by this evening, I'll come home. You have your breakfast, and there's peanut butter and jelly for lunch and lots of milk and fresh fruit. If you have a problem, call Molly's mother, okay?"

"We'll be fine, Mom." Cisco promised. "You should *go*."

"Right," Carley agreed. "Right." She needed to get—what? What did she need? She was so thrilled she'd forgotten whether or not she was even dressed.

She was. She needed only to pull on her boots, grab her keys and coat and gloves, and run to the car.

Cisco stood at the door, arms folded like a boarding school matron. "Do you have your cell?"

Carley fished around in her purse. "I do. Thanks for reminding me. I'll call!"

She jumped into her car and started the engine with such exuberance it roared.

At Vanessa's Carley found the front door unlocked. Vanessa was sitting on a kitchen chair, legs spread, huffing and puffing.

"My water broke," she told Carley. "My midwife Kiki says I should go to the hospital."

"She's right." Carley knelt around Vanessa's chair, soaking up the fluids with paper towels.

Vanessa heaved herself up.

Carley's senses clicked on to hyperalert. She double-checked the kitchen appliances. Everything was off. She held up Vanessa's coat while Vanessa struggled into it. She picked up Vanessa's bag. She held on to Vanessa's arm while she made certain the front door was shut and locked.

As they waded through the heavy snow to the car, Carley put her arm around Vanessa's waist, supporting her, protecting her from a fall. Just before they reached the car, Vanessa crouched down, groaning. Carley held on to her until the contraction passed.

In the car, she hit the heat up to high and flicked her windshield wipers into action. For a few moments, she tried to help Vanessa stretch the seat belt over her girth, but it was impossible, and they both ended up giggling helplessly.

She drove with great caution to the small hospital on Prospect Street. She used her turn indicator even when there were no other cars on the street. She didn't go over twenty-five miles an hour. From experience, she knew where potholes hid beneath the snow, and she steered around them. Carley's nerves were jumping. The Nantucket Cottage Hospital was small, with only nineteen beds and seven physicians, only one a surgeon. In January, some of the physicians were off on vacation. Oh, why was she worried? Vanessa had been attending childbirth classes, and she felt safe and comfortable with Kiki. Besides, Vanessa was a big-boned woman. She would be fine. The baby would be fine. Still, this was an event of great magnitude. Carley thought she'd have to do some deep breathing herself.

At the hospital, she helped Vanessa into the emergency room where Kiki was waiting with a wheelchair. Carley parked the car in the lot, then raced up the one flight of stairs—the hospital had only two stories—to the maternity ward and into the labor room.

Kiki was a young woman with flowing red hair, brilliant blue eyes, and the low, even voice of a hypnotist. As Carley bustled around, folding Vanessa's clothing, Kiki helped Vanessa change into a hospital gown and paper slippers.

"She's already six centimeters," Kiki informed Carley. "She's moving pretty fast for a primipara."

"How long did it take you, Carley?" Vanessa asked. "I forgot."

"Cisco took twenty-seven hours. Margaret came screaming out like a freight train."

"Don't sit down," Kiki advised her. "Walk around. Keep moving. Or if you want to sit; try the rocking chair. It's comfortable."

"Twenty-seven hours?" Vanessa was aghast. "How did you stand it?"

"It wasn't all bad. I wanted to have natural childbirth. Gus rubbed my back, helped me breathe. All the things I'm going to do for you."

"What time did your contractions start?" Kiki asked.

Vanessa put her hand on the wall, waited through a contraction, then answered. "I'm not sure, really. All yesterday I thought I had the flu; I heard a stomach flu's going around the school. I had diarrhea. I couldn't get comfortable in bed last night. I think they started at midnight, really. But they weren't consistent or regular. About four a.m., they started coming every four minutes." She laughed. "I thought, 'Is this a contraction? What's all the fuss about?'"

"Is there anyone you want me to call?" Carley asked.

Clearly Vanessa was thinking of her ex-husband at that moment; her face went soft and sad, and her eyes, just for a moment, were full of regret. "Nope!" When she replied, she did so jauntily. "You're my man for the day, Carley. Hope you can deal with that."

"Las Dos Enchiladas!" Carley joked.

A contraction squeezed Vanessa and she grimaced. After a while, she said, "That one really hurt."

The next few hours passed slowly for Carley, as she watched Vanessa endure the increasingly strong contractions. The time came when Vanessa's legs shook too hard to support her, so Kiki and Carley helped her into bed. Vanessa lay on her side, absorbed by her labor. Carley rubbed her back. She spooned ice chips into Vanessa's mouth, which kept going dry from panting.

When Carley left the warm room to use the bathroom, it was

as if she'd stepped out into an enormous universe of sounds and healthy people, and it came back to her with a powerful body memory, how imprisoned she'd felt when in labor, how she couldn't get away from it for even a moment, how she couldn't just go for a walk or even *think*. She had been as much frightened as hopeful.

Around three in the afternoon, Kiki informed Carley cheerfully, "She's eight centimeters! Not long to go!"

"Want me to rub your back some more?" Carley offered.

Vanessa's face was blotchy from strain. "No." Vanessa was standing again, leaning her weight on the side of the bed. This time the sound she made was an animal howl. Her body shuddered.

Carley went around the bed and stood next to Vanessa, putting a hand on each hip, holding her steady, not unlike the time in high school when she supported a friend while she vomited into the bushes. Vanessa moaned in pain, an extreme noise that pulled at Carley's own gut, echoes of her own two labors and of the passionate cries of sex.

Vanessa slumped against the bed as the contraction ended. "I can't do this anymore. I had no idea it would be like this. I can't make it."

"You're close, Vanny. You can *do* it. Your baby's coming!" Carley felt almost giddy.

A knock came at the door and Kiki stuck her head in. "Okay, ladies?"

Kiki checked Vanessa. "Ten centimeters. You're going to have a baby."

Vanessa clutched Carley's hand and grunted. The grunt turned into a long high wail of pain.

"I can't do it!" Vanessa screamed.

"Vanessa, remember we talked about transition?" Kiki soothed Vanessa's forehead. "You're almost through."

A nurse came in—Roma Caruso, who had children in school

with Carley's and Maud's. Vanessa screamed and clutched Carley's hand hard enough to crack bones.

Kiki announced, "Here we go." She crouched beneath Vanessa's legs, hands up to catch the baby.

Vanessa began to push. Carley on one side and Roma on the other held Vanessa up as she shuddered and grunted from the depths of her being. Carley's heart raced, her skin was covered with goose bumps, the hair on the back of her neck stood on end.

Vanessa roared like a lioness. The baby slid out into Kiki's waiting hands. The umbilical cord was there, a pumping red rope. Vanessa's legs trembled. Her teeth chattered. The baby wailed. Kiki cut and clamped the umbilical cord.

"Help her back to bed," Kiki ordered. She was busy with the baby, drying him, wiping him off. Roma and Carley hefted a moaning Vanessa up onto the bed. She was still panting. Kiki wrapped the baby in a blanket and put him in Vanessa's arms.

Vanessa brought him to her breast, gazing enraptured at his tiny face. "Hello, baby boy, my darling, my own." Her own face glowed with joy.

"He's *beautiful*." The miracle of this new life sent shivers through Carley, and an age-old desire streamed through her blood. A *baby*.

With trembling hands, Vanessa stroked his limbs. "Look. All his fingers. All his toes. He's perfect." Her eyes were shining. "Carley, I *did* it!"

"You did." Tears blurred Carley's sight. "He's an angel."

Blotchy-skinned, sweaty-haired, radiant, Vanessa announced, "*Paul*. His name is Paul."

Carley touched his tiny hand. "Hello, Paul."

Kiki was pushing on Vanessa's abdomen.

"That hurts," Vanessa complained.

"We have to get your placenta out," Kiki told her. "Sometimes it hurts a lot, but not for long. Put him on your breast. Let him nurse. That helps the placenta come out."

Vanessa touched her nipple to the baby's mouth. It took a few moments, but at last he latched on. Roma took over massaging Vanessa's lower abdomen, pushing down, while Kiki was between Vanessa's legs.

The air of the room wavered as if struck by a rainbow. Carley was gently crying as she watched Vanessa with her baby, so tiny, so intensely alive to his new world.

Then Carley heard Kiki say, in a low, urgent voice, "Get Fegley."

"What's going on?" Carley demanded.

"The placenta's being stubborn. Doesn't want to leave the uterus. It happens. Just a little hitch."

Roma rushed off, quickly returning with Dr. Fegley. The physician was dressed in scrubs and a gown tied in the back, a cap over her hair, and goggles hanging around her neck, ready to protect her eyes from blood if necessary. Dr. Fegley pressed Vanessa's abdomen. She said to Roma, "Start the pitocin."

"But the baby's out," Carley said.

"The placenta isn't." Kiki gave Carley a look that made her heart drop.

Roma wheeled the stand with the pitocin bag next to the bed and hooked up the pitocin. She deftly inserted an IV into Vanessa's wrist. Kiki massaged Vanessa's abdomen, and Carley could see from the way the midwife's muscles bunched that she was pressing hard.

Carley stroked Vanessa's hair. Vanessa didn't seem worried . . . she seemed drowsy. *Fading.* Carley noticed, with horror, how much blood had spilled out of Vanessa, how much was still flowing.

Dr. Fegley was between Vanessa's legs. "*Placenta accreta.*"

"What does that mean?" Carley asked.

Kiki's smile was false. Her voice shook. "It means the placenta is abnormally deeply attached to the uterus. Perhaps through the uterus. We can't get it all out. It's torn."

Dr. Fegley barked, "Get her on blood. Bag her."

Roma raced out of the room. Another nurse flew in behind Roma and gently snatched the baby from Vanessa. "Just going to clean him up a bit."

In the second Carley looked at the nurse, Vanessa's eyes had closed and her face had gone slack. The doctor's hand was fully in-side Vanessa's vagina. Vanessa's head fell back against the pillow. Dr. Fegley ordered, "Call a code."

Roma said to Carley, "You have to leave."

"But I'm her—"

Roma gave Carley a commanding look.

Kiki said, "Carley. Go."

Carley left the room as nurses ran in. More people were rushing down the hall, into Vanessa's room.

"Please," Carley begged at the door, "tell me what's happening. Will she be okay?"

"I hope so." Kiki was white.

"She's bleeding too much."

"Dr. Fegley knows what's she's doing. Look, I've got to get back. Wait in the visitors' lounge. We'll tell you when we can."

Carley stood helplessly in the hall, burning with a need to be in the room, helping Vanessa. She couldn't go to the visitors' lounge and read a damned magazine!

She should call someone, she could call Maud, she should call Maud and Toby! She rushed out of the hospital where cell phones were not allowed and stood in the bright, cold sunshine, punching in Maud's number. Then she stopped. Was she calling Maud for her own selfish purposes, because she was frightened, because she couldn't face this alone? Was she being selfish, cowardly? Okay, fine, what if she was? She *was* frightened! She punched in the number.

"Maud, something's wrong with Vanessa. She had the baby, the baby's fine, but the placenta won't come out and she's bleeding too much. They've called a code."

"Oh, fuck. I'll call Toby. We'll be right there."

Carley wanted to sink to her knees in the snow. Instead, she looked up at the sky, a clear, cold, heartless blue. "Oh, God, don't let her die. Please, I'm begging you. Let her live."

She hurried back inside, shivering with cold and fear. Perhaps the crisis had passed. Instead of taking the elevator, she flew up the stairs and down the hall. She pulled open the door to Vanessa's room. All she could see were doctors and nurses and machines and blood.

"Out!" a nurse yelled, striding toward Carley, and she looked angry as hell.

The visitors' lounge was empty. Magazines and a bowl of plastic flowers lay on a table between two vinyl sofas. Carley went to the windows and looked out at the snow-covered landscape. The familiar world was as cold and white as the moon.

She saw Toby's Mercedes SUV streak into the parking lot. He jumped out and raced to the door. As a doctor, he could enter Vanessa's room.

Maud got out more slowly. Carley left the lounge and went down to meet her in the foyer.

Maud asked, "Where is she?"

"Upstairs."

They walked up slowly.

"Which room?"

"The first one, but it doesn't matter. They won't let us in."

"How's the baby?"

"Perfect. All digits accounted for."

"Were you with her when she gave birth?"

"Yes. I picked her up this morning around eight and brought her to the hospital."

Maud studied Carley. "You need something to drink. Coffee or a Coke. A hit of caffeine. Come on, I'll buy you something."

"I'm not thirsty."

"You are, you're just not tuned in to yourself." Maud put a comforting arm around Carley. "Vanessa's going to be all right. Stop catastrophizing."

"You didn't see how she looks. All the blood."

"Cut it out, you're being morbid. Vanessa will be just fine. There's always a lot of blood with childbirth." Maud fed two dollar bills into the soda machine and pushed a button. The machine clunked and whirred and dropped down a Coke. "Here. Drink this. You look like shit." She put more bills in and got herself a ginger ale.

Carley sipped the cold liquid. The sugar and caffeine hit her in a rush. She took a deep breath.

"Better?"

"Better."

"Don't you remember," Maud recalled with a smile, "when I was in labor with Percy, I squeezed John's arm and said, 'If you don't make this pain stop, I'll bite you as hard as I can.' "

Carley laughed. "But that was labor, Maud. This is different. Her placenta was torn or something, it wouldn't come out, it wouldn't detach from the uterus."

"Someone will fix it. Stop *shaking*, you're giving me the creeps."

"God forbid," Carley snipped. She looked at her watch. "It's been over thirty minutes."

"Finish your drink and we'll go back."

Carley swigged it all down like medicine, and it did give her a burst of energy. "Let's go."

They headed back up the stairs and down the hall into the maternity ward. No one was at the nurses' station. Everything seemed unearthly quiet.

Toby came out of Vanessa's room. He looked at Maud, and then he looked at Carley.

Carley began to whimper.

Toby was beside her quickly, reaching out to hold her. Maud was trying to hug her.

"Ssssh," Maud soothed, "ssssh, Carley, it will be all right."

"No!" Clutching Toby's jacket in her fist, Carley pleaded, "Toby, please, no."

"I'm sorry." Toby's face was gray. "We lost her."

Maud stumbled backward. "Oh, Toby!"

"We *tried*. They did everything they could. They tried to resuscitate her, they did *everything* right." He fell against the wall, covering his face with his hands, and gave over to a full-hearted sobbing.

Carley crumpled to the floor.

44

·····

She woke to find herself lying on a hospital bed. Toby and Maud, their faces tear-streaked, sat in chairs next to her, one on each side.

"You fainted," Maud told her.

"Is Vanessa really *dead*?"

Toby's face made words unnecessary.

"This is unbelievable." Slowly Carley sat up and swung her legs over the side of the bed. She felt dizzy.

"I'm going to call Walker." Toby put his handkerchief in his pocket and rose.

"Wait." Maud put a restraining hand on Toby's arm. "Who's Walker?"

"Vanessa's lawyer." Grimacing, he murmured, "She used him for the divorce and rewriting her will."

"Her will? How can you think of such a thing right now?" Maud demanded.

"There's a child to consider," Toby reminded her stoically, and left the room.

Carley stumbled off the bed and over to the sink. She splashed her face with cold water. Oh, *Vanessa*, how could she be gone?

When she dried her face, Maud took her arm. "Let's go back to the visitors' lounge."

Carley allowed herself to be towed down the hall. "Maud, my brain's stopped."

"Mine, too. It's normal, honey. And I can only imagine how Toby must feel."

"Maud—the baby!"

"Poor little thing." Maud's eyes misted over. "Oh, dear God. He has no relatives at all! What's going to happen to him?"

Toby approached them as they stood in the corridor. "I phoned Lauren. She's going to pick up the girls and take them to her house. Lauren's offered to keep the girls for dinner, overnight if you want."

Carley nodded. "Thank you."

Toby continued, "As for the child—"

Kiki came down the hall, her face reddened from grief. Twisting her hands together, she approached Carley. "I need to tell you something."

"All right."

Kiki closed her eyes, then quickly blurted, "Vanessa told me that if anything happened to her, she wanted you to take the baby. She left instructions with her lawyer."

Maud burst out, "No! *I* should take him! I have boys! Carley, you have girls!"

Carley stared at Maud. "Are you kidding? You took Vanessa's *husband*! She wouldn't give you her baby, too!"

"Vanessa did say Carley," Kiki insisted, her voice quiet. "You can ask the lawyer."

"He'll be here soon," Toby said. He put his arm around Maud. "Honey. It's what Vanessa wanted."

"Oh, *Vanessa*," Maud cried, and buried her face in her hands and sobbed.

"We'll have to check the legalities," Toby said to Carley. "But I don't think you *have* to take the child . . ."

"But of course I have to!" Carley cried. "If that's what Vanessa wanted. And who else could tell him about his mother as well as I can? Poor little boy, little baby, I can give him a good home, he'll have sisters, he'll have a community, of course I'll take him!"

Maud sputtered, "You sold all your baby furniture at the tag sale."

"I'll use the stuff Vanessa bought," Carley said. "I'll have Frame help me move it over. I'll have to buy bottles and formula, though. Van was going to nurse."

"I want to see the baby," Maud said.

"You'd both better dry your faces and wash your hands first," Toby told them.

Obediently they did as he suggested, then gathered together at the nursery. Only one baby was there, lying in the arms of a nurse who sat in a rocking chair. When she saw them, she came toward them, holding the baby out.

Carley took him. It was automatic, how her arms formed a safe cradle for the infant, how she snuggled him against her breast and gazed down into his little face.

"Let me see," Maud begged.

Carley pulled back the blanket. The infant was red and wrinkled, with thin creased legs and clenched fists that he waved as he made peeping sounds. He had lots of black hair sticking up in all directions.

"Vanessa's hair," Carley whispered.

She touched his cheek and the little boy turned his head toward her hand. His blurred gaze seemed to search out her face. She unwrapped more of the baby, and they saw his feet and all his tiny toes.

"I have to hold him," Maud pleaded.

Reluctantly, Carley relinquished the infant into Maud's arms.

"This will be *our* baby," Maud told Carley.

"Oh, no," Carley said firmly. "This little boy needs one home, one mother, one family. He belongs to me." She held out her arms.

After a moment, Maud gave him over.

The infant had gotten cool with the blanket unwrapped. He waved his scrawny arms and legs and wailed in a thin high cry. Carley hurried to wrap the blanket around him. She held him against her chest, warming his little body all up and down, his tiny head pressed sideways against her shoulder. She kept one hand beneath his bum, and one hand roamed between his back and his soft, sweet-smelling, hot little head. This was the secret women knew, the ecstasy, the moment both out of time and connected to all women throughout all eternity. This was the center of the universe, a woman nurturing a mysterious, miraculous new life. Vanessa's child.

Tears of joy and grief welled in Carley's eyes. "I will be such a good mommy to you," she whispered to the little boy, kissing his head.

Footsteps sounded down the hall. Harold Walker, Vanessa's lawyer, approached at an even, almost ceremonial pace. Walker was a portly older man with a bow tie and a Vandyke beard. He wore a Brooks Brothers navy blue pinstriped suit exactly like one Gus had owned, and his thinning hair was combed into neat rows. He carried a slender leather briefcase.

He stopped and looked at them all. "I offer my condolences," he announced. "This is a terrible event. Terrible. I was very fond of Vanessa." For a moment, he choked up and could not continue. "I would rather not continue while standing in the hallway."

"We'll go to the visitors' lounge," Toby said. He placed his hand on Maud's back, ushering her toward the room. Carley followed with the baby in her arms. Harold Walker slowly proceeded behind her, and Kiki, unsure of her status, lingered in the background.

They stood in the visitors' lounge in an unofficial circle, not sure whether to stand or sit. Walker decided for them by taking a seat and indicating they should do the same.

As soon as everyone was seated, Walker cleared his throat. Reaching down, he unsnapped his briefcase and pulled out a heavy file. "I have here the last will and testament of Vanessa Hutchinson. As you know, she had no living relatives. She insisted on making provisions for her child, should she become deceased at any time after his birth. I will read it to you in all its legal language, but I'm sure you need to know the gist of it as soon as possible and so I will tell you. Vanessa Hutchinson, being of sound mind, asked that Carley Winsted become the legal guardian of her child."

Maud made a little moan. Carley held the baby tighter against her breast.

"Furthermore," Harold Walker intoned in his slow, stately speech, "Vanessa Hutchinson's assets, including the house and all her monies, are to go to Carley Winsted, to use as she wishes." His head wobbled slightly as he came to the final announcement. "That should amount to, once the house is sold, a sum of somewhere around two million dollars."

It was Kiki who reacted first. "Holy Mother of Angels!" She stood at the door to the visitors' lounge, half in, half out.

Harold Walker shot the midwife a stern reproaching glance.

"Sorry," Kiki muttered. "But that's a lot of money."

"The baby will be financially taken care of," Carley murmured, trying to think it through.

"Please understand," Harold Walker said, "this money is not left in trust for the child. It is left directly to you. Vanessa had complete faith in your ability to raise her child."

"She never talked this over with me," Carley said. Gently, rhythmically, she rocked the baby, patting his back, aware the motions were comforting her own body, too. "Why didn't she ever discuss this with me?"

"She didn't expect to die," the lawyer told her with brief practicality. "No one really does. She was wise to make this will. She came into my office only a few weeks ago, saying that she had recently learned how unexpected things happen in life, and she just wanted to be prepared." Harold Walker's face sagged as he continued, "She laughed about it. She was so full of life—well, extremely pregnant, but also, vivacious. She didn't expect to die. No one expected this to happen."

From the doorway, Kiki said, "Placenta accreta cannot be diagnosed in advance. It happens to one in every twenty-five hundred births, with a four percent fatality rate."

Carley stared at the midwife. The numbers wouldn't compute for her, and then Maud put her vague thoughts into words.

"In Vanessa's case, it was a one hundred percent fatality rate, and that's what matters to us." Her voice cracked as she spoke.

"At some time in the near future," Harold Walker said to Carley, "you will have to come in for a formal reading of the will, and to sign some paperwork. At present, I will take it upon myself to find the head of social services here at the hospital so that you can legally take the baby home with you. When you're ready, of course."

"He'll be fine in the hospital," Kiki rushed to assure them.

Carley brought the baby back against her body. He was awake, nuzzling. "I need to speak with the nurses about feeding him."

"Carley," Toby suggested, "why don't you let the nurses have the baby just for a while." Toby put a gentle hand on her arm. "Carley, I think you and I will have to be in charge of the funeral."

"The *funeral*." The word slashed her heart in half. "But it's so soon!" Carley protested. "Maybe—don't we—Vanessa—"

The lawyer said, "She left no instructions about her funeral."

"But aren't we rushing things?" A confusion of fears collapsed in Carley's chest, sending splinters of pain into her heart.

"Honey," Kiki said softly, "Vanessa's gone. We can't bring her back."

Toby said, "Carley, let's give the baby to the nurses, and I'll take you in to see Vanessa one last time."

It was not Vanessa who lay so still in the hospital room, a sheet covering her face. Vanessa, Carley's Vanessa, could never lie so still. The lustrous dark eyes were closed, the creamy skin was already slack, the body unresponsive as Carley bent over to embrace her friend one last time.

But surely all that had been Vanessa was not only flesh and could not be destroyed so easily. Perhaps Vanessa was somewhere nearby, invisible, spiritual, ethereal. Carley whispered to *this* Vanessa, promising to take care of her baby, to teach him who his mother was, to surround him with his mother's love. She bent over the bed, pressing her warm body against her friend.

"Carley." Toby touched her back. "We have to leave her."

Carley kissed Vanessa good-bye.

Maud, Kiki, and Harold Walker sat in silence in the visitors' lounge. Carley saw the exhaustion and strain on their faces and knew it reflected her own. The thought of the sweet new baby pulled on Carley's instincts like a drug, but she knew she had to attend to the past before she could go into the future. Yet, she was so extremely tired.

Maud's face drooped bleakly, as if she'd lost weight in the past few hours, and Carley knew that even though Maud had taken Vanessa's husband, still, Maud had loved Vanessa. Not as much as she loved Toby, true, but still, she had loved Vanessa.

Carley dropped down onto one of the ugly green vinyl chairs. She didn't think she had the energy to stand. "Maud," she said, "would you help us, please? With the funeral?"

Maud's eyes flew to Carley's. "Anything. I'll do anything."

"I think we should have it at St. Paul's. Vanessa went there. Will you phone the minister and make the arrangements?"

"Yes. What else?"

"This is Saturday. Let's make it Tuesday, okay? We can have the reception at my house because there's so much room. I have some food in the freezer . . ."

"We'll need alcohol and lots of it," Maud said. "I'll get it. Toby can help me carry it in and set it up."

"And maybe tomorrow you could call me and we can discuss songs Vanessa might like to have sung? Or poets she especially loved? And a scholarship of some kind, in Vanessa's name, let's think about that. She worked for so many good causes." This was coming back to her, Carley realized, this list of practical details, this moving forward, step-by-step, over the mundane, specific slates of necessary errands, like stepping on stones over a bottomless pool, crossing from death back to life. She had done this before, just over a year ago, when Gus died.

Toby's jaw was clenched. "I'll take care of seeing that Vanessa's body gets over to the mortuary."

Carley stared. *Vanessa's body.* "Thank you."

"What about the baby?" Maud asked.

"I'll talk to social services," Harold Walker reminded her. "Because of paperwork and legalities, it will be easier to allow the baby to remain in the hospital for a few days."

"And our nurses are wonderful," Kiki put in. "They'll take such good care of him, Carley, you know they will."

For a few moments, they didn't speak. Through the windows they could see the light draining from white to the dove gray of evening. Someone's stomach growled hungrily, and everyone smiled at this, this humble reminder that life was going on. Needs, desires, continued.

"We should go home," Toby said. "We're all exhausted."

"Carley," Maud reached out to touch Carley's arm, "come to our house. Have a drink with us, and dinner—"

"Thanks, but I need to be with the girls, and they're at Lauren's. I'll talk to you tomorrow."

Kiki brought out Carley's coat, gloves, and purse from the labor room where the morning had begun. Carley hugged them all, even Harold Walker, whom she hardly knew. He escorted her down the stairs and out to her car.

She sat in her SUV, arranged things as she always did, her purse on the floor of the passenger seat, her seat belt on, the key in the ignition, and then she paused. She was wading through time as if through high water. Cars rolled in and out of the parking lot while she sat there, and her thoughts were not racing, they were slow, and heavy with significance.

"Vanessa . . ." Carley whispered, looking down at her hands on the steering wheel. She set her hands in her lap and closed her eyes. At once her memory conjured up a clear image of Vanessa the day she returned to the island. The day she sat in Carley's living room and confessed that she was pregnant. The day Vanessa said, "It may be selfish of me to want this baby for myself. But I've never wanted anything more. Nothing has ever felt so right." And Carley thought of Maud in her kitchen, flushed with unabashed passion from her love affair with Toby. In her whole life, had Carley ever been selfish? It was clear to her at this moment what it was she wanted. What stopped her from taking it?

She took her cell phone out of her purse. She hit a number. She heard the electronic ring.

"Carley?"

"Wyatt," Carley said. "Please come home. I need you."

Wyatt arrived on Sunday afternoon. He'd left Vermont at six in the morning, driven fast, left his car in Hyannis to have shipped over on the Steamship car ferry, which took two hours, and grabbed a plane to the island, which took only twenty minutes.

Carley waited for him at the airport. She had spent the night at Lauren's, grateful for the warmth and noise of the Burr family. She'd sat Cisco and Margaret down and talked to them about Vanessa's death. Both girls cuddled against her, crying. Carley gave them a few moments to absorb the blow. Then she told them they were going to adopt the baby boy. Immediately Cisco and Margaret sat up, eyes wide. They peppered Carley with questions about the baby, and then to Carley's amazement, Cisco, temperamental teenaged Cisco, actually grabbed her younger sister's hands and together the girls jumped up and down, squealing with joy. *A baby!*

That morning Carley had spent on the phone with Toby and the minister and the mortician and the nurses at the hospital. She had dropped by the hospital to hold the baby for a few moments before going on to the airport.

Now Wyatt's plane had landed.

She saw him coming toward her over the tarmac. He wore the Tibetan wool hat Margaret had given him at Christmas and a navy blue North Face ski parka. His nose and cheeks glowed with the special rosiness that came from sun on snow. When he saw Carley waiting, his mouth crooked up in a smile that was almost shy.

Suddenly, she felt shy, too. She felt as if she were being strapped into a roller coaster, the most spectacular one on the planet, and the ride was about to begin. Her heart pounded. Here was her adventure, for if all went well, she would live with this man while she raised all three children, and she would live with him when they went off to college and began lives of their own. She would argue with him, and bring him tea and ask him to rub her back. She would—she would start with the first step, the first detail, the first day, today. She would ask him to move in with her and the kids. She would ask him to help.

He came through the sliding doors into the waiting room where people gathered at the low shelf for their baggage to be unloaded. He walked up to her and stopped just in front of her.

"Wyatt." He had come home. She threw her arms around his neck and kissed him full on the mouth, pressing her body against his as if she could meld with him.

He held her tight.

Because it was February, the three B&B rooms were unoccupied, but Carley wanted Wyatt as close to her as possible without upsetting her daughters, so that night he put his luggage in one of the guest bedrooms on the second floor, just a door away from Carley's bedroom. They agreed they'd talk with the girls about this later. Now was the time to focus on Vanessa's funeral, and then, to bring the baby home.

The funeral, and the reception at Carley's house, was a crowded, emotional affair. Half the town showed up to pay their respects. That day blurred past, full of tears and memories and laughter, and that night the girls slept in their own rooms, and Wyatt slept with Carley.

The next day Wyatt, Toby, and Frame moved all the baby's furniture and necessities from Vanessa's house into the guest room on the second floor that Carley and her girls had cleared out for the baby. Cisco and Margaret were all about the infant. As the days went by, Carley had to force them to go to school, to play with friends, to do homework. Maud came over every day, and Lauren, and Lexi, and even Beth Boxer. They took care of the little boy while Carley grabbed a much-needed nap. Between Wyatt and the baby, she didn't get much sleep at night.

They officially named the baby Paul Webster, because Vanessa had called the baby Paul when he was born, and Webster had been Vanessa's maiden name. Gradually, Paul's hair grew longer and darker, and often, at the grocery store, or in the pediatrician's waiting room, a stranger would say to Margaret or Cisco, "Your baby brother looks just like you!" Carley's daughters had their father's black thick hair, and while the baby's hair wasn't quite as dark, it was close. He did look like their brother, and that was very satisfying.

Wyatt helped Carley deal with all the legalities of Vanessa's death. He put the house on the market. Carley went through the house, carrying the baby in a pack on her chest, to choose the items of furniture or pictures that were especially "Vanessa" to her. She put these in the baby's room. Someday she'd explain them to him, when he was old enough to understand. She found a burial plot in one of the local cemeteries and arranged for a beautifully carved stone. She knew Cisco and Margaret sometimes visited Gus's plot, and she wanted Paul to be able to go somewhere on this earth to find a marker of his mother.

Carley phoned Annabel and Russell and over a crackling, buzzing connection, told them about Paul's birth and Vanessa's death. She told them she was legally adopting Paul. She held her breath, and after a moment, Annabel's voice came clear and strong: "Darling. I'm so sad about Vanessa. But you are doing the right thing, adopting that poor little child." From then on, her emails and her daughters' to Annabel and Russell were full of news about Paul's every cry and drool.

Sunday afternoon, Carley and Wyatt called Cisco and Margaret in for a special talk, to tell them that sometime soon, when they had time to think about it, they would be getting married, and that until then, Wyatt would be living with them, so he could help with all the cooking, and buying groceries, and picking up the girls from school.

Breathlessly, Carley waited for her daughters' reactions.

Margaret scrunched up her shoulders as her face brightened. "Can I wear a fancy pink dress and scatter rose petals at the wedding?"

Cisco staked her claim with a glower, daring them to disagree: "I'll hold the baby during the wedding."

Carley and Wyatt exchanged glances. They hadn't even had time to think about a *wedding* yet.

Carley said, "Those both sound like excellent ideas."

Little by little, Wyatt began to transfer his belongings into Carley's house. She had cleared out closets, so there was plenty of space for his clothing, but she was slightly alarmed at the amount of outdoor equipment he owned. Not just backpacks and tents, but the expensive dirt bike, a surf board, skis, snowshoes, waders and clamming gear. He was such an outdoor man. He was such a *traveler*. Could such a man really find happiness in a home with two little girls and a baby?

Could such a man find happiness with a woman tied down to a busy B&B?

One night in bed, Carley sat up, wrapped her arms around her knees, and asked, "Can we talk?"

Wyatt strode out of their bathroom, clad in the blue-and-white striped pajamas Carley had bought for him, now that he was living with her and the girls. "Shoot." He settled at the end of the bed, leaning against the footboard.

She could smell the fresh scent of toothpaste. She wanted to crawl the length of the bed and kiss his mouth.

"I've been thinking about the money Vanessa left me."

"Right."

"It's a magnificent gift. And perhaps we'll need it someday, in case of an emergency . . ."

"You all are *my* family now," Wyatt said. "*I'll* take care of you."

"Oh, Wyatt, that's not what I meant. I mean, yes, we are your family now, and I'm glad, and I'm grateful you'll take care of us, but what I'm trying to get at is—Wyatt, I don't want to give up the Seashell Inn."

"Okay. No one is saying you have to. But with Vanessa's money, you don't *have* to work. You have Paul to take care of now, in addition to your girls, and in the not too distant future," he finished, teasingly, "a very needy husband. Will you have the energy for the B&B, too? I'm not trying to persuade you one way or the other, Carley, but it's a question worth considering."

"I know it is, Wyatt, and I have considered it. The thing is, in a way I can't explain, the B&B nourishes me. It *gives* me energy. I enjoy it, every bit of it, and I'm looking forward to catching up with the news of the returning guests. I can't articulate it, but it's making my life broader, wider, more exciting. Why give up the B&B if it makes me happy? I've got plenty of help with the baby."

"And I'll do everything I can to help you in the summer, too."

"You will? Oh, Wyatt, thank you!" Carley tried to crawl across the bed like a sex kitten but got caught in the covers, finally tumbling against Wyatt's leg. "I want to kiss you."

"That can be arranged." Wyatt twisted on the bed, bringing his face down to hers, and pressed his warm, sweet-tasting lips against her mouth.

I can do this, Carley thought, *I can have so much happiness!* Then Wyatt put his hands on her body and she stopped thinking.

Wednesday evening, Toby was out on an emergency. Maud's boys were in their rooms. Carley and Maud sat on either side of the work-table in Maud's study, with cups of decaf sprinkled with chocolate close by. They were looking one final time at the cookbook. The printer wanted them *yesterday*, and since Maud couldn't leave her boys, Carley had come here. Wyatt was with the children. All the children.

"It's ready to go to the printer," Maud declared.

"I agree." Carley gave Maud a high five across the table. "The illustrations are beautiful, Maud."

"So are the recipes."

"Maud, I want to do another cookbook. I've invented a Vanessa cake."

"Chocolate, I'll bet."

"Completely. Streaked with fudge, dotted with chocolate chunks, plus a few mystery ingredients."

"Vanessa would love that." Maud pulled out a piece of paper and held it up. "We've been on the same wavelength. I'm adding a mermaid named Vanessa to my next book. She's kind of a fairy godmother."

Tears pricked Carley's eyes when she saw the drawing. There Vanessa was, dark hair flowing in the water, jewels covering her breasts, mermaid tail shimmering. "That's gorgeous!"

"It's just a sketch. I've got to write the story."

"And I've got to invent some more recipes. Maybe I can do an entire Vanessa cookbook."

"You'll gain weight with that one."

Carley chuckled and checked her watch. "No frantic phone calls! I think we've done it, Maud. The Great Experiment has succeeded."

"Who would ever think it possible? Wyatt alone in a house of children."

"Well, Cisco's still awake, doing homework. If Paul wakes up, she's perfectly capable of dealing with him. Although," she added, frowning, "Paul has a cold. I think Margaret brought it home from school. He sneezes and snuffles and seems miserable. Poor little guy."

"He'll be fine," Maud assured her.

"Hope so. He was sleeping when I left. Wyatt promised to phone if there was a problem."

Maud stretched her arms high above her head. "How's Wyatt doing?"

"He's good. Although I've talked with his sister Wendy about him. She said when they were children, he used to take the heads off her baby dolls."

Maud laughed. "Carley, all little boys do that! They take *everything* apart."

"I know. Gosh, Maud, it is such a responsibility, this little boy. I want to do everything right."

"No one does everything right," Maud reminded her.

"I don't know why I get so frightened."

"We all get frightened," Maud assured her. "And you've had some really bad stuff fall out of the sky onto your head. It's not surprising you're worried."

Carley hugged her friend. "Thanks, Maud, for everything." She gathered her papers and slid them into her book bag. She dug her keys out of her parka pocket. "Tell me when the printer thinks he can have the books ready. We can arrange a signing at the bookstores."

"Carley, this is going to be so much fun!"

Carley pulled on her down parka and gloves and wool cap before braving the fierce frigid wind. She shivered to her car over ice-glazed mounds and valleys of snow. Inside, she switched the heater to high. Even with the blower turned up, the interior of the SUV was still cold when she arrived home.

She used the automatic garage door opener, then hurried into the warmth of the house. She hung her parka on a hook and tossed her hat and gloves and car keys into the basket on top of the chest.

"Hello," she called lightly. Margaret might be asleep.

The downstairs was strangely quiet. Empty. That was odd. It was only after nine. She glanced in the den. The TV was blaring away on the sports network.

"Hello?" she called again as she walked up the stairs.

A pounding, roaring noise came rushing toward her as she ascended. What in the world?

She ran.

Mist wafted out of the bathroom into the hallway.

"In here!" Cisco called, opening the bathroom door.

"What's going on?"

Cisco's hair was hanging in dripping wet hanks. Even her sweater and jeans were damp. Her face was blotchy.

"Cisco? Oh, God, what's happened?" Carley stepped into the bathroom.

Wyatt sat on the side of the bath tub, which was filled with roiling hot water. The shower thundered full blast. Steam filled the air. Wyatt was holding Paul up against his shoulder. The baby was crying, hoarse little sobs.

"Shut the door." Wyatt's hair was wet, too. Water drops dripped down his crimson face. Globs of vomit slowly slid down the back of Wyatt's shirt.

"Mommy." Cisco took her mother's hand for comfort. "Mommy, the baby was crying and Wyatt and I got him. We tried to feed him the bottle, and he choked, and we burped him, he stopped choking, but he started making these terrible sounds, Mommy, he was *squeaking*. He couldn't get his breath."

Carley went ice cold with fear. "Croup." She started to reach for the baby, but Cisco's words stopped her.

"Wyatt said to come up here and turn on the hot water. Wyatt said steam would loosen the mucus and help him breathe, and it worked, Mommy, it worked!"

Carley's entire being longed to seize the little boy, to hold him in her arms, listen to his breathing, watch his chest rise and fall, look into his face.

But Wyatt was speaking to her as he held Paul against his chest, gently patting the baby's back. "My sister's baby had croup," he told Carley. "My sister had it, too, when she was little. I remember the drill. I've seen my mother do this."

Carley dropped to her knees next to Wyatt. "He vomited down your back."

"That's good. He got rid of some mucus."

"Mom," Cisco said, "Wyatt was *awesome*."

Astonished, Carley asked Wyatt, "But weren't you afraid?"

"I was terrified." Wyatt reached over to slow the volume of water. "But I could tell something had to be done immediately. I thought about having Cisco call Toby, or call you, or even call my mom, but by the time anyone got here . . . I just did it." Wyatt's smile was crooked and almost shy. "I think I did the right thing."

Drops of moisture slid down Carley's face and her clothes were growing sticky. Her skin prickled with heat. She wanted to comfort the baby, who actually seemed to be falling asleep on Wyatt's shoulder. She wanted to hug Cisco, who clearly had been frightened, and she wanted to kiss Wyatt fiercely all over. A loud freaked-out scream would feel good right now, too.

Instead, she acted as if this was just another normal evening. "Yes, Wyatt, you *did* do the right thing. Look at him. He's falling asleep. Come on, Cisco. Let's get you in dry pajamas and I'll tuck you in bed."

As she left the bathroom, she started to turn back, to softly call to Wyatt, "I'm going to give you a thank-you gift you'll never forget."

With a thrill in her heart, she realized that she didn't need to give him a present. He hadn't done it for *her*. He'd done it for Paul, spontaneously, without any motive except saving the baby. *Oh, Wyatt*, she thought, *you have no idea what a good father you are*.

Then she thought, with another leap of her heart, that Wyatt *did* know. He had known all along. She was the one who needed to know. To trust.

EPILOGUE

On an early July morning, Carley was in the kitchen slicing fruit for fruit cups. She'd already poured a cup of coffee for her B&B guest Melody, and had one for herself nearby.

Melody glanced quickly at the door, then asked, "Well? What do you think?"

Carley paused to rinse her hands. "I like him," she decided. "He's articulate and intelligent." She didn't add that anyone would be better than that Jack fellow who'd left Melody on the moors two years ago.

"And he's major nice," Melody crooned. "He's already graduated and he's working in his father's company, and I can tell he likes me *a lot.*" She widened her eyes at Carley, anticipating a positive reaction. "Don't you think he likes me a lot?"

Carley dried her hands and sat down at the table. "Here's what I really think, Melody. I think you're twenty years old, too young to get serious and way too young to think of marriage. You're a splendid young woman, and you've got a world of possibilities before you."

Melody looked crestfallen. "You don't like him."

Melody's new boyfriend, Quentin, entered the room, stopping their conversation. He kissed Melody's cheek and threw himself into a chair. "Good morning, all. It's going to be a scorcher out there."

Carley set coffee and a bagel with lox and cream cheese in front of him. Quentin politely declined the fruit and Carley politely declined from acting like his mother and telling him that fruit was good for him. She was already bossing enough people around.

Cisco strode into the room. "He's awake!" Since Paul's birth seventeen months ago, Cisco had grown even taller, with a wide-shouldered, lean and lanky build that made her look elegant on horseback. She was strong, too. Dealing with horses had strengthened her back and arms, and good thing, Carley thought, because Paul felt like he weighed about seventy pounds.

Cisco had already dressed Paul for the day in tee shirt and shorts, but left his feet bare. He wriggled in her arms, eager to get down.

"Good morning, darling!" Carley kissed Cisco first, because she didn't want to show favoritism to the baby. She kissed Paul. "Hello, big boy!"

Paul shrieked with joy, allowed himself to be hugged, then struggled away.

Jewel came into the kitchen, following Cisco. In spite of the tortoiseshell glasses and baggy clothes fifteen-year-old Jewel chose to wear, it was obvious that she was going to be a stunner. Jewel didn't ride, but she attended all the shows and in deference to Cisco's obsession, read every young-adult novel about horses, entertaining Cisco with summaries. More than that, she was perfectly happy to play babies with Cisco, and good thing, because when Cisco wasn't on a horse, she wanted to be with Paul.

"Gotta go." Quentin rose and held out his hand to Melody. "The beach is calling."

"Have fun!" Carley said. "Clean beach towels on the hooks."

Her guests went out into the hot day. Carley dropped happily into a chair. The other guests had already had breakfast and left. She could catch her breath.

Paul was toddling as fast as he could go, running after Tiger, who seemed to enjoy the morning chase routine. Mimi, who liked to observe from afar, perched on a blue quilted cushion on top of the cupboard, but Tiger strode around and around the kitchen table, tail high, just teasingly out of Paul's reach. If Paul got within a hair's touch, the cat easily zipped out the door and down the hall. Carley had learned to let Paul work off some of his morning energy.

The front door opened and Lexi stalked in, wearing fabulous

jeweled sandals and a batiked and beaded sundress. Her long blond hair was twisted into a high knot held with a stick. She kissed Jewel's cheek, then sank into a chair.

"Just checking in before I go work in the fields," she said.

"Please," Carley scoffed. "Your shop is air-conditioned and perfumed like a spa."

"Exactly. People come in for relief from the heat. That's why I'll be working like crazy." Reaching over, she picked up a fruit cup. "How is everyone?"

"Hot," Cisco told her. "We should get air-conditioning." She shot a look at her mother.

"We've been over this before," Carley told her older daughter. "It would cost a zillion dollars to air-condition this huge old house. Besides, it's perfectly cool in the yard, especially with the sprinkler going. Oh, yes, and may I just mention that the riding ring is not air-conditioned!" As she talked, she snatched Paul and swooped him up into his booster chair. Before he could object, she set a bowl of dry Cheerios in front of him. His fat little hand grabbed for the cereal.

"Jewel," Lexi said, "what's your schedule today?"

Jewel looked wary. She seemed to fear that her glamorous almost-stepmother was trying to lure her into the den of fashion, but Lexi knew well that Jewel, at least for the time being, didn't have the personality to work with the public.

"I was wondering if you could pick up some lunch for me and my assistant and bring it down."

Jewel looked over at Cisco, who looked over at Carley.

"We're going to the beach this morning," Carley said. "What time do you want lunch?"

"Anytime around one."

"That works for me," Carley said. If she could wear out Paul this morning, she could get him down for a nap this afternoon, and she could get something accomplished in her office. Cisco could change clothes and bike out to Lauren's to spend the afternoon with the horses. Later in the afternoon, Margaret could help with the baby while the big girls were gone. Margaret often complained that she didn't get to spend much time with Paul because of Cisco and Jewel, but this was a delicate issue since she was only seven. Margaret seemed torn between loving Paul and wanting to be a baby herself. Sometimes she asked Carley if she could have her milk from a bottle or sippy cup, and usually Carley allowed this, because thirty minutes later, Margaret would be stalking Jewel, asking what she was reading, if she wanted a bead bracelet, did she prefer vanilla or chocolate ice cream?

The phone rang. Cisco snatched it up. "For you, Mom."

"Hi, Carley," Maud said. "Is it crazy over there?"

"Is it ever not?" Carley retorted.

"Well, look, I'm taking the maniacs to the beach today. Want to meet me there? And since I'm making lunch for all of us, I'll make it for you guys, too. Just tell me how many of you there'll be."

"That would be fantastic," Carley answered. "There'll be—let's see, Cisco, Jewel, Margaret and me, that makes four, and Paul, but I'll bring his food."

"Great. Jetties at nine?"

"See you there."

"Must go." Lexi rose. "See you around one, Jewel. Oh. Here's some money for the food." She handed Jewel a wad of cash, blew a kiss at everyone, and stalked out the door on her very high heels.

"She's going to trip on the bricks and break her ankle," Jewel said, shaking her head.

"She's got to look chic," Cisco argued. She tugged Jewel's arm. "Let's go put on our bathing suits." They skipped up the back stairs, whispering and giggling. These days they giggled about everything.

"Good morning, everyone." Wyatt came in from the front hall, crouching so that Margaret, who rode his shoulders, wouldn't hit her head on the door frame. He wore a blue cotton button-down shirt with the sleeves rolled up and he looked so sexy that Carley wanted to shove him down on the table and have sex with him right there.

Instead, she reached up to accept her younger daughter as Wyatt slid her off his shoulders and into Carley's lap. Margaret was still in her cotton pjs, her hair tangled, sleep dust in the corner of her eyes.

"It's hot, Mommy," she whined.

Carley could guess where this was headed. Wyatt sometimes took Margaret into the office with him. She'd become fiercely attached to her stepfather and wanted to do everything with him. She was good, Wyatt said, happy to sit peacefully on the sofa, playing with paper dolls or coloring or reading. "We're going to the beach," Carley told Margaret. "We're going to meet Percy and Spenser."

Margaret still pouted.

"Try this." Carley stabbed a piece of watermelon onto her fork and lifted it to Margaret's mouth. "This is cool."

Wyatt poured himself a cup of coffee and leaned against the counter, looking at the crowd gathered around the table. A year ago he and Carley had been married here at home in a small private ceremony with only Cisco, Margaret, and Paul attending. Carley and Wyatt had reasoned that this would help their odd little family bond, and it looked as if they were right.

"Paul," he said. "Cheerios go in your mouth, not in your ears."

Paul giggled mischievously.

"Paul-y." Margaret slid off Carley's lap and stood next to Paul, smoothly pulling the cereal bowl out of reach. "Want some of my banana, Paul?"

"What chaos." Carley took a deep breath. She'd planned to tell him privately, but she couldn't wait another moment. "Wyatt, it's going to get more chaotic. Soon."

Wyatt reached for a bagel. "Really? Why?"

Carley didn't speak. She couldn't—the lump of happiness in her throat was too large.

Wyatt put the bagel down. "Carley?" In a flash, he read the message in her eyes. His jaw fell. "Are you kidding me?"

She shook her head and found her voice. "Not kidding."

"You're pregnant?"

"I am!"

"When is the baby due?"

"January."

Wyatt went pale.

"You're going to have a baby?" Margaret asked. Her eyes were wide. "Oh, goodie, a baby for *me*!"

"Are you okay?" Carley asked her husband.

With careful precision, Wyatt said, "We are going to have a baby."

Paul banged his spoon on the table and babbled.

Margaret put her face next to Carley's belly. "Are you a boy or a girl? If you can hear me, *kick*!"

Color was returning to Wyatt's face. He looked dazed. He looked *dazzled*. "This place is going to be wall-to-wall with children, Carley. Will you be able to run Seashell Inn this summer?"

"Oh, I think so," Carley told him. "These days I feel like I can do anything."

Heat Wave

A NOVEL

NANCY THAYER

A Reader's Guide

Nancy Thayer on *Heat Wave*

Are there any "ordinary" women? I don't think so.

My goal in writing has always been to capture the real lives of "ordinary" women. To do this, I draw on my own life, steal anecdotes from the lives of friends, and let it all be transformed by the alchemy of imagination.

For example: when I was in my early thirties with children three and five years old, my husband had an affair with my best friend. Suddenly I was divorced, living in a different state from my ex-husband, with no one to help with the children, not for a weekend or even an hour. I worried about so many things. How would I support myself and my children, financially and emotionally? How would we go on? Would anyone ever love me, a divorcée with two little children?

Recently, a friend of mine was widowed, and I realized that she was facing the same problems I had faced when I was divorced. In this way, Carley Winsted came to life. My divorce inspired Marina in *Beachcombers*, as well. In many of my novels, I find myself coming to grips with traumatic times in my life and working them through by writing about strong women facing change and not only surviving, but triumphing.

Another terrifying episode for me was when my daughter, at fourteen, left to attend a performance school to study ballet. She was a strong, talented, passionate girl, and when she returned for Thanksgiving, she'd lost a great deal of weight. Her fingertips were always ice-cold. Her shoulders were too wide for the classic tiny ballerina build. I was afraid she was becoming anorexic, but I also knew just how far arguing with her would get me—my children have always been champions at arguing. Fortunately, she was told her build wasn't right for ballet, and she left that school. And I was left with a powerful memory that blossomed into a girl named Cisco.

Three years after my divorce, I met a wonderful man who lived on Nantucket, and two years later I married him, bringing my children to live on the island. My husband's mother lived two blocks away from us. She was dignified, autocratic, reserved, and I might as well just say it: critical. I loved her and I understood that she was old-school Bostonian, but I grew up in Kansas with a family that was always hugging, kissing, arguing, laughing, talking, emoting. My mother-in-law was like a beautiful white owl peering down from the height of a tree while I, a yippy little terrier, bounced around the trunk. She has provided scenes for many books.

Throughout my life, my friends have been my sanity, my support, my saving graces. As I started writing *Heat Wave*, I wondered what would happen to Carley if suddenly, right when she needed them, her best friends became unavailable to her? So Maud and Vanessa sprang to life, becoming in their own ways, inaccessible. I've learned that it is possible to make a new friend who is a perfect match—just what you need—and so I had Carley meet Lexi. A true friend is not easy to find, I believe; it requires a kind of magic, but if we're lucky, we'll always be able to make new friends.

As I've grown older, I've been fortunate to become acquainted with younger women who are starting on their lives' journeys. They face the old questions: Will I find true love? Will I marry the right man? Will I have children? Will I do work I love? They find answers in new ways that I couldn't have dreamed of when I started writing. They are more enterprising than I was, and the world has changed immeasurably from when I was first divorced. Yet the desires remain the same, as do the challenges, and the things that sustain us: family, friends, laughter, love—and chocolate.

If you're reading this, I'm guessing you're like me and books are a big part of your life. In times both good and bad, fiction sustains me. I am always in the middle of one book, grateful for another voice to take me away for a little while, perhaps to a place not so different from my own. Other authors' novels invariably inspire me to try my very best with my own. I hope that you also get a feeling of connection and companionship with the characters I write about, that you find comfort and pleasure from the stories I tell, and maybe even learn something that proves helpful on your own life's journey.

Reading Group Questions and Topics for Discussion

1. Carley and Gus didn't begin their relationship with a grand passion or love for each other, but they did like each other a great deal and valued the same things. Is that a good enough foundation for a marriage?

2. Carley always believed that she had everything she wanted and she was everything she ever wanted to be: a mother, a wife, a good friend. Did she perhaps give up too quickly in finding what she really wanted to do in life? Did she sell herself too short?

3. Gus was secretive with their money, but Carley was more than happy to relinquish the financial affairs to him. Should she have been more assertive about being in the know about their finances?

4. While Annabel and Russell's offer to have Carley and the girls live with them seemed to have been made with good intentions, how much interference from grandparents is too much?

5. Even though Gus left the house to Carley, was it disrespectful of her to change her mother-in-law's family home into a B&B? Did Annabel have a right to be angry at her for making changes to her ancestral home and opening it up to strangers?

6. Did Carley inadvertently make a choice between Maud and Vanessa when she remained silent about the affair? Could she have handled the situation better?

7. Maud was so worried about her boys needing a man around the house. How important is it for a boy to have a man in his life? Was Maud just trying to assuage her guilt for stealing her best friend's husband?

8. Was Annabel using her grief to seduce Cisco into living with her? Should Carley have been more understanding about Annabel's grief?

9. Carley worries that it's too soon to start openly dating Wyatt. Is there ever a "right" time frame to begin to date? Does the time frame change if you have children?

10. Sarah and Sue tell Carley that "other peoples' concept of 'right' or 'wrong' doesn't matter when you're in love. What matters is the love." Do you believe this is true? What about in a situation such as Maud, Toby, and Vanessa's?

Read on for an excerpt from

SUMMER BREEZE

by Nancy Thayer

Published by Ballantine Books

When Aaron's Volvo pulled up to the curb of the Barnaby house, Bella felt just a bit giddy.

She'd met Aaron Waterhouse in December, just after she'd returned home to Dragonfly Lake to help her mother, and the connection had been instantaneous and electric.

Aaron was handsome, sweet, sexy, and smart. He was the first man she'd ever wanted to marry. Growing up, her own family had been happy—noisy and messy, but happy—and Bella wanted one like that for herself. Lots of children, toys on the floor, flour on the kitchen counter while she taught her son or daughter to make popovers, a husband who would come home from work with a smile on his face to toss his children into the air—and who could make her melt at the sight of him, the way she was melting now.

She could have all that with Aaron. He had just gotten his masters in architecture. He was putting out feelers for jobs, and he was sure to get a good one. He was so bright, so reliable. He wanted children. He was in love with her. She was in love with him, and the vision of their life together was enticing.

But there was one enormous problem: Aaron had been invited to interview for a job in San Francisco.

San Francisco excited Aaron. Bella didn't want to leave Massachusetts.

She'd left already, plenty of times. She'd seen foreign places. She'd traveled to Paris, to Italy, to Amsterdam. She'd lived in Utah and in Texas.

Now she wanted to get started with her own real life. She

wanted to live *here*, near Dragonfly Lake, a world she knew and cherished. It wasn't just the landscape and the closeness of her family. It was more than that—it was as if she were falling in love with a new vision of her self, as if at twenty-seven a mist was evaporating from a mirror, allowing her true image to show clear.

It was early June. Bella and Aaron had been together for five months, growing closer every day. She was pretty sure Aaron was about to propose to her. And she didn't know what her answer would be.

"Bell!" Her older brother Ben stuck his head into the living room. "I'm driving down to the Hortons with our beach chairs and the food."

"Okay," Bella answered. "Aaron and I will walk down."

Ben went out the door and headed to his Jeep Cherokee, with its four-wheel drive, good for the snowy months, and its back hatch, good for carrying lots of stuff. Ben was practical, scientific, and methodical. He had a PhD and a tenured position at the University of Massachusetts at Amherst. His life revolved in a precise circle like planets orbiting the sun.

Bella's life felt more like a slinky flopping down the stairs.

She grinned at her own joke. At least she still had her sense of humor. You couldn't live in a family of four Barnaby children, all with a first name that began with the letter B, without developing a sense of humor. And she *was* happy; and an optimist, glad to be home, full of hope for the future. Her life wasn't *tragic*. Just a puzzle.

Bella had spent the last two and a half years teaching third grade in Austin, Texas, until last Christmas, when her mother, while trying to put the angel on top of the tree, fell off the ladder and broke her leg. Bella's father taught high school English five days a week. Bella's older sister Beatrice was busy in her house an hour away with her three little children. Ben, of course, had his own apartment in Amherst, his students and lab. Seventeen-year-old Brady was still in high school. So Bella abbreviated her contract, left Austin after the first semester, and flew home to take over her mother's shop and to help around the house.

She was surprised to discover she didn't miss teaching. She was exhilarated to be back home, which for her was not just the comfortable house she'd grown up in on a lake surrounded by woodland, but the entire area where forests and farmlands stretched like a vast Eden on either side of the wide Connecticut River. Five of the best colleges in the world existed here, bringing students and faculty from all over the planet.

As a child, she'd hiked with her family up Mount Hadley and Mount Tom, and canoed on the Connecticut River. She'd visited Emily Dickinson's house several times, and heard Billy Collins speak when he was the country's poet laureate. She'd contemplated modern sculpture at the art museums and she'd witnessed a four-point stag, branched with heavy antlers, step over their lawn and down to the lake to drink in the early morning light.

She loved this area, her family, their house . . . and that was part of the problem. Perhaps she loved them too much.

Now, as she watched, Aaron stepped out of his Volvo. He waved at Ben as Ben backed the Cherokee out of the drive. Aaron had incredibly muscled arms and thighs, a residual trait from wrestling in high school and college. She loved the heft of them, the safety she felt in his arms. He had dark curly hair, and he wore glasses over his hazel eyes. He was her Superman, looking academic, restraining so much strength and sexuality.

He approached the house, tapped on the front door, and let himself in, as everyone did who knew the Barnabys well.

"Hi, Aaron."

"Hey, Bella."

Just the sight of him made her short of breath. He pulled her to him and kissed her thoroughly.

She gently pushed him away. "We should go."

"Right. I brought some wine. It's in the car."

Together they left the house, picked up the bottles of Pinot, and began walking along the narrow road winding around Dragonfly Lake. The lake was tucked in a hollow snuggled up against a gently rising mountain, or what was called a mountain in New England;

in Colorado, it would be downsized to a hill. It rose to a ridge running north and south, covered with evergreens, birch, and oaks,
home to deer, porcupine, fox, and numerous other creatures, including the clever raccoons who made human lives miserable if they
didn't use the proper tight-locking trash receptacles. Various styles
of houses surrounded the lake: A-frames, modernized log cabins,
seventies split-levels like the Barnabys' house, and a few fabulous
mini-mansions like the ones on either side of the Barnabys.

All the homes looked out on to the lake, which curved in a
capricious blue oval around the hill, its banks thick with grasses,
forest, and wild flowers. Much of the shore was dotted with
boathouses and docks, because the lake was big enough to sail on.
Here and there, man-made beaches of golden sand sloped to the
water. Everywhere there were trees, and over the lawns and road,
the sweet green leaves of spring were casting the first delicate shadows. Tulips opened their petals to the light; pansies spilled from
window boxes.

Aaron inhaled a deep breath of air. "Nice day for a cookout."

Bella nodded. "Mmm. Funny, it usually is. The Hortons have
held the first neighborhood summer cookout for years."

"How many people will be there?"

"Not a real crowd. Lots of these houses are just vacation homes.
Like the one to the right of us—"

"That place is just for vacations?" Aaron turned to look back at
the house.

"I know. An interior designer from Boston, Eleanor Clark, owns
it. She usually comes here in the summer. I heard she loaned it to
her niece this year while Eleanor goes around the world with her
new boyfriend. She's an artist—Natalie, not Eleanor—around our
age."

"Have you met Natalie?"

"Not yet. I think she'll be at the cookout. I hope so. I'd like to
meet her."

"I'd like to see the inside of that house," Aaron said.

Bella knocked his shoulders with hers. "Ever the architect."

. . .

Natalie noticed the man when he stepped out of the Jeep parked in front of the Horton's house. He was a hunk, with a stern countenance that gave him an air of intelligence. Judgment. *Responsibility.*

She thought: Now *there* was a face she would like to paint.

A wide brow—poets would call it "noble"—over romantically down-slanting pale blue eyes. A straight slender nose, neat ears, a long face with a firm jaw. Wrinkles at the corners of the eyes and across the forehead, not, she would bet, from laughing, but from thinking. Here in the five-college area, lots of people thought for a living. The man was perhaps thirty. His hair was golden brown, like toast; she would bet he'd been a towheaded child.

"That's my son," Louise Barnaby told Natalie. She was sitting next to Natalie, both of them in rockers on the front porch of the Hortons' house. Louise still had to baby her leg, although she could walk on it without a cane, and Natalie had brought her a glass of chilled white wine.

Louise was Natalie's first lake friend. She'd visited when Natalie moved into her Aunt Eleanor's house this week, presenting her with a casserole and a vase of fresh flowers. She'd insisted Natalie come to the cookout with Louise and her husband, Dennis, who was out on the front lawn, stabbing croquet wickets into the ground.

"He's awfully cute," Natalie said.

Louise smiled. "I know. The great thing is, he doesn't realize it."

Natalie was grateful for Louise's company. Louise was older, but still chic, her blond hair cut in a sexy shag, her trim body clad in chinos and a blue tee that brought out the azure of her eyes. Louise didn't look like a fifty-five-year-old who'd given birth to four children. For that matter, Dennis was tall, slender, with lots of floppy gray hair. He still looked pretty fine as well.

It was shallow of Natalie to be so judgmental, she knew, but she'd been afraid when she made the decision to move out here from Manhattan she'd find everyone sporting Birkenstocks, feeding chickens, and discussing compost.

Was she a snob? Really, she could only claim to be, at the most, a wannabe-snob. She didn't have the pedigree to be a real one.

Also, she was learning, there were different kinds of snobs. Here, near Amherst, Massachusetts, home of Amherst College where the old money went and Hampshire College where the hip gifted went and the University of Massachusetts at Amherst where Bill Cosby and Jack Welch had gone, near Smith College where poor, brilliant Sylvia Plath had gone and Mt. Holyoke College where Emily Dickinson *and* Wendy Wasserstein had gone, the snobbery would be intellectual.

Natalie felt awkward in her black jeans and black silk shirt. This was about as cookoutish as her New York wardrobe got. She'd just moved to Aunt Eleanor's house. She hadn't had time to buy different clothes yet.

Just for a moment, Natalie put her hand to her own head. At least her hair was growing out. Two years ago, when she had moved to Manhattan, she'd gone to a hairdresser and had it all chopped off into a severe, chic, scalp-clinging crop. It had been a part of her statement. She could still remember leaving the salon, head high and suddenly weightless, feeling the fresh air on her bare neck, knowing that now her real life was about to begin. She'd been twenty-eight. She'd struggled to get there. At times in her life, she'd despaired of getting there. For years she'd had to drop her studies to work, often two jobs, to pay for more studies, because her parents could never help her financially. If it hadn't been for her Aunt Eleanor, she would never have made it to Manhattan.

She dropped her hand. As soon as she'd decided to leave Manhattan, she'd begun to grow her hair out. Already dark curls clustered over her ears.

"We're ready!" Morgan called. "Shall I fasten Petey in his stroller?"

Her husband was in his study, tapping frantically at the computer. A sunny Saturday afternoon, and he was working.

"Josh?" She tried not to sound waspish. "The cookout."

"Coming."

Morgan took a deep breath. During the past year, she'd learned to achieve feats of patience she never before dreamed possible. First of all, her adorable boy, just a year old, had taught her a whole new range of deep breathing. Then Josh had taken this job with Bio-Green Industries—she had wanted him to take it, she had *encouraged* him to take it—and suddenly her husband was too busy to take out the trash, give her a hug, or notice their child.

Although, they did have their house. Their amazing, slightly overwhelming, new house.

The O'Keefes' new home was on the shores of Dragonfly Lake. It rose in its concrete-and-glass glory, modern, boxy, space-age. They were able to afford it because the couple who built it had to move to Spain and needed a quick sale. And, of course, because Josh's new job paid so well. They didn't *love* the house, but the location was sublime. A beachfront with sand for Petey to play on. A wilderness to hike in. Morgan and Josh enjoyed kayaking, canoeing, swimming, and dreamed of teaching their children all that and more in the clear, pure waters of this lake. Before the move, they'd been living in a condo on the outskirts of Boston, commuting to jobs on crowded expressways, not getting home until late, too tired to enjoy life, and completely uninspired by the views of malls, highways, and office buildings out their condo windows. This place had seemed like a little bit of heaven to them.

Sometimes, though, to Morgan, it was just a bit like the top circle of hell.

Morgan was a scientist, a hazardous materials expert. Until recently she'd worked in the biosafety department at Weathersfield University outside Boston. She was really good at her work. It challenged her, used all her mental and interpersonal skills; it gave her a sense of accomplishment, of keeping things safe in a turbulent world.

Since Josh had joined Bio-Green, Morgan's life required a whole new set of skills.

First of all, since Ronald Ruoff, CEO of BGI, Bio-Green

Industries, was Josh's new boss, paying Josh a salary he'd never even dreamed of before, it was incumbent upon Morgan to make nice to Josh's boss and his wife, Eva.

Morgan had made nice. She and Josh had gone out to dinner last week with Ronald and Eva, and Morgan had been as charming as she could be, which frankly was a big fat private pain for Morgan. She didn't like to do charming, and she *really* didn't like to pretend interest in vapid Eva's frivolous enthusiasms: massages, pedicures, shopping, and whether Kate Middleton was truly suitable for Prince William; Eva's personal and lengthy opinion was that Kate was beneath him and she didn't even get how her statement was funny. Morgan didn't understand how a woman perhaps only a decade older—Morgan was thirty, Eva somewhere in her forties, already Botoxed and face-lifted—could be so insipid. Especially with a husband like Ronald, who might not be the most debonair dog in the kennel, but at least was interested in saving the world. Or, more realistically, in making money while saving the world.

Morgan had hoped—she had *fiercely* hoped—that she would like Eva, that they would have interests in common, that they would make plans to get together, because even though her toddler Petey was the beating center of her heart, Morgan was quietly and sweetly going out of her mind being a stay-at-home mom. But if she had to spend more time with Eva Ruoff, she'd hang herself. Okay, that was a bit dramatic, she'd never want to leave Petey, or Josh, either, even though these days Josh annoyed her to no end. Was she going nuts?

Josh came into the living room, where Petey was babbling to himself as he swept his books off the coffee table and Morgan stood lost in her thoughts.

"Thinking about how to decorate?" he asked.

Morgan almost growled. They had to invite the Ruoffs over sometime, and the Ruoffs believed that their home should *make a statement*.

Josh sighed. "We agreed when I took this job. My part is working at the facility. Your part is networking, socializing, attracting investors."

"I'm not saying I won't do it." Morgan adjusted a *dove* pillow on their *smoke* sofa. "I'm just saying I'm not sure I *can* do it. It's not my field. Not my passion. Not even my interest. Plus, Petey is pretty much a full-time job."

"You could put him in day care."

"Josh, no. We talked about this. We agreed." Morgan snorted with contempt. "How ridiculous would that be, to put a baby in day care so I can spend time making a statement with the house!"

"You don't seem to take my job seriously," Josh muttered.

"What? How did we get to—" They were back on muddy ground, the swamp land of their marriage. She didn't want an argument this evening. They were going to a cookout. They were going to meet people. Calming down, she said pacifyingly, "I know you're working hard, Josh. I appreciate it. I do."

She put her arms around Josh, her husband, her beloved. With his thick, naturally frenzied red hair, sparkling green eyes, and freckled skin, it was difficult for him to appear as brilliant as she knew he was. Thirty-five, yet he looked like a kid. A good-natured, athletic, dreamy boy who fantasized about playing for the Red Sox. "Maybe we'll make some contacts at the cookout," she told him.

Josh kissed the top of her head and swept his son up into his arms. "Come on, Champ, we're going to a party."

Outside, they chose the smaller, easier stroller and strapped Petey in. They went down the driveway, past Morgan's SUV and Josh's black Cadillac Escalade that looked, Morgan thought, like something the CIA would use.

Be good, Morgan warned herself. *Look around!* It was June, perhaps her favorite month, warm and fresh and full of the promise of summer.

Bella and Aaron strolled along the lake road until they came to the Horton's house. Ben was parked in front, unloading the Jeep. Bella's father was on the front lawn, setting up the croquet wickets. Her mother was sitting on the front porch in a rocking chair. Next to her sat the new woman from next door, Natalie, very thin and sophisticated, all in black.

Aaron called, "Hang on, Ben, I'll help you." He handed his bottles of wine to Bella, and joined Ben at the Jeep. Together the men hefted the folding beach chairs out of the back of the Jeep and carried them around the Hortons' house to the lawn sloping down to the beach.

Bella cuddled the three bottles against her. She noticed the new woman studying Ben. *Good luck to you*, Bella thought.

Ben was good looking, with the Barnabys' blond hair and blue eyes. Half of her high school friends had had crushes on him, even while he'd been a total clueless geek, his nose always in a book, staying late to work on science projects for the science fair.

In college, he'd had a serious long-term girlfriend, another science nerd. Vickie could have been pretty if she'd cared to, but she was almost aggressively fashion-unconscious. Her nice figure had been hidden beneath baggy jeans and loose T-shirts. Usually they had arcane quotes on them, like "Resistance is not futile. It's voltage divided by current." In the winter, she wore hoodie sweatshirts instead of sweaters and often forgot to wear a coat. Ben and Vickie broke up after graduation. He went on to Stanford. She went to Harvard. Now she was doing post-doctorate work in London. They remained science buddies who emailed now and then.

When Ben was working on his doctorate in California, he dated other women; Bella knew because she flew out a couple of times to visit him. These women were a new breed, ambitious, intensely intellectual, and not interested in long term affairs. They were Bella's introduction to the less starry-eyed side of sexuality, and while she placed no value judgment on what Ben had with them, it made her vaguely sad. But then Bella was a hopeless romantic.

When Ben returned three years ago as an assistant professor at UMass/Amherst, he was grown-up, a serious adult. He rented an apartment in Amherst, but came home often for meals or to sail. It was only a fifteen-minute drive. Today he looked familiar, her normal brother, clad in khaki shorts and an old T-shirt.

Bella went up the steps to the front porch. "Hey, Mom."

"Join us, honey." Louise gestured toward the wicker sofa. "Natalie, this is my daughter Bella."

"Hi, Natalie." Bella smiled at the woman sitting next to her mother, even as she cringed just a little inside. Natalie looked so sophisticated with her cropped black curls and no jewelry. She looked like the smart girl in high school, the one who always rolled her eyes at Bella. Bella was smart, but she was petite, only five-two, with blue eyes, blond hair, and what older people always praised as a "sweet" face.

Natalie grinned shyly. "Hi, Bella. I think you and I might have met once or twice when we were kids. When Slade and I came to the lake for a week in the summer."

Bella nodded, although what she remembered most about next door was Eleanor Clark. She was glamorous, a wealthy interior designer from Boston's most chichi area. During July and August, her driveway was lined with convertibles and sports cars and even a Jaguar, with license plates from as far away as California. When Bella was younger and Bella's older sister Beatrice wasn't married yet, they used to hide in the attic with their parents' field glasses, spying on all the golden people languidly lounging on Eleanor's back deck in their very limited bathing suits. It was better than HBO.

Bella remembered also, vaguely, Natalie and her brother Slade from past summers when they visited their Aunt Eleanor: two scrawny, pale kids who seemed uncomfortable outdoors. Their mother and father never came to the lake house. The kids would wade from their aunt's beach into the lake, rushing right back out, clutching their arms, complaining that the water was too cold. The girl shrieked when she turned over a log and found bugs. The boy spent a lot of time in the forest, often carrying a book and studying tree trunks, which Bella had thought kind of weird and kind of intriguing.

If she remembered correctly, the brother had been pretty cute. Movie star cute. Black hair, like Natalie's.

"I remember," Bella told Natalie. She settled on the edge of the sofa, cradling the three bottles of wine in her arms. "Seems like a long time ago."

"It was," Natalie agreed. For a moment, she dropped her gaze, looking pensive.

Louise announced brightly, "Natalie's an artist."

Bella said, "Yes, I heard that. What sort of art?"

Natalie cleared her throat. "I paint. I've studied art for several years now, most recently in New York. But I've always had to work full-time as a waitress or sales clerk to pay the rent and buy food, so I've never had a chance to concentrate on my work. When Aunt Eleanor asked me to watch her summer house for her, it was an answer to my prayers." Talking about her work transformed her; she was prettier, more engaging. "What do you do, Bella?"

"I teach," Bella began. "Well, I *taught.* Hey, I've got to get these bottles into a cooler. No one wants warm white wine. Want to walk around to the back with me?"

Natalie glanced at Louise.

"Go on, you two," Louise said. "Grace asked me to sit out front and tell people where to put their stuff." As she spoke, an older couple came up the lawn to speak to her.

Natalie rose, extending a hand. "Here," she said to Bella. "I'll carry one of the bottles."

Bella and Natalie went down the steps and around the side of the house. Almost a dozen people were on the back lawn, setting up tables and chairs, firing up the grill, going in and out of the kitchen. Bella found a cooler full of ice for the wine.

"I don't like to talk about it in front of my mother," Bella confessed to Natalie, "but when you asked what I do—well, it's a complicated question. I've taught third grade for a few years. Last Christmas my mother broke her leg, so I came back to help her and to run her shop for her."

Natalie leaned against the deck railing. "Her shop?"

"Barnaby's Barn." Bella joined her against the railing, and they both gazed out at the water. "She sells children's things, mostly. Handmade clothing. Handmade wooden cradles. She's kind of an artist herself, but not like you. She makes these miniature collections called Lake Worlds." Bella always felt protective of her mother when she spoke about her creations.

"Lake Worlds?" Natalie prompted.

"When we were children, Mom invented stories for us about the creatures who lived around Dragonfly Lake. Darling Deer and her family for Beat—that's my older sister. Her name is really Beatrice. Timid Toad and his warty family for Ben, and Busy Bunny for me. Barton Bear for Brady."

Natalie's eyes flicked toward the woods. "Are there bears around here?"

"There could be, but don't worry, I've never seen one."

Natalie relaxed. "So go on."

"Well, our friends were crazy for the dolls, so Mom made more animals for birthday and Christmas presents, complete with miniature nests and lairs. I'll show you sometime. She began to get phone calls from parents, offering to pay her if she'd create a set of animals for their children. At the same time, a small barn just on the outskirts of Amherst came up for sale. So she got the idea for her shop. That was sixteen years ago."

"Cool."

"Yeah, the money helped a bit, especially when we all started college, but Mom didn't particularly care about the money. She enjoyed creating Lake Worlds and seeing children's faces when they came into the shop. But while her leg healed over the past few months, I've run the shop for her."

Natalie tilted her head, studying Bella. "Do you like running it?"

Bella looked back at Natalie. She liked her frank question. "Truthfully? I do, but . . . have you ever had a great idea at the back of your mind and it won't come quite clear?"

Natalie threw back her head and laughed. "All the time!"

Aaron approached them, glasses of Pinot Grigio in his hands. "Ladies?" he offered, with a pretentious bow.

"I'd love some." Natalie took a glass.

"Natalie, this is my boyfriend Aaron," Bella said. She stumbled over the introduction. What should she call him? He was certainly more man than boy. They weren't engaged yet, but they were definitely not merely friends.

Aaron turned toward Natalie, and Bella thought how proud she was to be his girlfriend—or whatever she was. Aaron wasn't provocative like an underwear ad, but he gave off an air of steadiness, rock solid capability, competence. If he'd been a surgeon, Bella would have let him operate on her. If he'd been a pilot, she'd have flown in any plane he flew.

But he was an architect, and he was aimed toward California.

Natalie was asking Aaron, "What kind of architecture do you prefer? Or perhaps the question should be, who are your favorite architects?"

More guests were arriving at the party, all carrying an offering: a bottle of wine or a casserole or a tray of deviled eggs. Bella saw her mother and father stroll down to the water's edge, leaning toward each other as they talked. Something had happened since Louise broke her leg, Bella thought. Her parents had always been a team, but now they seemed even closer. She'd talk it over with Ben, if she could drag his attention away from his work for a second or two.

As if summoned by her thoughts, Ben came up the steps to the deck and joined their group.

Natalie sensed an eager *click* in her chest when Ben approached. She believed she'd developed a certain sort of judgment from all her years of painting, like an organic and obstinate lock growing right below her diaphragm. She would arrange objects for a still life—a vase, a silver platter, a bunch of grapes—and the lock stayed stubbornly shut. She'd remove the grapes, lay a sheaf of daffodils across the platter, and *click!*—the reluctant lock snapped open. So she knew when a painting was right for her.

That same *click!* startled her when she saw Ben face-to-face. Something inside her opened to him. She thought she gasped; she hoped no one noticed.

Next to her, Bella stirred. "Natalie, this is my brother, Ben. Ben, this is Eleanor Clark's niece, Natalie . . . ?"

Natalie supplied her last name. "Reynolds."

Bella nodded. "Right. She's living here this summer."

Ben gave Natalie a preoccupied hello.

Natalie returned a lukewarm "Hi"; she didn't want to appear eager.

"Great day," Aaron said. "Have you been swimming yet?"

Ben answered, "Not yet. The water's still cold. But I got the canoe out last weekend."

Bella slid her arm through Aaron's. "Could you help me set out the salads? I think they're getting ready to eat." She deftly pulled Aaron away.

Ben stood near Natalie, saying nothing.

"So," Natalie asked, "you live on the lake, too, right?"

Without looking at her, Ben answered, "Not really. I mean, I grew up here, but technically, my parents' house is no longer my home. I'm thirty-two now. I moved out years ago. I live in Amherst."

"I see. What do you do?"

"I teach at UMass/Amherst," he said as he cast a sideways glance at her and blushed deeply.

Well, *ha!*, she thought, he was as *attracted* to her as she was to him. She angled her body toward him, lifting her face toward his. "What do you teach?"

"Chemical engineering." He stuck his hands in the pockets of his shorts, as if afraid of what they'd do left out on their own.

She confessed, "I'm not sure I know what chemical engineering is."

"Most people don't."

She persisted. "Give me a try."

He hesitated, then gave her an other quick glance. He blushed again. "I heard you say you're an artist."

She smiled wryly. "True. But that doesn't make me an *idiot*."

Ben checked her face, as if to be sure she wasn't ridiculing him, then told her, "Chemical engineering is more or less the combination of chemistry and physics with biosciences to create and construct new materials or techniques. Like nanotechnology or new fuels."

"Oh, well, if you put it that way, then it's perfectly clear," Natalie teased.

Ben had pale blue eyes streaked with white, like shards of icebergs, as if a shield of cold protected the deep and complicated depths. He had long thick lashes, too, and shaggy blond hair. But he wasn't surfer-boy tempting, he was grown-up tempting. He looked reflective, resolute.

And clueless. He didn't seem to get the fun in her voice. He seemed, in fact, insulted. She hurried to appease him, because she really didn't want to hurt his feelings.

"Maybe I could understand it a bit better if you gave me more details."

"I'm working on hierarchical porous materials."

"Okay . . ."

"We're looking for a way to convert wood-based biomass into oil."

"Fuel."

"Right."

"Got it. Sounds important."

"It could be. I hope it will be." He continued talking, enthusiastic now, explaining his lab, his grad students, the papers he'd had published in scientific journals she'd never heard of. As he talked, it was as if a light had gone on inside him. Natalie understood; she had her own light.

"There you are!" Louise Barnaby came onto the deck, carrying a toddler in her arms, followed by the appealing young couple Natalie had seen a couple of houses down from Aunt Eleanor's. "Natalie, I want you to meet Morgan and Josh O'Keefe. Oh, and I mustn't forget Petey, their son."

Petey clung to Louise with wide eyes.

"Say 'Hi,' Petey," Morgan urged. The boy blinked. "It will take him a while. With the move, all the new people, so much change . . . he's really a pretty gregarious little guy."

Louise asked, "Morgan, didn't you say Felicity Horton has babysat for Petey once or twice?"

"She has. Petey adores her." Morgan added, "I do, too. She's fifteen and still more Anne of Green Gables than Beyonce."

"Well, then, Petey, let's go find Felicity!" Louise carried the baby away.

"Hi. I'm Josh." Robust and red-haired, he sported a Rolex on his wrist.

Morgan held out her hand to Natalie. "I'm Morgan. You must be the artist, right?" She wore her long brown hair loose to her shoulders. She was tall, thin, and lanky, athletic looking.

The O'Keefes introduced themselves to Ben, and for a while the four chatted amiably about the lake, the party, the long-awaited arrival of summer.

Morgan turned to face the lake. "This is our favorite time of day. I love to sit on the deck with a drink and see the light show."

"It's *your* favorite time of the day," Josh corrected mildly. "I'm usually driving home from work, if I'm lucky enough to leave that early."

"Where do you work?" Natalie asked.

"At Bio-Green Industries."

"In that new facility on the outskirts of Amherst?"

"Right. We're working on plant technology, trying to find a way to propagate plants without the use of chemical enhancements."

"I'll drink to that!" Ben lifted his glass. He informed the others, "I'm a chemical engineer at the university. Working on bio-fuels."

In a wry voice, Morgan said, "Oh, Ben. Just the kind of person who makes my life miserable."

Puzzled, Natalie glanced at the two of them.

Ben asked Morgan mildly, "What do you do?"

"I was a Biological and Chemical Safety Officer at Weathersfield University outside Boston. I specialize in hazardous waste management." Noticing Natalie's perplexed expression, Morgan explained, "Chemical engineers and biosafety officers are natural enemies. Chemical engineers are more cavalier with the rules than chemists, they assume that because they're working with a small amount of chemicals they don't have to be as careful and they can skirt the rules . . ."

"And biosafety officers take up all our precious time insisting we fill out piles of forms and nitpicking our every move when we're trying to, oh, save the world!" Ben shot back. "*We* do not dump any chemicals down the drain. My lab is spotless."

"Gosh, I'd love to see it someday," Morgan replied wistfully.

Josh chuckled. "That's my wife. Hand her safety goggles and gloves and she's blissed out."

"I'll take you through any time," Ben told her. "Did you hear about the terrible accident at UNH?"

"No. What happened?" Morgan leaned forward, fixated.

All around them, families and couples gathered in clusters on the deck and in the yard, sipping beer and wine, yelling orders at their kids, telling jokes, laughing. A teenaged girl played on the beach with Petey. A yellow lab wagged through the crowd, looking hopefully for dropped crumbs. Delicious aromas drifted through the air.

Bella approached. "Hamburgers and hot dogs, hot and juicy, get them on the grill now! Fix your plates, you guys, then join me and Aaron down at the table on the grass. We're saving places for you."

Morgan scanned the back yard. "I'll get Petey . . ." She went off toward the small beach.

Their group separated, some toward the drinks table, some toward the grill.

Bella took Natalie's arm. "Having fun meeting your neighbors?"

Was it the wine, or the fresh air, or simply how easy it was to talk with Bella? In a whisper Natalie confessed, "I *am* having fun. Your brother's intriguing."

"Oh, please, don't *you* start," Bella moaned. "Ben's got the personality of a turtle."

"Bella." Her father passed her, a glass of wine in each hand. "Be nice."

Bella sighed theatrically. "This is what I get for living at home."

"It's a remarkable place to live," Natalie told her, and she meant it. It was idyllic, not just the scenery, but the sense of neighborhood. By the side of the house several teenagers played volleyball, jumping, yelling, snorting with laughter. At the other tables, families gathered with other families, and Grace and John Horton strolled among the guests, saying hello and asking if they had everything they needed. Grace would never be anyone Natalie would choose as a close friend. She was at least ten years older, and in her ironed white shorts and shirt and gold earring shaped like anchors, there was something a bit prissy about her. Natalie was certain Grace would find her artistic dreams too bohemian. But this seemed to be Grace's talent, to hold large, casual gatherings where neighbors got together to enjoy life.

At Natalie's table, the group broke off into separate islands of conversation. It amused Natalie to see how animated Ben was as he argued with Morgan about the Environmental Protection Agency's attempt to bring all universities and colleges into compliance with the current hazardous waste management laws. Odd, how Morgan, who'd seemed rather stiff, even aloof when she first came in, was vivacious now. Who knew what a few sweet words about waste management could do for a girl?

At her left sat Josh O'Keefe, leaning forward rather aggressively in his chair, pounding the side of one hand into the palm of the other like some revolutionary Russian, clearly trying to convince Aaron of something about Bio-Green. Natalie tuned in; was Josh actually trying to get Aaron to invest in Bio-Green? It sounded like it. Not the most charming way to converse at a cookout.

"Josh?" Bella asked sweetly, rising. "Would you help me clear the table?"

Josh said, "Of course," and stood up to help. Instantly he reverted back into the man Natalie had met on the deck, low-key, good-humored, easy-going.

She leaned back in her chair for a moment, letting the talk all around her fade into the background while she lost herself in pleasure at the sight of the water shining as if glazed with gold by the setting sun. She wouldn't allow herself to gawk constantly at Ben, but she was aware of him all through the evening, as if he were a song drifting through the air, or light from the rising moon.

When the party ended, Josh carried Petey home, the child's head lolling on his shoulder, rather than risk waking the boy by placing him in the stroller. Back at their house, he carefully laid his son in his crib.

"I'll take off his clothes and tuck him in," Morgan whispered.

Josh nodded and left the room. As Morgan undid the snaps of his Osh-Kosh overalls and slid them off his chubby body, Petey shifted in his sleep, but didn't wake. She checked his diaper—still dry; she'd just changed it at the Hortons' house. He'd be comfortable enough in his tiny white T-shirt, even if a few grains of sand were sifting off his clothes. Her child lay flat on his back, arms and legs spread, as if he were effortlessly falling through his sleep. His lips opened slightly as he puffed his sweet breath into the air. The sight of his innocent face made Morgan feel peaceful in every vein and bone. She etched his face on her brain for the inevitable days to come when he turned into Hyper-Active-Tantrum-Throwing Monster Boy.

In their bedroom, she pushed the button (how swank was that!) and the blinds buzzed shut across the wall of windows facing the lake. She undressed, hung up her clothes, pulled on one of Josh's long-sleeved T-shirts she'd appropriated for her own use as a night shirt.

She was tired. These days it seemed she was always tired, which was weird, because Petey at twelve months slept through most nights. She got comfortable in bed, plumped up her pillows, and waited for Josh to come back upstairs. Now was the sweet time, chatting lazily with him about the evening and the people they'd met. As tired as she was, she wouldn't mind making love tonight. It had been a while.

Josh didn't come up. She went out into the hall and leaned over the railing. "Josh?"

"I'm going to stay down here. I've got some work to catch up on."

Morgan bit back a bitter retort. He was always working, always in his study, even tonight. Since their move here, Josh had spent almost every night on the computer. Sometimes just an hour, often three or four. She didn't nag him about it. She'd known when he accepted the position that he'd have enormous, time-consuming responsibilities. Still.

Sometimes, when she'd had a bad day, missed her job and her friends, and allowed herself to morph into her Mad Morgan self, she wondered if *work* was all he was doing on his computer. Perhaps he was emailing some gorgeous sexy secretary from the office—but that was just *ridiculous*! She'd never had anxieties about Josh's fidelity before; she knew he loved her and adored Petey.

She stomped back to the bed, shoved her glasses on, grabbed up the report on the *Trans-Federal Task Force on Optimizing Biosaftey and Biocontainment Oversight,* and settled in. She would read until Josh came up to bed, and then she'd surprise him with an attack of sweet sex like she used to before they were married.

After an hour, she fell asleep, with the bedside lamp still on and her glasses sliding down her nose.

NANCY THAYER is the *New York Times* bestselling author of *Heat Wave*, *Beachcombers*, *Summer House*, *Moon Shell Beach*, and *The Hot Flash Club*. She lives on Nantucket.

Chat.
Comment.
Connect.

Visit our online book club community at
www.randomhousereaderscircle.com

Chat
Meet fellow book lovers and discuss what you're reading.

Comment
Post reviews of books, ask—and answer—thought-provoking
questions, or give and receive book club ideas.

Connect
Find an author on tour, visit our author blog, or invite one of
our 150 available authors to chat with your group on the phone.

Explore
Also visit our site for discussion questions, excerpts, author
interviews, videos, free books, news on the latest releases,
and more.

Books are better with buddies.
www.RandomHouseReadersCircle.com